NEW TOEIC

新多益

單字圖像記憶法

吳燦銘 ◎ 策劃

油漆式速記法 外語研發團隊

晨星出版

多益測驗（TOEIC）的全名是 Test of English for International Communication（國際溝通英語測驗），是針對英語非母語人士所設計之英語能力測驗，1979 年由美國教育測驗中心（Educational Testing Service，簡稱 ETS 協會）研發，目前已經成為全球最受歡迎的職場英語測驗，每年有超過 200 萬以上人次參加，被超過 165 個國家的企業廣泛接受，作為語言能力的參考依據。國內也有越來越多的大學系所要求學生在畢業前要通過多益成績門檻，可以稱為是目前最具公信與最方便報考的英語綜合測驗之一。

多益檢定的範圍不僅只於職場應用，還涵蓋日常生活上溝通與活動的場景與對話，測驗分數反映受測者在國際職場環境中與他人以英語溝通的熟稔程度。測驗型式為紙筆測驗，時間兩小時，總共有二百道單選題，分作兩大部分：聽力與閱讀。2006 年起，美國 ETS 協會為了研發更優化的考試內容及評量方法，宣布採用新版的聽力與閱讀測驗題型，稱為新多益（NEW TOEIC），並在聽力測驗中加入多國口音，包含美國、英國、澳洲、加拿大，2008 年 3 月正式在台灣實施。口說與寫作測驗（Speaking and Writing test）2008 年也在台灣正式登場，測驗方式透過網路進行，旨在評量受測者在職場環境中以英語進行口說與寫作的能力。

多益考試的其它相關資訊，請上 TOEIC 台灣區官方網站：
http://www.toeic.com.tw/。

在這個進入地球村的新世代，國際化的腳步日益快速，特別是面臨全球化不景氣時刻，失業問題已經變成各國政府最為頭痛的問題。這時擁有國際觀與外語能力的人才，往往就是各種企業優先選擇的最愛。學好外語成為現代人當務之急的功課，尤其英語是國際通用語言，不論是求學或就業，肯定都將會是你最佳的溝通工具。畢竟多學會一種語言，資源就多一倍，英語能力雖然不是職場的萬靈丹，但如果不懂英語，在世界競爭的舞台上卻是寸步難行。

單字不是萬能，少了單字卻萬萬不能

不論你認不認同背單字的重要性，英語能力和字彙量絕對是成正比的，許多人的聽力不好，歸咎原因多半還是因為有些單字根本聽不懂，當然後來也就愈聽愈迷糊了。參加多益測驗時也是如此，無論是在聽、說、讀、寫哪個部份，單字量確實就是得分最重要的關鍵。

對於大多數正在花時間背多益檢定單字的各位來說，最常見的現象就是每天抱著一本單字書猛 K，聚精會神地對著每個單字念念有詞，手上還拿著筆不停抄寫。時間一長就會發現，背一個單字是小問題，但是要想在短時間內背完大量單字，可就是一個如假包換的大工程了。

沒有記不住的單字，只有不好記的方法

美國 ETS 協會曾經宣布，在多益測驗題目中不會出現艱澀少見的專業辭彙，通常就是一些生活中普遍常用的單字。以本團隊多年的經驗來看，多益測驗中經常出現的單字大約只有 1000 到 1200 字左右，也就是各位一定要認識的必考單字。在本書中一共收錄了由電腦整理近二十年來，多益試題中最熱門的 2000 個單字，不但包括 1200 個必考單字，還附加 800 個常見的相關應考單字。簡單來說，只要背下這 2000 個電腦嚴選單字，多益檢定 800 分就不是問題了。

背單字就像刷油漆，凡刷過必留下痕跡

在本書的內容安排上，特別根據本團隊所發明的「油漆式速記法」原理，也就是「大量記憶」、「全腦學習」與「多層次滾動複習」三個理論為主要特色，

輕鬆幫助各位在 30 天內快速記下 2000 個單字。

1. 大量記憶

日本有句諺語說：「大雨使大地更加堅固！」而醫學專家則認為：「大量吸收訊息會使大腦更加靈光！」大腦是個非常特別的器官，如果能夠讓越大量的訊息進入大腦，神經迴路間的連結就會越緊密，記憶力也會越強。

簡單來說，各位輸入大腦記憶的單字量越多，反而能夠記得更快。在本書中會引導各位讀者在 30 天內背完 2000 個單字，每天以 60 到 70 個單字為一個單元，每天只要利用 1 至 2 小時就可以背完，這樣的規劃就是秉持大量記憶單字的原則。

日常生活中應該如何增進大腦吸收大量訊息的能力呢？「速讀」就是最好的方法之一。速讀的基本價值，就是為了大量記憶的目的，而忽略有些不切實際的精確要求。許多人總是認為一個單字看得越久越容易記住，這是非常錯誤的觀念！因為單字的記憶是屬於感官記憶，也是屬於速讀效果下的瞬間記憶力，不會因為你當下花更多的時間，就能背得更牢。其實每個單字平均一次只要花上 3 到 5 秒來記，5 分鐘之內就可讀完一個單元，而且可以達到同樣的記憶效果。

在速讀單字的過程中，請各位先學習認識（recognize）大量單字，要求自己看到這個單字的樣子，馬上就能想到中文解釋，千萬不要想馬上背下（memorize）這個單字的每一個字母。如果有些英文單字有好幾個不同的中文解釋，為了符合速讀的原理——先求有再求好，我們只要先記住其中之一的中文意思即可。

2. 全腦學習

人類大腦奇妙之處在於兩個半球分工不同，左右腦平分了腦部的所有構造及功能。通常我們做任何一項思考活動，左右腦都會同時參與，左腦是用邏輯進行思考，右腦則是以圖像進行思考。例如牛頓看了蘋果從樹上掉下來的景象，就提出了萬有引力定律。這個過程就是由左腦一邊觀察，提取右腦所描繪的圖像，同時在左右腦進行整合性的思維編碼。因此懂得運用全腦學習背單字的人，就能更輕鬆快速地記下大量單字。

一般人生活中利用比較多的是左腦，主要協助我們從事邏輯、數字、文字、分類等抽象活動。人類的語言能力，大都由左腦掌控。左腦對於語言性的反應有

先天的優勢能力，當我們進行各種閱讀時，左腦就擅長進行文法與語意的邏輯分析。右腦則具有自主性，能夠發揮獨自的想像力，大腦專家認為多數人終其一生約只運用了大腦的 3％，其餘的 97％都以沉睡狀態蘊藏在右腦的潛能中，所以用右腦進行圖像記憶，可以在最短的時間內，將大量訊息儲存於大腦中。

例如我們在背單字時，最好能把呆板的單字轉換成活潑生動的右腦圖像，就可到收事半功倍的記憶效果。不過初學者想要在背單字時，馬上達到右腦圖像記憶並不容易，也非一朝一夕就可以做到，因此本團隊特別結合速記專家，花費了大量的人力與物力，針對本書 2000 個單字，在每個單字旁製作了一個右腦圖像。當各位在速讀本書中的單字時，請同步記下這個單字的圖像。日後複習會發現一看到這些單字，腦海會先顯現圖像，然後才出現中文字意，這就是右腦圖像記憶的好處。

當各位利用右腦圖像記憶背下大量單字後，千萬不要沾沾自喜，在背單字的同時，不能只單靠右腦對單字的圖像記憶，還必須開始閱讀包含這個單字的句子，才能真正達到全腦學習的功用。記憶單字的最終目的不外乎是期望能達到永久記憶的效果，想要達到這種效果，就必須藉由左腦功能把這個單字放在句子裡的結構來分析，也就是同時進行「再確認」與「回憶」這兩種固化記憶的過程。

本書為每個單字都附上與多益測驗題型相關的兩個重要例句，各位如果想要在多益測驗中挑戰不可能的高分，每記下一個單字的時候，除了右腦圖像之外，最好還能記住至少一個相關例句。

3. 多層次滾動複習

複習是記憶之母，是把感官記憶移轉為長期記憶的一個重要過程。相信許多人都有吃過迴轉壽司的經驗，剛開始看到輸送帶上五花八門的壽司料理時，肯定是眼花撩亂，剛想選擇某些菜色，一溜煙又從眼前消失，連名稱跟價錢都看不清楚。不過迴轉了幾次之後，自然會慢慢記住想吃的壽司位置與價格。

為什麼最後會記住？因為我們已經重複看了好幾次迴轉臺上的壽司，關鍵在於「迴轉」，這也是本書主張「多層次滾動複習」的基本原理。「多層次」就是不斷地重複記憶，就好像在各位的大腦中刷上好幾層記憶油漆，進而能快速強化記憶力。複習，就像我們在大腦灑下記憶種子，複習的次數越多，記憶效果自然

會越好。

　　許多人對於「記不住」這個念頭有著與生俱來的恐懼，常常在背下一個單字時，害怕忘了剛剛才背過的上一個單字，於是忍不住又回想了一下。正因為想記的念頭越強，交感神經異常的收縮動作，反而使大腦記憶中樞陷入空轉，越是記不住。

　　所以我們強調以天數為單位記下大量單字，就算難免忘了一些也無妨，還是要記得放鬆心情。因為第一次所遺忘的單字，還可在第二次複習時進行補強，「油漆式速記法」的精神是——永遠期待下一次複習的機會，來彌補前一次不小心遺忘的單字。

　　本書中「多層次滾動複習」的精神，就是請各位每天要開始背一個新單元時，先利用速讀的方法將前面學習過的單元快速複習一遍，例如進行到第三天時，還是要先快速複習第一、二天學過的單元，越到後面所要複習的部分就越多。這樣的作法就像是從山上往下滾的雪球，滾得越久雪球就越大，背下的單字也會越多。

　　本書不僅僅是一本多益檢定的專業字彙書籍，更重要的是結合了速讀與速記技巧的輔助，只要各位願意花上 30 天的時間，按照書中所提供的「油漆式速記原理」來背單字，不論之前的英文程度如何，一定都能讓你的多益成績反敗為勝，順利獲取高分。

榮欽科技

吳燦銘 敬上

目　錄

1. 真人發音 MP3

掃描 Day01 到 Day30 每個單元左上角的 QR-code，即可下載每日學習進度的完整音檔；輸入網址加上單字編號，則可下載每個單字的個別音檔。還可以用電腦存檔下來，隨時隨地背單字、練聽力！

在網址後面手動 key 上單字編號，即可下載每個單字的個別音檔。

Day 01

用手機掃描就可以下載每日進度的完整音檔

範例：http://epaper.morningstar.com.tw/mp3/0103358/0001.mp3 0001單字音檔
http://epaper.morningstar.com.tw/mp3/0103358/0002.mp3 0002單字音檔
…… 依此類推

◎本書音檔由吳燦銘及其外語研發團隊製作提供，若有相關問題敬請洽詢h7373.michael@msa.hinet.net

2. 行動學習計劃表

背完當天的單字進度，還要記得用速讀法快速複習前面的單元。不知道怎麼安排進度？請搭配「行動學習計劃表」一起使用，完成當日的「背」與「複」兩項任務之後，就可以把日期旁邊的方框打勾，堅持 30 天，邁向 100%！

☐ Day01	☐ Day02	☐ Day03	☐ Day04	☐ Day05	☐ Day06
背 0001-0066 複 0001-0066	背 0067-0132 複 0001-0132	背 0133-0198 複 0001-0198	背 0199-0264 複 0001-0264	背 0265-0330 複 0001-0330	背 0331-0396 複 0001-0330
3.3%	6.7%	9.9%	13.2%	16.5%	19.8%

完成之後一天一天打勾，會很有成就感喔！

3. 油漆式單字記憶法 App

iOS 版下載

Android 版下載

4. 陪你上戰場——考前關鍵祕笈

精心挑選最重要的關鍵 500 字（編號後面標註★者），統整於本書最末提供快速複習使用。準備要出門迎接新多益檢定了嗎？記得撕下考前關鍵祕笈 500 字，陪你一起上戰場！

◆ My father always went to Japan at regular intervals.
我爸爸總是定期前往日本。

◆ There is an two minutes's interval to the next subway.
下一班地鐵間隔二分鐘。

0005 ★ 關鍵單字！

行動學習計劃表

	■ Day01	■ Day02	■ Day03	■ Day04	■ Day05	■ Day06
	背 0001-0066	背 0067-0132	背 0133-0198	背 0199-0264	背 0265-0330	背 0331-0396
		複 0001-0066	複 0001-0132	複 0001-0198	複 0001-0264	複 0001-0330
	3.3%	6.7%	9.9%	13.2%	16.5%	19.8%

■ Day07	■ Day08	■ Day09	■ Day10	■ Day11	■ Day12	■ Day13
背 0397-0462	背 0463-0528	背 0529-0594	背 0595-0660	背 0661-0727	背 0728-0794	背 0795-0861
複 0001-0396	複 0001-0462	複 0001-0528	複 0001-0594	複 0001-0660	複 0001-0727	複 0001-0794
23.1%	26.4%	29.7%	33%	36.3%	39.6%	42.9%

■ Day14	■ Day15	■ Day16	■ Day17	■ Day18	■ Day19	■ Day20
背 0862-0928	背 0929-0995	背 0996-1062	背 1063-1129	背 1130-1196	背 1197-1263	背 1264-1330
複 0001-0861	複 0001-0928	複 0001-0995	複 0001-1062	複 0001-1129	複 0001-1196	複 0001-1263
46.2%	49.5%	52.8%	56.1%	59.4%	62.7%	66%

■ Day21	■ Day22	■ Day23	■ Day24	■ Day25	■ Day26	■ Day27
背 1331-1397	背 1398-1464	背 1465-1531	背 1532-1598	背 1599-1665	背 1666-1732	背 1733-1799
複 0001-1330	複 0001-1397	複 0001-1464	複 0001-1531	複 0001-1598	複 0001-1665	複 0001-1732
69.3%	72.6%	75.9%	79.2%	82.5%	85.8%	89.1%

■ Day28	■ Day29	■ Day30				
背 1800-1866	背 1867-1933	背 1934-2000				
複 0001-1799	複 0001-1866	複 0001-1933				
92.4%	95.7%	100%				

勇於開始，才能找到成功的路

---

department

dɪˊpɑrtmənt

n. (大學) 系；
部門

人事部門

◆ He is in charge of the personnel department.
他負責人事部門的工作。

◆ The department store is always filled with people on weekends.
這間百貨公司每逢週末總是擠滿了人。

0001

---

sophomore

ˊsɑfəˏmor

n. (大學或高中) 二年級學生

◆ The sophomore class will go on a picnic tomorrow.
大二的班級明天要去野餐。

◆ I will be a sophomore soon because I have passed my final exam.
我已經通過期末考，即將成為大二生了。

0002

---

eclipse

ɪˊklɪps

n. (日、月的)
蝕 **v.** 黯然失色；
使……變暗

◆ There will be a lunar eclipse next Tuesday.
下週二將會出現月蝕。

◆ They go to the top floor to watch the solar eclipse.
他們到頂層去看日蝕。

0003

---

crime

kraɪm

n. (法律上) 罪；
不道德行為

◆ The criminal was sentenced to three years in prison for his part in the crime.
這個罪犯因為他參與這宗犯罪被宣判入獄三年。

◆ Bigamy is not a crime in some countries.
重婚在某些國家不算犯罪。

0004 ★

---

interval

ˊɪntəvḷ

n. (時間、場所的) 間隔；距離

0.0   0.5

0.5公分

◆ My father always went to Japan at regular intervals.
我爸爸總是定期前往日本。

◆ There is an two minutes's interval to the next subway.
下一班地鐵間隔二分鐘。

0005 ★

---

binocular

bɪˊnɑkjələ

n. (複) 雙筒望遠鏡

◆ The soldier scanned the battlefield with a binocular .
這位士兵用雙筒望遠鏡掃視戰場。

◆ Do not view the sun with this binocular.
不要使用雙筒望遠鏡看太陽。

0006

cobble
'kabl̩
n. 圓石 **v.** 匆匆
製作

◆ The old bus drove slowly over the cobble stones
這台老巴士慢慢開過圓石路。

◆ The table took him half a day to cobble up.
他花了半天時間就匆匆做成這張桌子。

0007

forgery
'fɔrdʒərɪ
n. 偽造的文件

◆ The man committed forgery because he copied the signature of the manager.
這男人犯了偽造文書罪，因為他偽造經理的簽名。

◆ At first sight of the painting, the artist told us that it was a forgery.
第一眼看到這油畫時，藝術家就告訴我們它是贋品。

0008

row
ro
n. 一列；一排 **v.**
使成列

◆ The captain told his soldiers to stand in a row.
這隊長叫他的士兵們站成一列。

◆ The girl standing in the front row is my sister.
站在前排的女孩是我妹妹。

0009

annual
'ænjʊəl
adj. 一年一次
的

十二月25日

◆ While I was in Venice, an annual carnival was held.
當我在威尼斯時，每年一次的嘉年華會正在舉行。

◆ Nineteen restaurants in this city didn't pass the annual sanitation inspection.
本市的十九家餐廳未通過一年一度的衛生檢查。

0010

consistent
kən'sɪstənt
adj. 一致的；
符合的

◆ Your conduct is not consistent with what you said.
你的行為和你所說的不一致。

◆ This testimony is not consistent with what she said earlier.
這個證詞和她早先的說法不符合。

0011

consensus
kən'sɛnsəs
n. 一致的共識

◆ No consensus has been reached about the safety of the project.
這企劃案的安全性還未達成一致的意見。

◆ They finally reached the consensus of this matter.
他們最後在這個問題上達成了一致共識。

0012

loaf
lof
n. 一條；一塊 **v.**
浪擲光陰

◆ The customer asks for a loaf of bread.
這個顧客要求一條麵包。

◆ The lazy boy loafed around the whole morning.
這個懶惰男孩浪費了一早的時光。

0013

alternative
/ɔlˈtɝnətɪv/
adj. 二者擇一的；替代的

西瓜還是橘子呢?

◆ I feel confused. Can you give me alternative suggestions?
我覺得很困惑，你可以給我替代的建議嗎？

◆ Most worlds' automakers make efforts to research in alternative-fuel technologies.
世界上大多數的汽車製造商努力於研究替代能源的技術。

0014 ★

population
/ˌpɑpjəˈleʃən/
n. 人口；全體居民

◆ The city has a population of nine million.
這個城市的人口有九百萬人。

◆ The population was sparse in the area.
這個地區的人口是稀少的。

0015 ★

census
/ˈsɛnsəs/
n. 人口調查；戶口普查

戶口普查!

◆ Using a census helps us understand the population.
利用人口調查可以幫助我們了解人口數目。

◆ In the United States there is a census every ten years.
在美國每十年有一次戶口普查。

0016 ★

artifact
/ˈɑrtɪˌfækt/
n. 人工製品；手工製品

◆ Bows and other artifacts were discovered during the excavations.
弓和其它手工製品被挖掘出來

◆ I have an ancient metal artifact from China.
我有一個來自中國的古老金屬藝品。

0017

sidewalk
/ˈsaɪdˌwɔk/
n. 人行道

◆ We walk on the sidewalk to be safe.
走人行道是為了保障我們的安全。

◆ Is it legal to park on the sidewalk?
在人行道上停車是合法的嗎？

0018

humanism
/ˈhjumənˌɪzəm/
n. 人道主義；人文主義

人道主義

◆ Humanism had flourished in last century gradually.
人文主義在上個世紀逐漸興盛起來。

◆ His essay analyses some aspects about the humanism.
他的論文分析了有關人道主義的觀點。

0019

access
/ˈæksɛs/
n. 入口；通路 **v.** 接近……

◆ The only access to the airport is along that narrow road.
到機場的唯一通路就是延著這條狹窄的公路。

◆ Please keep cleaning supplies and antifreeze in a place kids can't easily access.
請把清潔用品與防凍劑放到孩子拿不到的地方。

0020

billion
ˈbɪljən
n. 十億

◆ He's a scion of a rich family and the heir to a fortune of half a billion dollars.
他是這富有家庭的子孫，也是五億財富的繼承人。

◆ A billion dollars is a vast amount of money.
十億美金是筆很大的金錢。

0021

triple
ˈtrɪpl
adj. 三倍的；三重的 **v.** 增至三倍

◆ The company pay him triple pay for over-time work.
公司付他三倍的報酬作為加班費。

◆ The living room is triple the size it once was.
客廳擴大為原來的三倍大。

0022

arise
əˈraɪz
v. 上升；產生

◆ A beautiful sun arose from the sea.
美麗的太陽從海上升起。

◆ The accident arises from the driver's carelessness.
這場意外起因於駕駛員的粗心。

0023

superior
səˈpɪrɪə
adj. 上級的；優秀的 **n.** 上司

◆ Please wait until I get instructions from my superiors.
請等我獲得上司的指示。

◆ Peter offended his superior and then was fired.
彼得冒犯了他的上司，於是被解雇了。

0024

embark
ɪmˈbɑrk
v. 上船或飛機；著手從事

◆ The passengers embarked on the ship at 9 a.m.
這些乘客們在早上九點時上船。

◆ The scholar embarked on his research three years ago.
這位學者三年前就從事於他的研究。

0025

inferior
ɪnˈfɪrɪə
adj. 下級的；次級的

◆ The goods you sent us are inferior compared to the original sample.
你們送來的貨比原來樣品還要次等。

◆ This CD is inferior to the other one in its sound quality.
這張 CD 的聲音品質比其它的差。

0026

slogan
ˈsloɡən
n. 口號；廣告用語

◆ Time is money is the slogan of the old company.
「時間就是金錢」是這家老公司的口號。

◆ The black background of the sign made the slogan more distinctive.
這個標誌的黑色背景讓這個標語更為醒目。

0027 ★

verbal
ˈvɝbl
adj. 口頭的；
言語的

How are you doing?

◆ This is a verbal translation of this old poem.
這是這首古老詩歌的口頭翻譯。

◆ Our teacher teaches us how to use the verbal skills.
我們老師教導我們如何使用口述技巧。

0028

toast
tost
n. 土司

◆ I had two pieces of toast and an egg for breakfast.
我早餐吃了兩片吐司和一個蛋。

◆ I had ham and toast for breakfast.
早餐我吃了火腿與吐司。

0029

soil
sɔɪl
n. 土地；土壤

◆ The fecundity of the soil in the area brings much profit to the farmers.
這個地區土壤肥沃，給農民帶來許多利益。

◆ Earthworms move through the soil to maintain its fertility.
蚯蚓在土壤中的移動維持了它的肥沃。

0030

bountiful
ˈbauntəfəl
adj. 大方的；
寬大的；豐富的

◆ My boss gives bountiful presents to everyone at her office.
我的老闆給她辦公室中的每個人豐富的禮物。

◆ The bonus of this company is extremely bountiful.
這家公司的紅利是很大方的。

0031

stride
straɪd
v. 大步走；跨
過 **n.** 大步

◆ He strode out of the restaurant.
他從餐廳大步走出來。

◆ I was ten strides from the church.
我距離那教堂有十步之遙。

0032

embassy
ˈɛmbəsɪ
n. 大使館；大
使館（全體人
員）

◆ I've lost my passport. Should I contact the embassy as soon as possible?
我遺失護照了，應該儘速連絡大使館嗎？

◆ The consulate was upgraded to embassy status last year.
去年這間領事館已經升格為大使館。

0033 ★

roughly
ˈrʌflɪ
adv. 大約地；
約略地；粗暴地

大約一百萬!

◆ It will take roughly four hours from Kaohsiung to Taipei by train.
從高雄到台北坐火車大約要花四個小時。

◆ I was sorry that I had scolded so roughly to her.
我很抱歉對她如此粗暴地斥責。

0034

undergraduate
ˌʌndɚˈgrædʒuɪt
adj. 大學生的

◆ I studied in the Department of Foreign Languages during my undergraduate days.
我大學時代就讀外文系。

◆ She had an undergraduate degree in computer science.
她擁有電腦科學的學士學位。

0035 ★

academic
ˌækəˈdɛmɪk
adj. 大學的；學術的；學院的

◆ When you graduate from college, you will wear special academic dress.
當你從大學畢業時，將會穿著特別的學士服。

◆ I used to attend the academic lectures at school.
我過去曾經到學校參加許多學術性演講。

0036 ★

bold
bold
adj. 大膽的；英勇的

◆ It was hardly believable that such a young lady made a bold statement.
真是難以置信，這麼一位年輕的女孩做了一次大膽的評論。

◆ A bold man will never flinch when he faces difficulty.
一位英勇的人在面對困難時絕不退縮。

0037

female
ˈfimel
adj. 女人的；雌性的

◆ The female murderer was arrested in the morning.
這位女性謀殺犯早上被逮捕了。

◆ Male and female have different kind of hormones.
男人和女人擁有不同種類的荷爾蒙。

0038

knife
naɪf
n. 小刀；刀子

◆ He cut the beef with a knife.
他用刀子把牛肉切開。

◆ I use a knife with a serrated edge for cutting bread.
我使用一支邊緣有鋸齒的小刀來切麵包。

0039

cabin
ˈkæbɪn
n. 小屋；船艙

◆ My grandparents live in a white cabin near the beach.
我祖父母住在一間靠近海邊的白色小屋。

◆ She is going to lie down in her cabin.
她走到船艙裡躺下休息。

0040

pest
pɛst
n. 小害蟲；有害的人

◆ The pesticide killed off most of the insect pests.
農藥殺死了大多數害人的昆蟲。

◆ Rats and flies are regarded as pests.
老鼠和蒼蠅被認為是有害的。

0041

whisk
hwɪsk
n. 小掃帚 **v.** 揮動；打蛋

◆ The horse brushed away the flies with a whisk of its tail.
這匹馬用它掃帚似的尾巴來趕走蒼蠅。

◆ Whisk the egg first and then add the flour, please.
請先打蛋再加上麵粉。

0042

violin
ˌvaɪəˈlɪn
n. 小提琴

◆ Can the young child play the violin?
這年輕孩子會演奏小提琴嗎？

◆ The boy is endued with a talent of playing violin.
這男孩有拉小提琴的天賦。

0043

lane
len
n. 小道；車道

◆ They walked along the lane through the woods.
他們走這條小道穿越森林。

◆ That lane will take you to the famous temple.
這條小路會帶你到著名的寺廟。

0044

nap
næp
v. 小睡；打盹

◆ He napped for a while when he got home from work.
當他工作完回家後小睡了一會。

◆ He was awakened from his nap by the sudden doorbell.
他被突然的門鈴聲吵醒。

0045

cabinet
ˈkæbənɪt
n. 小櫥櫃；內閣

◆ There is no room for another cabinet in the living room.
客廳中沒地方放小櫥櫃了。

◆ Each member of the cabinet stated his opinions on the financial policy.
內閣中的每位成員對這個財務政策表示意見。

0046

peak
pik
n. 山頂；尖端；最高點

◆ Traffic is very heavy at peak hours.
尖峰時間的交通非常擁擠。

◆ Mount Fuji peaks are covered with snow all year.
富士山山頂整年都覆蓋著雪。

0047

worker
ˈwɝkɚ
n. 工人

◆ The factory has many workers.
那家工廠有很多工人。

◆ A higher salary can give young workers an incentive to work harder.
高薪能帶給年輕工作者更努力工作的動機。

0048

workaholic
ˌwɝkəˈhɔlɪk
n. 工作狂

◆ An workaholic is a kind of person who is addicted to work every day.
工作狂是一種每天沉溺於工作的人。

◆ I shouldn't define myself as a workaholic.
我不應該將自己定義為工作狂。

0049

tool
tul
n. 工具

◆ John had invented a tool for his factory.
約翰為他的工廠發明了一項工具。

◆ What is the function of this tool?
這個工具的作用是什麼？

0050

gear
gɪr
n. 工具；齒輪；排檔

◆ That warehouse store sells sports gear.
那家量販店有在賣運動器具。

◆ How do you tell when to change gear?
你如何確定何時換檔？

0051

engineer
ˌɛndʒəˈnɪr
n. 工程師

◆ He dreams to be a civil engineer.
他夢想成為一個土木工程師。

◆ I am studying to be a mechanical engineer.
我用功想成為機械工程師。

0052

wage
wedʒ
n. 工資；薪水

◆ The laborers call a strike to fight against their wage cuts.
勞工罷工反對他們的工資縮減。

◆ Our wages depend on production results.
我們的工資是以生產結果而定的。

0053 ★

factory
ˈfæktrɪ
n. 工廠

◆ Many people work at the factory.
很多人在這間工廠工作。

◆ The new factory will be completed next month.
新的工廠將在下個月完工。

0054

talent
ˈtælənt
n. 才能

◆ The little girl has a talent for art.
那位小女孩很有藝術天份。

◆ Kate has an apparently inborn talent for music.
凱特有明顯的天生音樂才華。

0055

substandard
səb'stændəd
adj. 不合標準的；在標準以下的

規格不合

◆ The product was absolutely substandard, the cartridges all leaked.
這產品絕對不合標準，所有墨水匣都有裂縫。

◆ All substandard products should be recalled immediately.
所有不合格的產品都要被立即回收。

0056

ominous
'ɑmənəs
adj. 不吉祥的

◆ A curse made by a witch is ominous and horrible.
巫婆所下的詛咒既不祥又可怕。

◆ 13 is regarded as a very ominous number.
十三被認為是一個非常不吉祥的數字。

0057

unfavorable
ʌn'fevrəbl
adj. 不利的；不適宜的

◆ The situation at present is unfavorable for them to initiatively attack the enemy.
目前情勢不利他們主動攻擊敵方。

◆ The weather is unfavorable to our schedules.
這種天氣對我們的時程計劃表不利。

0058

adverse
æd'vɜs
adj. 不利的；逆向的；有害的

◆ Smoking causes adverse effects on your health.
吸菸會造成不利於健康的影響。

◆ The flight encountered adverse weather conditions.
這架航班遇到不利的天候狀況。

0059 ★

missing
'mɪsɪŋ
adj. 不見了的；下落不明的

◆ The missing girl was found alive but unconscious.
下落不明的女孩被發現仍活著，但失去了意識。

◆ The missing teenager was declared deceased after 15 years.
這位失蹤的青少年在十五年後被宣告死亡。

0060

adversity
əd'vɜsətɪ
n. 不幸；厄運

◆ He met with adversities during his childhood.
他在童年時遭遇許多不幸。

◆ Food for the victims of natural adversity was replenished by the government.
因天災受害的災民，由政府來補足糧食。

0061

unfortunately
ʌn'fɔrtʃənɪtlɪ
adv. 不幸地；遺憾地

火災

◆ Unfortunately she died in a car accident.
很遺憾地她在一場車禍中身亡。

◆ He was unfortunately caught in the storm.
他不幸遇到暴風雨。

0062

insoluble

ɪnˈsɑljəbl

adj. 不能溶解
的；不能解決的

◆ Sand is insoluble in water.
沙不能溶解於水中。

◆ The physical problem seemed insoluble for these
students.
這個問題對這些學生而言似乎難以解決。

0063

real estate

ˈriəl əsˈtet

n. 不動產

◆ Mr. Smith is a professional real estate broker.
史密斯先生是位專業的不動產經紀人

◆ For example, a capital gain is a profit that results from
investments into a real estate.
例如資本利得是一種來自不動產投資的獲利。

0064

stale

stel

adj. 不新鮮的；
陳腐無趣的

◆ This bread is a little bit stale today.
今天的麵包有點不新鮮。

◆ We all are tired of his same stale old jokes.
我們對這些陳腐無趣的老笑話感到厭倦。

0065

immoral

ɪˈmɔrəl

adj. 不道德的

◆ Some people still think it is immoral to have sex before
marriage.
有些人仍然認為婚前有性行為是不道德的。

◆ It's immoral to copy other people's ideas.
抄襲別人的想法是不道德的。

0066

日日行，不怕千萬里

---

regardless
rɪˈɡɑrdlɪs
adv. 不管怎樣；
不顧

◆ I play basketball every day regardless of the weather.
不管天氣怎樣，我每天都打籃球。

◆ I want to take the job regardless of the pay.
不管報酬多少，我都想要這份工作。

0067

---

axis
ˈæksɪs
n. 中心軸；軸
線；核心

◆ The axis of a circle is its diameter.
圓的軸線就是它的直徑。

◆ Does the earth rotate on an axis?
地球是繞著中心軸旋轉的嗎？

0068

---

pertinent
ˈpɜtṇənt
adj. 中肯的；
切題的；有關的

◆ He offered several pertinent suggestions.
他提供了許多中肯的建議。

◆ I want to know all the details pertinent to the story.
我想知道所有有關這故事的細節。

0069

---

stroke
strok
n. 中風；游法
（游泳）；划法

◆ If you make yourself aware of cholesterol, you can reduce your risk for a heart attack or stroke.
假如你對膽固醇了解越多，就越能減少心臟病和中風的危險。

◆ I'm best at breast stroke, but I enjoy the crawl, too.
我最擅長蛙式，但也喜歡自由式。

0070

---

secondary
ˈsɛkənˌdɛrɪ
adj. 中等的；
次要的；第二的

◆ The government introduced generic secondary education years ago.
政府多年前採用了普遍的中等教育。

◆ All children must complete secondary education in Taiwan.
在台灣所有孩子都必須完成中等教育。

0071 ★

---

moderate
ˈmɑdərɪt
adj. 中等的；
適度的 ***v.*** 使和
緩

中等身材

◆ Moderate exercise will be of benefit to everyone.
適度的運動對每個人是有好處的。

◆ It is not moderate to spend a lot time daydreaming during the work.
工作時花很多時間做白日夢是不適當的。

0072

hardware
'hɑrd,wɛr
n. 五金

◆ The old man bought a hammer from the hardware store.
這老人從五金行中買了支榔頭。

◆ His father is a hardware merchant.
他的父親是位五金商人。

0073 ★

hatred
'hetrɪd
n. 仇恨；憎恨

◆ The couple has lived with hatred for many years.
這對夫婦懷著恨意生活在一起許多年。

◆ The sick murderer has suffered from a long-term pathological hatred of women.
這個兇手長期為病態地憎恨女人所苦。

0074

intervene
,ɪntɚ'vin
v. 介入調停；
干涉……

◆ Would you intervene when I give you a sign?
我給你一個手勢時，你可以介入調停嗎？

◆ The foreign exchange markets are often intervened by certain countries.
外匯市場常受到某些國家的干預。

0075 ★

care
kɛr
v. 介意……
n. 關心

◆ I don't care if you like me or not.
我不介意你喜不喜歡我。

◆ He doesn't seem to care about his parents.
他似乎不關心他的雙親。

0076

allow
ə'laʊ
v. 允許

歡迎寵物

◆ Swimming is not allowed in this abysmal lake.
這個深不見底的湖是不允許游泳的。

◆ Am I allowed to take pictures inside?
我可以在裡面拍照嗎？

0077 ★

permission
pɚ'mɪʃən
n. 允許；批准；
許可證

◆ Do we have your permission to make substitutions on this ?
你們是否同意這項目使用替代品呢？

◆ You will be fined if found trespassing onto the other people's property without permission.
如果沒有他人許可，擅闖民宅將會被罰款。

0078 ★

element
'ɛləmənt
n. 元素；成分；
要素

Calcium
20
Ca
40.078

◆ Vision, confidence and a little luck are the elements of success.
遠見、自信和一點點的好運氣是成功的要素。

◆ Carbon is an element, while carbon dioxide is a compound.
碳是元素，而二氧化碳是化合物。

0079 ★

content
ˈkɑntɛnt
n. 內容；要旨

◆ What are the contents?
裡面裝的是什麼？

content
kənˈtɛnt
adj. 滿足的

◆ He was very content with his doctoral thesis.
他對自己的博士論文很滿意。

0080 ★

reshuffle
riˈʃʌfl
n. 內閣改組；
重新洗牌

◆ The cabinet was reshuffled by the prime minister.
總理重新改組內閣。
◆ Did you hear about the personnel reshuffle recently?
最近你有聽到人事改組的消息嗎？

0081

insider trading
ɪnˌsaɪdə ˈtredɪŋ
n. 內線交易

◆ The financial manager could be accused of insider trading.
這位財務經理可能被控內線交易。
◆ This insider trading scandal scared off many potential investors.
這個內線交易的醜聞嚇退了許多潛在投資者。

0082 ★

company
ˈkʌmpənɪ
n. 公司；商號

◆ Tim works for a computer company.
提姆在一家電腦公司工作。
◆ Since when have you started working at this company?
你從什麼時候開始在這家公司工作的？

0083

highway
ˈhaɪˌwe
n. 公路

◆ My car ran out of gasoline and stopped in the middle of the highway today.
今天我的車子沒油，而且還停在公路中間。
◆ Please turn right at the intersection of two highways.
請在兩條公路相交的十字路口右轉。

0084

minute
ˈmɪnɪt
n. 分（鐘）；會
議記錄

◆ We will leave for the park in a minute or two.
再一到二分鐘，就要去公園了。
◆ The secretary keeps the minutes at an extraordinary general meeting.
祕書在臨時召開的大會中擔任會議記錄。

0085

branch
bræntʃ
n. 分公司；樹枝

◆ Do you have any branch offices in New York?
你們在紐約有任何分行嗎？

◆ The gardener cut off a branch from the big tree.
園丁從這棵大樹砍下一個樹枝。

0086 ★

share
ʃɛr
v. 分享……
n. 分擔

◆ My sister and I share a bedroom.
我姊姊和我共用一個房間。

◆ Tom shares his lunch with the poor homeless dog.
湯姆把午餐分給可憐的流浪狗。

0087

analyze
ˈænḷˌaɪz
v. 分析……；
解析……

◆ The isotope of the new element was analyzed.
這個新元素的同位素被分析出來。

◆ You should analyze the causes of failure.
你應該分析失敗的原因。

0088 ★

separately
ˈsɛpərɪtlɪ
adv. 分開地；
各自地

◆ Please wrap this item separately.
請分開包裝。

◆ I don't need to explain to you separately.
我不需要再另外跟你解釋。

0089

grade
gred
n. 分數；階級；
年級

◆ I hope I got a good grade on my science test.
我希望我的科學考試得到好成績。

◆ My younger sister will enter the third grade this year.
我妹妹今年要升上三年級了。

0090 ★

classification
ˈklæsəfəˈkeʃən
n. 分類；分等
級

◆ The classification of trash is one aspect of environmental protection.
垃圾分類是環境保護的面向之一。

◆ These all belong in a different classification.
所有這些都屬於不同的分類。

0091 ★

slice
slaɪs
v. 切成薄片

◆ Can you slice this mutton as thin as possible?
你能儘量將這羊肉切成薄片嗎？

◆ My father sliced the roast turkey for our family dinner.
我爸爸為家庭聚餐把烤火雞切成薄片。

0092

segment
ˊsɛgmənt
v. 切割…… **n.** 切片；部分

◆ This segment of the road near the village is very rough.
這條路接近村莊的路段是很崎嶇不平的。

◆ She painted a small segment of the wall.
她油漆了這面牆的一小部分。

0093

collusion
kəˊluʒən
n. 勾結；共謀

◆ The officials are in collusion with the criminals.
這些官員們和歹徒勾結。

◆ They discovered a politician acting in collusion with the gangsters.
他們發現一位政治人物和黑道勾結。

0094 ★

chemistry
ˊkɛmɪstrɪ
n. 化學

◆ I chose chemistry as my special field of study.
我選擇了化學作為我的專業科目。

◆ Your company is the leading company in the chemistry industry.
貴公司在化學工業界是首屈一指的公司。

0095

objection
əbˊdʒɛkʃən
n. 反對；厭惡

我反對!

◆ The Congress overrode the president's objection and passed the law.
國會不顧總統的反對通過了法律。

◆ The tax has increased, which has led to people's objections.
加稅引起許多人民的反對。

0096

oppose
əˊpoz
v. 反對某人或某事

NO!
速食

◆ The new reforms were opposed by reactionary elements within the party.
新的改革遭到黨內守舊份子的反對。

◆ The man execrated all who opposed him.
男子咒罵所有反對他的人。

0097 ★

refute
rɪˊfjut
v. 反駁

要不要抽煙? 不要!

◆ No one is able to refute his argument.
沒有人能反駁他的論點。

◆ I don't want refute a rumor at this moment.
此刻我不想去反駁謠言。

0098

ironic
aɪˊrɑnɪk
adj. 反語的；諷刺的

你很瘦喔!

◆ No one appreciated his ironic jokes.
沒有人欣賞這個反諷的笑話。

◆ I find it ironic that you don't like teaching, but you are a teacher.
我覺得很諷刺的是你不喜歡教書，但你卻是老師。

0099

contradict
kɑntrəˈdɪkt
v. 反駁……；
否認……

◆ Her statement was totally contradicted by the company.
她的聲明被公司完全反駁。

◆ Your actions contradict your principles.
你的行為與原則互相矛盾。

0100

genius
ˈdʒinɪəs
n. 天才；才能

◆ No one can deny the fact that Einstein was a great scientific genius.
每個人都承認愛因斯坦是個偉大的科學天才。

◆ Bill Gaze is an arrant genius.
比爾蓋茲是絕頂的天才。

0101

astronomer
əˈstrɑnəmə
n. 天文學家

◆ The astronomer scanned the heavens and watched the stars through a telescope.
這位天文學家透過望遠鏡瀏覽天空與觀察星星。

◆ I wished to be an astronomer when I am a child.
我還是小孩時，就希望成為一位天文學家。

0102

weather
ˈwɛðə
n. 天氣

◆ The weather looks bad.
天氣看起來不太好。

◆ How was the weather yesterday?
昨天的天氣如何？

0103

aerospace
ˈɛrəˌspes
n. 太空

◆ Could you tell me how to find the Aerospace Museum nearby?
你能告訴我如何找到附近的航太博物館嗎？

◆ The company was a pioneer of the world's aerospace industry.
這家公司是世界航太工業的先驅者。

0104

astronaut
ˈæstrəˌnɔt
n. 太空人

◆ The astronauts returned from the moon with lunar rocks.
太空人帶著月球岩石從月亮回來。

◆ Astronauts stay at the space capsule when doing science projects.
當進行科學計劃時，太空人待在太空艙內。

0105 ★

spacecraft
ˈspesˌkræft
n. 太空船（同
spaceship)

◆ Spacecraft could take human to other planets.
太空船能帶人類到其它行星。

◆ The spacecraft kept on flying at an altitude of 400 kilometers.
這架太空船持續在四百公里的高度飛行。

0106

solar
ˈsolə
adj. 太陽的

- ◆ It is very economical to generate electricity by solar power.
  使用太陽能來發電是經濟的。
- ◆ Solar energy is a regenerate resource.
  太陽能是一種再生的資源。

0107

cite
saɪt
v. 引用……；
舉出

據CNN報導…

- ◆ The judge cited various cases in support of his opinion.
  這位法官引用不同的案件來支持他的意見。
- ◆ Can you cite another case at like this one?
  你能舉出一個像這樣的案例嗎？

0108

cause
kɔz
v. 引起；招致

- ◆ The storm caused great damage to our crops.
  暴風雨對我們的農作物造成很大的傷害。
- ◆ 921 earthquake causes a serious disaster for everyone.
  地震對每個人而言都造成嚴重災難。

0109

curious
ˈkjurɪəs
adj. 引起好奇
的；奇怪的

- ◆ I'm a curious person, and I like to learn new things.
  我是個充滿好奇心的人，喜歡學習新的事物。
- ◆ Children are always curious about everything they see.
  孩子對他們所看見的一切總是好奇的。

0110

quotation
kwoˈteʃən
n. 引號；引文；
報價單

- ◆ He finished his speech with a quotation from Confucius.
  他演講的結尾引用了孔子的話。
- ◆ Can you give me a quotation for building the house?
  你能給我一份建造這房子的估價單嗎？

0111

elicit
ɪˈlɪsɪt
v. 引誘出……；
使……顯現

- ◆ The police tried to elicit enough information from the witnesses by patiently questioning.
  警方試著耐心問話，好從目擊者身上引出足夠訊息。
- ◆ I tried to elicit his interest in learning a second language with me.
  我嘗試引出他和我學習第二外語的興趣。

0112

lead
lid
v. 引導……；
帶領……

- ◆ The waitress led us to our seat.
  服務生帶領我們入座。
- ◆ I have been leading a very regular daily life.
  我一直過著規律有序的生活。

0113

mental
ˋmɛntl̩
adj. 心理的；
精神的；智力的

◆ The man has some mental problems.
那個男人心理上有一些問題。

◆ The lady is suffering from severe mental disorder .
這位女士正被精神錯亂所苦。

0114

spirit
ˋspɪrɪt
n. 心靈；精神

◆ What do you think about work spirit?
你認為工作的精神是什麼？

◆ The positive team spirit led the team to win the state championship this year.
球隊的正面團隊精神讓他們贏得了這次的洲際冠軍。

0115

pushcart
ˋpʊʃˌkɑrt
n. 手推車

◆ Do you know how many things on the pushcart?
你知道手推車上都放了哪些東西嗎？

◆ He peddled flowers from a pushcart.
他推著手推車賣花。

0116

wrist
rɪst
n. 手腕

◆ The nurse put her fingers on my wrist to feel my pulse.
這位護士把手指放在我的腕上量脈搏。

◆ My brother fell downstairs and broke his wrist.
我弟弟跌下樓而且摔斷手腕。

0117

cellular phone
ˋsɛljʊləˌfon
n. 手機
(同 cell phone)

◆ I left my cellular phone in the room.
我把行動電話留在房間裡。

◆ Can you describe what your cellular phone looks like?
你能形容一下你手機的樣子嗎？

0118

workmanship
ˋwɝkmənˌʃɪp
n. 手藝；工藝

◆ The impressive vase is of classical workmanship.
這是件令人印象深刻的古典工藝花瓶。

◆ The inferiority of the workmanship makes the factory bankrupt.
工藝做得太差使得工廠破產。

0119

craft
kræft
n. 手藝；技藝；
詭計

◆ I learned the cooking craft from my mother.
我從母親那兒學會了廚藝。

◆ The famous hotel lobby has a display of local craft.
這間知名飯店的大廳有陳列當地手工藝品。

0120

proponent
prə'ponənt
n. 支持者；擁護者

◆ She is a strong proponent of women's rights.
她是女權的強力支持者。

◆ Who is the firm proponent of nonviolence?
誰是反暴力的堅定支持者？

0121

---

dominate
'dɑmə.net
v. 支配……；在……上佔優勢

◆ Consumers dominate the market and the market decides the price.
消費者支配市場，市場決定價格。

◆ He once dominated the country for ten years.
他一度掌控這個國家十年。

0122

---

portfolio
port'folLo
n. 文件夾；作品集；投資組合

◆ He eventually searched out a dusty portfolio from the attic.
他最後從閣樓中找到一個布滿灰塵的文件夾。

◆ I think my stock broker need to diversify my portfolio.
我認為我的股票經紀人應該使我的投資組合多元化。

0123 ★

---

stationery
'steʃən.ɛrɪ
n. 文具

◆ We may buy a variety of stationery in the bookstore.
我們在書店裡能買到各種文具。

◆ There are many kinds and size of staplers in the stationery store.
在這家文具店中有許多種類和尺寸的訂書機。

0124 ★

---

literature
'lɪtərətʃə
n. 文學；文學作品；文獻

◆ Tina likes to read literature more than listen to music.
和聽音樂相比，汀娜更喜歡閱讀文學著作。

◆ I borrow books of classical literature regularly from the municipal library.
我定期從市立圖書館借古典文學的書來看。

0125

---

means
minz
n. 方法；手段；財力

◆ By means of nanotechnology, the company invented an innovative computer chip.
靠著奈米技術，這家公司發明了創新的電腦晶片。

◆ He employed all available means to reach his goal.
他使用了所有可能的方法來達成目標

0126

---

method
'mɛθəd
n. 方法；規律

◆ If you follow this calculation method, you can solve this problem easily.
如果你依照這個方法去計算，很容易就可以解開這道題目。

◆ Eating less and exercising more is a good method to lose weight.
少吃多運動是減重的一個好方法。

0127 ★

convenient
kən'vinjənt
adj. 方便的；
便利的

◆ What's the most convenient way to get to Central Park?
去中央公園最方便的方法是什麼？

◆ Many people think contact lens are more convenient than glasses.
許多人認為隱形眼鏡較傳統的眼鏡方便。

0128 ★

calendar
'kæləndə
n. 日曆；行事曆

◆ You should have a daily calendar to make notes of all your appointments.
你應該用一本日曆手冊來記錄所有的約會。

◆ What year of the Western calendar were you born？
你是西元的哪一年生的呢？

0129 ★

wane
wen
v. 月(缺)；使減少；使減弱

◆ Why should the moon have wax and wane?
為什麼月亮會有盈缺？

◆ She told me her interests in French have waned.
她告訴我對法文的興趣已經減弱了。

0130

platform
'plæt.fɔrm
n. 月台；講台

◆ The platform was filled with people when the train was approaching.
火車進站時，月台上擠滿了人。

◆ The train from Kaohsiung to Taipei will depart from platform six.
高雄到台北的火車即將要從六號月台出發。

0131 ★

carpenter
'kɑrpəntə
n. 木匠

◆ We need a carpenter to repair our house.
我們需要一位木匠來修房子。

◆ When will the carpenters begin to floor the room?
什麼時候木匠要開始鋪地板？

0132

行動是知識的卓越果實

---

owe
o
v. 欠……(債)；
歸功於……

◆ We owe the rich man a lot of money.
我們欠這有錢人許多錢。

◆ How much do I owe you?
我欠你多少錢？

0133

---

ratio
ˈreʃo
n. 比例

◆ The ratio of man to woman is 1:3 in Taiwan.
在台灣男女的比例是一比三。

◆ The ratio between the two parties is one to two.
這兩個政黨的人數比是一比二。

0134 ★

---

cement
səˈmɛnt
n. 水泥 v. 使鞏
固；使黏緊

◆ That sidewalk is made of cement.
這個人行道是水泥製的。

◆ It is very important for our nation to cement trade relations with other nations.
鞏固我們國家與其它國家的貿易關係是很重要的。

0135

---

bucket
ˈbʌkɪt
n. 水桶

◆ Children often use a bucket and a shovel to play in the sand.
孩子們經常拿水桶與鏟子在沙地上玩。

◆ The naughty boys can't wait to douse him with a bucket of water during the Water Festival.
潑水節時這些頑皮的孩子等不及把一桶水潑在他身上。

0136

---

plumber
ˈplʌmə
n. 水管工人

◆ If your water stops running, you should call a plumber.
假如停水了，你應該叫水管工人來。

◆ You have to call a plumber carefully check of the pipes.
你必須找水管工來對這些水管仔細檢查。

0137

---

fire
faɪr
n. 火；火災

◆ The famous department store was on fire.
這間著名的百貨公司著火了。

◆ It is praiseworthy for his courage to save people from the fire.
他從大火中救人，勇氣值得讚許。

0138

match
mætʃ
n. 火柴；婚姻
對象 *v.* 適合

◆ He reached for the matches.
他伸手拿火柴。

◆ Your shirt and tie match pretty well.
你的襯衫與領帶很相配。

0139

flame
flem
n. 火焰；火舌

◆ A volcano spouts flame and lava in Italy.
義大利的一座火山噴出火焰及熔岩。

◆ Many fire engines are playing on the flames.
許多消防車正在救火。

0140

blaze
blez
n. 火焰；閃光；
火災

◆ The building burned for hours before the blaze was put out.
這棟建築物燒了數小時火勢才撲滅。

◆ Several cars and motorcycles had been burnt to the ground before the blaze was controlled.
在這場火災被控制住之前，許多汽車與摩托車被完全燒毀了。

0141

parental
pə'rɛntl
adj. 父母親的

◆ Ivy wanted to be a singer but succumbed to parental pressure and was trained as a dentist.
艾薇想當歌手，但屈從於父母的壓力，成為牙醫。

◆ You had better change your parental strategy.
你最好改變你做父母的管教方式。

0142

royalty
'rɔɪəltɪ
n. 王權；王室；
版稅

◆ How much do you agree to pay in royalties?
你同意要付多少權利金？

◆ The writer can receive a 10% royalty on each copy of his book sold.
這位作家每賣一本書可收百分之十的版稅。

0143 ★

generation
.dʒɛnə'reʃən
n. 世代；一代

◆ Up to my grand grandfather's generation my family were local farmers.
從我曾祖父那一代起，我們家就都是當地的農民。

◆ The new generation tried to break the shackles of convention.
新的世代嘗試打破傳統的束縛。

0144

worldly
'wɜldlɪ
adj. 世俗的；
世間的

◆ He left all his worldly goods to charity.
他把所有世俗的財產留給慈善機構。

◆ My professor stood aloof from worldly success.
我的教授對世俗的成功漠不關心。

0145

master
ˈmæstə
n. 主人；碩士
v. 使精通

◆ The cruel master beat his dog with a whip.
這位殘酷的主人鞭打他的狗。

◆ He masters programming and the Internet.
他精通程式設計以及網際網路。

0146 ★

kingpin
ˈkɪŋˌpɪn
n. 主要人物；
領袖

◆ Tourism is the economic kingpin of Thailand.
旅遊業是泰國的主要經濟命脈。

◆ He's the kingpin of the whole baseball team.
他是整個棒球隊的主要人物。

0147

main
men
adj. 主要的；
首要的

◆ The main building material of this house is concrete.
這棟房子的主要建材是混凝土。

◆ A strong storm blocks the main road.
一陣強烈的暴風雨阻塞了主要的道路。

0148

major
ˈmedʒə
n. 主修科目
v. 主修……
adj. 主要的

◆ There are twelve required courses in my major.
我的主修科目有十二門必修課。

◆ Do you have a major credit card?
你有任何主要信用卡嗎？

0149 ★

chairman
ˈtʃɛrmən
n. 主席
(同 chairperson)

◆ The chairman made a few conventional remarks in the meeting.
這位主席在會議中說了些客套話。

◆ The chairman called the meeting to order.
主席宣布會議開始。

0150

doctrine
ˈdɑktrɪn
n. 主義；學說

資本主義

◆ This new esthetic doctrine was generally accepted by the public.
這個新的美學主義普遍被大眾所接受。

◆ Most people were astonished at her doctrine.
大多數人因為她的學說而驚訝。

0151

subjective
səbˈdʒɛktɪv
adj. 主觀的；
個人的

很**主觀**喔！

◆ He is so subjective that he never accepts anyone else's suggestions.
他主觀到從來不肯接受別人的意見。

◆ My father has a subjective bias against Japanese and Chinese people.
我父親對日本人與中國人有主觀的偏見。

0152 ★

representative
ˌrɛprɪˈzɛntətɪv
n. 代表；代理人；典型人物

◆ The tiger is a common representative of the cat family.
老虎是貓科動物中最常見的代表。

◆ Many representatives from various countries attend the summit conference regularly.
來自各國的許多代表定期出席高峯會議。

0153 ★

contingent
kənˈtɪndʒənt
n. 代表團 **adj.** 有條件的；附帶的

歐洲代表團

◆ A large contingent from China was present at the conference.
一個龐大的中國代表團出席這場會議。

◆ Further investment must be contingent upon the company's profit performance.
進一步投資必須是有條件的，視公司的獲利表現而定。

0154

delegate
ˈdɛləˌget
n. 代表團；委派代表 **v.** 授權……

◆ She delegated him to take part in a chess competition.
她委派他代表參加一場西洋棋競賽。

◆ Each party delegates one member to attend the election of Taipei city mayor.
各個政黨推派一名成員參選台北市市長選舉。

0155 ★

repulsive
rɪˈpʌlsɪv
adj. 令人噁心的；使人嫌惡的

走開！

◆ The dirty street was repulsive.
這骯髒的街道令人噁心。

◆ The mayor's speech was tedious and repulsive.
這位市長的演講乏味而且令人作嘔。

0156

marvelous
ˈmɑrvələs
adj. 令人驚嘆的；奇異的

◆ He earned a scholarship because of his marvelous achievement in the school.
他因為在學校的出色成就而贏得獎學金。

◆ I wish I could dive in the marvelous sea.
我希望能在令人驚嘆的的大海中潛水。

0157

substitute
ˈsʌbstəˌtjut
v. 以……代替 **n.** 代理人；代用品

我來代替你!

◆ Is there any chance that we can substitute this for you？
有沒有任何可能由我們來幫你替換這個呢？

◆ Vitamins should not be used as a substitute for a healthy diet.
不能以吃維他命當作健康節食的替代方案。

0158 ★

stake
stek
v. 以……打賭 **n.** 賭注；柱

◆ The life of the serious patient is at stake.
這個重病患者的生命危在旦夕。

◆ The gardener put up a stake to support the newly planted tree.
這位園丁豎立一根柱子來支持這棵新種的樹。

0159

abundant
əˋbʌndənt
adj. 充裕的；豐富的

◆ The area is abundant in gold and natural resources.
這個區域有充足的黃金和天然資源。

◆ The library provides abundant resources and information for the local people.
這間圖書館提供了當地人充足的資源與資訊。

0160

---

concave
kɑnˋkev
adj. 凹面的

◆ The teacher taught us how to use the concave lens.
老師教我們如何使用凹面鏡。

◆ The outside surfaces of my eyeglasses are convex, and the insides are concave.
我眼鏡的外部平面是凸面的，裡面則是凹面的。

0161

---

exit
ˋɛksɪt
n. 出口；退場

◆ The exit is located next to the stage.
出口在舞台旁邊。

◆ Which exit should I take for Time Square?
到時代廣場要走哪個出口？

0162

---

origin
ˋɔrədʒɪn
n. 出身；起源

◆ The origin of that dance song is Latin.
這首舞曲源自於拉丁人。

◆ Scientists try to speculate on the origin of the earth.
科學家們嘗試猜測地球的起源。

0163 ★

---

publisher
ˋpʌblɪʃɚ
n. 出版商

◆ The publisher promoted the second edition of Harry Porter.
出版社為《哈利波特》再版促銷。

◆ The author wrote a summary of his book to send to a publisher.
這位作者寫了他的書的摘要寄給一家出版社。

0164

---

appear
əˋpɪr
v. 出現；出庭

◆ Rainbows sometimes appear after raining.
下雨過後，有時會出現彩虹。

◆ He does not appear to be happy.
他看起來不快樂。

0165

---

emerge
ɪˋmɝdʒ
v. 出現；露出

◆ The rainbow emerged soon after the rain.
雨後隨即出現了彩虹。

◆ I saw the naughty boy emerge from the bushes.
我看到這位頑皮的男孩從灌木叢出現。

0166

yield
jild
v. 出產 (水果) ；
使屈服；讓與

◆ The hijackers refuse to yield to release the hostages.
劫機者拒絕屈服釋放人質。

◆ The soldier would rather die than yield to the enemy.
這士兵寧可死也不願意向敵方投降。

0167 ★

output
'aʊt,pʊt
v. 出產……
n. 生產；作品

◆ South Africa is very productive in outputting diamonds.
南非在鑽石方面是很多產的。

◆ You must increase your output to meet our demand.
你必須增加你們的生產來滿足我們的需要。

0168 ★

bid
bɪd
n. 出價
v. 投標……；吩咐……

(500元！)

◆ We'd like a chance to bid on this business.
我們希望有機會投標到這筆生意。

◆ Are there no bids for this beautiful house?
那棟漂亮的房子都沒人出價嗎？

0169

merit
'mɛrɪt
n. 功績；優點

◆ One of her great merits is her ability to listen.
她的眾多優點之一就是傾聽的能力。

◆ Teachers judge students on their own merits and not on how rich their parents are.
老師們判斷學生是依照他們的優點，而不是他們父母多有錢。

0170

spicy
'spaɪsɪ
adj. 加有香料的；辛辣的

◆ We like to eat spicy kimchi soup.
我們喜歡吃辛辣的韓國泡菜湯。

◆ Spicy food does not agree with the elderly.
辛辣的食物不適合老人。

0171

stress
strɛs
v. 加重音；使強調 **n.** 壓力

[ə`priʃ ɪ͵et]

◆ My English teacher stressed the importance of writing.
我的英文老師強調寫作的重要。

◆ We don't want to be under too much stress.
我們不願意有太大壓力。

0172

accentuate
æk'sɛntʃʊ͵et
v. 加重音；強調……

bonəs

◆ My boss accentuated that everyone should come on time.
我老闆強調每個人都要準時到達。

◆ My coach is right to accentuate the positive.
我的教練強調有信心是對的。

0173

encryption
ɪnˈkrɪpʃən
n. 加密

◆ Encryption technology is often used to achieve data security.
密碼技術經常用在資料防護上。

◆ You can change the encryption key for your confidential file.
你可以幫機密檔案更換加密的金鑰。

0174 ★

include
ɪnˈklud
v. 包括；包含

◆ Does the price include the rent and the water fee?
這個價錢包含了房租跟水費嗎？

◆ The price includes both television and video recorder.
價錢包括了電視和錄影機。

0175 ★

package
ˈpækɪdʒ
n. 包裹

◆ I will call you and let you know when we ship the package.
當我們運送這個包裹時，會打電話讓你知道。

◆ I'd like to insure this package, please.
這個包裹我打算投保。

0176

radius
ˈredɪəs
n. 半徑

◆ What is the radius of this circle?
這個圓的半徑是多少？

◆ I have searched for jobs in a two-mile radius around my home.
我一直在尋找離我家半徑兩公里內的工作。

0177

hemisphere
ˈhɛməsˌfɪr
n. 半球體

◆ America is located on the northern hemisphere.
美國是位於北半球。

◆ Tactile and visual sensations are controlled by the right hemisphere of the brain.
觸覺及視覺是由右半邊大腦掌管。

0178

ancient
ˈenʃənt
adj. 古代的；古老的

◆ He likes to collect ancient objects.
他喜歡收藏古物。

◆ The art museum has a good collection of ancient gold and silver coins.
這家藝術博物館有很好的古金幣與銀幣收藏。

0179

weird
wɪrd
adj. 古怪的；怪異的

◆ I was scared by the weird sounds in the forest.
我被森林裡傳來的古怪聲音嚇了一跳。

◆ He cannot stand Virgo people's weird fear of dirtiness.
他不能忍受處女座的人那種怪異的潔癖。

0180

sentence
ˈsɛntəns
n. 句子 *v.* 宣判……

◆ Can you read the next sentence for me?
請你為我讀下一個句子。

◆ If the subject is singular, use a singular verb in English sentence.
在英文句子中，如果主詞是單數，就要用單數動詞。

0181

assemble
əˈsɛmbl
v. 召集……；集合；裝配……

◆ The students were assembled in the school garden.
這些學生在校園集合。

◆ Everyone had already assembled in the boardroom.
所有人都已經到會議室集合了。

0182

available
əˈveləbl
adj. 可用的；有空的

◆ Are there some other days you are available?
還有沒有其他有空的時間？

◆ Is this machine available in Taiwan?
這種機器在台灣買得到嗎？

0183 ★

horrible
ˈhɑrəbl
adj. 可怕的；可憎的

◆ This movie is so horrible, I regret seeing it.
這部電影太可怕了，我很後悔去看。

◆ It is horrible to walk along in the tenebrous street.
在暗巷中獨自走路是很恐怖的。

0184 ★

awful
ˈɔful
adj. 可怕的；嚇人的

◆ To be candid with you, you look awful with heavy make-up.
坦白跟你說，你畫濃妝很嚇人。

◆ At the party, she looked awful with her furbelows.
在這個宴會上，她的俗麗衣飾讓她看來嚇人。

0185 ★

terrible
ˈtɛrəbl
adj. 可怕的；嚇人的

◆ The traffic is terrible at rush hour.
交通狀況在顛峰時間很糟糕。

◆ Reports have just come in of a terrible crash between two airlines.
剛才插播了兩架飛機相撞的可怕新聞。

0186

chance
ˈtʃæns
n. 可能性；機會

◆ It's a good chance to beat the enemy.
這是打敗敵人的好機會。

◆ I will give you one more chance to be good.
我再給你一次改過自新的機會。

0187 ★

probable
ˈprɑbəbl
adj. 可能的；
可能發生的；有
希望的

他可能睡著了！

◆ It seems probable that he will arrive on time.
他似乎能夠準時到達。

◆ Your new hypothesis is considered probable.
你的新假設被認為是可行的。

0188 ★

feasible
ˈfizəbl
adj. 可實行的；
可能的；合理的

◆ It is feasible to earn money first and then go abroad to study.
先賺錢然後到國外念書是可行的。

◆ This fertile land is feasible for cultivation.
這塊肥沃的土地適合耕種。

0189 ★

suspicious
səˈspɪʃəs
adj. 可疑的；
懷疑的

◆ His sneaky behavior on the street made the police suspicious.
他在街頭鬼鬼祟祟的行徑引起了警察的懷疑。

◆ The police were suspicious of the bank clerk for his peculation.
警方懷疑這位銀行行員盜用公款。

0190

reliable
rɪˈlaɪəbl
adj. 可靠的；
可信賴的

◆ The candidate's honest statements made the voters feel that he would be reliable.
這位候選人誠實的聲明使選民感到可以信賴。

◆ Mary is so reliable that the employer appreciates her very much.
瑪麗很可靠，所以老闆非常欣賞她。

0191

portable
ˈportəbl
adj. 可攜帶的

◆ She uses a portable computer to keep a diary when she travels.
當她旅行時，都使用可攜式電腦來寫日記。

◆ I have bought a small-screen portable TV yesterday.
我昨天買了一台可攜式小螢幕電視。

0192 ★

quarter
ˈkwɔrtə
n. 四分之一；
一刻鐘；(美金)
二十五分

◆ You need to pay a quarter of a million dollars to buy this company.
你需要付二十五萬美金來買這間公司。

◆ Would you mind giving me some quarters for this dollar?
我可以拿這一元美金和你換一些二角五分的硬幣嗎？

0193 ★

outsourcing
ˈaut.sɔrsɪŋ
n. 外包工作；
外購

◆ The challenges of outsourcing become especially acute when the work is being done in a different country.
當在不同的國家從事工作時，外包任務的挑戰變得特別嚴重。

◆ Outsourcing can't solve your financial problem.
外包工作不能解決你的財務問題。

0194 ★

superficial
ˌsupɚˈfɪʃəl
adj. 外表的；表面的；淺薄的

◆ It is superficial to judge people by appearance.
看外表來判斷人是膚淺的。

◆ The book is talking about something superficial.
這本書談論的是一些相當淺薄的事。

0195

foreign
ˈfɔrɪn
adj. 外國的

◆ Can you speak any other foreign language?
你會說其他的外國語言嗎？

◆ This is my first visit to a foreign country.
這是我第一次到國外參觀。

0196

trauma
ˈtrɔmə
n. 外傷；傷口

◆ There are several traumas on his arm.
他的手臂上有許多傷口。

◆ People say that time is the best medicine to cure one's trauma.
人們說時間是治癒心靈創傷最好的藥。

0197

affair
əˈfɛr
n. 外遇；事情

◆ Did you know he was having an affair?
你知道他有外遇嗎？

◆ We have no right to intercede with the internal affairs of other countries.
我們沒有權力去仲裁其它國家的內部事務。

0198 ★

exterior
ɪkˈstɪrɪə

n. 外貌 **adj.** 外部的

◆ The exterior walls of the buildings in the city are painted white.
這個城市中建築物的外牆都被漆上白色。

◆ The cases have tough exterior materials to protect against knocks.
這些箱子的外表材料相當結實，可以耐受撞擊。

0199

coincidence
koˈɪnsədəns

n. 巧合；碰巧

◆ You two are wearing the same pants. What a coincidence!
你們兩人穿同樣的褲子。真巧！

◆ They encounter each other by an uncanny coincidence.
不可思議的巧合使他們相遇。

0200

huge
hjudʒ

adj. 巨大的；極大的

◆ Peter owed me a huge amount of money.
彼得欠了我一大筆錢。

◆ He can achieve the goal because of his huge efforts.
他能達成目標是由於他極大的努力。

0201

tremendous
trɪˈmɛndəs

adj. 巨大的；驚人的；可怕的

◆ The terrorists plan to make a tremendous explosion in LA.
恐怖分子計劃要在洛杉磯製造一場極大的爆炸。

◆ He has tremendous aptitude for art.
他對藝術有極大的才能。

0202

citizen
ˈsɪtəzn

n. 市民；公民

◆ The citizens in the city came to the aggregate number of a million.
這城市的市民總數達到一百萬。

◆ He is an eminent citizen of America.
他是一位傑出的美國公民。

0203 ★

mayor
ˈmeə

n. 市長

◆ The mayor in the city impresses the citizens with his good image.
這個市長的好形象讓市民印象深刻。

◆ The mayor often speaks in public with a megaphone.
市長經常使用擴音器對公眾演說。

0204

mediocre
ˋmidɪͺokəˋ
adj. 平凡的；中等的

◆ The novel describes the way of life of the mediocre people there.
這部小說描述一個平凡人的生活方式。

◆ The mediocre performance bored the audience.
這場平庸的演出讓觀眾感覺無聊。

0205

market
ˋmɑrkɪt
n. 市場

◆ I enjoy going to the night market.
我喜歡去逛夜市。

◆ Our latest product will be on the market at the end of this month.
我們的新產品將於這個月底上市。

0206

welfare
ˋwɛlͺfɛr
n. 平安；福利；福祉

◆ What sort of welfare do you provide?
你們有提供哪些福利呢？

◆ Many benefits accrue to society with perfect social welfare.
完美的社會福利增加了社會許多好處。

0207 ★

smooth
smuð
adj. 平坦的；平穩的

◆ The music changed from a smooth melody to a staccato rhythm.
這音樂從一個平穩的旋律改變到斷音的節奏。

◆ The strong wind tousled her smooth hair.
這陣強風弄亂了她平順的頭髮。

0208

plane
plen
n. 平面；飛機
adj. 平坦的

◆ The platform must be completely plane.
這個月台必須是完全平坦的。

◆ Please keep your performance on a high plane.
請讓你的表現維持高水平。

0209 ★

requirement
rɪˋkwaɪrmənt
n. 必需品；必要條件

◆ You can't seem to meet our sales requirements.
你似乎無法達成我們的銷售要求。

◆ The refugees' main requirements are food and water.
難民的主要必需品是食物與水。

0210

pack
pæk
v. 打包……
n. 一盒；一包

◆ We'll need all our orders packed that way from now on.
今後我們所有訂單都要這樣包裝。

◆ When will you pack for your trip?
你何時收拾行李？

0211

typist
ˈtaɪpɪst
n. 打字員

◆ I substituted for the dexterous typist during her absence.
這個熟練的打字員不在時，由我來代替她。

◆ Typists transcribe tape recordings of conversations and enter them into the database.
打字員抄寫了錄音帶的對話記錄，並將他們放回資料庫中。

0212

yawn
jɔn
v. 打呵欠 **n.** 乏味的事

◆ His long boring speech made us yawn.
他冗長無聊的演講讓我們打起了哈欠。

◆ The speech is one big yawn from start to finish.
這場演講從頭到尾都十分乏味。

0213

salute
səˈlut
v. 打招呼；向……致敬

◆ Japanese salute each other with a bow.
日本人彼此鞠躬表示敬意。

◆ The general ordered his soldiers to fire a salute.
這位將軍命令他的士兵鳴放禮砲。

0214

maul
mɔl
v. 打傷……；傷害……；虐待……

◆ He had been mauled by a big dog.
他被一隻大狗攻擊受傷了。

◆ The troops were severely mauled before evacuating the isolated island.
這個軍隊撤出這孤島時被重創。

0215

shatter
ˈʃætə
v. 打碎；粉碎

◆ The boy shattered the window with a stone to express his anger.
這個男孩用石頭砸破窗戶發洩怒氣。

◆ The bottle will shatter if you drop it carelessly.
假如你不小心讓它掉下來，這個瓶子會碎掉。

0216

call
kɔl
v. 打電話；稱為……

◆ Call me when you get home.
到家後打個電話給我。

◆ My dad's boss calls him everyday.
我爸的老闆天天打電話給他。

0217

bet
bɛt
v. 打賭…… **n.** 賭注

◆ He bet one hundred dollars on the black horse.
他賭這隻黑馬一百元美金。

◆ I made a bet that he would win the game.
我打賭他會贏得這場比賽。

0218

sneeze
sniz

v. 打噴嚏

◆ She sneezes every time that she smells pepper.
她每次一聞到胡椒粉就會打噴嚏。

◆ When I get a cold, I sneeze a lot.
當我感冒時，很會打噴嚏。

0219

disturb
dɪˈstɝb

v. 打擾……；使不安

◆ They were fined for disturbing the peace.
他們因為妨礙安寧而被罰款。

◆ I cannot endure being disturbed during work.
我無法忍受工作時受到打擾。

0220 ★

interrupt
ɪntəˈrʌpt

v. 打斷；妨礙

◆ It is impolite to interrupt a conversation suddenly.
突然打斷人家交談是不禮貌的。

◆ Bill is precipitate to interrupt the conversation without understanding the situation first.
比爾沒有先了解情況，就魯莽地打斷談話。

0221 ★

shiver
ˈʃɪvə

v. 打顫；發抖

◆ She is shivering with cold as she waits for a bus in the snow.
當她在雪中等巴士時冷得顫抖。

◆ He was shivering when he faced the frigid wind.
當他面對這冷風時冷到發抖。

0222

future
ˈfjutʃə

n. 未來

◆ No one knows what will happen in the future.
沒人知道未來會發生什麼事。

◆ Going to college will help you have a better future.
上大學會幫助你擁有比較好的未來。

0223 ★

prospective
prəˈspɛktɪv

adj. 未來的；預期的

◆ We have received letters of application from several prospective candidates.
我們收到數封預期可以成為候選人的申請書。

◆ The prospective employees try to create good impressions during their job interviews.
未來的僱員試圖在工作面談中製造好印象。

0224

undetected
ˌʌndɪˈtɛktɪd

adj. 未被發現的

◆ Of course, we have no statistics on crimes that go undetected.
當然我們沒有未發現犯罪的統計資料。

◆ The disease often remains undetected for a long time.
這種疾病常常很久都沒有被發現。

0225

square
skwɛr
n. 正方形；方塊；平方

◆ Can you draw a square?
你會畫正方形嗎？

◆ The field is fifty square meters.
這塊田地為五十平方公尺。

0226

---

renounce
rɪˋnauns
v. 正式放棄；宣布退出

我要退出比賽!

◆ Susan decided to renounce her claim to the inheritance.
蘇珊決定放棄她的財產繼承權。

◆ The famous writer renounced family for a life of adventure abroad.
這位知名作家為了海外的冒險生活放棄家庭。

0227

---

formal
ˋfɔrml̩
adj. 正式的；形式上的

◆ I would like to make a formal complaint.
我想提出一個正式的控訴。

◆ Every guest in this party was requested to wear formal gowns.
這場宴會的每位來賓都必須穿正式禮服。

0228 ★

---

normal
ˋnɔrml̩
adj. 正常的；常態的

36℃

◆ In Western society, it is quite normal for everyone to have his own lawyer.
在西方社會中，每個人都有自己的律師是相當正常的。

◆ The prison service aimed to rehabilitate the criminals so that they can lead normal lives when they leave prison.
監獄的用意在改造罪犯，使他們在出獄後能過正常生活。

0229 ★

---

correct
kəˋrɛkt
adj. 正確的
v. 改正

◆ Are you sure the amount is correct?
您確定這數目是正確的嗎？

◆ My fictitious answer is not necessarily correct.
我假想的答案不必是正確的。

0230

---

perpetrate
ˋpɝpəˏtret
v. 犯……罪行；做……錯事

◆ I perpetrated an error in handling the business.
在我處理這項業務時犯了一個錯誤。

◆ What kind of person can perpetrate this terrible crime?
什麼樣的人能夠犯下這麼糟糕的罪行？

0231

---

commit
kəˋmɪt
v. 犯罪……；委託；授與

◆ Gill committed an error in handling the business.
在處理這項業務時，吉爾犯了一個錯誤。

◆ John refuses to commit a crime.
約翰拒絕犯罪。

0232

raw
rɔ
adj. 生的；未煮過的；皮破肉損的

◆ Do you want your vegetables cooked or raw?
你想把蔬菜煮熟或生吃？

◆ The raw and bleeding wound was bound up by bandage.
這個皮開肉綻又流血的傷口被用繃帶包紮起來。

0233

---

flaw
flɔ
v. 生裂縫 *n.* 瑕疵

◆ Can you spot the flaw in their proposals?
你能舉出他們提案中的缺點嗎？

◆ Arrogance is the greatest flaw in his character personality.
傲慢是他性格上的最大缺點。

0234

---

rust
rʌst
v. 生鏽；變遲鈍 *n.* 鏽

◆ The great advantage of this tool is that it doesn't rust.
這個工具最大的好處是不會生鏽。

◆ Iron will easily react with water and air to produce rust.
鐵容易和水與空氣反應產生鐵鏽。

0235

---

tie
taɪ
v. 用……綁起來；與……聯繫 *n.* 領帶

◆ Please tie these books with the string.
請把書用繩子捆起來。

◆ This blue tie does not match with your suit.
這條藍色的領帶和你的西裝不配。

0236

---

scrub
skrʌb
v. 用力擦洗；刷洗

◆ She patiently scrubbed the dirty marks on the table.
她有耐心地擦洗桌上的痕跡。

◆ The maid has to scrub off all the oil muck before evening.
這位女僕在下午前必須擦洗掉所有油汙。

0237

---

capitalize
ˈkæpətḷ.aɪz
v. 用大寫書寫；供給（資本）

◆ Should we capitalize our name?
我們的名字需要大寫嗎？

◆ My boss decided to capitalize all his property.
我老闆決定把所有財產轉為資本。

0238

---

secondhand
ˈsɛkəndhænd
adj. 用過的；二手的

◆ How much is the secondhand calculator?
這台二手計算機要多少錢？

◆ I want to buy a dictionary from a secondhand bookstore.
我想去舊書店買本字典。

0239

consist

kənˈsɪst

v. 由……組成；由……構成

◆ The complicated machine consists of several component parts.
這台複雜的機器由許多零件所組成。

◆ The machine consists of a pair of concentric cylinders.
這台機器是由一對同軸的圓筒所組成。

0240 ★

application

ˌæpləˈkeʃən

n. 申請書；申請

◆ I'd like to make an application for a telephone.
我想申請一支電話。

◆ Complete your application in ink, please.
請用鋼筆填寫申請書。

0241 ★

white-collar

ˌhwaɪtˈkɑlɚ

adj. 白領階級的

◆ White-collar workers refer to salaried professionals or educated workers in a company.
白領工作者是一家公司內的受薪專業人員或受過教育的工作者。

◆ We had to lay off thousands of white-collar workers last year.
去年我們必須資遣數千名白領工作人員。

0242

skin

skɪn

n. 皮膚；外皮
v. 擦破皮

◆ Skin is the human body's first defense against bacteria.
皮膚是人體抵抗細菌的第一道防線。

◆ Spa water is very good for the skin because of the minerals it contains.
溫泉水因為含有礦物質，所以對皮膚很好。

0243

object

ˈɑbdʒɪkt

n. 目標；物體

◆ UFO stands for Unknow Flying Object.
UFO 代表不明飛行物體。

◆ I paint a lot of still objects, but I'm not very good at portraits.
我畫許多靜物，但不太擅長畫人像。

0244 ★

eyewitness

ˈaɪˈwɪtnɪs

n. 目擊者

◆ The eyewitness was accused of perjury.
這個目擊者被控作偽證。

◆ He was the only eyewitness of the crime.
他是這場罪行的唯一目擊者。

0245

legislature

ˈlɛdʒɪsˌletɚ

n. 立法機關

◆ The legislature impeached the governor for his graft.
州議會以貪汙罪彈劾這位州長。

◆ The legislature passed many bills yesterday.
立法院昨天通過了多項法案。

0246

transaction
træn'zækʃən
n. 交易；處理；買賣

◆ It is safe to sign covenant during the business transaction.
進行商務交易時，要簽署契約才安全。

◆ Internet has caused a revolution in business practices and transaction.
網際網路已經對商務的進行及交易引起了一場革命。

0247 ★

traffic
'træfɪk
n. 交通

◆ Turn right at the first traffic light and then you'll see the post office.
在第一個交通號誌右轉，你就可以看到郵局了。

◆ New measures have been taken to solve traffic problems.
新措施已施行以解決交通問題。

0248

arbitrate
'ɑrbə.tret
v. 仲裁；公斷

◆ You have to arbitrate the quarrel between Bill and Jack.
你必須仲裁比爾和傑克之間的爭論。

◆ Someone must arbitrate between them.
必須有個人在他們之間仲裁。

0249

constitute
'kɑnstə.tjut
v. 任命……；構成……；設立……

◆ This move constitutes an expression of love.
這個動作構成了愛的表現。

◆ Twelve months constitute one year.
十二個月構成一年。

0250 ★

tenure
'tɛnjə
n. 任期；保有

◆ During the mayor's tenure, she made many improvements.
在市長任期內，她做了許多改善。

◆ The tenure of office of an Taiwan president is four years.
台灣總統的任期是四年。

0251 ★

enterprise
'ɛntə.praɪz
n. 企業；進取心

◆ My boss think that the name of our new enterprise should be copyrighted.
老闆認為我們新企業的名字必須要申請版權。

◆ His job was to liaise between the government and the enterprises.
他的工作是負責政府與企業之間的聯絡。

0252 ★

fierce
fɪrs
adj. 兇猛的；猛烈的

◆ Lions and tigers are both fierce animals.
獅子和老虎都是兇猛的動物。

◆ The kid was frightened by the fierce cat.
這個小孩被這隻凶惡的貓嚇壞了。

0253

luminous
/ˈlumənəs/
adj. 光亮的；發亮的

◆ You should wear luminous clothing when riding a bicycle at night.
夜晚騎腳踏車時，你應該穿會反光的衣服。

◆ The full moon is luminous tonight.
今晚的滿月很明亮。

0254

slippery
/ˈslɪpərɪ/
adj. 光滑的；狡猾的

◆ The roads are very slippery with ice.
路上結冰非常的滑。

◆ The road was slippery after the heavy rain.
這場大雨之後，路面非常光滑。

0255

optical
/ˈɑptɪkl/
adj. 光學的；視力的

◆ Pilots are guided by infrared optical systems that show images clearly even at night.
駕駛員靠著即使在晚上都能將影像顯示清楚的紅外線光學系統所引導。

◆ Both telescopes and microscopes are optical instruments.
顯微鏡和望遠鏡都是光學儀器。

0256

national
/ˈnæʃənl/
adj. 全國性的

◆ The national expense has exceeded the budget.
國家的花費已經比預算還要高。

◆ The 4th of July is a national holiday in America.
七月四日是美國的國定假日。

0257 ★

global
/ˈglobl/
adj. 全球的；球形的；世界性的

◆ In recent years, the global temperature has continued to rise.
近幾年來全球溫度一直持續上升中。

◆ Because of global warming, the polar ice caps are melting.
因為全球暖化，南北極的冰帽融化了。

0258 ★

staff
/stæf/
n. 全體人員；全體職員

◆ The staff of this company are very outstanding.
這個公司的全體職員都是非常傑出的。

◆ The company dismissed a superfluity of staff.
這家公司遣散了多餘的員工。

0259 ★

accomplice
/əˈkɑmplɪs/
n. 共犯

◆ The drug smugglers were arrested, but one accomplice got away.
毒品走私販被逮捕，但有一名共犯逃逸。

◆ He was charged with being an accomplice to the crime.
他被控是這項犯罪活動的共犯。

0260

list
list
v. 列出……
n. 目錄；名冊

◆ He listed the names of the guests who were invited to the seminar.
他列出受邀參加研討會的來賓名單。

◆ See! Your name is on the waiting list. You still have chance to enter this school.
看！你的名字出現在備取名單中，你還是有希望考取的。

0261

procession
prə'sɛʃən
n. 列隊行進；隊伍

◆ Thousands of people joined the demonstration procession.
數以千計的人參加示威遊行。

◆ The military march was a long procession.
這個軍事遊行的隊伍很長。

0262

crisis
'kraɪsɪs
n. 危機；難關

◆ The economic crisis has lasted for several years.
經濟危機持續了許多年。

◆ The company is unable to pay the emoluments to the employees during its financial crisis.
這間公司在財務危機時期，無法給付員工薪資。

0263 ★

danger
'dendʒɚ
n. 危險

◆ The woman is in danger of losing her baby.
這個女人有流產的危險。

◆ Only a dastard would run away from helping someone in danger.
只有懦夫會逃避去幫助身陷危險的人。

0264

不怕慢，只怕站

dangerous
ˈdendʒərəs

adj. 危險的；不安全的

◆ Leaving these barbs here may be dangerous for children.
把鉤子留在這裡對孩子們來說是危險的。

◆ It is dangerous for a girl to dawdle over alone in the night.
一個女孩子在夜間單獨遊蕩很危險。

0265 ★

hazardous
ˈhæzədəs

adj. 危險的；冒險的

◆ Hazardous nuclear waste is a big menace to public safety.
危險的核廢料對大眾安全是種重大威脅。

◆ It is an offence to carry hazardous material onto a plane.
攜帶違禁品上飛機是違法的。

0266

merge
mɜdʒ

v. 合併；吞併

◆ The company plans to merge its subsidiaries into one.
這家公司計劃把它的子公司合併成一個。

◆ The two roads merge a mile ahead
這兩條路在前面一英里處會合。

0267

eligible
ˈɛlɪdʒəbḷ

adj. 合格的；合意的

◆ Only citizens are eligible to vote.
只有公民才有資格投票。

◆ Jordan is the most eligible bachelor in the world.
喬丹是世界上最夠格的單身漢。

0268 ★

rational
ˈræʃənḷ

adj. 合理的；理性的

這很合理！

◆ Gemini people are mostly quite rational.
雙子座的人大多相當理性。

◆ A statesman must be a rational person.
一位政治家必須是理性的。

0269

reasonable
ˈrizənəbḷ

adj. 合理的；講道理的

很合理喔！

◆ If the price is reasonable, I will rent the house.
如果價錢合理，我就會租下這間房子。

◆ Our sales target for the next year are very reasonable.
我們下年度的銷售目標是非常合理的。

0270

simultaneous
.saɪm1'tenɪəs
adj. 同時的；
同時發生的

◆ This event was almost simultaneous with that one.
這個事件和那件事幾乎同時發生。

◆ Do you need simultaneous interpretation service?
你需要同步翻譯嗎？

0271

compassion
kəm'pæʃən
n. 同情；憐憫

◆ His suffering arouses her compassion.
他的痛苦引起她的同情。

◆ The doctor had great compassion for her patients.
這位醫生很同情她的病人。

0272 ★

synonym
'sɪnə.mɪn
n. 同義字

fall ; autumn
秋天

◆ This book will help you review and strengthen your knowledge of synonyms.
這本書將幫助你複習和加強同義詞的知識。

◆ Could you tell me the synonym and antonym of this word?
你能告訴我這個字的同義字和反義字是什麼嗎？

0273 ★

peer
pɪr
n. 同輩；同事

◆ I want to discuss the homework with my school peers.
我想和學校同學討論功課。

◆ The peer pressure is one of the reasons of juvenile delinquency.
同儕壓力是青少年犯罪的原因之一。

0274

reputation
.rɛpjə'teʃən
n. 名聲；名譽

◆ A company recall does a lot of harm to its reputation.
一家公司回收產品對聲譽會造成很大傷害。

◆ This Chinese restaurant attracts many visitors because of its good reputation.
這家中國餐館的好評吸引很多客人。

0275 ★

propose
prə'poz
v. 向……提議；
提供意見；求婚

◆ You will be interested to see what we propose.
你們一定有興趣看看我們的提議。

◆ He proposed to his girlfriend with sincerity.
他真誠地向他女友求婚。

0276

rush
rʌʃ
n. 衝；匆忙；
搶購

◆ Many vehicles are on the road during rush hour.
交通巔峰時間路上有許多車輛。

◆ There's been a big rush for the robot product lately.
這種機器人產品最近銷路很好。

0277

backward

/ˈbækwəd/

adj. 向後的
adv. 向後地

◆ The backward student lacks a mathematics background.
這位落後的學生缺乏數學背景。

◆ There is a crisis of literacy in this backward country.
這個落後國家有讀寫能力的危機。

0278

consult

/kənˈsʌlt/

v. 向某人請教；
與……商量

◆ I need time to consult with my colleagues.
我需要時間與同事商量。

◆ I'll do nothing without consulting my parents.
任何事我都會跟父母商量之後才去做。

0279

retrospect

/ˈrɛtrə.spɛkt/

v. 回顧……；
回想…… **n.** 懷
舊

◆ In retrospect it was the happiest day of my life.
回顧過去，這是我此生中最快樂的日子。

◆ In retrospect, I wish I had taken the chance.
回顧往事，我希望能把握機會。

0280

therefore

/ˈðɛr.fɔr/

adv. 因此；所
以

◆ He drank too much, therefore we drove him home.
他喝太多了，因此我們必須開車送他回家。

◆ He was down with the flu, and therefore he didn't give the market report.
他患了流行性感冒，因此沒辦法做市場報告。

0281

factor

/ˈfæktə/

n. 因素；要素

◆ Price will be a crucial factor for developing a product.
開發一件商品，價格是關鍵性的因素。

◆ One of many factors of his death was that he used drugs.
他死亡的其中一個原因是吸毒。

0282

undermine

/ˌʌndəˈmaɪn/

v. 在……挖地
道；破壞……的
基礎

◆ The prisoners undermined the jail wall and escaped successfully .
這些囚犯在監獄下挖地道，並且成功逃脫。

◆ The factious group is trying to undermine the government.
這個黨派團體正在設法暗中破壞政府。

0283

ramble

/ˈræmbl/

v. 在……漫步；
蜿蜒伸展

◆ We rambled through the countryside on our bicycles.
我們騎著腳踏車穿過鄉間閒逛。

◆ We went for a ramble through the garden.
我們穿過花園散步。

0284

overseas
.ovə'siz
adv. 在國外

◆ Another new overseas branch will start to operate next month.
另一家新的海外分公司將於下個月起開始營運。

◆ She is listening to an overseas broadcast program.
她正在聽海外的廣播節目。

0285 ★

abroad
ə'brɔd
adv. 在國外；到國外

◆ Are you willing to take business trips abroad?
你願意到海外出差嗎？

◆ My friend will go abroad in the fall.
我的朋友將在秋天出國。

0286 ★

aboard
ə'bord
adv. 在船（或飛機、車）上

◆ He put her aboard an airplane bound for Boston.
他把她送上了一艘往波士頓的飛機。

◆ When should I transact the procedure of going aboard?
什麼時候我應該辦理登機手續？

0287

basement
'besmənt
n. 地下室

◆ There is an underground parking lot in the basement.
地下室有地下停車場。

◆ The fire broke out in the basement yesterday.
昨天地下室著火了。

0288

gravity
'grævətɪ
n. 地心引力；嚴肅

◆ Gravity acts between planets and spacecrafts.
重力在行星和太空船之間起作用。

◆ He preserved his mask of gravity even with acquaintances.
即使遇到熟人，他都保持嚴肅的假面具。

0289

status
'stetəs
n. 地位；身份；狀態

◆ The consulate was upgraded to embassy status last year.
去年這間領事館已升格為大使館。

◆ What's the status on your project?
你的計劃進行得怎麼樣？

0290 ★

address
ə'drɛs
n. 地址 *v.* 向……演說

email address

◆ How far is this address from here?
這個地址離這裡多遠？

◆ The chairman is going to address to the public.
主席將在群眾前發表演說。

0291

ground
graʊnd
n. 地面；土地

◆ Do not play on the wet ground.
不要在溼的地上玩。

◆ How long are we going to be on the ground?
多久之後我們會降落呢？

0292

earthquake
ˈɝθ.kwek
n. 地震

◆ An underwater earthquake caused a tidal wave.
一個海底的地震引起海嘯。

◆ 921 earthquake caused a serious disaster for everyone.
九二一大地震對每個人而言都造成嚴重災難。

0293

site
saɪt
n. 地點

Taipei 101

◆ This is the site of our new home.
這是我們新家的地點。

◆ Our company has a good site in downtown Manhattan.
我們公司在曼哈頓市中心的一個好地點。

0294

rocky
ˈrɑkɪ
adj. 多岩石的；搖晃的

◆ The sea beats against the rocky coast from day to day.
海浪一天又一天地拍打著岩岸。

◆ My father drives carefully up the rocky lane.
我爸爸很小心地從岩石路上駕駛過去。

0295

multinational
ˌmʌltɪˈnæʃənl
adj. 多國的；跨國公司的

◆ She is now serving in a multinational corporation.
他目前在一家跨國公司服務。

◆ The auditor examines the accounts of all departments in the multinational corporation.
這位查帳員檢查這家跨國企業每個部門的帳目。

0296 ★

fruitful
ˈfrutfəl
adj. 多產的；肥沃的；富有成效的

◆ The work will be more fruitful under this plan.
這份工作在這個計劃下成效會更好。

◆ He is really a fruitful novelist.
他是一位多產的小說家。

0297

prolific
prəˈlɪfɪk
adj. 多產的；豐富的；肥沃的

◆ Mice and cockroaches are prolific breeders.
老鼠和蟑螂是多產的繁殖者。

◆ Mozart was a prolific composer.
莫扎特是一位多產的作曲家。

0298

multimedia
ˌmʌltɪˈmidɪə
n. 多媒體

◆ We bought a set of multimedia computers.
我們買了一組多媒體電腦。

◆ Our school holds a multimedia laboratory.
我們學校有一間多媒體實驗室。

0299

overcast
ˈovɚˌkæst
adj. 多雲的；陰暗的 *v.* 使憂鬱

◆ He looked with grief at the overcast sky.
他悲傷地看著陰暗的天空。

◆ The sky was overcast with heavy clouds.
天空布滿烏雲而顯得陰暗。

0300

yummy
ˈjʌmɪ
adj. 好吃的；美味的

◆ The roasted turkey is very yummy.
這烤火雞是很好吃的。

◆ I like eating apples because they are yummy.
我喜歡吃蘋果，因為好吃。

0301

exist
ɪgˈzɪst
v. 存在於

◆ Cinderella doesn't exist in the real world.
灰姑娘在真實世界中並不存在。

◆ The revolutionist plans to overturn the existing government.
革命者計劃推翻現存的政府。

0302

backlog
ˈbækˌlɔg
n. 存貨；積蓄

◆ After the long vacation there was a huge backlog of undelivered mail at the post office.
長假後郵局中積壓了大量未寄出的郵件。

◆ Our company is faced with a backlog of orders we can't deal with.
我們公司積壓了一堆無法處理的訂單。

0303

safety
ˈseftɪ
n. 安全

◆ The safety of nuclear power plant is a very important issue.
核能發電廠安全是一個非常重要的議題。

◆ No consensus has been reached about the safety of the project.
這企劃案的安全性還未達成一致的意見。

0304

security
sɪˈkjurətɪ
n. 安全；保安

◆ The attainment of financial security didn't make him complacent.
財務安全方面的成就並沒有使他感到自滿。

◆ The new security system has a very sensitive motion sensor.
新的保全系統有非常敏感的動作感應器。

0305 ★

arrange
əˈrendʒ
v. 安排；預備

♦ I have to arrange my affairs before going away.
離開之前我必須把事情安排好。

♦ Would you arrange for me to sit next to my friend?
可以讓我和我的朋友坐在一起嗎？

0306 ★

---

temple
ˈtɛmpl
n. 寺廟

♦ There are many temples in Taiwan.
台灣有許多廟宇。

♦ I had never crossed the threshold of a temple before.
我以前從未踏進寺廟的門檻。

0307

---

shriek
ʃrik
v. 尖聲喊叫 *n.* 尖叫聲

♦ The teenage girls shrieked when the rock star appeared.
當搖滾明星到達時，這些年輕女孩發出尖叫聲。

♦ A shriek stirred me from sleep.
一聲尖叫把我從睡夢中驚醒。

0308

---

state
stet
n. 州 *v.* 陳述……事物

♦ Mexico abuts some of the richest states of the United States.
墨西哥緊臨美國最富庶的幾個州。

♦ The agent gave away state secrets to the enemy .
這位探員把國家機密洩露給敵人。

0309

---

mode
mod
n. 式樣（服裝）；方式；語氣

♦ She was not used to a lavish mode of living.
她不習慣浪費的生活方式。

♦ I try to change my whole mode of life.
我嘗試改變我所有的生活方式。

0310

---

success
səkˈsɛs
n. 成功的事或人

♦ This activity was held to celebrate the success of their plan.
這個活動是為了慶祝他們計劃成功而舉辦。

♦ He's very unassuming about his glorious success.
他對於他輝煌的成就非常謙虛。

0311

---

cost-conscious
kɔst ˈkɑnʃəs
n. 成本意識 *adj.* 有成本意識的

♦ My boss is a businessman with good cost-conscious.
我老闆是個非常有成本意識的商人。

♦ More and more cost-conscious customers know how to compare prices in global recession.
在全球不景氣中，越來越多有成本意識的消費者知道如何比較價格。

0312

growth
groθ
n. 成長；增加；
發育

◆ The growth of the company is getting better and better.
這家公司的成長是越來越好。

◆ Most industrial labors under a misapprehension believe the economic growth can be achieved without damaging the environment.
大多數勞工都誤解了，相信經濟成長可以在不危害環境的情況下達成。

0313

perpendicular
ˌpɝpənˈdɪkjələ
adj. 成垂直的；
陡峭的

◆ The two lines are perpendicular to one another.
這兩條線彼此互相垂直。

◆ The high wall is out of the perpendicular.
這高牆有點傾斜。

0314

accomplishment
əˈkɑmplɪʃmənt
n. 成就；成績

◆ It took him several decades to have the accomplishment today.
他花了數十年才有今日的成就。

◆ Parents send their children to learn how to play piano as their accomplishments.
父母送他們的孩子去學鋼琴當做才藝。

0315

ripe
raɪp
adj. 成熟的；可
食用的

◆ Fruit tastes delicious when it is ripe.
水果成熟了吃起來就好吃。

◆ Are the peaches ripe enough to eat yet?
這些桃子已經熟到可以吃了嗎？

0316

mellow
ˈmɛlo
adj. 成熟的；甘
美多汁的(水果)

◆ I enjoy listening to mellow music to relax after a long work day.
在一天漫長的工作後，我享受聆聽柔和的音樂來放鬆自己。

◆ Grandmother gave me a bunch of mellow grapes.
祖母給我一串甜美多汁的葡萄。

0317

buckle
ˈbʌkl
n. 扣環 (皮帶)

◆ The kid cannot fasten the shoe buckle by himself.
這個小男孩不會扣緊他的鞋帶扣。

◆ He unfastened the buckles and took off the shirt.
他解開這些扣子，並脫掉襯衫。

0318

income
ˈɪnˌkʌm
n. 收入

一小時100元！

◆ She got a waitress job to supplement her income.
她找了份女服務生的工作來增加收入。

◆ She assisted me with my income tax return.
她幫我填寫所得稅申報書。

0319

earnings

ˋɝnɪŋz

n. 收入；工資；利潤

◆ The woman's exiguous earnings cannot afford such a high rental.
這位女子微薄的收入無法負擔這麼貴的房租。

◆ I spends only a fraction of my earnings.
我只花了我收入的一小部分。

0320

consignee

ˌkɑnsaɪˋni

n. 收件人；收貨人；受託人

◆ These shipping documents are normally sent by courier to the consignee.
這些託運文件通常由快遞送到收件者手上。

◆ What are the difference between the shipper and the consignee?
託運人和收貨人有什麼不同？

0321 ★

receive

rɪˋsiv

v. 收到；接受

◆ To receive the discounted price, you must wait until after Christmas.
想得到特價必須等到聖誕節之後。

◆ My decision received the support from my company.
我的決定得到公司的支持。

0322

addressee

ˌædrɛˋsi

n. 收信人

◆ This letter is intended only for the named addressee.
這封信只打算給指定收件人。

◆ You have to write down the name of the addressee.
你必須寫下收信人的名字。

0323

affiliate

əˋfɪlɪˌet

v. 收為會員；接納……為成員；追溯……來源

◆ We are affiliated with a local golf club.
我們成了一所當地高爾夫俱樂部的會員。

◆ If we affiliate, we will have a better chance to develop.
假如我們參加，未來將會有更好的發展機會。

0324

reap

rip

v. 收割；獲得

◆ The farmers were busy reaping the rice in the field.
農夫們忙著在田裡割稻。

◆ You cannot reap where you have not sown.
要怎麼收穫，先那麼栽。

0325

shrink

ʃrɪŋk

v. 收縮；減少

◆ Hot water shrinks woolen clothes.
熱水讓羊毛衣服縮水。

◆ The price of stocks shrinks a lot during recession.
不景氣時股票價格跌了不少。

0326

gifted
ˋɡɪftɪd
adj. 有天賦的

◆ Picasso was a gifted but impecunious painter.
畢卡索是有天分卻窮困的畫家。

◆ My younger sister is gifted with a good voice.
我妹妹天生有副好嗓子。

0327

immune
ɪˋmjun
adj. 有免疫力的
n. 免疫者

◆ Having more fruits and vegetables is very helpful to your immune system.
更多的蔬菜與水果將有助於你的免疫系統。

◆ Cancer is a kind of an disease that attacks human immune system.
癌症是一種侵襲人體免疫系統的疾病。

0328

promising
ˋprɑmɪsɪŋ
adj. 有前途的；
有希望的

◆ He is a promising graduate student at one of the top universities in Taiwan.
他是一位台灣頂尖大學中相當有前途的研究生。

◆ The student wants to be a promising youth.
這學生想要成為一位有前途的年輕人。

0329

baleful
ˋbelfəl
adj. 有害的；凶
惡的

◆ She gave him a baleful look when he talked about a mistress.
當他談到情婦時，她凶惡地看了他一眼。

◆ The robber has a fierce baleful look.
這個強盜有一副殘忍邪惡的長相。

0330

千里之行，始於足下

---

aerobics
[.ɛə'robɪks]
n. 有氧運動

◆ I enjoy taking aerobics classes which make me feel flexible and energetic.
我喜歡參加讓人感到身體放鬆和精力充沛的有氧舞蹈課程。

◆ The famous movie star does aerobics twice a week.
這位有名的電影明星一週做兩次有氧運動。

0331

---

beneficial
[ɛfɪ'nənɛd,]
adj. 有益的；有利的

Is Banana beneficial for Diabetics ?

◆ The group insurance is beneficial to all the staff.
團體保險對所有的員工都有利。

◆ Her largess was beneficial for me.
她的慷慨對我相當有助益。

0332 ★

---

advantageous
[sædvən'tedʒəs,]
adj. 有益的；有利的；有助的

◆ We are able to offer you very advantageous terms.
我們能夠提供你非常優惠的條件。

◆ It is highly advantageous to our troops.
這對我們的軍隊非常有利。

0333 ★

---

healthful
['hɛlθfəl]
adj. 有益健康的

◆ Does the hospital cafeteria provide a healthful diet?
醫院的自助餐提供的是有益健康的飲食嗎？

◆ The Asians prefer more healthful peanut oil.
亞洲人喜歡較健康的花生油。

0334

---

orderly
['ɔrdəlɪ]
adj. 有秩序的

◆ Subject transitions will be swift, quiet, and orderly.
換科目、換教室時，應該要迅速、安靜、有秩序。

◆ The people lined up in an orderly way.
這些人井然有序地排好隊伍。

0335

---

capable
['kepəbl]
adj. 有能力的；有才華的

◆ The administrator showed that he was capable of working independently.
這位行政人員展示他獨立工作的能力。

◆ Kenny is capable of using casuistry to win a debate.
肯尼擅長以詭辯贏得辯論。

0336 ★

comprehensive
ˌkɑmprɪˈhɛnsɪv
adj. 有理解力
的；綜合的；廣
泛的

◆ Gary can get the point easily because he has a comprehensive mind.
蓋瑞理解力強，容易抓到重點。

◆ My school is a comprehensive university, which contains five colleges with a total of twenty-one departments.
我的學校是一所綜合性大學，總共包括了五所學院共二十一個科系。

0337 ★

remunerative
rɪˈmjunəˌretɪv
adj. 有報酬的；
有利益的

◆ High technology is a highly remunerative job.
高科技是一份高報酬的工作。

◆ In order to have good living standards, he accepts any remunerative chore.
為了有好的生活水準，什麼工作他都接。

0338

malignant
məˈlɪgnənt
adj. 有惡意的
的；惡毒的

◆ Smoking is malignant to your health.
抽煙對你的健康有害。

◆ I had a malignant tumor removed.
我切除了一個有害的腫瘤。

0339

ambitious
æmˈbɪʃəs
adj. 有雄心的；
野心勃勃的

◆ An ambitious man usually works hard.
一個有雄心的男人總是努力工作。

◆ An ambitious politician must have a canny political advisor offering the suggestions.
有雄心的政治家必須要有一位精明能幹的政治顧問提供建議。

0340

contagious
kənˈtedʒəs
adj. 有傳染性
的；感染性的

◆ His job easily exposes him to contagious diseases.
他的工作讓他容易接觸到傳染病。

◆ AIDS is a contagious disease.
AIDS 是種傳染性疾病。

0341 ★

guilty
ˈgɪltɪ
adj. 有罪的

◆ I felt guilty after blaming him.
責備他之後，我覺得很內疚。

◆ The man was found not guilty of murder by reason of insanity.
這個男人因為精神錯亂，被判謀殺罪不成立。

0342 ★

persuasive
pəˈswesɪv
adj. 有說服力的

◆ She gave a persuasive speech about the need for more funding for the project.
她為了籌募更多計劃經費，發表了有說服力的演說。

◆ Statistical evidence can make your project more persuasive.
統計上的證據能讓你的計劃更具說服力。

0343 ★

helpful
/ˈhɛlpfəl/
adj. 有幫助的；有益的

◆ It is very fortunate that that you have so many helpful friends.
你很幸運有這麼多肯幫助人的朋友。

◆ Having more fruits and vegetables is very helpful to your immune system.
更多的蔬菜與水果將有助於你的免疫系統。

0344

adhesive
/ədˈhisɪv/
adj. 有黏性的
n. 黏著劑

◆ It could be stuck with such adhesive.
用這樣的黏著劑才能把它黏住。

◆ You should seal the parcel with adhesive tape.
你應該用膠帶把這包裹密封起來。

0345

polite
/pəˈlaɪt/
adj. 有禮貌的

◆ It is a polite action to offer the seat to the elders on the bus.
在公車上讓位給老人家是有禮貌的行為。

◆ Be polite to your friends.
對你的朋友要有禮貌。

0346

relevant
/ˈrɛləvənt/
adj. 有關的；切題的

◆ I will do my best to give you any information that is relevant to you.
我們會盡量把與你有關的資訊提供給你。

◆ His statement is totally relevant to the subject.
他的言論與主題完全有關。

0347

moreover
/morˈovɚ/
adv. 此外；並且

◆ Moreover, children will have less time to play with their peers due to extra studies.
此外，因為額外的學習，孩子們將沒有多少時間能與同儕玩耍。

◆ Moreover, I will thank all the people who helped me before.
此外，我將要感謝所有過去曾幫過我的人。

0348

besides
/bɪˈsaɪdz/
adv. 除此之外

◆ I enjoy eating vegetables besides being healthy.
我喜歡吃蔬菜，除此之外還能有益健康。

◆ John likes playing basketball. Besides, he also likes going swimming.
約翰喜歡打籃球；除此之外，他還喜歡去游泳。

0349

veteran
/ˈvɛtərən/
n. 老兵；老手；專家

◆ He is one of the veterans from the Second World War.
他是一位參加過第二次世界大戰的退伍軍人。

◆ Francis is a 25-year army veteran.
法蘭西思是一位有二十五年經驗的陸軍老兵。

0350

sophisticated
sə'fɪstɪˌketɪd
adj. 老練的；世故的；複雜的

◆ He is suave, sophisticated, well-educated gentleman.
他是位溫和、有教養且受過良好教育的紳士。

◆ The professional hackers succeed in intruding highly sophisticated weapons systems.
這些專業的駭客成功入侵了尖端防禦系統。

0351

examination
ɪgˌzæmə'neʃən
n. 考試 (同 exam)

◆ Did you take the entrance examination this year?
你今年有參加入學考試嗎？

◆ How many examinations did you have in the mid-term?
你期中考考了幾科？

0352 ★

ponder
'pɑndɚ
v. 考慮；沉思

我想想

◆ She pondered his marriage proposal for weeks.
她對他的求婚考慮了好幾個星期。

◆ I wanted to ponder the next move for a while.
我想要好好仔細考慮下一步。

0353

muscle
'mʌsl̩
n. 肌肉

◆ His healthy and strong muscles attract many girls' attention.
他健壯有力的肌肉吸引了很多女孩子的注意。

◆ Contraction of muscles is a natural reaction of the body.
肌肉的緊縮是很自然的身體反應。

0354

buffet
bu'fe
n. 自助餐；食物台

◆ I recently had a buffet meal at John's Wedding.
我最近一次吃自助餐是在約翰的婚禮上。

◆ Do you prefer regular menu or buffet?
你希望點固定菜單還是自助餐？

0355

automatic
ˌɔtə'mætɪk
adj. 自動的；必然的

自動洗衣機

◆ Automatic washing machines save housewives a lot of time in doing housework.
自動洗衣機為家庭主婦節省很多做家事的時間。

◆ Is it an automatic camera?
這是一台自動相機嗎？

0356 ★

suicide
'suəˌsaɪd
n. 自殺

◆ I was shocked that she went bankrupt and committed suicide.
她破產和自殺的消息讓我相當驚訝。

◆ It takes a bit of nerve to commit suicide.
自殺是需要一點膽量的。

0357

nature
'netʃə
n. 自然；天性

◆ The resources of nature are exhaustible.
自然界的資源是會被用完的。

◆ The selfish old miser had a stand-off nature.
這個自私的老守財奴有冷漠的天性。

0358

brag
bræg
v. 自誇；吹噓

我很美吧！

◆ He often brags about how well he plays baseball.
他常愛自誇棒球打得有多好。

◆ The captain is always bragging about his military valor.
隊長總是吹噓他的軍人氣概。

0359

supreme
sə'prim
adj. 至上的；最高的

The Winner

◆ Washington was a man of supreme character.
華盛頓是一位擁有至高人格的人物。

◆ The verdict of the supreme court shall not be appealed against .
最高法院的判決不容上訴。

0360

sovereign
'sɑvrɪn
adj. 至高無上的

統一王室繼承人

◆ Who holds sovereign power in the kingdom?
這個王國中誰掌握最高權力？

◆ Is there any sovereign remedy for a cancer?
癌症有任何靈丹妙藥嗎？

0361

blood
blʌd
n. 血；血統

◆ My father suffers from high blood pressure.
我爸爸為高血壓所苦。

◆ Exercise can prompt your circulation of blood.
運動能促進血液循環。

0362

ancestry
'ænsɛstrɪ
n. 血統；祖宗；祖系

華裔美國人

◆ She is born of a good ancestry.
她家世良好。

◆ He is an American of Chinese ancestry.
他是一位華裔美國人。

0363

baggage
'bægɪdʒ
n. 行李（美式用法）

◆ Do you have any carry-on baggage?
您有隨身行李嗎？

◆ How much baggage do you wish to check in?
你有多少行李要託運？

0364

baggage claim
ˋbægɪdʒ ˏklem
ph. 行李領取處

行李提領

◆ Where is the baggage claim area?
行李提領區在哪裡？

◆ Here are your boarding pass and ticket with your baggage claim tag.
這是您的登機證、機票和行李領取證。

0365

---

assassinate
əˋsæsṇˏet
v. 行刺；糟蹋

◆ President Kennedy was assassinated in Dallas in 1963.
甘迺迪總統於1963年在達拉斯被行刺。

◆ An intrigue to assassinate the president was uncovered by government agents.
行刺總統的陰謀被政府探員識破了。

0366 ★

---

executive
ɪgˋzɛkjutɪv
adj. 行政的；執行的；高級享受的

◆ He is a member of the executive committee.
他是其中一位執行委員。

◆ My dad was promoted Chief Executive Officer of the company.
我爸爸晉升為這家公司的執行長。

0367

---

march
mɑrtʃ
n. 行軍；步調
v. 強行帶走

◆ The army was now on the march to Baghdad.
這支軍隊正在向巴格達進軍。

◆ The soldiers marched at a slow pace.
士兵們以緩慢的速度前進。

0368

---

wardrobe
ˋwɔrdˏrob
n. 衣櫥；全部衣服

◆ Helen showed me her new wardrobe yesterday.
海倫昨天帶我去看她的新衣櫥。

◆ The big wardrobe takes up too much space.
這個大衣櫃佔了太大的空間。

0369

---

estimate
ˋɛstəˏmet
v. 估計……；評價……；估算

◆ It is hard to estimate how much we lost during the financial tsunami period.
金融海嘯期間我們的損失難以估算。

◆ It is very difficult to estimate the amount of booty and war material captured.
要估計出戰利品與接收的戰爭物資數量是非常困難的。

0370 ★

---

assess
əˋsɛs
v. 估價；估計；徵稅

一百萬元！

◆ How do you assess my paintings in the exhibition?
你對我正在展覽中的油畫估價多少？

◆ How do you assess our products in the trade fair?
你對這次商展中我們的產品評價如何？

0371

reach
riːtʃ
v. 伸手；到達

◆ Space and time can reach unlimited range.
時間與空間的範圍是沒有邊界的。

◆ How long will it take to reach Taiwan?
要多久時間才能到達台灣？

0372

plausible
ˈplɔzəbl
adj. 似乎合理的；貌似真實的

◆ His explanation for the absence sounds fairly plausible to me.
我覺得他為缺席所作的解釋聽起來頗合理。

◆ What he said is plausible, but not necessarily correct.
他的話似乎合理，但不必然正確。

0373

undervalue
ˌʌndəˈvælju
v. 低估價值；輕視

◆ You should not undervalue knowledge before an audience.
你不應該在群眾前貶低知識的價值。

◆ Don't undervalue his contribution to the war.
不要低估他對這場戰爭的貢獻。

0374

whisper
ˈhwɪspə
v. 低語；沙沙作響

◆ It's rude to whisper in front of others.
在別人面前耳語是無禮的。

◆ His wife often heard him whisper to another girl.
他的太太經常聽到他跟其它女孩竊竊私語。

0375

occupy
ˈɑkjəˌpaɪ
v. 佔領……；使忙碌；擔任職務

◆ It seems that you've been occupied with tasks since you left school.
看來你從離開學校後就一直忙於工作。

◆ Our troop succeeded in occupying the enemy base.
我軍成功占據敵軍基地。

0376

surf
sɜːf
v. 作衝浪運動；在網路上迅速瀏覽資料

◆ My father will not allow us to go surfing if we don't take a nap.
如果我們不睡午覺，爸爸就不讓我們去衝浪。

◆ I surf the Internet six hours a day.
我每天上網六個小時。

0377 ★

infer
ɪnˈfɜː
v. 作出……推論；結論出……

◆ I infer that the studious person will succeed in the future.
我推論這位用功的學生將來會成功。

◆ I inferred a conclusion from the facts.
我從這個事實推測出結論。

0378

66

result

rɪˈzʌlt

v. 作為……結果；導致於 n. 結果

拿到證照了

◆ What's the result of the baseball game?
籃球比賽的結果如何？

◆ High unemployment is a direct result of the recession.
高失業率是經濟蕭條的直接結果。

0379 ★

---

overcome

ˌovəˈkʌm

v. 克服……；擊敗……

◆ Tina spends lots of time overcoming her inner fear to speak out.
汀娜花了很多時間克服大膽發言時內心的害怕。

◆ The patient had a titanic struggle to overcome the painful disease.
病人以很強的鬥志戰勝令人痛苦的疾病。

0380 ★

---

duty-free

ˌdjutɪˈfri

adj. 免稅的

免稅商店

◆ Have you bought any duty-free goods?
你有買任何免稅商品嗎？

◆ Are there any duty-free shops in the transit lounge?
過境休息室裡有免稅商店嗎？

0381

---

complimentary

ˌkɑmpləˈmɛntərɪ

adj. 免費贈送的；讚賞的

不用錢喔！

◆ I've got complimentary tickets for a movie.
我有幾張電影招待券。

◆ My manager was very complimentary about my work.
我的經理對我的工作表現非常讚賞。

0382

---

behalf

bɪˈhæf

n. 利益；代表

◆ This celebration is on behalf of the war hero.
這場慶祝活動是為了這位戰爭英雄而舉辦的。

◆ The board of directors have to make decisions on shareholders' behalf.
董事會成員必須依照股東的利益來做決策。

0383 ★

---

benefit

ˈbɛnəfɪt

n. 利益；好處；恩惠

◆ Many people receive benefits from working hard.
大多數人從工作努力中獲得利益。

◆ The company earns lots of benefits from the computer games.
這家公司從事電腦遊戲獲利不少。

0384 ★

---

interest rate

ˈɪntərɪst ˌret

n. 利率

台灣銀行
利率是3%！

◆ What's the interest rate for the savings account?
儲蓄帳戶的利率是多少？

◆ What is the annual interest rate?
年利率是多少？

0385 ★

delete
dɪˈlit
v. 刪除

◆ Her name was deleted from the list.
她的名字被從名單上刪除了。

◆ I deleted all the e-mails he sent to me yesterday.
我刪除了昨晚他寄來的電子郵件。

0386

---

assistant
əˈsɪstənt
n. 助手；助教

◆ He worked as an assistant for the president.
他當過總統助理。

◆ I hear that you are in need of an assistant.
我聽說你們需要一位助手。

0387 ★

---

effort
ˈɛfɚt
n. 努力；成就

◆ I will make an effort to finish the work.
我會努力完成工作。

◆ The authority made great effort to extirpate the drug abuse.
官方當局為杜絕毒品濫用做了極大的努力。

0388 ★

---

procure
proˈkjʊr
v. 努力取得；設法……得到

◆ Joy procured some supplies for his experiment.
喬伊努力設法為他的實驗取得了一些供給品。

◆ The manufacturers procure the trust from the consumers by great quality of the goods.
製造業者設法以高品質的商品獲得消費者的信任。

0389

---

hijack
ˈhaɪdʒæk
n. 劫持（飛機）；強取（貨運）

◆ The terrorists machinated to an air hijack.
這群恐怖份子策劃空中劫機。

◆ Do you know about the recent hijack in Japan？
你知道最近在日本的劫機事件嗎？

0390 ★

---

shortly
ˈʃɔrtlɪ
adv. 即刻；不久

◆ The village was evacuated shortly before the explosion.
這個村莊在爆炸前不久撤離。

◆ The drama was over shortly before six.
這齣戲將在六點前結束。

0391

---

immediately
ɪˈmidɪɪtlɪ
adv. 即刻地；馬上地

◆ I think we should get down to the bottom line immediately.
我認為我們應該馬上開始處理帳務盈虧結算。

◆ The incipient cancer can be cured, but you must start treatment immediately.
癌症初期可以被治癒，不過必須立刻展開治療。

0392

forthcoming

/ˌforθ'kʌmɪŋ/

adj. 即將到來的；樂意幫助的

雨快來了！

◆ Next Saturday is the forthcoming presidential election.
下週六是即將到來的總統選舉。

◆ They talked about the school and a forthcoming track and field competition .
他們談論到學校與即將到來的田徑比賽。

0393

inhale

/ɪn'hel/

v. 吸入⋯⋯

好香喔！

◆ I love to inhale the fresh air in the forest.
我喜歡吸入森林中的新鮮空氣。

◆ They inhaled a stale musty smell when entering the attic.
當進入這閣樓時，他們吸入了陳腐發霉的味道。

0394

absorb

/əb'sɔrb/

v. 吸收⋯⋯；使專心；融會貫通

◆ I can't absorb all the information the teacher gave me.
我無法吸收這位老師教我的所有資訊。

◆ I think painting and photography are both absorbing hobbies.
我認為繪畫和攝影都是引人入勝的嗜好。

0395

assimilate

/ə'sɪml̩.et/

v. 吸收⋯⋯；消化⋯⋯；同化

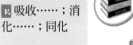

◆ The children of the immigrants easily assimilated into American culture.
新移民的小孩容易被美國文化同化

◆ The student is easy to assimilate new concepts.
這個學生容易吸收新觀念。

0396

要怎麼收穫，先那麼栽

whistle ˈhwɪsl̩ **v.** 吹口哨；呼嘯而過 	◆ My friend gave a loud whistle of gladness. 我朋友吹了一聲響亮的口哨表示高興。 ◆ The wind whistled through a crevice in the window. 風從窗戶的縫隙中呼呼地吹進來。 0397
spectacular spɛkˈtækjələ **adj.** 壯觀的；引人注目的 	◆ There is a spectacular waterfall in the national park. 在國家公園中有一座壯觀的瀑布。 ◆ The new movie was a spectacular success. 這部新電影獲得了引人注目的成就。 0398
setback ˈsɛt.bæk **n.** 妨礙；挫折 	◆ This minor setback has drained away our confidence. 這個小挫折削弱了我們的信心。 ◆ This setback has drained away my passion. 這個挫折逐漸消磨我的熱情。 0399
interfere ˌɪntəˈfɪr **v.** 妨礙……；干涉…… 	◆ She always interferes in other people's domestic affairs. 她總是干涉其他人的家務事。 ◆ Don't interfere with my business. 別干預我的事情。 0400 ★
hinder ˈhɪndə **v.** 妨礙……；阻礙…… 	◆ Her lack of experience cannot hinder her efficiency on work. 缺乏經驗並不妨礙她的工作效率。 ◆ Too many rules seem to hinder innovation. 太多規定似乎會妨礙改革。 0401
hamper ˈhæmpə **v.** 妨礙……行動 **n.** 障礙物 	◆ The policy will promote rather than hamper reform. 這個政策將會提升而不是妨礙改革。 ◆ The storm hampered us from going out. 這個暴風雨妨礙我們外出。 0402

unanimous
ju`nænəməs
adj. 完全同意的；全體一致的

◆ The jury was unanimous that the defendant was not guilty.
陪審團一致認為被告無罪。

◆ The committee agreed to the plan in a unanimous decision.
委員會一致決定同意這項計劃。

0403

accomplish
ə`kɑmplɪʃ
v. 完成……；實現……

◆ I have accomplished every task that the boss asked of me.
我已完成老闆交代我的所有任務。

◆ I will accomplish my goals at any cost.
無論如何都要完成我的目標。

0404 ★

tail
tel
n. 尾巴；尾部
v. 尾隨

◆ The dog was frenzied because the naughty boy pulled on its tail.
這隻狗被激怒了，因為頑皮的男孩拉了牠的尾巴。

◆ The peacock spreads his beautiful tail.
這隻孔雀展現牠美麗的尾巴。

0405

shape
ʃep
n. 形狀 **v.** 使成形

◆ The sun has the shape of a circle.
太陽是圓形的。

◆ The intensity of breath sounds depends on the location of auscultation and on the body shape.
呼吸聲的強度視聽診的位置和患者的體型而定。

0406

refrain
rɪ`fren
v. 忍住……；抑制……；禁止……

◆ I couldn't refrain from crying.
我無法忍住哭泣。

◆ Wendy refrained from having midnight snacks to reduce her weight.
溫蒂為了減重克制自己不吃宵夜。

0407

volunteer
.vɑlən`tɪr
n. 志願者；義工

◆ Is there any volunteer to take care of this litter of puppies?
有誰自願來照顧這窩小狗？

◆ She was given a badge of honor as a volunteer for the hospital.
因為當醫院的義工，她獲得一枚榮譽勳章。

0408 ★

rapid
`ræpɪd
adj. 快速的；急促的

◆ The patient had a rapid recovery.
病患快速復原了。

◆ Building a rapid transit system will be a mammoth job.
建造一個快速傳輸系統是一項巨大工程。

0409

simulate
ˈsɪmjə.let
v. 扮作……；
偽裝……；模
仿……

◆ He simulated that he was sick.
他假裝生病了。

◆ A sheet of metal can be shaken to simulate thunder.
搖晃一片金屬就可模擬雷聲。

0410

rail
rel
n. 扶手；欄杆；
鐵軌

◆ The old lady kept her hand on the rail as she climbed the steps.
這位老太太爬樓梯時，手一直扶著欄杆。

◆ The cargo will be shipped by rail.
這些貨物要靠鐵路運送。

0411

sanction
ˈsæŋkʃən
v. 批准；准許
n. 約束力

◆ The bill has gotten an official sanction.
這項法案得到官方的批准。

◆ The church refused to sanction the king's second marriage.
教會拒絕批准國王的第二段婚姻。

0412

ratify
ˈrætə.faɪ
v. 批准……；認
可……

◆ The government delayed ratifying the treaty.
政府延遲批准這項合約。

◆ The board ratified the agreement finally.
董事會最後批准了這項協議。

0413 ★

wholesale
ˈhol.sel
n. 批發

◆ Our stationery business is wholesale only.
我們的文具生意只做批發而已。

◆ The clothing company is one of the best places to buy wholesale merchandise for your store.
這家服裝公司是你為店面批貨的最佳去處之一。

0414

criticism
ˈkrɪtə.sɪzəm
n. 批評的言論；
評論文章

◆ He might be mad if he heard the criticism.
他如果聽到批評也許會發火。

◆ The writer is impervious to criticism.
這位作家不會受評論的影響。

0415

resist
rɪˈzɪst
v. 抵抗……；使
反抗

◆ It is hard to resist the temptation of iced drinks in the hot summer.
炎炎夏日裡要抗拒冷飲是困難的。

◆ The old man is too weak to resist other diseases.
那位老人太虛弱了，以至於無法抵抗其他的疾病。

0416

mechanic
məˈkænɪk
n. 技工

◆ Almost all of the mechanics will encounter this problem.
幾乎所有的技師都會遇到這個問題。

◆ We took our vehicle to the mechanic for its yearly safety inspection.
我們把車開到技師那裡做年度安全檢查。

0417

skill
skɪl
n. 技巧；技術

◆ What kind of skills do you have?
你有什麼專長呢？

◆ The architect has good spatial skills in building a house from plans on paper.
建築師掌控空間的技巧很好，可以把紙上的設計圖蓋成房子。

0418

transcript
ˈtræn.skrɪpt
n. 抄本；副本；成績單

◆ The transcript was sealed and marked.
這份副本已經被封起來並且加上標記。

◆ Here is the transcript from my university.
這是我的大學成績單。

0419 ★

split
splɪt
v. 把……切開；使劃分；使分攤

◆ Shall we split the check？
我們一起分攤費用好嗎？

◆ The party split into several factions.
這個政黨分裂成許多派別。

0420

exclude
ɪkˈsklud
v. 把……排除；不考慮……

◆ You can't exclude the possibility that it will rain.
你不能排除會下雨的機率。

◆ The labor leader refused to exclude the possibility of a strike.
這位勞工領袖拒絕排除罷工的可能性。

0421

exaggerate
ɪgˈzædʒə.ret
v. 把……誇張化；使擴大

◆ The threat of attack was greatly exaggerated.
攻擊的威脅被誇大了。

◆ Don't take his words too seriously, he exaggerated the importance of his project.
別把他說的話看得太嚴重，他誇大了企劃案的重要性。

0422 ★

withhold
wɪðˈhold
v. 抑制；阻擋；扣留

◆ VIP cards were withheld from some members of the club.
這家俱樂部的某些會員被扣留 VIP 卡。

◆ I withheld payment until the workers had completed the job.
我保留著應付款項直到工人們完成工作。

0423

repress
rɪˈprɛs
v. 抑制；撲滅

◆ We repress the student riots with the help of the army.
我們靠軍隊來幫忙平息這場學生示威。

◆ I could hardly repress my laughter.
我幾乎無法抑制我的笑聲。

0424

seize
siz
v. 抓住；把握

◆ My father seized my arm to hold me back.
爸爸抓住我的手臂把我拉回來。

◆ The army seized control of the riot yesterday.
軍隊昨天已控制住暴動。

0425

grab
græb
v. 抓取；奪取；霸佔

◆ Can you grab my cell phone on my desk?
你能快點到我的桌上去拿手機嗎？

◆ He grabbed hold of the theft and flung him to the ground.
他捉住竊賊並把他摔到地上。

0426

scratch
skrætʃ
v. 抓傷……；劃破……

◆ I saw the kitten scratch its ears.
我看到小貓在抓牠的耳朵。

◆ Will you scratch that sticker off the jeep window?
請你把吉普車窗上的貼紙刮掉好嗎？

0427

ballot
ˈbælət
n. 投票；選票

◆ The electoral computer made the ballot count more efficient.
這台選舉用的電腦讓選票計算更有效率。

◆ Who will you cast a ballot for?
你要投票給誰？

0428 ★

vote
vot
v. 投票 **n.** 選票

◆ In 1918, British women got the right to vote.
西元 1918 年英國女人獲得投票的權利。

◆ All stockholders were allowed to vote in their annual election.
所有的股東都被允許在年度選舉中投票。

0429

poll
pol
n. 投票所；投票

◆ Conducting a poll can help the company know the consumers' needs.
做民意測驗可以幫助一家公司了解消費者的需求。

◆ In the nineteenth century, women were excluded from the polls.
十九世紀時女人被排除在投票所之外。

0430

invest
in'vɛst

v. 投資；賦予；
使打扮

◆ Jack invested much money in real estate.
傑克投資了很多錢在房地產。

◆ Consider carefully before investing money in the stock.
把錢投進股市之前要想清楚。

0431 ★

cast
kæst

v. 投擲；鑄造

◆ The little boy casts the stone against the window.
小男孩對著窗戶丟石頭。

◆ She cast a pebble into the lake.
她向湖中投了一塊小圓石。

0432

shot
ʃɑt

v. 投籃；發射
n. 打針

◆ The basketball player made the shot at the last second and made a basket.
這位籃球選手在最後一秒時投籃得分。

◆ I think you need a shot right now.
我認為你現在需要打一針。

0433

scoop
skup

n. 杓子；鏟子

◆ Could I have a scoop of vanilla ice cream?
能給我一杓香草冰淇淋嗎？

◆ The clerk gave him an extra scoop of chocolate.
店員給了他額外的一杓巧克力。

0434

pace
pes

n. 步調；步幅；
節奏

◆ She walks so fast that I can't keep pace with her.
她走得很快，我趕不上她的腳步。

◆ I can see a bee one hundred paces away .
我能看到一百步以外的蜜蜂。

0435

daily
'delɪ

adj. 每日的；日
常的

◆ She takes the train to work daily.
她每天都搭火車上班。

◆ Her daily regimen always includes an hour of exercise.
她的日常養生之道包含運動一小時。

0436

determination
dɪˌtɝmə'neʃən

n. 決心；決斷
力

◆ Tina pursued her singing career with great determination.
汀娜下定極大決心要追求她的歌唱事業。

◆ It is not tears but determinations that make pain bearable.
不是眼淚，而是決心使得痛苦能夠忍受。

0437

resolution

.rɛzəˈluʃn̩

n. 決心；決議

◆ Mike's friends admired his resolution to quit drinking alcohol and smoking.
麥克的朋友佩服他戒酒與戒菸的決心。

◆ His remarks evinced a strong resolution to succeed.
他的言論中展示出想要成功的強烈決心。

0438

---

crucial

ˈkruʃəl

adj. 決定性的；重要的

◆ This is a crucial moment and you must hold on to the last second.
這是個決定性的時刻，你必須要堅持到最後一秒鐘。

◆ One of the crucial features of Switzerland is that it is a nonaligned country.
瑞士很重要的一個特色就是中立國。

0439 ★

---

glower

ˈglauə

v. 沉著臉；怒視

◆ The teacher glowered at his students.
這位老師怒視他的學生。

◆ They just stood and glower each other.
他們只是站著互相怒視對方。

0440

---

confiscate

ˈkɑnfɪs.ket

v. 沒收；將……充公

◆ I'll have to confiscate those because you aren't allowed to bring fresh fruit into the United States.
我必須沒收這些，因為您不能帶新鮮水果進入美國。

◆ The traitor's property was confiscated since he was put into prison.
這個賣國賊因為入獄，財產遭到沒收充公。

0441 ★

---

lackluster

ˈlæk.lʌstə

adj. 沒有光澤的；毫無生氣的

◆ I felt tired and lackluster this morning.
今早我感覺疲倦、沒有生氣。

◆ No one predicted that the super star would give such a lackluster performance in the play.
沒有人預料到這位超級巨星在這場表演中會如此失常。

0442

---

impatient

ɪmˈpeʃənt

adj. 沒有耐性的；不耐煩的

◆ This teacher is very impatient with her students.
這位老師對她的學生很沒有耐性。

◆ People are more impatient and easy to get angry under the noisy circumstances.
人在吵雜的環境下比較沒耐心，也容易生氣。

0443

---

secure

sɪˈkjur

adj. 牢固的；安心的 **v.** 使安全

◆ The jail was secure with iron bars and a high fence.
這間有鐵欄杆與高圍牆的監獄是安全的。

◆ The anchor secured the boat's location during the storm.
錨能使暴風雨中的船定位更牢固。

0444

wild
waɪld
adj. 狂野的

◆ Many wild animals are extinct because they have been hunted by human beings.
很多野生動物因為人類的獵殺而瀕臨絕種。

◆ Many conservationists make much effort to save wild birds.
許多保育人士非常努力在挽救野生鳥類。

0445

salesman
'selzmən
n. 男銷售員

◆ The salesman deceived me into buying a fake.
這位業務員騙我買了一個仿冒品。

◆ The salesman wore a blue necktie with white dots.
這位業務員打了一條藍底白點的領帶。

0446

system
'sɪstəm
n. 系統

◆ The present system of education is too complicated for people to understand.
現行的教育體制太複雜了，讓大眾很難了解。

◆ The government built up a heating system that utilizes wind energy.
政府建造了一個利用風力發動的暖氣系統。

0447

peculiar
pɪˈkjuljə
adj. 罕見的；獨特的

◆ This house is very peculiar in lots of ways.
這間房子在許多方面都很特別。

◆ I have my own peculiar way of cooking dishes.
我做菜有自己獨特的方式。

0448 ★

mentor
'mɛntə
n. 良師

大師好!

◆ My former boss is my mentor who gives me advice in my career.
我的前任老闆是在職場上給我建議的良師。

◆ One good mentor can change your life forever.
一位好的良師能永遠改變你的一生。

0449

character
'kærɪktə
n. 角色；人格

◆ They are the two main characters in the movie.
他們是這部電影中的兩個重要角色。

◆ My older brother is a man of stable character.
我哥哥是一個具有穩定人格的人。

0450 ★

corner
'kɔrnə
n. 角落 *v.* 追到一角

◆ Please stop the car at next corner.
請在下一個街角停車。

◆ He carefully examined every corner of this room.
他仔細檢查了這個房間的每個角落。

0451

contraband

'kɑntrə.bænd

n. 走私；私貨
adj. 違禁的

◆ The truck was found to be carrying thousands of pounds worth of contraband through customs.
這輛卡車被發現載運價值數千磅的走私貨，在通過海關時被查獲。

◆ The businessman was accused of trading in contraband.
這商人被指控走私交易。

0452 ★

smuggle

'smʌɡl

v. 走私；偷運

◆ The gang smuggled drugs into that country.
這些罪犯走私毒品進入這個國家。

◆ Customs officials uncovered a plot to smuggle weapons into the country.
海關官員們揭發一樁走私武器到這個國家的陰謀。

0453

soccer

'sɑkɚ

n. 足球

◆ World Cup is the most famous soccer game in the world.
世界盃是世界上最有名的足球賽。

◆ He was selected as the best soccer player in the school.
他被選為學校裡最好的足球選手。

0454

frail

frel

adj. 身體虛弱的；意志薄弱的

◆ Mrs. Warner is too frail to live by herself.
華納太太過於虛弱，以至於不能自行生活。

◆ Her health has been frail for years.
她的身體狀況已經虛弱了好幾年。

0455

garage

gəˈrɑʒ

n. 車庫；汽車修理廠

◆ My car broke down, and a truck towed it to the garage.
我的車拋錨了，一台卡車把它拖到車庫中。

◆ He used to work in a garage as a mechanic.
他曾經在汽車修理廠當技工。

0456

hardship

'hɑrdʃɪp

n. 辛苦；困苦

◆ She suffered financial hardship during the economic recession.
她在經濟不景氣時遇到財務困難。

◆ He believes that no insurmountable hardship can beat him.
他相信沒有困難能打倒他。

0457 ★

vicious

'vɪʃəs

adj. 邪惡的；墮落的；兇猛的

◆ That vicious dog attacks and bites people.
這隻凶惡的狗會攻擊及咬人。

◆ The author portrayed the professor as a vicious drunkard in this novel.
在小說中，作者將這位教授描寫成一個墮落的酒鬼。

0458

protect
prə'tɛkt
v. 防護；保護

◆ A helmet can protect your head from harm.
安全帽可以保護你的頭部免於受到傷害。

◆ She protected herself from the sun with suntan lotion.
她用防曬乳液來保護自己避免受到日曬。

0459 ★

runner-up
'rʌnə 'ʌp
n. 亞軍；第二名

◆ It's highly probable that he will be the runner-up in this game.
他很有可能成為這場競賽的亞軍。

◆ He won the runner-up on the golf tournament finally.
他最後在高爾夫球錦標賽中奪得亞軍。

0460

sink
sɪŋk
v. 使……下沉
n. 水槽

◆ Your aim is to sink the enemy's ship.
你們的目標是擊沉敵人的船隻。

◆ Mother spent two hours cleaning the sink.
媽媽花了兩小時來清理這個水槽。

0461

delay
dɪ'le
v. 使……延誤；耽擱

◆ How long will this flight be delayed?
這班飛機將會延遲多久？

◆ The speech is delayed because the speaker hasn't shown up.
因為講者沒有出現，所以演說被迫延遲。

0462 ★

---

drop
drop
v. 使……落下；
下車 **n.** 一滴之
量

◆ The tree's leaves drop to the ground in the fall.
這棵樹的葉子在秋天時落在地上。

◆ Would you drop me at the main entrance of the hotel?
請您載我到旅館正門入口處下車好嗎？

0463

---

disband
dɪsˈbænd
v. 使……解散；
使……退役

◆ He formed a political group, which disbanded a year later.
他成立了一個政治團體，一年之後解散。

◆ The government tried to disband the illegal party.
政府嘗試解散不合法的政黨。

0464

---

bore
bor
v. 使……厭煩

◆ These complaint letters really bored me.
那些抱怨信真令我心煩。

◆ The mathematics class is very boring.
數學課非常無聊。

0465

---

leak
lik
v. 使……漏出；
使滲透 **n.** 縫隙

◆ The sedan is leaking oil.
這輛轎車在漏油。

◆ A leak in the pipe made the bathroom floor wet.
水管有個裂縫，所以浴室地板都溼了。

0466

---

erupt
ɪˈrʌpt
v. 使……爆發；
使噴出；發疹

◆ The volcano suddenly erupted and many people were injured.
火山突然爆發，造成很多人受傷。

◆ An active volcano may erupt at any time.
一座活火山可能隨時會爆發。

0467

---

astonish
əˈstɑnɪʃ
v. 使……驚訝；
使吃驚

◆ The magician's amazing trick astonished Helen.
這位魔術師的驚人技巧讓海倫嚇了一跳。

◆ It is very astonishing to hear you got married for 3 times.
聽到你結過三次婚真是讓人驚訝。

0468 ★

realize
ˈrɪəˌlaɪz
v. 使了解；使領悟；將……實現

◆ Do you realize that most of our work is completed at night?
我們大部分都在晚上工作，你明白嗎？

◆ He finally realized the importance of knowledge.
他終於了解知識的重要性。

0469 ★

humanize
ˈhjumənˌaɪz
v. 使人性化；教化……；使文明

◆ The officials all seek to humanize the government in various ways.
所有官員都在尋求讓政府體系人性化的各種方式。

◆ The government should modify regulations and humanize the prison system.
政府應該修改規定讓監獄體系更人性化。

0470

convince
kənˈvɪns
v. 使人信服；使確信

◆ The numbers don't convince that this financing will come through.
這些數據無法使人確信這個財務計劃可以順利完成。

◆ Your explanation might have convinced Betty.
你的解釋已經說服了貝蒂。

0471

distract
dɪˈstrækt
v. 使分心；轉移注意

◆ I hope Ethan's new hi-fi won't distract him from his studies.
我希望伊森的新音響不會讓他在讀書上分心。

◆ Don't let online games distract your attention
不要讓線上遊戲分散你的注意力。

0472

diverge
dəˈvɜdʒ
v. 使分歧（道路）；使離題

◆ The witness's statement in court diverges from the police report.
這位目擊者在法院的證詞和警方的報告有所分歧。

◆ Our tastes diverge from each other.
我們的品味各有不同。

0473 ★

detach
dɪˈtætʃ
v. 使分開；使分離

◆ He detached the buttons from his shirt.
他解開衣服上的鈕扣。

◆ We should detach good fruits from bad.
我們應該把好的水果與壞的水果分開。

0474

separate
ˈsɛpəˌret
v. 使分離 **adj.** 分開的

◆ We need our order separated into three different boxes.
我們訂購的貨需要分裝成三個箱子。

◆ Your personal identification number(PIN) will arrive in a separate envelope.
你的個人識別碼會用不同的信封寄來。

0475 ★

upgrade
ʌpˋgred
vt. 使升級；提高……品質

◆ I upgraded my computer in order to improve its performance.
我為了改善效能而將電腦升級。

◆ We must upgrade the pay and status of nurse.
我們必須提高護士的薪水及地位。

0476 ★

---

revolt
rɪˋvolt
vt. 使反感；厭惡……；反抗……

◆ What he said yesterday revolted me.
他昨晚講的話讓我覺得反感。

◆ The people revolted against the tyrant.
人民反抗這位暴君。

0477

---

electrify
ɪˋlɛktrə͵faɪ
vt. 使充電；使震驚

◆ We are electrifying the battery.
我們正在為電池充電。

◆ The national railways had been electrified long ago in Taiwan.
在台灣，鐵路早已電氣化。

0478

---

join
dʒɔɪn
vt. 使加入；使聯合

◆ Are you interested in joining our club?
你有興趣加入我們的俱樂部嗎？

◆ I had joined many song contests when I was a child.
小時候我參加過許多歌唱比賽。

0479

---

fail
fel
vt. 使失敗；使失去作用

◆ He was afraid that he would fail the exam.
他很怕考試會不及格。

◆ He became feckless after he failed in his business.
他生意失敗後個性變得很軟弱。

0480

---

poise
pɔɪz
vt. 使平衡；使穩健 *n.* 姿勢

◆ We admired the graceful poise of the ballerina.
我們欣賞這位女芭蕾舞者的優雅姿勢。

◆ The dancer tried her best to poise herself.
這位舞者盡力保持平衡。

0481

---

appease
əˋpiz
vt. 使平靜；使撫慰

◆ The father often talk about the inspirational story to appease his sorrowful mood.
這位父親經常講勵志的故事來安撫他悲傷的心境。

◆ The government had reformed the policy in order to appease these critics.
政府為了安撫這些評論家而改革政策。

0482 ★

infuriate
ɪnˈfjʊrɪˌet
v. 使生氣；使大怒

◆ The ridiculous news infuriated me.
這個荒謬的消息讓我生氣。

◆ It infuriated me to find that he had left home.
我發現他已經出門讓我很生氣。

0483

---

adjourn
əˈdʒɝn
v. 使休會；使中止；延期

◆ The committee decided to adjourn the meeting until next Thursday.
委員會決定休會到下週四。

◆ Capitol Hill will adjourn early this year.
美國國會決定今年提前休會

0484

---

interact
ˌɪntɚˈækt
v. 使交互作用；使互動

◆ An event interacts as both cause and effect.
一個事件會受到原因和結果的交互影響。

◆ You must understand the way the kids interact.
你必須了解孩子們互動的方式。

0485

---

imperil
ɪmˈpɛrəl
v. 使危及；使⋯⋯陷於危險

◆ The poisonous gas imperiled thousands of inhabitants of the city.
這種毒氣危及城市中數以千計的居民。

◆ Any military attacks will imperil peace in this area.
任何軍事攻擊都會危及這個區域的和平。

0486

---

jeopardize
ˈdʒɛpɚˌdaɪz
v. 使危險；冒⋯⋯的危險

◆ The people's lives were in jeopardy during the war.
在戰爭期間這些人的生命是處於危險之中。

◆ Failing a test will not jeopardize your future.
考試不及格不會危及你的將來。

0487

---

incorporate
ɪnˈkɔrpəˌret
v. 使合併；使包含；組成公司

◆ The incorporated company starts to dismiss some lazy employees.
這家股份有限公司開始解雇懶散的員工。

◆ We will incorporate your ideas in this new proposal.
在新的企劃案中，我們將會併入你的想法。

0488 ★

---

consolidate
kənˈsɑləˌdet
v. 使合併；使鞏固；使加強

◆ The president decided to consolidate with other companies.
董事長決定要和其他公司合併。

◆ He bribes his manager to consolidate his position.
他賄賂經理來鞏固自己的位置。

0489

qualify
/ˈkwɑləˌfaɪ/
v. 使合格；使適任

- ◆ After qualifying, teachers spend at least one year working in the school.
  資格認定通過之後，教師們至少要花一年在校工作。
- ◆ You seem well qualified to do the job.
  你看來滿能夠勝任這份工作的。

0490 ★

concur
/kənˈkɝ/
v. 使同意；同時發生

- ◆ Wealth and happiness don't always concur.
  財富與幸福不會總是同時並存。
- ◆ Three car accidents concurred at night.
  三場車禍在晚上同時發生。

0491 ★

survive
/səˈvaɪv/
v. 使存活；使……劫後餘生

- ◆ She was lucky to survive the airplane crash.
  在這場墜機事件中她很幸運地存活下來。
- ◆ We are very glad to know that he has survived the serious car accident.
  我們很高興得知他在那場嚴重的車禍中倖免於難。

0492 ★

soothe
/suð/
v. 使安撫；使平靜；減輕

- ◆ Rocking often soothes a crying baby.
  搖晃經常能安撫哭泣的嬰兒。
- ◆ My aunt often gave a candy to soothe me when I was crying.
  我哭的時候，阿姨常常給我一顆糖安慰我。

0493

fuss
/fʌs/
v. 使忙亂；使抱怨 **n.** 小題大作

- ◆ She is fussy about minor things.
  她對這些小事小題大作。
- ◆ Don't make so much fuss over losing a cent.
  不要為弄丟了一分錢而大驚小怪。

0494

succeed
/səkˈsid/
v. 使成功；使繼續

- ◆ I'm sure you'll succeed if you work hard.
  我很確定只要你努力，一定會成功。
- ◆ To succeed is not so difficult as you think.
  成功不如你所想的那麼困難。

0495 ★

ruin
/ˈruɪn/
v. 使成廢墟；使毀壞

- ◆ Cheating in the game ruined that player's reputation.
  在比賽中作弊，破壞了這位運動員的聲望。
- ◆ The stately mansion has gone to rack and ruin.
  這座宏偉的大樓已經破舊荒蕪。

0496 ★

gather

ˈɡæðɚ

v. 使收集；使聚
集；逐漸增加

◆ He is gathering materials for a new book.
他正在為一本新書收集資料。

◆ The soldiers gathered here to commemorate their victory.
這些士兵聚集在這裡慶祝他們的勝利。

0497

diversify

daɪˈvəsəˌfaɪ

v. 使有變化；使
多元化

◆ The new chairman of the television station wants to diversify the programs.
電視台的新董事長想讓節目更有變化。

◆ Everyone should diversify their investments.
每個人都應該讓投資多元化。

0498 ★

pollute

pəˈlut

v. 汙染；弄髒

CO_2

◆ The river was polluted by the waste water from the factory.
這條河川受到工廠汙水的汙染。

◆ Garbage has polluted the environment.
垃圾汙染了附近的環境。

0499 ★

contaminate

kənˈtæməˌnet

v. 使汙染；使弄
髒

◆ Air pollution has contaminated our living condition.
空氣汙染弄髒了我們生存的環境。

◆ Much of the coast has been contaminated by nuclear waste.
這個海岸已經大多被核廢料汙染。

0500 ★

puzzle

ˈpʌzḷ

v. 使困惑 **n.** 謎
語；拼字遊戲

◆ She used her intelligence to win the puzzle contest.
她以智慧贏得猜謎比賽。

◆ Her decision was a puzzle to everyone.
她的決定對每個人來說都是個謎。

0501

embarrass

ɪmˈbærəs

v. 使困窘；使拮
据

好帥哦！

◆ Asking about age or weight always embarrasses females.
問及年紀或體重總是令女性尷尬。

◆ Your compliments really embarrass me.
你的恭維實在讓我覺得不好意思。

0502

beset

bɪˈsɛt

v. 使困擾；使苦
惱；鑲嵌

◆ We were beset by mosquitoes last night.
我們昨晚為蚊子所苦。

◆ The country was beset with many financial problems.
這個國家被許多財政問題所苦惱。

0503

complete

kəm'plit

v. 使完成 **adj.** 完全的；徹底的

◆ After the draft is completed, we can work out any minor problems.
草約完成後，我們就能來處理任何較小的問題。

◆ Would you please give me a complete list?
你可以給我一份完整的清單嗎？

0504 ★

drain

dren

v. 使弄乾；從……排出水 **n.** 下水道

◆ My sister washed the lettuce and drained it.
我妹妹沖洗萵苣，並且把它弄乾。

◆ Unlike bathrooms in many countries, there is no drain in the floor.
與許多國家浴室不同的是，那裡沒有排水孔。

0505

blur

blɜ

v. 使弄髒；使汙黑；使模糊

◆ The heavy fog blurred my vision during the storm.
濃霧在大風雪中模糊了我的視線。

◆ The building appeared as a blur in the mist.
這棟建築物在霧中顯得一片模糊。

0506

sprain

spren

v. 使扭傷

◆ Have you ever sprained your ankle during a game?
你曾在比賽中扭傷過腳踝嗎？

◆ John fell off the roof and sprained his ankle.
約翰從屋頂上跌下來扭傷了腳。

0507

restrain

rɪ'stren

v. 使抑制；限制……行動

◆ High prices restrain consumer spending.
高價抑制了消費者的花費。

◆ Those onlookers had to be restrained by police.
那些旁觀者遭到警察的制止。

0508

plunge

'plʌndʒ

v. 使投入；使跳入 **n.** 跳入

◆ They have finally decided to take the plunge and get married.
他們最後決定冒險嘗試結婚。

◆ The police was about to plunge into something.
警察準備要採取某些行動了。

0509

surrender

sə'rɛndə

v. 使投降；使自首；使放棄

◆ The terrorists surrender to the police and release the hostages.
這些恐怖分子向警方投降並釋放人質。

◆ The U.S. government will not surrender to terrorist threats and start to fight back.
美國政府不會向恐怖分子屈服，並且開始反擊。

0510

capitulate
kə'pɪtʃə.let
v. 使投降；使屈服

◆ Our president will never capitulate to pressure from outside.
我們的總統不會向外在的壓力屈服。

◆ Their forces capitulated eventually after the bombardment of the country began.
開始對這個國家轟炸後，他們的軍隊終於投降。

0511

torture
'tɔrtʃə
v. 使折磨；使拷問 n. 折磨

◆ His heart ache is sheer torture!
他的心痛完全是種折磨。

◆ Most criminals are under torture.
大部分罪犯都遭受被拷打。

0512

improve
ɪm'pruv
v. 使改良；使改善

◆ It is going to cost us more to improve quality control than to make refunds.
改善品管所花費的成本高於退款。

◆ We have to improve the company's financial condition as soon as possible.
我們必須儘快改善公司的財務狀況。

0513 ★

reform
.rɪ'fɔrm
v. 使改革；使進 n. 改革

◆ The new chairman reformed the company's financial management.
這位新董事長改良了這家公司的財務管理。

◆ We can carry out the reform if we have a fully representative policy.
如果有完整而具代表性的政策，我們就可以實現改革了。

0514

update
ʌp'det
v. 使更新

◆ Would you mind updating those files?
你可以更新那些檔案嗎？

◆ The feedback from the class enables us to update the lessons.
課堂上的回饋能讓我們為課程補充最新資訊。

0515 ★

renovate
'rɛnə.vet
v. 使更新；翻新；革新

◆ Father renovated the old house and sold it.
爸爸翻新老房子並且賣掉它。

◆ I've decided to renovate the garden and garage next week.
我決定下週重新裝修花園與車庫。

0516

stray
stre
v. 使走失；使離題 adj. 走失的

◆ He beat the stray dog with a goad.
他用這支棍子打流浪狗。

◆ The crying boy strayed from his parents while they were visiting the zoo.
當他們參觀動物園時，這位哭泣的男孩與父母走散了。

0517

mission
ˈmɪʃən
n. 使命；任務

◆ This mission is too hard to achieve.
這個使命太困難以致於無法達成。

◆ He has exhausted all his energy to finish the mission.
他竭盡全力來完成這項任務。

0518 ★

compromise
ˈkɑmprəˌmaɪz
v. 使和解；使調停

◆ I agree to compromise with you if you say sorry.
如果你道歉，我同意與你和解。

◆ I think it is better for you to compromise with Monica.
我認為你跟莫妮卡講和比較好。

0519 ★

affix
əˈfɪks
v. 使固定；附加；貼上

◆ My English literature teacher asked us to affix a note to our reports.
我的英國文學老師要求我們在報告中附上註釋。

◆ The supervisor affixed his seal to the document.
這位主管將他的印章蓋在文件上。

0520

disregard
ˌdɪsrɪˈgɑrd
v. 使忽視；漠視⋯⋯ **n.** 不注意

◆ We cannot disregard his coming late to work so often.
我們不能漠視他上班經常遲到。

◆ My boss did this in disregard of any advice.
我的老闆不顧任何勸告去做了這件事。

0521

detain
dɪˈten
v. 使拘留；使延遲

◆ The problem shouldn't detain us very long.
這個問題不會耽誤我們很久。

◆ Could you allow me to detain you for a moment？
允許我耽誤你一下嗎？

0522

release
rɪˈlis
v. 使放開 **n.** 釋放；發布（新聞稿）

◆ The fisherman decided to release the whale back into the sea.
這位漁夫決定把鯨魚放回大海中。

◆ We don't need to issue a press release about this matter.
有關這個議題，我們不需要發布新聞稿。

0523 ★

relax
rɪˈlæks
v. 使放鬆；使輕鬆

◆ He relaxes himself from pressure by taking a deep breath.
他深深吸一口氣讓自己從壓力中放鬆。

◆ I love reading prose because it keeps me relaxed.
我鍾愛看散文，因為它能使我放鬆心情。

0524 ★

slacken
ˈslækən

v. 使放鬆；使鬆弛；使緩和

◆ You shouldn't slacken off in your study.
在你學習時不應該鬆懈。

◆ When will this sharp pain slacken off?
什麼時候這種劇痛可以減輕？

0525

obey
oˈbe

v. 使服從；遵守命令

◆ Soldiers are expected to obey their commander's orders.
士兵被認為應該服從指揮官的命令。

◆ Foreign nationals should also obey the government ordinance.
外國僑民也應該遵守政府的法令。

0526

stain
sten

v. 使沾汙；汙點；著色劑

◆ My jacket was stained with ink.
我的夾克被墨水沾汙了。

◆ You must wash out this stain by tomorrow.
你必須在明天以前洗淨這個汙點。

0527

fluctuate
ˈflʌktʃʊ.et

v. 使波動；使起伏

◆ As everyone knows, the exchange rate fluctuates almost daily.
大家都知道匯率幾乎每天波動。

◆ She fluctuated between happiness and sorrow.
她在快樂與憂傷中起起伏伏。

0528 ★

---

vacate
ˋveket
v. 使空出；使撤離

◆ When should we vacate the room?
什麼時候我們該讓出房間？
◆ You must vacate the hotel room by Monday.
你必須在星期一之前遷出旅館。

0529

---

obstruct
əbˋstrʌkt
v. 使阻礙；故意妨礙

◆ The road was obstructed by the car accident for hours.
這條道路因車禍而阻塞了幾個小時。
◆ The fallen trees obstruct the road during the storm.
暴風雨中這些倒下的樹木阻礙了道路。

0530

---

weaken
ˋwikən
v. 使削弱；使變弱

◆ The massacre of hundreds of soldiers weakened the army.
數以百計的士兵被殘殺削弱了這支軍隊的實力。
◆ The dictator tried his best to weaken the power of the clergy.
這位獨裁者盡全力去削弱神職人員的權力。

0531

---

advance
ədˋvæns
v. 使前進；提出…… *n.* 預付

◆ The suggestion which George advanced may be a good way to solve the problem.
喬治所提出的建議可能是解決問題的好方法。
◆ The artist advanced a new aesthetic theory.
這位藝術家提出了一套新的美學理論。

0532

---

smack
smæk
v. 使勁拍打 *n.* 掌摑

◆ I'll smack your bottom if you do that again.
如果你再調皮，我就打你的屁股。
◆ She gave the kid a smack on his face.
她在這小孩的臉上打了一巴掌。

0533

---

retreat
rɪˋtrit
v. 使後退；使退縮 *n.* 休養所

◆ You can't retreat from the responsibility in this business deal.
你不能迴避在這個商業交易中的責任。
◆ The old man lived in a mountain retreat after he retired.
這位老人退休後住在山上的休養所。

0534

check
tʃɛk
v. 使查核；核對…… **n.** 支票

◆ Checking all the names was a slow and arduous job.
查核所有姓名是一項緩慢且費力的工作。

◆ Do you accept credit cards or traveler's checks?
你們有收到信用卡或旅行支票嗎？

0535 ★

highlight
ˈhaɪˌlaɪt
v. 使突出；強調…… **n.** 最精彩部分

◆ Homographs in this dictionary are highlighted so that I can easily tell them apart.
在這本字典中同形異義字被標示出來，所以我能輕易辨別。

◆ Her performance is one of the highlight of the match.
她的表演是這比賽中的精彩項目之一。

0536 ★

afflict
əˈflɪkt
v. 使苦惱；加痛苦於……

◆ John has no money and is afflicted with debts.
約翰沒錢，又為欠債而苦。

◆ I don't want to afflict you with my personal problems.
我不想讓你為我的個人問題所苦惱。

0537

downgrade
ˈdaʊnˌɡred
v. 使降級；貶低；看輕

◆ Most employees in my company have been downgraded.
我公司的多數員工被降職了。

◆ You can't downgrade the young people.
你不能貶低年輕人。

0538

splash
splæʃ
v. 使飛濺；濺起

◆ Great drops of rain splashed on the window.
斗大的雨滴濺溼了窗戶。

◆ As for the style of Chinese painting, I prefer the splash-ink painting.
以國畫的風格而言，我比較喜歡潑墨畫。

0539

modify
ˈmɑdəˌfaɪ
v. 使修改；使改正

◆ You need to modify your composition, or you will fail this course.
你必須修改你的作文，否則這科就會不及格。

◆ I am forced to modify my plan.
我被強迫修改我的計劃。

0540

expand
ɪkˈspænd
v. 使展開；使擴大

◆ The company tries to expand its business in Thai.
這家公司試圖在泰國擴展業務。

◆ Would you expand on the event a little further?
請你再進一步談談這場事件好嗎？

0541 ★

facilitate
fəˋsɪləˌtet
v. 使容易；促進……

◆ Computers can facilitate people's daily work.
電腦能幫助人們每天的工作。

◆ Many modern inventions facilitate our work.
許多現代發明能讓我們的工作更容易。

0542

---

saturate
ˋsætʃəˌret
v. 使浸透；使溼透

◆ His work clothes was saturated with sweat.
他的工作服被汗水浸溼了。

◆ Our clothes were saturated to the skin with the heavy rain.
這場大雨讓我們的衣服都溼透了。

0543

---

disappear
ˌdɪsəˋpɪr
v. 使消失；隱沒不見

跑去哪兒？

◆ The rainbow disappeared very quickly.
彩虹很快地消失了。

◆ The mysterious man gave me some sibylline words and disappeared without a trace.
神祕男子給了我幾句預言，就消失得無影無蹤。

0544

---

subside
səbˋsaɪd
v. 使消退；使沉陷；使平息

◆ The violent typhoon is subsiding little by little.
這場激烈的颱風漸漸地消退了。

◆ People's bias against her is gradually subsiding.
人們對她的偏見正逐漸平息。

0545

---

addict
əˋdɪkt
v. 使耽溺於；使成癮 **n.** 上癮者

◆ My uncle is addicted to gambling and drinking.
我的叔叔沉溺於賭博與飲酒。

◆ The drug addict vowed that he would never touch that again.
吸毒犯發誓他再也不會再碰那玩意兒了。

0546

---

bemuse
bɪˋmjuz
v. 使茫然；使發呆

◆ The physical problem bemuses many students.
這個物理問題讓課堂上許多學生困惑。

◆ This mysterious book bemused me for days.
這本神祕的書籍讓我困惑了好幾天。

0547

---

obsess
əbˋsɛs
v. 使迷住；使分心

◆ He is obsessed with computer games without studying hard.
他不努力用功而沈迷電玩。

◆ Most people are obsessed with money.
大多數的人對金錢是著迷的。

0548

retire
rɪˈtaɪr
v. 使退休；使退役

◆ The jury has retired to think about its verdict.
陪審團退席去考慮判決。

◆ Obviously, even he is retired, he can't live a tranquil life for the past reputation.
顯然即使他退休了，仍因為過去名聲而無法過著平靜的生活。

0549 ★

starve
storv
v. 使飢餓；使餓死

◆ Most refugees either die from the cold or starve to death.
大多數難民不是凍死就是餓死。

◆ I am starving and what do you serve here on the airplane?
我快餓扁了。機上供應什麼樣的餐點呢？

0550

soar
sor
v. 使高飛；使上漲

◆ The temperature soared to 36 degrees today.
今天的溫度上升到三十六度。

◆ In the experts' estimation, the price of stock will soars tomorrow.
專家預估，股價明天會大幅上揚。

0551

cease
sis
v. 使停止；使結束

◆ The president ordered his troops to cease to attack another country.
總統命令他的軍隊停止對其它國家攻擊。

◆ The people are praying that the war will cease soon.
人們正在祈禱這場戰爭將會盡快結束。

0552

heap
hip
v. 使堆滿；使堆積 n. 堆

◆ The skyscraper collapsed in a heap of ruin.
這座摩天大樓倒塌成了一堆廢墟。

◆ This heap of old clothes is for charity.
這堆舊衣服是作為慈善之用。

0553

reinforce
ˌriɪnˈfors
v. 使強化；使增強

◆ His impolite manner reinforced my dislike of him.
他無禮的舉止加深我對他的厭惡。

◆ The walls are reinforced with steel rods.
這些牆用鋼筋來強化。

0554

spin
spin
v. 使旋轉；吐絲

◆ The spider is diligent in spinning its web between two trees.
這隻蜘蛛勤奮地在兩棵樹之間織網。

◆ A successful politician must have a canny spin doctor offering the suggestions.
成功的政治家必須要有一位精明能幹能提供建議的公關顧問。

0555

revolve
rɪˈvɑlv
v. 使旋轉

◆ The moon revolves around the earth every day.
月球每天繞地球旋轉。

◆ The earth revolves once a year around the sun .
地球每年繞太陽旋轉一次。

0556

rotate
ˈrotet
v. 使旋轉；使輪
流；由……輪值

◆ The bird rotated from east to west.
這隻鳥由東向西旋轉。

◆ The weather vane rotated from north to south.
這個氣候風向標由北向南旋轉。

0557 ★

whirl
hwɜl
v. 使旋轉；嘗
試…… n. 漩渦

◆ The typhoon whirled the trees around in a circle.
颱風把樹木吹得團團轉。

◆ You had better give it a whirl.
你最好嘗試看看。

0558

tarnish
ˈtɑrnɪʃ
v. 使晦暗；使失
去光彩；使敗壞

◆ Air and humidity tarnish silver.
空氣與溼氣會使銀失去光澤。

◆ The news will tarnish his image.
這消息會敗壞他的形象。

0559

mingle
ˈmɪŋgl
v. 使混合；使相
混

◆ We can not mingle oil and water .
我們不能把油和水混合在一起。

◆ I mingled at the party and talked with many people.
我混在舞會中和許多人交談。

0560

refresh
rɪˈfrɛʃ
v. 使清涼；使恢
復精神

◆ After a long sleep, I drink a cup of coffee to refresh myself.
睡了很久後，我喝了一杯咖啡來提神。

◆ This glass of iced coffee will refresh you.
這杯冰咖啡會讓你感覺清涼。

0561

skyrocket
ˈskaɪˌrɑkɪt
v. 使猛漲；突然
地往上衝

◆ The price of houses skyrocketed from $100,000 to $200,000 in two years.
這間房子的價格從十萬美金猛漲到二十萬美金。

◆ Does the patient's blood pressure skyrocket ?
這位病人的血壓有急速上升嗎？

0562

prevail
priˈvel
v. 使盛行；使流行；勝過……

◆ It is believed that good will prevail over evil.
人們相信善良將戰勝邪惡。

◆ Justice will prevail over evil.
正義將會戰勝邪惡。

0563

migrate
ˈmaɪɡret
v. 使移居；使遷移

◆ Some birds migrate to warmer climates in the winter.
冬天時有些鳥會遷移到較溫暖的氣候區。

◆ Many people migrate to urban areas from rural areas.
許多人從鄉村地區遷移到都市地區。

0564

suffocate
ˈsʌfəˌket
v. 使窒息；把……悶死

◆ The thick smoke nearly suffocated me.
這股濃煙差點讓我窒息。

◆ The stale air made everyone nearly suffocate.
這汙濁的空氣讓每個人幾乎窒息。

0565

coincide
ˌkoɪnˈsaɪd
v. 使符合；使一致；使巧合

◆ My tastes and habits coincide with my sister's.
我的品味與習慣和我妹妹一致。

◆ His suggestion and our schedule just coincide.
他的建議和我們的時程正好相符。

0566

tickle
ˈtɪkḷ
v. 使逗笑；使發癢；使滿足

◆ The rough towel tickles my skin.
這粗糙的毛巾讓我皮膚發癢。

◆ I was greatly tickled at the funny joke .
這個有趣的笑話讓我開懷大笑。

0567

connect
kəˈnɛkt
v. 使連結；使聯想

◆ May I connect my USB drive to your computer?
我可以將隨身碟連接到你的電腦嗎？

◆ Where should I proceed to change for a connecting flight to Miami?
請問要轉往邁阿密的下一班飛機，要在哪裡搭乘？

0568

paralyze
ˈpærəˌlaɪz
v. 使麻痺；使無能為力

◆ The stroke left the patient paralyzed on one side of his body .
中風讓這位病人身體一邊麻痺。

◆ My fingers were paralyzed by the cold.
我的手指因為寒冷而麻痺。

0569

embed
ɪmˈbɛd
v. 使嵌入；使插入

◆ The diamond is embedded in the expensive ring.
這顆鑽石鑲在這個昂貴的戒指上。

◆ Those good days will be embedded in his memory forever.
那些美好的日子將會永遠藏在他的記憶中。

0570

resurrect
ˌrɛzəˈrɛkt
v. 使復活；恢復使用；再流行

◆ It is said that this mysterious medicine can resurrect the dead.
據說這種神祕的藥能讓死人復活。

◆ That thunder is enough to resurrect the dead.
那陣雷聲大到能讓死人復活。

0571

circulate
ˈsɝkjəˌlet
v. 使循環；使流通

◆ Money circulates slowly in a recessional economy.
金錢在不景氣時流通緩慢。

◆ Gossip tends to circulate quickly.
八卦消息很快速地流傳開來。

0572

mourn
mɔrn
v. 使悲傷；使哀悼

◆ The widow mourned for her deceased husband.
這位寡婦為她死去的丈夫感到哀痛。

◆ I really mourn the loss of that gold necklace.
我確實為我丟掉的金項鍊感到悲傷。

0573

smolder
ˈsmoldɚ
v. 使悶燒

◆ The fire burned brightly, then smoldered quietly.
這場火燒得火光明亮，然後安靜地悶燒。

◆ The fires still smolder beneath the ruins after bombing.
轟炸過後，火仍然繼續在廢墟中燃燒。

0574

cripple
ˈkrɪpl
v. 使殘障 **n.** 殘障人士

◆ He was crippled in the accident.
這場車禍讓他變殘障。

◆ The cripple walks with the help of a crutch.
這位殘障者借助拐杖來走路。

0575

relieve
rɪˈliv
v. 使減輕；使寬心

◆ I took a comfortable shower to relieve my pressure of the day.
我沖了個舒服的澡消除一天的壓力。

◆ The doctor prescribed some paregoric to relieve the patient's pain.
這位醫生開了些止痛藥來減輕病人的痛苦。

0576

gush
gʌʃ
v. 使湧出;話不停地講 **n.** 湧出

◆ There was a gush of blood as the wound opened again.
當傷口又裂開時,血流如注。

◆ He gushed about his love for his country.
他滔滔不絕說自己對國家的愛。

0577

revoke
rɪˈvok
v. 使無效;廢除……

◆ Her driver's license was revoked by the police.
她的駕照被警察撤銷了。

◆ The government may revoke his driver license.
政府可能會撤銷他的駕照。

0578

happen
ˈhæpən
v. 使發生;碰巧……

◆ What would it happen to the price if we doubled the order?
如果訂單加倍的話,價格要怎麼算?

◆ John would certainly have attended the judiciary proceedings if the flat had not happened.
假如爆胎沒有發生的話,約翰確定會參加這場審判程序。

0579

anger
ˈæŋgə
v. 使發怒 **n.** 生氣

◆ Nothing you say can assuage my anger.
無論你說什麼都無法減輕我的憤怒。

◆ He exploded with anger when he knew his son cheated during the exam.
當他知道他兒子考試作弊時,簡直氣炸了。

0580

develop
dɪˈvɛləp
v. 使發展;使進化;沖洗底片

◆ Shanghai developed into a major city of China.
上海發展成為中國的主要城市。

◆ The project is developed just in its embryonic stage at the moment.
這個計劃此只是在初期發展階段。

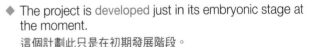

0581 ★

stink
stɪŋk
v. 使發臭 **n.** 臭氣

◆ Drinking beer will make your breath stink.
喝啤酒會讓你的呼吸有股臭味。

◆ There is a stink of dogs in the room.
房間裡有狗的臭味。

0582

inflate
ɪnˈflet
v. 使脹大;使充氣

◆ Ray inflated the volleyball.
雷為這顆排球充氣。

◆ Steel has inflated in price.
鋼鐵價格漲價了。

0583

burgeon
ˋbɝdʒən
Vt 使萌芽；使急速成長

◆ The new plant is burgeoning very quickly.
這棵新的植物很快就發芽。

◆ The little village burgeons soon after the sound arrangement and construction.
小城在健全的規劃和建設下很快發展起來。

0584

evolve
ɪˋvɑlv
Vt 使進化；使發展

◆ Some scientists think that humans evolved from monkeys.
一些科學家認為人類是由猴子進化而來。

◆ Human beings evolve from apes.
人類是從人猿進化而來。

0585

injure
ˋɪndʒɚ
Vt 使傷害；受……的損害

◆ The soldier injured his backbone and was paralyzed during the war.
這位士兵在此戰役中傷了脊椎而導致癱瘓。

◆ Some passengers were injured when the train suddenly jerked to a halt.
這列火車突然搖晃然後停止，一些乘客受傷了。

0586

slant
slænt
Vt 使傾斜；使歪斜 n 傾斜

◆ The carpenter slanted the roof to make water to run off easily.
這位木匠使屋頂傾斜以便讓水容易流掉。

◆ The fish line is slanting to the left .
這條魚線向左傾斜。

0587

tilt
tɪlt
Vt 使傾斜；使翹起

◆ The table suddenly tilted, so all the glasses crashed onto the floor.
這個桌子突然傾斜，因此所有的杯子都掉到地上。

◆ My uncle often likes to tilt his head forward .
我叔叔常常喜歡把頭往前傾斜。

0588

topple
ˋtɑpl
Vt 使傾覆；使翻倒；使推翻

◆ A stack of plates toppled over onto the floor.
一堆盤子翻倒在地板上。

◆ That house is going to topple down.
那房子即將會倒塌。

0589

slide
slaɪd
Vt 使滑行；悄悄地走 n 幻燈片

◆ Sometimes I spent a whole morning practicing sliding.
有時候我會花一整個早上練習滑壘。

◆ Where could I buy some slides or picture postcards?
請問哪兒可以買到幻燈片或風景明信片呢？

0590

slip
slɪp

v. 使滑倒 **n.** 失足；紙條

◆ Mary feels embarrassed when she slipped on the street.
瑪麗在路上滑倒而感到丟臉。

◆ May I have your passbook and deposit slip？
可以給我你的存摺和存款單嗎？

0591

perturb
pɚˋtɝb

v. 使煩惱；使心煩

◆ Don't perturb about such a trifling matter.
不要為這種微不足道的小事來煩惱。

◆ What perturbs me is her sudden appearance.
令我不安的是她突然出現。

0592

bother
ˋbɑðɚ

v. 使煩擾；使打攪

◆ Don't bother me with such a trivial problem.
不要用這些瑣碎的問題來煩我。

◆ Don't turn the stereo up to maximum volume! It will bother other people.
不要把音響的音量開到最大，會吵到其他人。

0593

solve
sɑlv

v. 使解決；給……解答

◆ I can't solve this problem without your help.
沒有你的幫忙，我無法解決這個問題。

◆ The problem cannot be solved if one side is adamant in not negotiating.
如果一邊堅決不協商，問題便無法解決。

0594 ★

無論走多慢都不要停下腳步

---

liberate
ˈlɪbəˌret

🔢 使解放……；
擺脫……限制

你自由了！

◆ Those kind people did their best to liberate slaves.
那些善良的人們盡他們的能力在解放奴隸。

◆ Our task is to liberate those oppressed nations.
我們的工作是解放那些被壓迫的國家。

0595

---

span
spæn

🔢 使跨越；架
起……；跨度

◆ The bridge has a span of 60 meters.
這座橋跨度六十公尺。

◆ The government built a bridge to span the river.
政府建造一座橋來跨越這條河。

0596

---

pervade
pəˈved

🔢 使遍布；彌漫
於

◆ There is a smell of coffee pervading the coffee shop.
這間咖啡店裡瀰漫著巧克力的味道。

◆ Internet technology will soon pervade the world.
網際網路科技將會很快普及於世界。

0597

---

drip
drɪp

🔢 使滴下；滴下
液體；滴水聲

◆ Sweat is dripping from the worker's forehead.
汗水從這個工人的額頭上滴下來。

◆ We heard the drip of the rain all day.
我們整天都聽到雨水的滴答聲。

0598

---

refine
rɪˈfaɪn

🔢 使精煉；除
去……雜質；使
精美

◆ Petroleum is refined from crude oil.
石油是從原油中提煉。

◆ She used so many refined words in her article.
她在她的文章中使用了如此多的精美文字。

0599

---

corrode
kəˈrod

🔢 使腐蝕；削
弱……力量

強鹽酸

◆ Rain would corrode the metal pipes.
下雨會腐蝕這些金屬管子。

◆ This acid may corrode metal.
這種酸可能會腐蝕金屬。

0600

---

sustain
səˈsten
v. 使維持；使支撐；使繼續

打穩地基最重要

◆ The foundations were enough to sustain the weight of the house.
這地基足夠支撐房子的重量。

◆ The judge sustained the defendant's objection.
這位法官支持這個被告的異議。

0601

decay
dɪˈke
v. 使腐爛；使衰退 n. 蛀牙

◆ Power decays the human mind.
權力腐化人心。

◆ Muggy weather makes fruits decay easily.
悶熱的天氣讓水果容易腐爛。

0602

spurt
spɝt
v. 使噴出；使冒出 n. 爆發

◆ Water began spurting from a hole in the pipe.
水從這個水管的洞中噴出。

◆ A spurt of blood came out of his wounded leg.
一股鮮血從他受傷的腳噴出。

0603

affect
əˈfɛkt
v. 使影響；使感動

◆ The family background of a person may affect his personality.
家庭背景可能影響一個人的性格。

◆ No one likes an affected smile, as it looks so artificial.
沒有人喜歡不自然的微笑，因為它看起來很假。

0604 ★

rage
redʒ
v. 使憤怒；使盛怒

東西被偷了

◆ The boss was gnashing his teeth with rage.
這位老闆氣得咬牙切齒。

◆ He flew into a rage and tore the letter into pieces.
他勃然大怒，並且把信撕成碎片。

0605

pause
pɔz
v. 使暫停；使中斷 n. 暫停

◆ He paused for a few seconds before he gave his answer.
他講出答案前停頓了幾秒。

◆ He decided to finish it without pause.
他決定毫不猶豫地完成它。

0606 ★

slump
slʌmp
v. 使暴跌；使下降

◆ Sales slumped by 15% last year.
上年度業績掉了百分之十五。

◆ Share prices slumped on a febrile USA stock exchange.
熱門的美國證券交易所股價大跌。

0607

obfuscate
əbˈfʌskɛt
ｖ. 使模糊；使困惑

◆ Don't obfuscate the main issue.
不要故弄玄虛。

◆ His strange behavior obfuscated me a lot.
他奇怪的行為讓我很困惑。

0608

acquaint
əˈkwent
ｖ. 使熟識；使認識

◆ When did you become acquainted with Buddhism?
你什麼時候開始接觸佛教的？

◆ Please acquaint my parents with my arrival.
請通知我父母我來了。

0609

mitigate
ˈmɪtə.get
ｖ. 使緩和；使減輕

◆ This lotion mitigates her itching.
這種乳液能減緩他的發癢。

◆ Measures need to be taken to mitigate the environmental pollution of burning more coal.
必須採取措施來減少燃燒更多的炭對環境所造成的汙染。

0610

assuage
əˈswedʒ
ｖ. 使緩和；使減輕

◆ Whatever you say, nothing can assuage my anger.
無論你說什麼都無法減輕我的憤怒。

◆ Some people think that alcohol is the best medicine to assuage suffering.
有些人認為酒精是撫平痛苦的最好良藥。

0611

inflict
ɪnˈflɪkt
ｖ. 使遭受；使負擔；使煩惱

◆ He inflicted a great deal of suffering on his wife.
他讓太太非常痛苦。

◆ Don't inflict your belief on your children.
不要將你的信仰強加於小孩。

0612

cover
ˈkʌvə
ｖ. 使遮蓋；使覆蓋 ｎ. 被單

◆ I will cover the baby with a blanket.
我會替嬰兒蓋毯子。

◆ My sister had her cover washed.
我姊姊洗了她的被單。

0613

quake
kwek
ｖ. 使震動；使搖晃 ｎ. 地震

◆ The little boy stood there quaking with fear.
這個小男孩站在那裡害怕地發抖著。

◆ It is predicted that there will be an quake of cosmic proportions soon.
根據預報，那裡很快將有一場天大的地震。

0614

vibrate

'vaɪbret

v. 使震動；使擺動

◆ The vocal cords vibrate as air passes over them.
聲帶在空氣經過時會震動。

◆ His words vibrated with scare.
他的話因恐懼而顫抖。

0615

provoke

prə'vok

v. 使激怒；引起……刺激

◆ He provokes her by telling her that she is too ugly.
他說她太醜而激怒了她。

◆ His remarks about her weight provoked her anger.
他有關她體重的言論激起了她的怒火。

0616

intensify

ɪn'tɛnsə.faɪ

v. 使激烈；使強烈

◆ We will intensify the development of rural economy.
我們將要加強農村經濟的發展。

◆ You should intensify your sense of responsibility.
你應該加強你的責任感。

0617

strike

straɪk

v. 使擊出；使撞擊

◆ This van struck my car from behind.
這部廂型車從後頭撞上我的車。

◆ I thought he was going to strike out.
我本來以為他會三振出局。

0618 ★

polish

'palɪʃ

v. 使擦亮；使磨光

◆ Father asked me to polish his shoes.
爸爸要求我把鞋子擦亮。

◆ You should use wax to polish on wooden floor.
你應該在木製地板上打蠟。

0619

strand

strænd

v. 使擱淺；使滯留

◆ The fishers had been stranded by a storm.
這些漁夫被暴風雨困住了。

◆ We were imagining having some dessert when we were stranded in the desert.
當我們被困在沙漠時，我們幻想著正在吃甜點。

0620

unify

'junə.faɪ

v. 使聯合；使統一

◆ He unified the small states into a single nation.
他統一了這些小州成為一個單一的國家。

◆ There are three ways to unify Korea.
統一韓國有三種方法。

0621

flush
flʌʃ
v. 使臉紅；使沖洗 *adj.* 豐富的

◆ His face flushed for a moment with embarrassment.
他的臉因為困窘而臉紅。

◆ The company is flush with capital.
這家公司有豐富的資金。

0622

diffuse
dɪˈfjuz
v. 使擴散；使散布 *n.* 四散的

◆ A teacher's job is diffusing knowledge to students.
一位老師的工作是傳播知識給學生。

◆ His speech was so diffuse that I missed his point.
他的演講沒有邊際，以至於我抓不到重點。

0623

simplify
ˈsɪmpləˌfaɪ
v. 使簡化；使容易

◆ The teacher simplified the explanation to make the children understand.
老師簡化說明來讓這些孩童明白。

◆ The subject is very difficult to simplify further.
這個主題很難來進一步簡化。

0624

concern
kənˈsɝn
v. 使關心；與……有關 *n.* 關心

◆ The rumor concerns the relationship between two political figures.
謠言牽涉到兩位政治人物之間的關係。

◆ There is concern that the giant panda will soon become extinct.
他們關心大熊貓很快會絕種。

0625

bend
bɛnd
v. 使彎曲；使彎折 *n.* 轉彎處

◆ You cannot expect a rich man to bend the knee to a poor man.
你不能期待一個有錢人對窮人屈膝。

◆ Is there some kind of landmark at that bend?
那個轉彎處有什麼地標嗎？

0626

spread
sprɛd
v. 使攤開；使散布；使伸展

◆ She spread a colorful tablecloth on the table this morning.
今天早上她在桌上鋪了一塊鮮豔的桌布。

◆ The burning rubber spread acrid smoke across the city.
燃燒橡膠所散布的刺鼻煙霧穿越了這個城市。

0627

amuse
əˈmjuz
v. 使歡樂；使開心

◆ She amused her friends by mimicking her sister.
她模仿她姊姊來逗朋友開心。

◆ Good comedies will amuse the audience.
好的喜劇將給觀眾帶來歡樂。

0628

spill
spɪl
v. 使灑出；使潑
出 **n.** 溢出物

◆ I spilt the bottle of milk on the ground.
我把這瓶牛奶灑在地上了。

◆ The oil spill imperiled thousands of marine life.
漏油危及到數以千計的海洋生物。

0629

quiver
ˈkwɪvɚ
v. 使顫動；使抖
動

◆ The breeze makes the leaves quiver.
微風使得這些樹葉搖動。

◆ The rabbit quivered its nose all the time.
這隻兔子總是抖動牠的鼻子。

0630

stir
stɜ
v. 使攪動；使撥
動 **n.** 轟動

◆ Stir the sauce quickly to prevent it lumping.
快速攪動這調味醬以免它結塊。

◆ The latest magazine caused quite a stir.
這新版的雜誌引起很大的轟動。

0631

transform
trænsˈfɔrm
v. 使變化；使變
形

◆ Frogs are transformed from tadpoles.
青蛙由蝌蚪變化而來。

◆ Remodeling transformed an old and dark house into a cheerful one.
重新整修讓一間老舊黑暗的房子轉變成令人愉快的地方。

0632 ★

soften
ˈsɔfən
v. 使變軟

◆ The special material has begun to soften up.
這特殊的物質開始軟化。

◆ This cream will help to soften up your skin.
這種乳霜會幫助妳的皮膚更柔軟。

0633

scare
skɛr
v. 使驚恐

◆ Her screams scared the robber away.
她的尖叫聲把搶匪嚇跑了。

◆ The child was scared by the ghost on TV and had a nightmare that night.
孩子被電視上的鬼怪嚇到，當晚就做了惡夢。

0634

frighten
ˈfraɪtn
v. 使驚恐

◆ The child was frightened by a viper.
這孩子被這條毒蛇嚇壞了。

◆ The people who had been dispersed feel confused and frightened.
被驅散的人群們感到迷惑與驚恐。

0635

dismay
dɪs'me
v. 使驚慌；使
沮喪 n. 氣餒

◆ The expensive cost of tuition made him feel dismay.
這昂貴的學費讓他覺得不知所措。

◆ We enjoyed the meal but were a bit dismayed at the bill.
我們享受這頓飯，但是對帳單有點不知所措。

0636

appall
ə'pɔl
v. 使驚駭

◆ She was appalled by the horrific film.
她被這部恐怖電影驚嚇到。

◆ We were appalled by his harsh words.
我們對他尖酸的言論感到驚訝。

0637

startle
'startl̩
v. 使驚嚇

◆ I was startled when he came in.
他進來時我嚇了一跳。

◆ My coach was startled by the sudden fiasco.
我的教練對這突如其來的慘敗大吃一驚。

0638

round-trip ticket
'raʊnd ˌtrɪp 'tɪkɪt
n. 來回票

◆ How much is the price of a round-trip ticket from Kaohsiung to Taichung?
從高雄到台中的來回票多少錢？

◆ Do you buy a single fare or a round trip ticket?
你要買單程還是來回票？

0639

visitor
'vɪzɪtə
n. 來訪者

◆ Many visitors spend their holidays in Hawaii.
許多遊客到夏威夷渡假。

◆ There's been a steady flow of visitors to the amusement park through the summer.
整個夏天都有固定的遊客人潮來到遊樂場。

0640

source
sors
n. 來源；泉源

維生素 A

◆ What is the source of the Yellow River?
黃河的源頭在哪裡？

◆ Carrots are a good source of vitamin A.
紅蘿蔔是很好的維生素 A 來源。

0641 ★

supply
sə'plaɪ
v. 供給……；
補充…… n. 補
給品

營養午餐

◆ This paper goods company supplies us with printing paper.
這紙品公司提供我們列印紙。

◆ When will you get a new supply next month?
下個月什麼時候你們會補新貨？

0642 ★

depend
dɪˈpɛnd
v. 依靠……；
視……而定

◆ Whether we go to the meeting or not depends on you.
我們參不參加這次會議由你決定。

◆ That depends on how much work is involved.
那要看牽涉到多少工作量而定。

0643

reliant
rɪˈlaɪənt
adj. 依賴的；依
靠的

◆ The orphanage is heavily reliant upon charity.
這家孤兒院大量依賴贊助。

◆ Tom is far too reliant on his parents for financial support.
湯姆在財務上太依賴他的父母。

0644

warden
ˈwɔrdn̩
n. 典獄長

◆ It is neither easy nor interesting to be a warden.
當一位典獄長既不容易也不有趣。

◆ The prisoner was taken to the warden's office.
這個囚犯被帶到典獄長的辦公室。

0645

ritual
ˈrɪtʃʊəl
n. 典禮；儀式
adj. 儀式的

◆ A rite of passage is a ritual that marks a change in a person's social status.
成年禮是一種對於個人社會地位改變的儀式。

◆ We make our ritual visit to the temple every month.
每個月上教堂是我們的例行儀式。

0646

due
dju
adj. 到期的；應
歸還的

你借的書
到期了！

◆ The due date of the bill is December 25th.
這張帳單的付款到期日是十二月二十五日。

◆ Hard copies of weekly essays are due on Mondays at 6 p.m.
每週論文的紙本必須在週一下午六時之前交出。

0647

uniform
ˈjunəˌfɔrm
n. 制服 **adj.** 相
同的；一致的

◆ They all wear uniforms at the store.
這家商店的員工都穿制服。

◆ These students at the school wear uniform clothing.
這所學校的學生穿相同的服裝。

0648 ★

sting
stɪŋ
v. 刺；叮；使疼
痛

◆ Denny was stung by a bee at the picnic.
丹尼野餐時被一隻蜜蜂螫到。

◆ My eyes are stinging from the heavy smoke .
我眼睛被濃煙薰得很痛。

0649

shrill
frɪl
adj. 刺耳的；尖聲的

◆ He heard the shrill voice of a woman next door.
他聽到隔壁傳來女人的尖叫聲。

◆ She emitted one shrill cry and then escaped.
她尖叫了一聲，然後就逃走了。

0650

pierce
pɪrs
v. 刺穿；穿過

◆ He used a sword to pierce his enemy's stomach.
他用一把劍刺穿敵人的腹部。

◆ We use the tools to pierce holes on the floor.
我們使用這些工具在地板上打洞。

0651

piquant
ˈpikənt
adj. 刺激的；辛辣的

◆ He added spices to the soup to give it a piquant taste.
他在湯中加入香料，讓它嚐起來有辛辣的口感。

◆ Vegetable salads are often added with a piquant sauce.
蔬菜沙拉經常加上辛辣的調味料。

0652

scale
skel
n. 刻度；規模；秤；天平

◆ His ruler has one scale in centimeters and another in inches.
他的尺有公分與英吋兩種刻度。

◆ Put your baggage on this scale, please.
請將你的行李放在秤上過磅。

0653

association
əˈsosɪˌeʃən
n. 協會；聯想；社團

◆ They formed an association to promote employee's welfare.
他們成立協會促進員工福利。

◆ Have you joined the teachers' association?
你有參加教師協會嗎？

0654 ★

coordinate
koˈɔrdn̩ˌet
v. 協調……；使調合

◆ A four-year-old child cannot easily coordinate his movements.
四歲大的小孩無法協調自己的動作。

◆ You need a lot of experience to coordinate the logistics of such a large event.
你需要許多經驗來協調這個大案子的物流。

0655

agreement
əˈgrimənt
n. 協議；協定；同意

◆ We have reached an agreement for this proposal.
對此提案我們達成共識。

◆ I came to an amicable agreement with my boyfriend after our argument.
在我們爭吵後，我和我男朋友達成友好的協議。

0656 ★

victim
ˈvɪktɪm

n. 受害者；犧牲者；受災者

◆ The funeral ceremony for the victims of the airliner crash was held last week.
空難罹難者的葬禮在上週舉行。

◆ The government took cursory action to aid the earthquake victims.
政府採取了粗略的行動來幫助地震的受害者。

0657

beneficiary
ˌbɛnəˈfɪʃərɪ

n. 受益人

保險受益人
王小明

◆ The man made his oldest son his beneficiary in case of his death.
這位男士將他的長子指定為死後的受益人。

◆ The mayor promises that once the policy is put into practice, all the citizens would be the main beneficiaries.
市長承諾一旦該政策付諸實行，所有的市民將是最大的受益人。

0658

employee
ˌɛmplɔɪˈi

n. 受雇者；員工

◆ A big company can offer good employee welfare.
大公司能提供好的員工福利。

◆ The director condescended to have lunch with the employees in the canteen.
這位局長屈尊到福利社與員工共進午餐。

0659 ★

palatable
ˈpælətəbl

adj. 味美的；令人愉快的

◆ Roger's dishes are always highly palatable.
羅傑做的菜總是很美味。

◆ This cocktail is palatable and not very expensive.
這杯雞尾酒很美味，價錢也不貴。

0660

鍥而不捨，金石可鏤

---

taste
test
n. 味道；品味
v. 品嚐出

◆ The adjunct of fruit makes the cereal taste good.
水果的添加物讓麥片更好吃。

◆ A thick woolen rug does not fit my taste.
厚羊毛地毯不太適合我的品味。

0661

---

groan
gron
v. 呻吟著說；受
苦難 *n.* 呻吟

◆ The wounded soldier uttered a groan.
這個受傷的士兵發出呻吟聲。

◆ He gave a loud groan when he heard the news.
當他聽到這個消息，大叫了一聲。

0662

---

command
kə'mænd
v. 命令……；支
配……；控制權

馬上去做！

◆ I have a good command of English and Japanese, as
well as a little Spanish.
我精通英文、日文和一點西班牙文。

◆ I command you to stop at once.
我命令你立即停止。

0663 ★

---

fate
fet
n. 命運；天意

◆ Nobody can predict the fate of the hostages.
沒有人能預測人質的命運將會如何。

◆ The fate of a man hinges on how much effort he makes.
一個人的命運視他做了多少努力而定。

0664

---

snarl
snorl
v. 咆哮 *n.* 吼叫

汪汪

◆ The coach snarled at the players who were late.
這位教練對這些遲到的運動員咆哮。

◆ She answered her husband with an angry snarl.
她滿懷怒火吼叫地回答她丈夫。

0665

---

solid
'salɪd
adj. 固體的；堅
實的；純的

◆ People like to buy solid furniture.
大家喜歡買堅固的家具。

◆ Water becomes solid when it freezes.
水結冰時會變成固體。

0666

ramp
ræmp
n. 坡道；活動梯

◆ Ramps are needed at exits and entrances for wheelchair users.
出口與入口的坡道對輪椅的使用者是需要的。

◆ He moved down the ramp happily.
他快樂地朝著斜坡往下走。

0667

---

directory
də'rɛktərɪ
n. 電話簿；目錄

◆ Would you like your number listed in the telephone directory?
你希望你的號碼列在電話簿上嗎？

◆ You will find a list of some of the industry trade press with corresponding contact information in the directory.
你將在這本工商目錄中找到一份與工商業刊物相符合的聯絡訊息列表。

0668 ★

---

commission
kə'mɪʃən
n. 委託；佣金；委任

◆ How much of this estimated salary is commission on sales?
在預估薪資裡面，有多少是銷售的佣金呢？

◆ He had a commission to build a house on this land.
他接受委任在這片土地上蓋一座房子。

0669 ★

---

seasonal
'siznəl
adj. 季節的

◆ The weather became cold because of a seasonal change.
因為季節性的改變，氣候變冷了。

◆ Where can I find casual or seasonal work?
我去哪裡能找到臨時或季節性的工作？

0670

---

religious
rɪ'lɪdʒəs
adj. 宗教的；謹慎的

◆ It is very hard for me to get used to a traditional religious ceremony.
我很難習慣傳統宗教儀式。

◆ Religious beliefs are personal and should not be forced.
宗教信仰是涉及個人的，而且不應該被強迫。

0671 ★

---

officer
'ɔfəsɚ
n. 官員

◆ The generous officer helped the poor children.
這位慷慨的官員幫助這個可憐的孩子。

◆ The President awarded a badge of honor to the police officer.
總統頒贈榮譽獎章給這名警官。

0672

---

bureaucracy
bju'rɑkrəsɪ
n. 官僚主義

請願抗議

◆ In order to reduce the national budget, the government plans to eliminate unnecessary bureaucracy.
為了刪減國家預算，政府計劃淘汰官僚體系。

◆ He could not bear the bureaucracy in his company, so he quit his job last week.
他不能忍受公司裡的官僚主義，所以上週辭職了。

0673 ★

bedrock
ˈbɛdˌrɑk
n. 岩床；根基；基礎

◆ The bedrock in Kaohsiung protects the buildings from damage in an earthquake.
高雄的岩床保護這些建築物在地震中避免被破壞。

◆ Ancient Indian culture is the bedrock of all.
古老的印度文化是所有文化的根基。

0674

---

bottom
ˈbɑtəm
n. 底部；底層

◆ She washed away the brownish sediment at the bottom of the tank.
她洗去這個水槽底部褐色的沉澱物。

◆ She added a postscript at the bottom of her letter.
她在信的底部加上附筆。

0675

---

conquer
ˈkɑŋkɚ
v. 征服；戰勝；贏得掌聲

克服懼高症

◆ Napoleon conquered both France and Josephine, but he did not keep either forever.
拿破崙雖然征服了法國和約瑟芬，卻未永遠留住兩者。

◆ I finally conquer my bad habits.
我終於克服我的壞習慣。

0676

---

advice
ədˈvaɪs
n. 忠告；消息

明天出門要帶雨衣！ TV

◆ Thanks for your advice. I now know what to do.
謝謝你的建議，現在我知道要怎麼做了。

◆ The bureau of public health issues advice and warning to the public about adulterated food irregularly.
衛生局不定期針對混雜劣等物質的食物向民眾發出建議與警告。

0677 ★

---

ignore
ɪgˈnor
v. 忽視……；不理……

等等我！

◆ Don't ignore the details on the contract.
不要忽略了合約的細節。

◆ The teacher ignores the spelling mistakes made by the students.
老師不理會學生所犯的拼字錯誤。

0678

---

disposition
ˌdɪspəˈzɪʃən
n. 性情；性格

◆ My sunny disposition makes me so many friends.
我的陽光性格讓我交了不少朋友。

◆ Her humorous disposition brings happiness to people around her.
她幽默的性情給她身邊的人帶來快樂。

0679

---

ownership
ˈonɚˌʃɪp
n. 所有權

◆ The department store is under new ownership in downtown Taipei.
台北市區的一間百貨公司易主了。

◆ Who is the ownership of this baggage?
這個行李是誰的？

0680

admit
əd'mɪt

v. 承認；容許入場

◆ I was admitted to the graduate school of National Taiwan University.
我被國立台灣大學的研究所錄取了。

◆ He admitted that he had blundered again.
他承認他又犯了大錯。

0681 ★

acknowledge
ək'nɑlɪdʒ

v. 承認……；回覆；打招呼

我認罪!

◆ It is now generally acknowledged that Hitler was responsible for German collapse.
現在普遍認為希特勒必須為德國的瓦解負責。

◆ The prime minister acknowledged his political mistake in public yesterday.
總理昨天承認了他在政治上的錯誤。

0682 ★

concede
kən'sid

v. 承認……；讓與

我認輸了!

◆ He conceded that he took the money that was left on the table.
他承認拿了放在桌上的錢。

◆ They must concede that I have tried my best.
他們必須承認我已經盡力了。

0683 ★

cater
'ketə

v. 承辦飲食；迎合

◆ This luxurious restaurant caters especially to foreign customers.
這家豪華餐廳特別提供宴食服務給外國客戶。

◆ Many products on the market nowadays are catered to individual needs.
現在市場上許多商品是迎合個人需求的。

0684

grievance
'grivəns

n. 抱怨；不滿

受夠了 ……

◆ Her employers redressed her grievances by increasing her salary.
她的雇主用加薪來補償她的不滿。

◆ The king died with a grievance in his heart.
這個國王心中懷著怨懟而終。

0685

complain
kəm'plen

v. 抱怨……；訴苦……

為什麼貨沒送到?

◆ They always complain about an increase in price.
他們總是抱怨價格調漲。

◆ I've really got nothing to complain about.
我確實沒有任何抱怨。

0686 ★

grumble
'grʌmbl

v. 抱怨……；對……不滿

對不起!

◆ There is no use in grumbling.
抱怨一點用都沒有。

◆ Many employees will grumble about having to do the work.
許多員工即將為了做這份工作而抱怨。

0687

thumb
θʌm
n. 拇指

◆ When he dunked, the coach gave him a thumbs-up.
他灌籃後，教練對他豎起大拇指。

◆ The four fingers, a thumb and a palm are the main parts of the hand.
手部主要是由四隻手指，一隻大姆指和手掌所組成。

0688

stretch
strɛtʃ
v. 拉長；張開；伸出

◆ These exercises are designed to stretch the muscles of your legs.
這些運動的設計是為了伸展腿部肌肉。

◆ I stretched out my hand for the cup.
我伸出手去拿茶杯。

0689

zip
zɪp
n. 拉鍊；拉拉鍊
v. 快速移動

◆ The problem is the zip isn't working now.
問題是現在拉鍊壞了。

◆ Will you sew me a new zip on my pants ?
你能幫我在褲子縫上新拉鍊嗎？

0690

abandon
əˋbændən
v. 拋棄；丟棄；使放縱

◆ The children abandon their bicycles and run to the river.
孩子們將腳踏車丟在一旁，然後跑到河裡。

◆ You had to abandon your abortive attempts.
你必須放棄你的失敗嘗試。

0691

discard
dɪsˋkɑrd
v. 拋棄……；丟棄……

◆ After discussing things with his boss, he discards his original thoughts.
和老闆討論之後，他放棄了原有的想法。

◆ Let's discard some of these old documents.
讓我們丟棄一些舊文件。

0692 ★

clap
klæp
v. 拍手；喝采
n. 雷鳴聲

◆ The baby was scared by a redoubtable clap of thunder.
嬰兒被一聲可怕雷鳴嚇到了。

◆ The clap of thunder startled the speaker.
這個演講者被如雷的掌聲驚嚇到。

0693

auction
ˋɔkʃən
n. 拍賣 *v.* 把……賣掉

◆ My boss bid 1 million dollars for the antique car at the auction.
我老闆在拍賣會出價一百萬美金買這台古董車。

◆ We will put the laptop up for auction.
我們將把這台筆電拍賣。

0694 ★

cane
ken
n. 拐杖;甘蔗

◆ My grandma is advancing slowly with the aid of a cane.
我祖母靠這一根拐杖慢慢前進。

◆ This kind of sugar cane is quite a sweet and juicy.
這種甘蔗既甜又多汁。

0695

---

refuse
rɪˋfjuz
v. 拒絕……**n.** 廢物

◆ We refuse to sell to you are acting illegally.
如果你們行為不合法,我們拒絕售貨給你們。

◆ The movie star refuses to talk about her marriage.
這位電影明星拒絕談論到她的婚姻生活。

0696 ★

---

extract
ɪkˋstrækt
v. 拔取;用力取出 **n.** 摘錄

◆ The oil which is extracted from olives is used for cooking.
從橄欖中提煉出來的油可用來烹飪。

◆ Could you extract any information from the reporter?
你能從這記者那裡打聽到任何訊息嗎?

0697

---

unplug
ʌnˋplʌg
v. 拔掉插頭

◆ Please unplug the TV before you leave home.
當你離開家時請拔掉插頭。

◆ Turn off and unplug the computer before cleaning.
在清理電腦時要關機與拔掉插頭。

0698

---

haul
ˋhɔl
v. 拖……;拉…… **n.** 搬運

◆ A crane had to be used to haul the truck out of the river.
要將這台卡車拖離河中必須使用起重機。

◆ When you order new products, you will have a free haul.
當你訂購新產品時,你將會獲得一次免費搬運。

0699

---

drag
dræg
v. 拖拉……;用滑鼠拖曳

◆ Where are you dragging this case to?
你要把這個箱子拖到哪裡去?

◆ How much longer is this going to drag on?
這件事還要拖多久?

0700

---

exile
ˋɛksaɪl
v. 放逐;流亡國外

◆ They exiled the journalist from their country.
他們把這位記者流亡國外。

◆ The statesman was exiled because he is always the dissident.
這個政治家被流亡國外,因為他總是扮演異議份子。

0701

set
sɛt
v. 放置；指定
n. 一組

◆ It is more convenient to set up an intercom in every office.
每間辦公室都放上內部通話裝置會更方便。

◆ The smart boy made a radio set for himself.
這個聰明的男孩自己做了一組收音機。

0702

wanton
'wɑntən
adj. 放縱的；無節制的；淫蕩的

◆ The woman was described as wanton in insane ways.
這個女人被形容成瘋狂的放蕩。

◆ It seemed still a wanton impulse in some way.
在某種意義上它似乎仍是種放蕩的衝動。

0703

loosen
'lusn̩
v. 放鬆；解開

◆ The baby would not loosen its grip on my arm.
這個嬰兒沒有鬆開我的手臂。

◆ Could you loosen the lid of this bottle？
你能把這個瓶子的瓶蓋鬆開嗎？

0704

expensive
ɪks'pɛnsɪv
adj. 昂貴的；高價的

◆ Air freight is more expensive than ocean freight.
空運比海運還要昂貴。

◆ The wedding dress is made of expensive brocade.
這件結婚禮服是由昂貴的錦緞做成。

0705

manifest
'mænə.fɛst
adj. 明白的；明顯的

◆ Happiness was manifest on the bride's face.
快樂在這個新娘的臉上是明顯的。

◆ Her manifest lack of interest in the project has caused her partner's hatred.
她對這個計劃明顯興趣缺缺，已造成夥伴的怨懟。

0706

sensible
'sɛnsəbl̩
adj. 明智的；合理的；注意到的

◆ That she did not buy the dress was a sensible decision.
她沒買下那件洋裝是明智的決定。

◆ The double agent is sensible of the danger of his position.
這個雙面間諜知道他的處境很危險。

0707

obvious
'ɑbvɪəs
adj. 明顯的；明白的

◆ It is obvious that the man is drunk.
很明顯的這個男人已經醉了。

◆ The politician who had scandal shows his obvious antagonism towards the press.
這位有醜聞的政治人物對媒體露出明顯的敵意。

0708 ★

dizzy

/ˈdɪzɪ/

adj. 昏眩的；頭暈的

◆ I feel chilly and dizzy. Can you give me a hot towel, please?
我覺得又冷頭又暈。可以給我一條熱毛巾嗎？

◆ Watching the clock's pendulum made me dizzy.
看著時鐘的鐘擺使我感到頭暈。

0709

buoyant

/ˈbɔɪənt/

adj. 易浮的；愉快的；上漲的

◆ Salt water is more buoyant than fresh water.
鹹水比淡水更有浮力。

◆ Most children are usually more buoyant than adults.
大部份的孩童通常比成人們快樂。

0710

fragile

/ˈfrædʒəl/

adj. 易碎的；易消失的

◆ Glass is certainly more fragile than diamond.
玻璃當然比鑽石易碎。

◆ The porters are trained to be careful when carrying the fragile parcels.
搬運工被訓練成在搬運易碎包裹時要小心。

0711

frangible

/ˈfrændʒəbəl/

adj. 易碎的；脆弱的

◆ Most frangible toys are not suitable for young children.
多數容易破掉的玩具不適合年紀小的孩子。

◆ The glasswork is frangible and must put it carefully.
玻璃製品是易碎的，必須小心置放。

0712

palpable

/ˈpælpəbl/

adj. 易察覺的；可摸到的

◆ The big bird's heartbeat was very palpable.
這隻大鳥的心跳非常容易察覺。

◆ The letters of protest have already had a palpable influence to the government.
抗議信件對政府已有顯著影響。

0713

flexible

/ˈflɛksəbl/

adj. 易彎曲的；有彈性的；可變通的

◆ Rubber and plastic both are flexible materials.
橡膠和塑膠都是有彈性的材質。

◆ Excellent leaders should be flexible rather than dogmatic.
優秀的領導者應該變通而不武斷。

0714 ★

serve

/sɝv/

v. 服務……的需要；為……盡力

◆ He serves as the priest in a famous church.
他在一所著名的教堂當牧師。

◆ We will serve breakfast from six to nine in the coffee shop tomorrow morning.
我們明早將從六點到九點在咖啡室供應早餐。

0715

overdose
ˈovəˌdos
v. *n.* 服藥過量

◆ He died of a drug overdose.
他的死因是服藥過量。

◆ The woman went into a deep coma after taking an overdose of sleeping pills.
這女人在服用過量的安眠藥之後，進入重度昏迷。

0716

weapon
ˈwɛpən
n. 武器；兵器

◆ Knives and guns are dangerous weapons.
刀與槍是危險的武器。

◆ The crowd in the market picked up eggs to use as weapons.
群眾在市場撿起雞蛋當武器。

0717 ★

depression
dɪˈprɛʃən
n. 沮喪；意志消沉；不景氣

◆ By 1932, the depression had reached its nadir.
到了西元 1932 年，不景氣到達了最低點。

◆ The threat of an economic depression hangs over Europe.
經濟不景氣的威脅籠罩著歐洲。

0718 ★

cure
kjʊr
v. 治療；使痊癒

◆ The medicine can cure your cold.
這個藥能治好你的感冒。

◆ His illness was cured by a potent medicine.
他的病被一種特效藥治療好了。

0719

treatment
ˈtritmənt
n. 治療；處置

◆ The best treatment for the flu is to rest and drink lots of hot water.
流感最好的治療方法就是休息和多喝熱開水。

◆ The patient got proper treatment for his ailment.
這個病人的疾病得到適當的治療。

0720

therapy
ˈθɛrəpɪ
n. 治療法

◆ The man's physical force is debilitated by the special therapy.
這個男人的體能因為這項特別治療而衰弱。

◆ The Chinese herb doctor is good at acupuncture and breathing technique therapy.
這位中醫擅長針灸與氣功療法。

0721

remedy
ˈrɛmədɪ
n. 治療法；醫治
v. 治療⋯⋯

◆ She took a cold remedy to relieve her sneezing and headache.
她採取一種冷凍療法來治療她的打噴涕和頭痛。

◆ Many scientists strive for a breakthrough in H7N9 remedy.
許多科學家們努力爭取在 H7N9 治療上的突破。

0722

infuse
ɪnˈfjuz
v. 注入……；傾注……；灌輸……

◆ Would you infuse a kettle of tea for me?
你能幫我泡一壺茶嗎？

◆ The general's speech infused new life into the troops.
這位將軍的演說為軍隊灌輸了新生命。

0723

notice
ˈnotɪs
v. 注意到

◆ I did not notice that you entered the classroom.
我沒注意到你進入教室。

◆ I notice from your resume that you've studied abroad for two years.
我從你的簡歷中注意到你曾在國外留學兩年。

0724 ★

strife
straɪf
n. 爭吵；衝突；不和

◆ The strife between Mary and Helen was settled last week.
瑪麗和海倫間的衝突在上週解決。

◆ She was upset because of the family strife.
她因為家庭的紛爭而沮喪。

0725

contend
kənˈtɛnd
v. 爭論……；爭奪……；主張……

◆ Three tennis players contended for the prize.
三位網球選手爭奪這項獎品。

◆ The old woman has contended with her illness for a long time.
這位年老的女士和她的疾病戰鬥了很久。

0726

edition
ɪˈdɪʃən
n. 版；版本

莎士比亞全集 中文版

◆ The new edition of the famous dictionary will come out soon.
這本知名字典的新版將要問世。

◆ Have you read the unabridged edition of that novel?
你有讀過那部小說的完整版嗎？

0727 ★

學如逆水行舟，不進則退

---

physical
ˈfɪzɪkl̩
adj. 物理的；身體的；實際的

◆ Physical is Greek to this lazy student.
這個懶惰的學生對物理學一竅不通。

◆ The man's physical force is debilitated by the special therapy.
這個男子的體力因這項特別的治療而衰弱。

0728

---

proof
pruf
n. 物證；證據；考驗

犯案工具

◆ There is positive proof that she stole money.
有確切的證據顯示她偷了錢。

◆ The lawyer presents a complete proof to save the innocent person from the prison.
律師提出完整的證據營救出牢裡無辜的人。

0729

---

helicopter
ˈhɛlɪˌkɑptə
n. 直升機 *v.* 乘直升機

◆ The helicopter hovered over the mountain to search for the victims.
這架直升機在山上盤旋以搜尋罹難者。

◆ A damaged boat was winched by a helicopter.
一艘毀壞的船被直升機吊拉起來。

0730

---

straight
stret
adv. 直接地；筆直地 *adj.* 直的

◆ Go straight along this street, and the bank is at the third corner.
沿著這條街直走，銀行就在第三個轉角處。

◆ Just go straight to the end of road and you'll find the building.
只要直走到路的盡頭，就會看到大樓。

0731

---

intuition
ˌɪntjuˈɪʃən
n. 直覺

◆ I always make a decision based on my intuition.
我總是以直覺來下決定。

◆ He had an intuition that there was something wrong.
他直覺認為有些事錯了。

0732

---

instinct
ˈɪnstɪŋkt
n. 直覺；本能；天性

敏銳的偵探本能

◆ My mother has good instinct about choosing the right clothes for me.
我媽媽對於如何幫我選對的衣服有很好的直覺。

◆ It's maternal instinct that causes mothers to try their best to protect their children.
母性的本能引起母親盡最大的努力來保護他們的小孩。

0733

aware
ə'wɛr
adj. 知道的；察覺的

◆ She is aware of Bill's rude comments behind her back.
她知道比爾在她背後說了些不禮貌的話。

◆ His father must be aware of the fact that he is destitute.
他爸爸一定知道他窮困潦倒的事實。

0734 ★

sense
sɛns
n. 知覺；意義；理性

◆ Jerry realized that he had no sense in his legs after the operation.
手術後傑瑞發覺他的雙腿毫無知覺。

◆ It's common sense that polar bears live in the Arctic.
北極熊住在北極圈是個常識。

0735

social
'soʃəl
adj. 社交的；社會的；關於社會的

◆ Her lack of self-confidence makes her rather maladroit in social situations.
缺乏自信使得她在社交場合中顯得相當笨拙。

◆ Tammy had such a good social life and manner when she was at college.
大學時，泰咪的社交生活十分活躍。

0736 ★

society
sə'saɪətɪ
n. 社會

◆ Western societies have different views on education compared to eastern societies.
西方社會的教育觀念與東方社會有所不同。

◆ There was a caste system in Indian society.
在印度社會中有世襲階級制度。

0737

blank
blæŋk
n. 空白表格處

◆ Please fill in the blanks with your personal information.
請在空白處填上您的個人資料。

◆ Please fill "F" for female or "M" for male in the blank.
請在空格處填入「F」代表女性，或「M」代表男性。

0738

empty
'ɛmptɪ
adj. 空的；空腹的 **v.** 使……清空

◆ You can use an empty bottle as a makeshift vase.
你能使用一個空瓶子當替代花瓶。

◆ The market is glutted with large and expensive houses lying empty and unsold.
市場上充斥又大又貴、空蕩蕩未售出的房子。

0739

hollow
'hɑlo
adj. 空洞的；凹下的 **v.** 挖空

◆ We heard a hollow boom of thunder.
我們聽到一陣低沉的雷聲。

◆ The students have to hollow the egg before coloring it.
學生們在上色之前必須先把蛋挖空。

0740

vacant
ˈvekənt
adj. 空著的；空虛的

◆ Is there a table vacant?
有任何桌子空著嗎？

◆ She has had a vacant mind since she broke up with her boyfriend.
她與男朋友分手時，腦海中一片空白。

0741

spare
spɛr
adj. 空閒的；未佔用的；多餘的

◆ I spent almost all my spare time studying photography.
我幾乎花了所有的空閒時間學攝影。

◆ Do you have a spare tire?
你有備用輪胎嗎？

0742

corporation
ˌkɔrpəˈreʃən
n. 股份（有限）公司

◆ The multinational corporation monopolizes the textile market.
這家跨國大公司壟斷了紡織市場。

◆ Our corporation is one of the largest technology companies in Taiwan.
我們公司是台灣的大型科技公司之一。

0743 ★

shareholder
ˈʃɛrˌholdə
n. 股東

◆ Do you know who the main shareholders in the company are?
你知道本公司主要的股東們是誰嗎？

◆ Dividends will be sent to shareholders next week.
下週股息將會送到股東們的手中。

0744 ★

stock
stɑk
n. 股票

◆ You need to analyze the stocks first before investing your money.
在投資前，你要先分析股票。

◆ The fledgling investor put the whole capital into the stock market without a second consideration.
菜鳥投資人不多考慮就把所有的資金投入股市。

0745

fertilizer
ˈfɝtlˌaɪzə
n. 肥料

◆ What is fertilizer and why do plants need it?
什麼是肥料，為什麼植物需要呢？

◆ That farmer uses natural fertilizer on his land.
那個農夫在他的土地上使用天然肥料。

0746

ballet
bæˈle
n. 芭蕾舞

◆ She kept at her ballet lessons even though her toes were in great pain.
即使她的腳趾很痛，她仍然持續上她的芭蕾舞課程。

◆ The President is coming to see the most popular ballet this evening.
總統在下午時前往觀賞最有名的芭蕾舞表演。

0747

spend
spɛnd
v. 花錢；支出

◆ How much do you spend a month?
你一個月花多少錢？

◆ How much were you planning to spend?
你計劃花多少錢？

0748

scorn
skɔrn
v. n. 表示輕蔑；
對……不屑一顧

◆ She looked at the poor student with terrible scorn.
她極輕蔑地注視著這個貧窮的學生。

◆ You've no right to scorn a poor loser.
你沒有權利去輕蔑一個可憐的失敗者。

0749

behave
bɪˈhev
v. 表現出……；
舉止

◆ He behaves counter to his promise.
他的行為和他的承諾相反。

◆ The well-behaved boy refused to join their capers.
這位行為良好的男孩拒絕加入他們的惡作劇。

0750 ★

express
ɪkˈsprɛs
v. 表達……；
用……表示

◆ I don't know how to express my appreciation.
我不知道如何表示我的感謝。

◆ Words can't express how happy I am.
言語無法表達我的快樂。

0751

show
ʃo
n. 表演 **v.** 顯示出

◆ I went to the show with my family.
我和家人一起去看這場表演。

◆ What is being shown at the New York Movie Theater now?
紐約戲院現在正上映什麼片子？

0752

orientation
ˌorɪənˈteʃən
n. 迎新聚會；
定位；方向

◆ The building faces the east-west orientation.
這幢建築物是東西向。

◆ His sexual orientation was a lot more straight than gay.
他的性向不像同志，更像異性戀男性。

0753

metal
ˈmɛtl̩
adj. 金屬的

◆ The gold necklace was adulterated with other metals.
這條金項鍊攙雜其它的金屬。

◆ You'd better take your watch off, or you'll set off the metal detector.
你最好拿掉手錶，否則將會觸動金屬探測器。

0754

trek

trɛk

v. 長途跋涉；移居；拉車

◆ It took us a week to trek to leave the desert.
我們花了一週長途跋涉才離開沙漠。

◆ Einstein trekked from Germany to the United States.
愛因斯坦從德國移居到美國。

0755

porch

pɔrtʃ

n. 門廊；入口處

◆ Put the umbrella on the porch to drain before you enter the house.
在你進房之前，要把雨傘放在走廊上晾乾。

◆ I met that person at the porch of the drugstore.
我在藥房的走廊遇到這個人。

0756

concierge

ˌkɑnsɪˈɛrʒ

n. 門房

◆ My brother is a concierge at a five-star hotel.
我弟弟是一個五星級飯店的門房。

◆ The concierge can arrange to get you tickets to the movie.
這位門房可以幫你拿到這場電影的門票。

0757

outpatient

ˈaʊtˌpeʃənt

n. 門診病人

記得多休息！

◆ Could you show me your outpatient appointment card?
你能秀你的門診預約單給我看嗎？

◆ Where are the outpatient department?
門診部在哪裡？

0758

clog

klɑg

v. 阻塞

◆ The road to the train station is clogged with traffic.
往火車站的道路因為交通而阻塞。

◆ Don't clog your mind with useless facts.
別讓你的思緒塞滿無用的事實。

0759

thwart

θwɔrt

v. 阻撓……；反對……

別跑

◆ The plans for having a picnic on the mountain have been thwarted by the rain.
到山上野餐的計劃因下雨而阻撓。

◆ I don't think that will thwart our determination.
我不認為那會阻撓我們的決心。

0760

additional

əˈdɪʃən̩l

adj. 附加的；添加的；額外的

附加郵費是200元！

◆ We need additional people to help us finish the drawing.
我們需要額外人手幫忙完成草圖。

◆ Could you make one additional recommendation?
您可以再提一個建議嗎？

0761

proviso
prə'vaɪzo
n. 附加條件；
但書

◆ I agreed to buy the car with the proviso that the dealer would provide the loan for it.
我同意買這台車的但書是車商將提供車貸。

◆ I'll come, on the proviso that it will be fine.
我會來，但書是一切沒問題。

0762

appendix
ə'pɛndɪks
n. 附錄

◆ You'd better look it up in the appendix of this dictionary.
你最好去查閱這本字典的附錄。

◆ There is an appendix at the back of the encyclopedia.
在這本百科全書後面還有一份附錄。

0763 ★

adolescent
͵ædl'ɛsn̩t
adj. 青少年期的

◆ Most adolescents like to go out dancing or singing with their friends.
大多數青少年喜歡與朋友們去跳舞和唱歌。

◆ It is generally known that most adolescents are anti-social behaviorists.
一般都認為大多數青少年是反社會行為者。

0764 ★

remarkable
rɪ'mɑrkəbl̩
adj. 非凡的；值得注意的

◆ After studying a lot, Rita has made remarkable progress on her job.
莉塔努力用功，在課業上有了顯著的進步。

◆ The soldier's feats of courage in battle were remarkable.
這名士兵戰場上的英勇功績非凡。

0765

illegal
ɪ'ligl̩
adj. 非法的

◆ It's illegal to enter another's house without permission.
未經同意進入他人的房子是違法的。

◆ It is illegal to sell cigarettes to those who are under 18.
將香煙販售給十八歲以下的人是非法的。

0766 ★

insult
'ɪnsʌlt
v. 侮辱……；
對……無禮
n. 羞辱

◆ He insulted me about my haircut when I saw him last night.
我昨晚看到他時，他侮辱我新剪的頭髮。

◆ His words were tantamount to an insult to me.
他的話無異於對我是一種羞辱。

0767

keep
kip
v. 保留……；保持……

◆ Please keep your room neat.
請保持房間的整潔。

◆ She keeps a journal of daily feelings.
她用日記寫下每天的心情。

0768

retain
rɪˈten
v. 保留……；
持續維持；雇
用……

◆ The sea retains the sun's warmth longer than the land.
海洋比陸地能維持更久的太陽溫暖。

◆ The company retained the best lawyer as their counselor.
這家公司雇用這位最好的律師做他們的顧問。

0769 ★

defend
dɪˈfɛnd
v. 保衛……；防
禦……；替某人
辯護

◆ Everyone should defend his country, whatever the cost may be.
每個人都該不計代價保護他的國家。

◆ The neutral develops enormous military force to defend its land.
此中立國發展強大的軍事力量來捍衛國土。

0770 ★

guard
gɑrd
v. 保衛……；護
送…… **n.** 守衛

◆ He worked as a guard at the state penitentiary.
他在州立監獄當一名警衛。

◆ An officious old guard came over and told me to walk softly in the museum.
一個好管閒事的老警衛走過來告訴我：在博物館走路輕一點。

0771

maintenance
ˈmentənəns
n. 保養；維修；
主張

◆ Old cars need a lot of maintenance.
老車需要一大堆保養。

◆ He's taking classes in computer maintenance.
他正在上電腦維修課。

0772 ★

insurance
ɪnˈʃurəns
n. 保險；保險
金

◆ We're filing a claim with our insurance company.
我們正向我們的保險公司提出賠償要求。

◆ The insurance company compensates workers for injuries suffered at their workplaces.
這家保險公司賠償在他們工作場所遭受傷害的工人們。

0773 ★

pledge
plɛdʒ
v. 保證……；
用……抵押
n. 抵押品

◆ He pledged that he would redress his ways.
他保證會矯正他的方式。

◆ We all had to pledge allegiance to our nation.
我們所有人都保證效忠國家。

0774

warranty
ˈwɔrəntɪ
n. 保證書；保證；
擔保

◆ How long is the warranty on this refrigerator?
這個冰箱的保固期有多久？

◆ The manufacturer gives a one-year warranty against any problem with its products.
這個製造公司給他的產品一年保固期。

0775 ★

bail
bel
n. 保釋金 *v.* 保釋……

◆ She paid 6000 dollars bail for her husband.
她為她的丈夫付了六千美金的保釋金。

◆ The magistrate refused his bail.
這位地方法官拒絕他的保釋。

0776

assurance
əˈʃurəns
n. 信心；自信

◆ He gives me repeated assurance that he won't break a promise.
他再次向我保證不會違背承諾。

◆ The speaker lacked assurance in front of the audience.
這位演講者在群眾面前缺乏自信。

0777

confidence
ˈkɑnfədəns
n. 信心；信賴

◆ You need more confidence while giving a speech.
你演講時需要更多自信。

◆ His frailness came from a dearth of confidence.
他的脆弱源自於缺乏信心。

0778 ★

correspondence
ˌkɔrəˈspɑndəns
n. 信件；通信；一致

◆ I used to keep up a regular correspondence with my pen pal.
我過去和筆友經常魚雁往返。

◆ We have carried on a correspondence for years.
我們已經持續通信好幾年了。

0779

envelope
ˈɛnvəˌlop
n. 信封

◆ Mother wrote the address and name on the envelope.
媽媽在信封寫上姓名與地址。

◆ He folded the letter and put it in an envelope.
他把信摺好，並且放入信封中。

0780

message
ˈmɛsɪdʒ
n. 信息；消息

◆ Do you want to leave a message?
您要留下任何訊息嗎？

◆ He left a message for his family not to go home tonight.
他留了個訊息給家人說他今晚不回家。

0781

signal
ˈsɪgnl̩
n. 信號；暗號

◆ A green light is a signal to go.
綠燈是可以通行的信號。

◆ The policeman objurgated the driver for turning without a signal.
警察責罵這位駕駛轉彎時沒打信號。

0782

rely

rɪˈlaɪ

v. 信賴；依靠

◆ We should not rely on our parents forever.
我們不該永遠依賴我們的父母。

◆ The habitants have to rely on the river for their water.
這些居民的用水必須依賴這條河。

0783

risk

rɪsk

v. 冒著……危險
n. 危險

◆ I don't think he will risk buying some enterprise bonds.
我不相信他會冒著風險買一些企業債券。

◆ John is a venturous man, unafraid of risks.
約翰是個大膽的人，不怕危險。

0784

venture

ˈvɛntʃɚ

n. 冒險；投機
v. 使冒險

◆ They are the adventurers on the venture to the jungle.
他們是叢林探險的冒險者。

◆ They have planned well for the venture into the jungle.
他們好好計劃到叢林探險。

0785

champion

ˈtʃæmpɪən

n. 冠軍；優勝者
v. 支持……

◆ He is the champion of 100-meter sprint.
他是百米賽跑的冠軍。

◆ The bill championed by the famous lawmaker should be in the bag.
這位知名立委所支持的法案應該是沒問題。

0786

peel

pil

v. 削皮；剝去……的皮 **n.** 皮(蔬果)

◆ The chef peeled the potatoes before cooking them.
這位主廚在煮菜前先削馬鈴薯皮。

◆ The monkeys know how to peel the bananas.
這些猴子知道怎麼剝香蕉皮。

0787

former

ˈfɔrmɚ

adj. 前者的

◆ Why don't you think you got the job in the former interview?
你想你為何沒有在上次的面試中得到工作？

◆ Many laws made by the former reign have been annulled since the coup.
前朝許多法律自從政變後便失效了。

0788

forward

ˈfɔrwəd

n. 前鋒 **adv.** 前進的 **v.** 轉交

◆ I played forward in a school team when I was a college student.
念大學的時候，我在校隊打前鋒。

◆ He put forward a plan for improving the economic situation.
他提出一個改進經濟狀況的計劃。

0789

reluctant
rɪˈlʌktənt
adj. 勉強的；不情願的

◆ Karen seemed reluctant to learn how to cook.
凱倫似乎很勉強地學做菜。

◆ I won't be reluctant to work overtime.
我不會勉強加班。

0790

hallmark
ˈhɔl.mɑrk
n. 品質證明；標誌

◆ Oyster omelets and chopped meat and rice have been the hallmarks of this night market.
蚵仔煎與魯肉飯是這個夜市的招牌菜。

◆ Pessimism is the hallmark of his most movies.
悲觀主義是他大部分電影的標誌。

0791

delude
dɪˈlud
v. 哄騙；使人迷惑

◆ The dishonest man deluded the girl that he would marry her.
這位不老實的男人哄騙這個女孩將會娶她。

◆ The man deluded the old woman to lend him money for emergency.
這位男子騙老婦人借他錢應急。

0792

contract
ˈkɑntrækt
n. 契約；合同
v. 訂契約

◆ It is necessary to sign a written contract during the business deal.
在生意往來期間必須簽訂書面合約。

◆ The contract can be cancelled by mutual agreement.
這份合約經過雙方同意可以取消。

0793 ★

menace
ˈmɛnɪs
v. 威脅……；脅迫…… **n.** 威脅

給我滾

◆ These horrible weapons are a menace to world peace.
這些可怕的武器對世界和平是種威脅。

◆ A drunk driver is a menace to all road users.
一位酒醉駕駛對道路上所有使用者都是一種威脅。

0794

勝利是屬於最堅忍的人

---

guest
gɛst
n. 客人

歡迎光臨

◆ How many guests did you invite to this party?
這場舞會中你邀請了幾位客人？

◆ Mr. Smith is one of my important guests.
史密斯先生是我重要的客人之一。

0795

---

objective
əb'dʒɛktɪv
adj. 客觀的；基於事實的

客觀的決議

◆ Making a judgment should be objective, or it causes unfairness.
做判斷應該要客觀，否則將造成不公。

◆ What Mary has advised you was very objective.
瑪麗對你的勸告是如此的客觀。

0796

---

ballyhoo
ˌbælɪ'hu
n. 宣傳；廣告
v. 大肆宣傳

◆ New Year's Eve celebrations are full of ballyhoo.
除夕的慶祝活動充滿了廣告宣傳。

◆ Many candidates ballyhoo their campaigning in the street.
許多候選人在街上大舉進行他們的競選活動。

0797 ★

---

propaganda
ˌprɑpə'gændə
n. 宣傳活動；宣傳品

全館特價

◆ The producer spends a lot of money publishing the propaganda for the products.
製造商花了許多錢替產品印製宣傳品。

◆ The advertiser was fined for the mendacious propaganda.
這位廣告商因不實宣傳而被罰款。

0798

---

measure
'mɛʒɚ
n. 度量；措施
v. 度量……長度

◆ I cannot understand the axiom of probability measure.
我不了解機率計量的基本定理。

◆ Are you for or against the controversial measure?
你支持還是反對這項有爭議的措施？

0799 ★

---

found
faʊnd
v. 建立；創立；創辦

創辦音樂學院

◆ The man contributed half of his savings to found a school.
這男人奉獻他一半的儲蓄來建立這所學校。

◆ The Japanese founded a colony in Taiwan before.
日本人以前在台灣建立了一個殖民地。

0800 ★

constructive
kənˈstrʌktɪv
adj. 建設性的；積極的

積極跑步瘦身成功

◆ The advisor put forward constructive criticism.
這位顧問提出了一個建設性的批評。

◆ No one wants to pay attention to her because her opinions are not constructive.
沒有人注意她，因為她的意見沒有建設性。

0801

architect
ˈɑrkəˌtɛkt
n. 建造者；建築師

◆ I hoped to be a scientist but turned out to be an architect.
我曾希望做個科學家，但後來卻當了個建築師。

◆ Every man is the architect of his own fortune.
每個人是自己命運的建築師。

0802

seldom
ˈsɛldəm
adv. 很少地；難得地

很少穿禮服

◆ My family seldom misses church.
我家人很少不去教堂。

◆ I seldom wear dresses unless it's for a formal occasion.
除非是在正式的場合，不然我很少會穿禮服。

0803

well
wɛl
adv. 很好地；相當地

◆ Our waiter are not doing very well.
我們的服務生表現不是很好。

◆ I have a well-paid job but with long office hours.
我的薪水優渥，但是工作時間很長。

0804

attorney
əˈtɝnɪ
n. 律師；法定代理人

◆ Her dream is to become a famous attorney.
她的夢想是成為一個著名的律師。

◆ My uncle was selected as the district attorney.
我叔叔被選為地方檢察官。

0805 ★

offspring
ˈɔfˌsprɪŋ
n. 後代；子孫

◆ All of his offspring are very outstanding.
他所有的子孫都相當優秀。

◆ The doctor's offspring are diligent and intelligent.
這位醫生的後代是勤奮且有智慧的。

0806

delinquent
dɪˈlɪŋkwənt
adj. 怠惰的；過期未付款的

好冷,沒地方住

◆ He has been delinquent on his mortgage payment for two months.
他的抵押貸款已經兩個月沒繳了。

◆ The poor man is delinquent in paying his rent.
這個窮人沒錢付房租。

0807

courier
ˈkʊrɪə
n. 急件信差；
導遊

◆ I sent a message to my partner via the courier.
我經由信差傳遞訊息給我的夥伴。
◆ The parcel was delivered by a courier this morning.
這份包裹今天早晨由信差送來。

0808

daze
dez
n. 恍惚 *v.* 使恍
惚；使眩暈

◆ The car accident left him in a daze.
這場車禍使他神智恍惚。
◆ The splendor of the palace dazed him.
這個宮殿的壯觀讓他暈眩。

0809

comeback
ˈkʌm.bæk
n. 恢復；復位

永不放棄

◆ I've never lost the faith that he'd have a comeback.
我從未喪失他會東山再起的信心。
◆ The big city made a splendid comeback after a long time.
這個大城市經過長時間後恢復了往日風光。

0810 ★

indicate
ˈɪndə.ket
v. 指示；指出；
暗示

在這邊

◆ The author indicated in his book that he is an atheist.
作者在他書中表示他是個無神論者。
◆ A comparison of the two players indicates that Sunday's golf game will probably be close.
根據這兩位選手的比較，指出了週日的高爾夫比賽可能實力相當。

0811

instruct
ɪnˈstrʌkt
v. 指示……；通
知……；指導

◆ The teacher instructs students about the environmental protection.
這位老師教導學生環保相關議題。
◆ My job is to instruct her in French.
我的工作是指導她法文。

0812 ★

direction
dəˈrɛkʃən
n. 指示說明；
方向

廁所

◆ You are going in the wrong direction.
你走錯方向了。
◆ The factory is under the direction of the government.
這間工廠是由政府領導管理。

0813 ★

assign
əˈsaɪn
v. 指定；分派

你做這。 她做那。

◆ Every student was assigned to a teacher in the cram school.
在補習班中，每位學生都分配一個老師。
◆ The boss assigns tasks to the employees.
老闆分派工作給員工們。

0814

appoint
ə'pɔɪnt
v. 指派任務；任命……

◆ He was appointed as a manager of the Japanese branch company.
他被指定為日本分公司的經理。

◆ He was appointed as the diplomat to Germany.
他被指定為駐德外交官。

0815

guideline
'gaɪd.laɪn
n. 指導方針

◆ The police think the law only as a general guideline.
警察認為法律是一般的指導方針。

◆ Can you give me a guideline as a employee in your company？
能給我做為你公司員工的指導方針嗎？

0816

count
kaʊnt
v. 按順序數；計算；指望……

◆ My little sister can count from one to ten.
我的妹妹會從一數到十。

◆ That was the only way they could count on.
那是他們唯一能指望的方式。

0817

defiant
dɪ'faɪənt
adj. 挑戰的；不屈的；大膽的

◆ The student talked to his teacher with a defiant manner.
這個學生用一種反抗的態度跟他的老師說話。

◆ The man shows a defiant attitude to laws.
這個人對法律採取一種反抗的態度。

0818

unearth
ʌn'ɝθ
v. 挖掘出；發現

◆ They unearthed a skeleton from the field.
他們從田地中挖掘出一具骸骨。

◆ The team will unearth the buried treasure here successfully.
這個團隊將會成功地在此挖掘出埋藏的寶藏。

0819

government
'gʌvɚnmənt
n. 政府

◆ The government declared a ban on using plastic bags.
政府宣布了一個使用塑膠袋的禁令。

◆ The government officer became rich because of the graft and corruption.
這位政府官員因為貪汙與收賄而富有。

0820 ★

policy
'pɑləsɪ
n. 政策；方針

◆ Whatever policy is adopted, the key is for clear leadership to be displayed.
無論採取什麼政策，關鍵是清楚的領導力展現。

◆ The government adopts the policy to make Taiwanese our second official language.
政府採取政策讓台語成為我國第二官方語言。

0821 ★

coup
ku
n. 政變

◆ Many laws made by the former reign have been annulled since the coup happened.
自從政變發生後，前朝許多法律便失效了。

◆ The coup leaders could face life imprisonment.
這些政變領袖可能面臨終身監禁。

0822 ★

regime
rɪˈʒim
n. 政體；制度

沙皇政體

◆ Under the old regime women had no right to vote.
女人在古老的制度下沒有投票權。

◆ Since the king was overthrown by the rebels, its regime became an acephalous anarchy.
自從國王被反抗者推翻後，它的政權便呈現群龍無首的無政府狀態。

0823

story
ˈstorɪ
n. 故事

愛麗絲夢遊仙境

◆ This movie is based on a true story.
這部電影是根據真實故事改編而成。

◆ The story is too tedious for a child.
這個故事對一個小孩來說太無聊了。

0824

breakdown
ˈbrekˌdaʊn
n. 故障；拋錨

◆ My car had a breakdown on my way home.
在我回家的路上車子拋錨了。

◆ My mother suffered a nervous breakdown.
我媽媽有神經衰弱的毛病。

0825

constellation
ˌkɑnstəˈleʃən
n. 星座；群集

◆ The Big and Little Dipper are well known constellations.
大小北斗星是相當知名的星座。

◆ What comes to mind when you think of constellations?
當你想到星座時，腦海中會出現什麼？

0826 ★

shelf
ʃɛlf
n. 架子；擱板；沙洲

◆ I put some old books on the top of the shelf.
我把舊書放在架子的頂端。

◆ We can use an elevator to lift the shelf onto the truck.
我們可以使用起重機將架子舉起到卡車上。

0827

dye
daɪ
v. 染上顏色；染色 *n.* 染料

◆ I'd like to have my hair dyed.
我想要染髮。

◆ This dye is not the color I used before.
這種染料不是我以前用的顏色。

0828

cave
kev
n. 洞穴；山洞

◆ The man has lived alone in the cave for ten years.
這個男人單獨在這洞穴中住了十年。

◆ The narrow cave reverberated with the sound of the water drop.
這個狹窄的洞穴回響著水滴聲。

0829

---

flat
flæt
adj. 洩了氣的；
走了氣的（飲
料）；平坦的

◆ He got a flat tire of the rear wheel of his bicycle.
他腳踏車的後輪胎爆胎了。

◆ It's totally unreasonable that they sell flat drinks only.
他們只賣淡而無味的飲料，真是沒道理。

0830

---

current account
ˈkɜnt əˈkaunt
n. 活期存款帳戶

◆ What's the difference between a current account and a fixed account?
活期存款帳戶與定期存款帳戶有何不同？

◆ You may open a current account at a bank.
你可以在銀行開一個活期存款帳戶。

0831

---

alive
əˈlaɪv
adj. 活著的

◆ The missing girl was found alive but unconscious.
這個失蹤的女孩被發現還活著，不過失去了意識。

◆ It is a miracle that the man is alive.
這個男人會活著是個奇蹟。

0832

---

gory
ˈgɔrɪ
adj. 流血的；血
腥的

◆ Jack came home with a gory arm.
傑克回家時手臂流血了。

◆ The violent movie is just a little too gory.
這部暴力電影有點太過血腥。

0833

---

flu
flu
n. 流行性感冒

◆ The flu virus infected almost the whole company.
感冒病毒幾乎讓全公司受到感染。

◆ Is the bird flu epidemic coming soon?
禽流感近期會大流行嗎？

0834

---

meteor
ˈmitɪɚ
n. 流星

◆ We saw three meteors streak across the sky last night.
我們昨晚看到三顆流星劃破天際。

◆ The beautiful meteor arched across the sky.
這美麗的流星以弧形狀越過天空。

0835

abortion
əˈbɔrʃən
n. 流產；墮胎

◆ The abortion issue is one of the great moral dilemmas.
墮胎議題是重大道德兩難問題之一。

◆ The committee discussed the morality of abortion.
委員會討論了墮胎的道德性。

0836

bomb
bɑm
n. 炸彈

◆ A car bomb exploded after the car started.
一枚汽車炸彈在車子發動後爆炸。

◆ The enemy tries to threaten us with nuclear bombs.
敵軍想要以核子彈威脅我們。

0837

explosive
ɪkˈsplosɪv
n. 炸藥 *adj.* 爆炸性的；暴躁的

◆ The building was blown to pieces by explosives.
這棟建築物被炸藥炸得粉碎。

◆ The lonely old man has an explosive temper.
這個孤獨的老人性格暴躁。

0838 ★

sacrifice
ˈsækrəˌfaɪs
v. 為……犧牲；祭品 *n.* 犧牲行為

◆ Frogs used to be the sacrifice for the dissection of the experiment.
青蛙以前是解剖實驗的犧牲品。

◆ It's not worth sacrificing your health for career development.
為了事業發展而犧牲健康並不值得。

0839

vindicate
ˈvɪndəˌket
v. 為……辯護；澄清……嫌疑

◆ No matter what happens, I will try my best to vindicate my honor.
無論發生什麼事，我都要為我的名譽辯護。

◆ How can you vindicate your behavior to the jury?
你怎麼對陪審團辯護你的行為呢？

0840

glassware
ˈglæsˌwɛr
n. 玻璃器皿

◆ The famous shop sells beautiful glassware.
這家有名的商店販賣美麗的玻璃器皿。

◆ The clerk folded the glassware in newspapers.
這位店員用報紙把玻璃器皿包起來。

0841

scar
skɑr
n. 疤痕

◆ He had a scar on his leg from an accident.
他的腳因為意外留下一道疤痕。

◆ The scar on my forehead is very noticeable.
我額頭上的疤是非常明顯的。

0842

vaccine
ˈvæksɪn

n. 疫苗 **adj.** 疫苗的

◆ We try to use the antibody as a vaccine against the special flu viruses.
我們嘗試使用抗體來做為對抗這種特殊流感病毒的疫苗。

◆ How long will this vaccine give you immunity?
這疫苗給你多久的免疫力？

0843

reciprocal
rɪˈsɪprəkl̩

adj. 相互的；互惠的；回報的

◆ Reciprocal understanding is essential to friendship.
相互的了解對於友誼是必須的。

◆ Such agreement between two companies provides reciprocal rights and obligations.
這兩個公司之間的這種協定提供了互惠的權利和義務。

0844

similar
ˈsɪmələ

adj. 相似的

◆ There is a subtle difference between these two photos although they are similar.
這兩張照片看來很像，但還是有細微的不同。

◆ My point of view is similar to yours.
我的觀點和你的類似。

0845

shield
ʃild

n. 盾；屏障；護罩

◆ The knight protected himself from the rival's attack by a shield.
這位騎士靠盾牌來保護自己防止對手的攻擊。

◆ Do you want your wind shield cleaned ?
你要清洗擋風玻璃嗎？

0846

research
rɪˈsɝtʃ

n. 研究；調查

◆ The research on children's brain development has an astonishing result.
這項針對孩子腦部發展所作的研究有驚人的結果。

◆ Tina does her research with tenacity.
汀娜持之以恆地做研究。

0847 ★

seminar
ˈsɛmənɑr

n. 研討會；討論會

◆ Our tutor asked us to hold a seminar twice a week.
我們的助教要求我們每週開兩次研討會。

◆ We will attend a seminar about feminist activism in Taiwan next month.
下個月我們將要參加一個台灣女權行動主義的研討會。

0848 ★

scientific
ˌsaɪənˈtɪfɪk

adj. 科學（上）的

◆ There were many scientific discoveries last year.
去年有許多科學上的新發現。

◆ A professional historian must have an scientific mind.
一位專業的歷史學家必須有科學的頭腦。

0849 ★

wear
wɛr
v. 穿；戴

◆ Why didn't you wear your watch?
你為什麼沒有戴手錶？

◆ You two are wearing the same pants. What a coincidence!
你們兩人穿同樣的褲子。真巧！

0850

prominent
ˈprɑmənənt
adj. 突出的；顯著的

◆ Generally speaking, her research in medicine is more prominent than that in biology.
大體說來，她在醫學的研究比生物學方面更為卓越。

◆ A prominent point in the discussion is finding a solution for the current program.
這次研討的顯著重點是要對現今的計劃找到解決方案。

0851

breakthrough
ˈbrek.θru
n. 突破；完成

◆ Have you had a breakthrough in your work?
你在工作上有所突破嗎？

◆ The discovery is a major technological breakthrough.
這個發現是個重要的技術突破。

0852 ★

abrupt
əˈbrʌpt
adj. 突然的；唐突的

陡峭危險

◆ The road is full of abrupt turns.
這條路上有很多急轉彎。

◆ The accident is too abrupt for me to accept.
這起意外太突然，令我難以接受。

0853

sudden
ˈsʌdn̩
adj. 突然的；意外的

◆ His sudden visit surprised me.
他突然的來訪嚇了我一大跳。

◆ She looks so dismal because of the sudden incident.
由於突發的意外，她看起來非常憂鬱。

0854

raid
red
n. 突襲；突然搜查

◆ The police made a raid on the pub last night.
警察昨晚突襲這家酒吧。

◆ The enemy launched a submarine to raid our warships.
敵軍派遣一艘潛水艇來突襲我們的戰艦。

0855

souvenir
ˌsuvəˈnɪr
n. 紀念品

◆ I have some souvenirs that I bought at the duty-free shop.
我有一些在免稅商店買的紀念品。

◆ Where can I buy some souvenirs?
我在哪裡可以買到紀念品？

0856 ★

monument
ˈmɑnjəmənt

n. 紀念館；紀
念碑

◆ The government built a monument for soldiers who were
killed in battles.
政府建造一個在戰役中死去士兵的紀念碑。

◆ I miss all the delicious food and places of historic
monuments there.
我懷念那裡所有好吃的食物以及歷史古蹟。

0857

restrict
riˈstrɪkt

v. 約束……；
以……限制

◆ The author restricted her article to the current political
issues.
這位作者將她的文章限定在目前的政治議題上。

◆ The police checked the restricted area thoroughly.
警察徹底檢查了這個管制區。

0858

gourmet
ˈɡʊrme

n. 美食鑑賞家

◆ The publication had asked the famous gourmet to write
for them.
這家出版社要求這位知名的美食家為他們寫文章。

◆ The famous restaurant offers a gourmet menu .
這間著名的餐廳提供美食家菜單。

0859

intrigue
inˈtrig

v. 耍陰謀；激起
興趣 *n.* 陰謀

◆ An intrigue to assassinate the president was uncovered
by government agents.
攻擊總統的陰謀被政府探員發現。

◆ The title of this book intrigues me.
這本書的書名激起我的興趣。

0860

stomach
ˈstʌmək

n. 胃

◆ One boxer gave his opponent a punch in the stomach.
一位拳擊手對他對手的胃部用力猛擊。

◆ A couple of hours after eating, he got a terrible stomach
ache.
在飯後二個小時，他覺得肚子很痛。

0861

登高必自卑，行遠必自邇

background
ˈbæk.graʊnd
n. 背景；經歷

◆ How do you get along with people whose backgrounds are different from you?
你怎麼和那些背景與你不同的人相處呢？

◆ Could you tell me something about your background?
可以談一談你的經歷嗎？

0862 ★

fatal
ˈfetl
adj. 致命的；命運的

◆ He struck the man with a fatal blow to his chin.
他在這個男人的臉頰上打了致命的一拳。

◆ My grandmother died peacefully without suffering any fatal pain.
我祖母安詳的過世，沒有遭受任何致命的痛苦。

0863 ★

lethal
ˈliθəl
adj. 致命的；毀滅性的

◆ It is unwise to carry lethal weapons
攜帶致命武器很不明智。

◆ Nuclear weapons are lethal to the whole population.
核子武器對全人類是致命的。

0864

demanding
dɪˈmændɪŋ
adj. 苛求的

◆ A demanding boss always expects his employees to do everything cautiously and quickly.
一個苛求的老闆總期待他的員工們每件事都做得小心又快速。

◆ It is a demanding role and she needs to work so hard.
這是一個要求很高的角色，她必須如此努力地工作。

0865

fastidious
fæˈstɪdɪəs
adj. 苛求的；愛挑剔的

◆ The sales manager used to be a bit more fastidious.
這位業務經理過去常常有點吹毛求疵。

◆ The parents were very fastidious about their children's behavior.
這對父母對孩童的行為非常苛求。

0866

bitter
ˈbɪtə
adj. 苦的；難堪的

◆ Caffeine is a bitter substance found in coffee or tea.
咖啡因是一種在咖啡或茶中帶苦味的物質。

◆ The medicine tastes bitter.
藥嚐起來很苦。

0867

demand
dɪˈmænd
v. 要求……；請求 n. 查問

◆ The employer has a high demand for the employees.
這位雇主對員工們的要求很高。

◆ The magazine is very much in demand.
這本雜誌需求很大。

0868

cab
kæb
n. 計程車

◆ He asked the doorman to call a cab for his wife.
他要求門房為他太太叫輛計程車。

◆ A cab will be here in ten minutes.
十分鐘後計程車就來了。

0869

scheme
skim
n. 計劃；方案；陰謀

◆ In order to get the treasure, he carried out the scheme to kill his companions.
為了得到寶藏，他耍陰謀殺了同伴。

◆ We have a scheme for reaching high efficiency in a short time.
我們計劃在短時間內達到高績效。

0870 ★

calculate
ˈkælkjəˌlet
v. 計算；估計

◆ Can you calculate the area of this circle?
你能計算出這個圓形的面積嗎？

◆ The remark is calculated to hurt her feelings.
這則評論蓄意要傷害她的感情。

0871 ★

tally
ˈtælɪ
v. 計算……；使符合 n. 得分

◆ The company tallied the expenses of last year.
這家公司計算上一年的花費。

◆ His figures don't tally with yours.
他的數字和你的不符合。

0872

accountable
əˈkauntəbl
adj. 負有責任的；可說明的

◆ Every adult is accountable for his own behavior.
每個成年人要對自己的行為負責。

◆ He is not accountable to you for his actions.
他的行動沒有必要對你說明。

0873

burden
ˈbɝdn̩
n. 負荷 v. 使重載

◆ Too heavy of a burden makes one unhappy.
過重的負擔會令人不快樂。

◆ The variety of examinations has become a heavy burden to students.
各式各樣的考試變成學生一種沉重的負擔。

0874 ★

orbit
/ˈɔrbɪt/
n. 軌道

◆ Most planetary orbits are not circles but ellipses.
大部分行星的軌道都不是圓形而是橢圓。

◆ The spacecraft is now in orbit around earth.
這台太空船現在正在圍繞地球的軌道。

0875

military
/ˈmɪlətɛrɪ/
adj. 軍人的；軍事的

◆ He is too obese to be in the military.
他太胖了以致於無法服兵役。

◆ He has finished one year's military service.
他已經服完一年的兵役。

0876 ★

imminent
/ˈɪmənənt/
adj. 迫切的；迫近的

快要開學了

◆ She is getting nervous because the date is imminent.
她顯得很緊張，因為這個日期逼近了。

◆ The patient who has cancer fears imminent death.
這位癌症病人害怕即將來臨的死亡。

0877

impending
/ɪmˈpɛndɪŋ/
adj. 迫近的

海嘯來了!

◆ The sailors are ready for the impending typhoon.
這些水手為即將來臨的颱風作準備。

◆ People playing at the beach were warned of the impending storm.
在海灘遊玩的民眾被警告暴風雨要來了。

0878

restate
/riˈstet/
v. 重申；重述

我再說一次...

◆ Before the formal contract is drawn up you should restate the main points of the agreement.
在正式合約簽定前，你應該重述一下這份協議的重點。

◆ How can I restate this thesis statement in my conclusion?
我如何能在我的結論中重申這項論點？

0879

significant
/sɪgˈnɪfəkənt/
adj. 重要的；重大的；顯著的

美國、古巴復交

◆ The act of the two leaders shaking hands is a significant step toward peace.
兩位領導者的握手動作對和平是個重要里程。

◆ Temporal power and wealth are significant to him.
世俗的權力和財富對他而言是重要的。

0880 ★

pivotal
/ˈpɪvətl/
adj. 重要的；關鍵的；樞軸的

◆ These negotiations are pivotal to the future of our firm.
這些談判對我們公司的未來非常重要。

◆ Logistics management has a pivotal role for our company.
物流管理對我們公司有舉足輕重的角色。

0881

relocate

.ri'loket

v. 重新安置；搬遷

◆ I have decided to relocate to New York City.
我決定重新遷移到紐約市。

◆ My boss decide to relocate our company in Taipei.
我老闆決定將公司遷往台北。

0882

retrieve

ri'triv

v. 重新得到；取回……

◆ I ran back to the restaurant and retrieved my bag.
我跑回餐廳來取回我的手提袋。

◆ The wreckage of the crashed plane and remains of passengers were retrieved from the ocean.
從海裡尋回空難飛機的殘骸及旅客的遺體。

0883 ★

renew

ri'nju

v. 重新開始；使更新

電腦更新中...

◆ The contract will be renewed annually.
這個合約將會每年更新一次。

◆ If you want to keep this book longer, you can renew it by calling us.
假如您想借這本書借久一點，您可以來電續借。

0884 ★

rally

'ræli

v. 重新集合；恢復健康；大會；振作

◆ Over 10,000 soldiers were rallied at the airport to honor the President's visit.
超過一萬名士兵被集合在機場，對這位總統的蒞臨表示敬意。

◆ They made great efforts to rally their supporters.
他們盡最大努力來集合他們的支持者。

0885

stranger

'strendʒə

n. 陌生人

別和陌生人說話

◆ Who is the stranger talking to your sister?
和你姊姊說話的陌生人是誰？

◆ It was unwise of you to lend money to a stranger.
借錢給陌生人是不明智的。

0886

lower

'loə

v. 降低；減低；放下

定價:1000元
500元

◆ Would you lower down your voice during the game?
看球賽時可以降低你的音量嗎？

◆ The lower price lures many consumers.
這份較低的價格吸引了許多消費者。

0887

depreciation

dɪ,priʃɪ'eʃən

n. 降價；貶值（貨幣）；瞧不起

外幣 銀行 買入 買出
美元　XX銀行 32　31.9

美元又貶值了!

◆ How much is the depreciation charge?
折舊費用是多少？

◆ A depreciation of a currency's value usually makes imports more expensive.
貨幣貶值通常讓進口更昂貴。

0888

area
ˋɛrɪə
n. 面積；地區

◆ Can polar bears live in tropical areas?
北極熊在熱帶地區能生存嗎？

◆ Many government officials live in this area.
許多政府官員住在這個地區。

0889

concert
ˋkɑnsɚt
n. 音樂會、演奏會

◆ The musician will give a concert next week.
那位音樂家在下星期將舉行一場音樂會。

◆ How about going to the charity concert with us tonight?
今晚跟我們一塊去慈善音樂會如何？

0890

sound system
saund ˋsɪstəm
n. 音響系統

◆ How do you know if your sound system is working well?
你怎麼知道你的音響系統運作良好？

◆ A good sound system does not need to cost a lot of money.
一套好的音響系統並不必花許多錢。

0891

wind
wɪnd
n. 風

◆ The wind is blowing from the west.
現在吹西風。

◆ Do you want your wind shield cleaned?
你要清洗擋風玻璃嗎？

0892

style
staɪl
n. 風格；款式

◆ Could you cut my hair in her style?
您能幫我剪和她同樣的髮型嗎？

◆ You'll find several different American styles of architecture on this street.
在這條街上你會發現幾種不同美式風格的建築物。

0893 ★

scenery
ˋsinərɪ
n. 風景

Notre-Dame
du Paris

◆ The mountain scenery is so beautiful.
山中的景色真是美麗。

◆ I'll photograph all the beautiful things in the world, especially natural scenery.
我將拍下世上所有美好的事物，尤其是天然的美景。

0894

aviator
ˋevɪˌetɚ
n. 飛行員

◆ To be an successful aviator is not easy.
成為一個成功的飛行員不容易。

◆ Do you know who the first aviator in the world is?
你知道誰是世界上第一位飛行員嗎？

0895

runway

ˈrʌn.we

n. 飛機跑道

◆ The runway has been extended to take large planes.
這條跑道擴大到能夠承載大飛機。

◆ After a crash landing, the plane slid off the runway and crashed into some trees nearby.
經過緊急著陸後，飛機滑出跑道並撞倒了附近的一些樹木。

0896

fragrance

ˈfreɡrəns

n. 香味

好香哦!

◆ This kind of perfume emits an enticing fragrance.
這種香水發出誘人的味道。

◆ I can smell the fragrance of lilies after showers.
陣雨過後我能聞到百合花的香味。

0897

amend

əˈmɛnd

v. 修正…… *n.* 賠罪；補償

◆ It is time that you had better amend your style of living and studying.
現在是你改變生活和讀書方式的最佳時機。

◆ My boyfriend made amends for his absence by giving me some flowers.
我男朋友為了他的缺席而送花來賠罪。

0898 ★

revise

rɪˈvaɪz

v. 修改；修訂

◆ She received a higher grade after revising her essay.
她修改了她的論文後得到更好的成績。

◆ The student made many corrections from the revised composition.
學生在修改過的作文中做了很多更正。

0899 ★

slender

ˈslɛndə

adj. 修長的

九頭身

◆ As she has a beautiful slender figure, this dress will fit her.
因為她身材優美苗條，所以這件衣服適合她穿。

◆ Each model on the platform has a slender figure.
每個在伸展台上的模特兒都有修長的身材。

0900

fix

fɪks

n. 修理；固定

◆ My father will fix the broken window.
我爸爸將修理破掉的窗戶。

◆ My washing machine needs to be fixed, what number should I call?
我的洗衣機需要修理，我應該打電話找誰呢？

0901

mend

mɛnd

v. 修理；縫補

◆ I need a seamstress to mend my torn pants.
我需要一位女裁縫師來修補我破掉的褲子。

◆ We need an electrician to mend the washing machine .
我們需要一個電工來修理洗衣機。

0902

restore
rɪˈstor
v. 修復……；復原……；使復職

◆ The government promises to restore the stock market in this season.
政府承諾本季重振股票市場。

◆ If breathing is not restored, the patient may start to twitch.
假如呼吸沒有恢復，這位病人就會開始痙攣。

0903

culture
ˈkʌltʃə
n. 修養；文化

◆ I would try hard to adapt myself to this new culture.
我會努力嘗試使自己去適應新文化。

◆ We should do our best to protect our own culture.
我們應盡力保護我們自己的文化。

0904 ★

warehouse
ˈwɛr.haʊs
n. 倉庫；貨倉

◆ We don't have space in the warehouse for it.
我們倉庫沒有空位了。

◆ The outdated magazines are stacked in a warehouse.
這些過期的雜誌堆積在倉庫裡。

0905

personal
ˈpɜsn̩l
adj. 個人的；私人的

◆ There is no personal animosity between the neighboring countries.
這些鄰國間沒有私人恩怨。

◆ Life is too short to turn every personal affront into a battle.
人生苦短，不要太計較個人的毀譽。

0906

worth
wɜθ
adj. 值…… **n.** 價值

$250,000

◆ Is there anything worth watching on channel 5 at 8:00 this evening?
今晚八點五號頻道有什麼值得觀賞的節目？

◆ The expert's appraisal is that the diamond is worth two million dollars.
這位專家評估這顆鑽戒價值兩百萬美元。

0907

memorable
ˈmɛmərəbl̩
adj. 值得紀念的

◆ It was a memorable trip for me.
對我來說這是趟難忘的旅程。

◆ This is the most memorable day of my life.
這是我一生中最難忘的一天。

0908

part-time
ˈpɑrtˌtaɪm
adj. 兼任的

我是打工族!

◆ I'd like to have a part-time job.
我想要一份兼職的工作。

◆ That's why I am looking for a part-time job now.
這就是我現在在找打工機會的原因。

0909

strip

strɪp

v. 剝光……；強奪…… **n.** 脫衣舞

- ◆ The robber asked the girl to strip off her clothes.
  這位強盜要求這個女孩脫掉衣服。
- ◆ The pirates stripped every valuable from the ship.
  這些海盜們搶奪了這艘船上的貴重物品。

0910

raw material

ˏrɔ məˈtɪrɪəl

n. 原料

- ◆ We are faced with a shortage in raw materials.
  我們面臨原料不足的問題。
- ◆ All the raw materials are imported in my factory.
  在我們的工廠中所有原料都是進口的。

0911

pardon

ˈpɑrdn̩

n. 原諒 **v.** 寬恕

- ◆ The prisoner's plea for a pardon was repudiated.
  這囚犯赦免的請求被否決了。
- ◆ May I ask your pardon if I have offended you?
  如果我有冒犯你，能夠得到你的寬恕嗎？

0912

excuse

ɪkˈskjuz

v. 原諒……；寬恕…… **n.** 藉口

I'm sorry!

- ◆ He is absent without any excuses.
  他缺席連藉口都沒有。
- ◆ I have no excuse for not finishing my homework.
  對於功課沒做完，我沒任何藉口。

0913 ★

personnel

ˏpɜsn̩ˈɛl

n. 員工；人事部門

- ◆ This section of the factory is for authorized personnel only.
  工廠的這區域只容許授權的人員進入。
- ◆ She's on attachment to the personnel department of our company.
  她是暫時隸屬於我們公司的人事部門。

0914 ★

suit

sut

n. 套裝；西裝

- ◆ John had a black suit on today.
  約翰今天穿了一套黑色西裝。
- ◆ He wore an unsightly suit to the party.
  他穿了件不體面的西裝去舞會。

0915

tolerant

ˈtɑlərənt

adj. 容忍的；寬恕的

沒關係！

- ◆ The mayor is not very tolerant of any criticism.
  這位市長不太能容忍任何的批評。
- ◆ My manager was tolerant of different views.
  我們經理能容忍不同意見。

0916 ★

volume
ˋvɑljəm
n. 容量；體積；音量

15c.c

♦ These beautiful illustrations enhanced the book's sales volume.
這些漂亮的插圖提高了這本書的銷售量。

♦ This chart shows the growth of the sales volume during the past six months.
這份圖表顯示了過去半年間的銷售額成長。

0917

feature
ˋfitʃə
n. 容貌；特徵

特徵是皮膚較黑

♦ I need to see more features before I make an ofter.
當我出價購買時，我必須要看到更多特色。

♦ The professor will give a lecture on geographical features in a tropical area.
這位教授將要做一場熱帶地區地理特徵的演講。

0918 ★

reveal
rɪˋvil
v. 展現；使顯示；透露出

♦ Everyone felt sorry when Tom revealed his miserable childhood.
湯姆透露了他的悲慘童年，每個人都感到難過。

♦ The investigation revealed political chicanery and bribery at the highest levels.
這份調查揭露了最高階層的政治詭計和賄賂。

0919

display
dɪˋsple
v. 展覽……；陳列

服裝店

♦ The artist displays his work in front of the public.
這位藝術家在大眾前展示作品。

♦ The toys were displayed in the window.
這些玩具在櫥窗中展示。

0920 ★

island
ˋaɪlənd
n. 島；島嶼 (同 isle)

♦ Indonesia includes more than ten thousand islands.
印尼包含了超過一萬座的島嶼。

♦ Taiwan is an island, which is surrounded by the ocean.
台灣是一個被海洋環繞的島嶼。

0921

seat
sit
n. 座位

♦ There is someone sitting in my seat.
有人坐在我的座位上。

♦ You have bought two seat tickets, haven't you?
你有買兩張對號票嗎？

0922

yard
jɑrd
n. 庭院；碼

♦ The kids are playing games in the back yard.
孩子們在後院中玩遊戲。

♦ The chicks are raised in the yard.
這些小雞飼養在後院中。

0923

daunt
dɔnt
v. 恐嚇……；使氣餒

◆ The prosecutor won't be daunted by authority and power.
這位檢察官不為權勢所恫嚇。

◆ What he said would not daunt me.
他所說的話無法嚇到我。

0924

regret
rɪˈgrɛt
v. 悔恨；遺憾

◆ Amy deeply regretted shouting at her friends.
艾咪後悔對朋友們叫囂。

◆ He regrets for the follies of his youth.
他後悔年輕時的荒唐。

0925

donate
ˈdonet
v. 捐贈給

◆ Mary donated all her money to the charity.
瑪麗把所有的錢捐給慈善機構。

◆ It's very noble of you to donate a great sum of money to help the elderly.
捐獻那麼大一筆錢給老人是很崇高的。

0926 ★

capture
ˈkæptʃɚ
v. 捕獲……；拍攝……；使留存

◆ The murderer killed the man and was captured very soon after.
兇手殺了這個男人，而且隨即被捕。

◆ You want to set up a keystroke that captures a menu.
你能設定一組按鍵來保存一個功能選單。

0927 ★

effect
ɪˈfɛkt
n. 效用；影響；結果

◆ Smoking causes adverse effects on your health.
吸菸會造成不利健康的影響。

◆ The effects of the flood would exacerbate the agricultural problems.
洪水的影響將會加重農業的問題。

0928

要為成功找方法，不為失敗找理由

---

onlooker
ˈɑnˌlʊkə
n. 旁觀者

◆ The onlooker guaranteed the fact to be true.
這個旁觀者保證這個事實是真的。

◆ The onlooker certified that he did not kill the taxi driver.
這位旁觀者證實他沒有殺這個計程車司機。

0929

---

trip
trip
n. 旅行

◆ How about making a trip over this weekend？
這個週末去旅行怎麼樣？

◆ I am going to take a trip to Japan next week.
我下星期要去日本旅行。

0930

---

tour
tur
n. 旅遊；旅程

◆ Do you have one day tour package that goes to the Statue of Liberty?
你們有自由女神像的一日套裝旅遊行程嗎？

◆ What time does the tour start？
這個旅行團幾點出發呢？

0931

---

timetable
ˈtaɪmˌtebḷ
n. 時刻表

◆ You can find the correct time for your train in this latest timetable.
你可以在這份最新的時刻表中，找到火車的正確時刻。

◆ Look up the time of the next bus in the timetable.
查一下公車時刻表下一班車的時間。

0932 ★

---

fashion
ˈfæʃən
n. 時尚；流行款式

◆ The Milan fashion show is very famous.
米蘭的時裝展非常有名。

◆ Fashion trends are changing all the time.
流行趨勢總是一直在改變。

0933

---

jet lag
dʒɛt læg
n. 時差

◆ I get jet lag for three days after traveling overseas.
我出國旅遊三天後還會有時差。

◆ Do you have much trouble with jet lag?
時差對你很困擾嗎？

0934

fashionable

'fæʃənəbl

adj. 時髦的；流行的

◆ Curly hairstyles are not very fashionable at the moment.
捲髮造型現在並不是很流行。

◆ Where can I buy the fashionable T-shirt like yours?
我在哪裡可以買到跟你一樣時髦的 T 恤？

0935

picturesque

.pɪktʃə'rɛsk

adj. 栩栩如生的；美麗的

◆ When I saw the picturesque village, I was touched beyond words.
當我看到這個如圖畫般的村莊，我感動莫名。

◆ I lived in a picturesque fishing village before.
我之前住在一個風景如畫的漁村中。

0936

frame

frem

n. 框架；骨架；思想狀態

◆ The frame of the chair is made of wood.
這張椅子的骨架是木頭做的。

◆ The plastic frame tends to twist under pressure.
這個塑膠框架在壓力下會變形。

0937

comb

kom

n. 梳子 **v.** 梳頭髮

◆ Where is my pink comb?
我的那隻粉紅色梳子在那裡？

◆ This is the way we comb our hair.
我們用這樣的方式梳頭髮。

0938

odor

'odɚ

n. 氣味；味道；名聲

◆ A warm musky odor transpired when she passed by me.
她經過我身邊時散發出一股溫和的麝香味。

◆ The flowers gave off a special odor.
這些花朵發出特殊的香味。

0939

scent

sɛnt

n. 氣味；香味；線索

◆ The scent of lilies is in the air.
空氣中有百合花的香味。

◆ I like the scent of the tulip flower .
我喜歡鬱金香花的香味。

0940

balloon

bə'lun

n. 氣球

◆ The balloon burst and scared my cat.
氣球爆炸嚇壞了我的貓咪。

◆ The kid popped all the birthday balloons after the birthday party.
生日舞會後這孩子「砰」地弄破所有的生日氣球。

0941

asthma
ˈæzmə
n. 氣喘

◆ The little boy cannot do the keen exercises because he has a congenital asthma.
小男孩無法做激烈運動，因為他天生氣喘。

◆ My grandfather has got another attack of asthma.
我祖父氣喘發作了。

0942

meteorology
ˌmitɪəˈrɑlədʒɪ
n. 氣象學

◆ This is a textbook about meteorology.
這是一本有關氣象學的教科書。

◆ Meteorology is mainly the study of weather and weather forecasting.
氣象學主要是氣候與氣候預測的研究。

0943

waste
west
v. 浪費；使消耗

◆ Don't waste time in arguing over petty things.
不要浪費時間為雞毛蒜皮的小事爭吵。

◆ Leaving the air conditioning operation all the time wastes electricity.
整天開著冷氣機是很浪費電的。

0944 ★

tub
tʌb
n. 浴缸

◆ Is there a tub in your bathroom?
你的浴室裡有浴缸嗎？

◆ The baby liked to dabble in the tub.
這小嬰兒喜歡在澡盆裡玩水。

0945

altitude
ˈæltəˌtjud
n. 海拔；高度

2000公尺

◆ What is the altitude of this temple in the mountain？
在山上的這座寺廟海拔是多少？

◆ We are flying at an altitude of 30000 feet.
我們在三萬英呎上飛行。

0946 ★

seaweed
ˈsiˌwid
n. 海草

◆ This kind of medicine is extracted from seaweed.
這種藥是從海藻提煉。

◆ The fish lives in seaweed beds in warm water.
這種魚生活在溫暖的海草中。

0947

seal
sil
n. 海豹；印章

◆ The first time I saw a seal was in a zoo.
我第一次看到海豹是在動物園。

◆ The supervisor affixed his seal to the document.
這主管將他的印章附在文件上。

0948

soak
sok
v. 浸泡；吸收

◆ He soaked the sponge in water to make it soft.
他將海綿放在水中浸溼，讓它變柔軟。
◆ The spray from the waves soaked my clothes.
這些波浪的浪花使我的衣服溼透了。

0949

disinfect
ˌdɪsɪnˈfɛkt
v. 消毒……；
使淨化

◆ The nurse disinfected the wound before dressing it.
這位護士在包紮傷口前先消毒。
◆ Could you disinfect the microphone for our guests?
你能幫我們的客人消毒麥克風嗎？

0950

information
ˌɪnfəˈmeʃən
n. 消息；知識

◆ Tell me some more information about this news.
多告訴我一點關於這則新聞的資料。
◆ Where can I query the information about the flights?
我在哪裡可以問到關於航班的資料？

0951 ★

expenditure
ɪkˈspɛndɪtʃə
n. 消費；消費
量；消耗時間

BUY NOW!

◆ Executing a policy needs a lot of expenditure and time.
執行政策需要相當多的經費與時間。
◆ Armament expenditure is a burden in Taiwan every year.
軍備花費是台灣每年的重擔。

0952 ★

consumer
kənˈsumə
n. 消費者；用
戶

◆ What are the consumer rights?
什麼是消費者權利？
◆ The consumer price index compares current costs of goods and services with past costs.
消費者物價指數把目前的貨品與服務成本與過去的成本作比較。

0953 ★

negative
ˈnɛgətɪv
adj. 消極的；
否定的

◆ I have a negative opinion about your proposal.
我對你的提案持否定的意見。
◆ She gave me a negative answer.
她給了我一個否定答案。

0954 ★

perish
ˈpɛrɪʃ
v. 消滅；毀滅；
死亡

◆ Hundreds of passengers perished when the ship went down.
當這艘船沉沒，數以百計的乘客死亡。
◆ Do these beautiful flowers perish in winter？
這些美麗的花朵在冬天會枯萎嗎？

0955

eliminate

ɪˈlɪmə.net

v. 消滅……；消除……；排除……

◆ All defective genes will be eliminated in the experiment.
所有有缺陷的基因在此次實驗中將被消除。

◆ The government decides to eliminate the crimes.
政府決定消滅犯罪。

0956 ★

roast

rost

v. 烘烤…… **adj.** 烘烤的

◆ I had roast chicken for lunch today.
我今天中午吃烤雞。

◆ My mother roasted a turkey for Thanksgiving.
感恩節時我媽媽烘烤了一隻火雞。

0957

particular

pəˈtɪkjələ

adj. 特別的

◆ I have a particular fondness for Japanese literature.
我對日本文學有特別的喜愛。

◆ Do you have any particular subject you like to paint?
你有特別喜歡作畫的題材嗎？

0958

special

ˈspɛʃəl

adj. 特別的；特殊的

Special Price

$1999

◆ He will give us a special price for the sofa.
他會給我們這組沙發特別的價格。

◆ Do you have any special requests for your room?
對您的房間有什麼特別要求呢？

0959

specific

spɪˈsɪfɪk

adj. 特定的；具體的

ROOMS

有什麼特別要求呢？

◆ The cirrus of insects has a specific purpose.
昆蟲的觸毛有特別的功用。

◆ Capital punishment is the practice of executing someone as punishment for a specific crime.
死刑是一種因特殊犯罪而將某些人處死的執行。

0960

excellent

ˈɛksələnt

adj. 特優的；傑出的

◆ One of the excellent points about this computer is that it rarely needs servicing.
這種電腦的優點之一是很少需要維修。

◆ It's excellent material and we have quoted you the lowest price.
這是極佳的質料而且我們已經開最低的價錢給你了。

0961 ★

flight

flaɪt

n. 班機；飛行

◆ This flight has been delayed for one hour.
這班飛機已延後一小時。

◆ I am catching a connecting flight to New York.
我要轉機到紐約。

0962

weary
'wɪrɪ
adj. 疲乏的；
疲倦的

◆ He was so weary that he slouched back in his seat.
他疲累到垂頭喪氣地躺在椅子上。

◆ Most people are growing weary of the gulf war.
大多數人民越來越厭倦波斯灣戰爭了。

0963

fatigue
fə'tig
n. 疲倦；疲勞

◆ Working overtime caused me great fatigue.
加班工作讓我很疲倦。

◆ Over fatigue may make people have stertorous breath during sleep.
過度疲勞可能會使人睡覺時打呼。

0964

ache
ek
v. 疼痛；渴望
n. 痛苦

◆ The waiter is aching all over with fatigue.
這位男服務生累得全身疼痛。

◆ Her heart aches for the poor children on TV.
她對電視上的貧窮兒童覺得心疼。

0965

sore
sor
adj. 疼痛的

◆ I can hardly eat any food because of my sore throat.
因為喉嚨痛讓我幾乎沒辦法吃下任何食物。

◆ His sore throat recurs every winter.
他的喉嚨痛每年冬天都會發生。

0966

malady
'mælədɪ
n. 疾病；弊病

◆ The baby suffered from a rare malady when he was born.
當這嬰兒出生時，患了一種罕見疾病。

◆ There is no specific remedy for the strange malady.
對於這種陌生的疾病沒有特別的治療方法。

0967

ward
wɔrd
n. 病房；行政
區

◆ The patient was put in an isolation ward.
這位病人住在隔離病房。

◆ The general hospital have a medical ward and a surgical ward.
這家綜合醫院有內科病房與外科病房。

0968

ounce
aʊns
n. 盎斯

◆ An ounce is one sixteenth of a pound.
一盎斯等於十六分之一英磅。

◆ How many calories can one ounce of sugar supply?
一盎司糖能夠提供多少卡路里？

0969

blink
blɪŋk
v. 眨眼 *n.* 一瞬間

- ◆ The thief ran fast and disappeared around the corner in the blink of an eye.
  這個小偷快速跑著，在轉角處一眨眼就不見了。
- ◆ A sudden lightning that made me blink.
  一道突然的閃電讓我眨了一下眼。

0970

fracture
ˈfræktʃɚ
n. 破口；裂縫

- ◆ The fracture of his left hand is very serious.
  他左手的骨折非常嚴重。
- ◆ I am sure there is a fracture in the water pipe.
  我確定這水管中有裂縫。

0971

bankrupt
ˈbæŋkrʌpt
adj. 破產的

- ◆ The bankrupt man hypothecated his last house to bank for a loan.
  破產人抵押他最後一間房子向銀行借貸。
- ◆ Her unbridled spending made her bankrupt.
  她毫無節制花錢而導致破產。

0972 ★

rupture
ˈrʌptʃɚ
n. 破裂 *v.* 使破裂；使鬧翻

- ◆ The negotiation among these countries came to a rupture.
  這些國家間的談判破裂了。
- ◆ I saw the rupture of the pipeline.
  我看到這條輸油管裂口。

0973

crack
kræk
n. 破裂；爆炸聲 *v.* 使爆裂

- ◆ When she heard a crack of thunder, she cried.
  當她聽到這爆炸般的雷聲就哭了。
- ◆ There is a crack at the bottom of this bowl.
  這個碗的底部有一條裂縫。

0974

sabotage
ˈsæbə.tɑʒ
n. 破壞 *v.* 蓄意破壞……

- ◆ The sabotage of the main bridge stopped the enemy invasion.
  這主要橋樑的破壞行動阻止了敵人的侵略。
- ◆ The fire at the building was caused by sabotage.
  這場建築物的大火是蓄意破壞所引起。

0975

destroy
dɪˈstrɔɪ
v. 破壞……；毀掉……；使失效

- ◆ The city was destroyed in the war.
  這城市在戰爭被摧毀了。
- ◆ The grains have been destroyed by the depredation of insects.
  這些穀物被蟲害毀壞了。

0976 ★

secretary
/ˈsɛkrətɛrɪ/
n. 祕書

◆ She is the secretary of this manager.
她是這位經理的祕書。
◆ You can talk with the deputy secretary during my absence.
你可以在我缺席時跟我的代理祕書談。

0977

conclave
/ˈkɑnklev/
n. 祕密會議

◆ Several mayors of the country held a conclave to reform.
這個國家的許多市長開了個改革的祕密會議。
◆ I met my partner at that conclave last year.
我在去年的祕密會議中遇到我的伙伴。

0978

congratulate
/kənˈgrætʃəˌlet/
v. 祝賀；恭賀

◆ I went to congratulate Vicky when I knew she was going to get married.
當我知道維琦將結婚時，我前去恭喜她。
◆ I congratulate you on your great victories.
我恭喜你有了偉大的勝利。

0979

divine
/dəˈvaɪn/
adj. 神的；神聖的

◆ Before having a meal, we pray and thank the divine grace.
用餐前，我們祈禱感謝神的恩典。
◆ The divine tree in Ali Mountain was blighted to death.
阿里山的神木因為枯萎而死去。

0980

sacred
/ˈsekrɪd/
adj. 神聖的；不可侵犯的

◆ A person should make a sacred vow before accepting baptism.
在受洗之前，要先立下神聖的誓約。
◆ The Bible is the sacred book of Christianity.
聖經是基督教的神聖書籍。

0981

solemn
/ˈsɑləm/
adj. 神聖的；莊重的

◆ The archaic church looks so solemn.
這間古代的教堂看起來非常神聖。
◆ His jocose manner was inept for such a solemn occasion.
他開玩笑的態度對如此莊嚴的場合而言很不妥。

0982

myth
/mɪθ/
n. 神話；虛構的故事

◆ Students learn about the myths of ancient Greece and Rome.
學生們學習有關古代希臘和羅馬的神話。
◆ In Greek myths, Nemesis was the goddess of retribution and vengeance.
希臘神話中，娜米西斯是復仇女神。

0983

miracle
ˈmɪrəkḷ
n. 神蹟；奇蹟

◆ He is alive by a miracle after the severe car accident.
他奇蹟似地從這場嚴重車禍中活過來。

◆ Heavy industry is also one of the critical forces that lead to the economic miracle of Taiwan.
重工業也是促成台灣經濟奇蹟的關鍵力量之一。

0984

---

lease
lis
n. 租約

◆ How long is the lease?
租期是多久？

◆ The lease expires in three years' time.
這份合約三年後到期。

0985

---

falter
ˈfɔltɚ
v. 站不穩；蹣跚；支吾其詞

◆ The drunken old man faltered along the street.
這喝醉老人蹣跚地沿著街道往前走。

◆ The young man is beginning to falter in his beliefs.
這年輕人的信仰開始動搖。

0986

---

stand
stænd
v. 站立；忍受
n. 路邊攤

◆ They need to stand in a line.
他們必須站成一直線。

◆ I can't stand your bad habits anymore.
我再也無法忍受你的壞習慣了。

0987

---

texture
ˈtɛkstʃɚ
n. 紋理；質地（織物等）；結構

◆ This kind of cloth has a smooth texture.
這種布料有光滑的質地。

◆ Sand has a granular texture.
沙子有種粒狀的結構。

0988

---

vein
ven
n. 紋理；靜脈（血管）；礦脈

◆ The veins on her face are so apparent.
她臉上的血管是如此明顯。

◆ There is a rich vein of silver in the mountain.
在這山中蘊藏有豐富的礦脈。

0989

---

vegetarian
ˌvɛdʒəˈtɛrɪən
n. 素食者

◆ She is a vegetarian, so she eats vegetables for each meal.
她是素食者，所以每餐都吃蔬菜。

◆ That's the reason why you're a vegetarian, isn't it?
這就是你吃素的原因，不是嗎？

0990 ★

sketch
skɛtʃ
v. 素描……；繪草圖 *n.* 草案

◆ I can simply sketched one with a pencil in a few minutes.
我可以用鉛筆在幾分鐘內簡單地畫出一張素描。

◆ She did a sketch of the baseball player.
她對這位棒球選手畫了一張素描。

0991

deficiency
dɪˈfɪʃənsɪ
n. 缺乏；不足量

沒油了!

◆ Many diseases are caused by certain vitamin deficiencies.
許多疾病的引起是因為缺乏某些維他命。

◆ The old man has a slight calcium deficiency.
這位老人有點缺鈣。

0992

lack
læk
v. 缺乏……；沒有…… *n.* 缺乏

我缺乏睡眠

◆ She always lacks of confidence in front of the public.
在大眾面前她總是缺乏信心。

◆ Wilson is suffering from lack of appetite.
威爾森正為缺乏食慾所苦。

0993

shortcoming
ˈʃɔrt.kʌmɪŋ
n. 缺點；缺陷

又來不及了

◆ Greed is the woman's chief shortcoming.
貪心是這個女人主要的缺點。

◆ Not being punctual is her biggest shortcoming.
不守時是她最大的缺點。

0994

drawback
ˈdrɔ.bæk
n. 缺點；短處；障礙

太重，拿不動

◆ The only drawback to the book is that it is too heavy.
這本書唯一的缺點就是太重。

◆ There is a drawback to this new computer.
這台新電腦有一個缺點。

0995 ★

羅馬不是一天造成的

---

defect
dɪˈfɛkt
n. 缺點；過失

◆ Laziness is Mary's fatal defect.
懶惰是瑪麗無可挽回的缺點。

◆ She tries her best to correct all her defects .
她盡力改正她所有的缺點。

0996 ★

---

wing
wɪŋ
n. 翅膀；廂房

◆ A colorful bird stood on a tree and fluttered its wings.
一隻鮮豔的鳥站在樹上鼓動著雙翅。

◆ The house was amplified with a new wing.
這間房子擴大了一個新的廂房。

0997

---

cultivate
ˈkʌltə.vet
v. 耕種……；培養

◆ Tina starts to cultivate her hobby during the summer vacation.
汀娜在暑假期間開始培養她的嗜好。

◆ Only two thirds of the land can be cultivated.
只有三分之二的土地可以耕作。

0998

---

capability
.kepəˈbɪlətɪ
n. 能力；性能

◆ The salesman explained the sedan's technical capabilities.
這位業務員解說了這台轎車的技術性能。

◆ The professor lost the capability of doing important research.
這位教授喪失做重要研究的能力。

0999

---

viable
ˈvaɪəbḷ
adj. 能生存的；可行的

◆ The patient's willpower will make him viable regardless of his cancer.
不管他的癌症，這位病人的意志力將會使他生存下來。

◆ There are two viable methods to this problem.
這個問題有兩個可行的方式。

1000

---

competent
ˈkɑmpətənt
adj. 能幹的；有競爭力的

◆ He was an competent and respectable sales manager.
他是一位非常能幹且受人尊敬的業務經理。

◆ He is born to be upright so he must be competent as a judge.
他秉性正直，所以一定能勝任法官。

1001

lucrative
ˈlukrətɪv
adj. 能獲利的；賺錢的

◆ She has a lucrative business selling leather goods.
她有一份能獲利的銷售皮革生意。

◆ His software company sounds like a very lucrative business.
他的軟體公司聽起來像非常賺錢的生意。

1002 ★

voyage
ˈvɔɪɪdʒ
n. 航行；航海

◆ The voyage from England to India may take six months.
從英國到印度的航行可能要花上六個月。

◆ The typhoon precluded the sailors from sea voyages.
這場颱風阻止了這些船員的海上航程。

1003

sail
sel
v. 航行於；駕駛船隻

◆ The north wind favored their sailing at dawn.
這個北風有利於他們黎明時的航行。

◆ The ship sails up north from the Pacific Ocean to the Arctic.
那艘船北上太平洋，要到北極去。

1004

navigate
ˈnævəˌget
v. 航行於；駕駛船隻；導航

◆ I saw many ships navigate the ocean.
我看到許多船隻航行海洋。

◆ Who first navigated the Atlantic ?
是誰先橫渡大西洋？

1005

saucer
ˈsɔsə
n. 茶碟

◆ Mother always puts a cup on a saucer.
媽媽經常把茶杯放在茶碟裡。

◆ She offers me tea in her delicate saucer.
她以精緻的茶碟請我用茶。

1006

lawn
lɔn
n. 草地；草坪

◆ The gardener is mowing the lawn at this moment.
這位園丁此時正在割草。

◆ I have to trim the lawn and the hedge regularly.
我必須定期去修剪草地和籬笆。

1007

draft
dræft
n. 草稿；通風裝置 *v.* 打草稿

◆ He'll send you a draft of the contract in the email.
他將會把合約的草案以電子郵件寄給你。

◆ Making a draft before writing a composition can save you time.
寫作文前先打草稿可以節省時間。

1008 ★

desolate

/ˈdɛsḷɪt/

adj. 荒涼的；無人煙的 *v.* 使荒蕪

◆ We saw only a few people in the desolate town.
在荒涼的鎮上我們只看到了一些人。

◆ The land was desolated by the drought.
這塊土地因為乾旱而荒蕪。

1009

absurd

/əbˈsɝd/

adj. 荒謬的；可笑的

◆ It is absurd to go out in such terrible weather.
這麼壞的天氣還要出門，實在是荒謬。

◆ It was absurd of you to suggest such a thing.
你這樣的建議真是荒謬。

1010

haggle

/ˈhægḷ/

v. 討價還價

◆ She haggled with the fishmonger over the price.
她為了價格跟魚販討價還價。

◆ Let's not haggle over a few dollars.
不要為了一點錢討價還價。

1011 ★

bargain

/ˈbɑrgɪn/

v. 討價還價 *n.* 交易

◆ We got a great bargain when we bought this car.
我們買這台車是個很棒的交易。

◆ I made a satisfactory bargain with him.
我和他做了一筆令人滿意的交易。

1012 ★

discuss

/dɪˈskʌs/

v. 討論……；商議……

◆ I have some questions to discuss with you.
我有一些問題要和你討論。

◆ We have to discuss the matter face to face.
我們必須當面討論這件事。

1013 ★

scold

/skold/

v. 訓斥；責罵

◆ Don't scold the child without any reason.
不要沒理由就斥責孩子。

◆ The impenitent boy was scolded by his parents.
這個不知悔悟的男孩被他的父母責罵。

1014

reporter

/rɪˈportɚ/

n. 記者

◆ This reporter was sued for slander.
那位記者因為毀謗罪被告。

◆ The spokesman tried to shun the reporters' queries.
這位發言人試圖規避記者們的問題。

1015

remember

rɪˈmɛmbə

v. 記得做；記住要

◆ I can't remember where the post office is.
我想不起來郵局在哪裡？

◆ Remember to close the window when it rains.
下雨時，別忘了把窗戶關上。

1016

memorize

ˈmɛməˌraɪz

v. 記憶……；背熟……

◆ Many learners do not have good method to memorize English vocabulary.
許多學習者沒有好方法來記住英文字彙。

◆ The most effective memory mode of the human being's cerebrum is to memorize phrases.
人類大腦最有效率的記憶方法是記憶詞組。

1017

monetary

ˈmʌnəˌtɛrɪ

adj. 財政的；貨幣的

◆ We can't give you a monetary refund though.
我們還是不能給你現金退款。

◆ The government announced further changes in the monetary system.
政府宣布了貨幣制度的未來變革。

1018 ★

property

ˈprɑpətɪ

n. 財產；所有物；特性

◆ Our government made efforts to protect the intellectual property rights during these years.
這幾年來我們政府竭盡努力在保護著作財產權。

◆ A speculator may try to amass great property.
投機商可能嘗試積聚大量房地產。

1019

wealth

wɛlθ

n. 財富；豐富

◆ Saudi Arabia made its wealth by selling oil.
沙烏地位阿拉伯靠賣油致富。

◆ He has no aspiration for fame or wealth.
他不渴望名聲與財富。

1020 ★

contribution

ˌkɑntrəˈbjuʃən

n. 貢獻；捐款；投稿

◆ She made a contribution of $200 to the fund each week.
她每星期捐助二百元給基金會。

◆ Einstein make a great contribution to science and physics.
愛因斯坦對科學與物理學做出了重大貢獻。

1021

contribute

kənˈtrɪbjut

v. 貢獻……；捐助……

◆ She did not contribute anything to the work.
她對這件工作沒有絲毫貢獻。

◆ Several gases in the atmosphere contribute to global warming.
大氣層的好幾種氣體會引起全球暖化。

1022 ★

surge

səɜdʒ

v. 起伏（海浪）；
起波濤 *n.* 高漲

◆ The ship began to surge forward once more.
這艘船再一次開始破浪前進。

◆ There has been a surge in car prices recently.
最近汽車的價格高漲。

1023

---

effective

ɪˈfɛktɪv

adj. 起作用的；
生效的

fluoride

◆ More and more commuters are finding that carpool is one of the most effective ways to help reduce travel time and costs.
越來越多的通勤者發現共乘是一種最有效幫助減少旅遊時間和成本的方法。

◆ Some dentists believed that the addition of fluoride in water is effective as a prophylactic treatment.
有些牙醫相信水中加氟是一種有效預防疾病的方式。

1024 ★

---

wrinkle

ˈrɪŋkl

v. 起皺紋

◆ When the old man thinks about something, he wrinkles his forehead.
當這位老人想起了一些事時，就皺起了額頭。

◆ The old man has a wrinkled forehead.
那個老人的額頭布滿皺紋。

1025

---

revile

rɪˈvaɪl

v. 辱罵；誹謗

@#%!&...

◆ The beggar reviled the rich man for his lack of sympathy.
這位乞丐辱罵這位有錢人缺乏同情心。

◆ The old lady reviled the man who drove her off.
這老女人辱罵趕走她的男人。

1026

---

overtake

ˌovɚˈtek

v. 追上；趕上；
突然遭遇

◆ One runner overtook another runner and passed him.
一位跑者追上另一位跑者，並且超越他。

◆ I had to walk very fast to overtake you.
我必須走很快才能趕上你。

1027

---

chase

tʃes

v. 追求；狩獵

◆ Maggie is a glamorous young lady so many men chase after her.
瑪姬是個迷人的年輕淑女，所以有許多男士在追求她。

◆ The policemen are chasing the theft.
警察正在追捕竊賊。

1028

---

pursue

pɚˈsju

v. 追趕……；追
求……

◆ Everyone should pursue his own happiness in the limited life span we have.
每個人應該在有限的人生中，追求自己的幸福。

◆ She loves to use abrasive words to hurt men who pursue her.
她喜歡用刻薄的言語來傷害追求她的男士們。

1029

refund
rɪˈfʌnd
v. 退還；償還

◆ Would you like a refund or an exchange?
你想要退貨還是換貨？

◆ You can get the refund if you show the receipt.
如果出示收據，你就可以得到退款。

1030 ★

fugitive
ˈfjudʒətɪv
n. 逃亡者；逃犯
adj. 逃亡的

◆ The police beat the city for the fugitive.
員警在城中搜捕這個逃犯。

◆ The fugitive is wanted for murder by the police.
警察正在通緝這位犯下謀殺罪的逃犯。

1031

escape
əˈskep
v. 逃脫；逃走

◆ The criminal escaped from the prison.
這個罪犯從監獄逃出來了。

◆ If you meet any carnivorous beast in the mountains, you had better immediately escape.
要是在山裡遇到任何肉食性的獸類，你最好立刻逃跑。

1032 ★

flee
fli
v. 逃離；消失

◆ The robbers fled when they saw the police.
當他們看到警察時，這些強盜逃走了。

◆ You should not flee from your duty.
你不應該逃避你的責任。

1033

ingredient
ɪnˈgridɪənt
n. 配料；成份

◆ What are the ingredients of the bread?
麵包的原料有哪些？

◆ All ingredients are mild and oil-free.
所有的成分都是溫和且去油的。

1034 ★

quota
ˈkwotə
n. 配額；限額

◆ Our sales quotas for employees should be increased.
我們職員的銷售配額要增加。

◆ The government put a strict quota on imports.
政府對於進口產品設定了嚴格的配額。

1035 ★

bar
bar
n. 酒吧；棒；條
v. 阻止……

◆ I want to sing at a karaoke bar tomorrow.
我想要明天到卡拉 ok 酒吧唱歌。

◆ People are barred from entering this building.
此大樓禁止進入。

1036

nail
nel
n. 釘子

◆ Mallets are used for hitting nails into wood.
木槌是用來把釘子釘入木頭。

◆ It was not easy to get the rusty nail out.
拔出這支生鏽的釘子不容易。

1037

sparkling
ˈsparklɪŋ
adj. 閃閃發光
的；起泡沫的

◆ I enjoy looking at my daughter's sparkling big eyes.
我喜歡看著我女兒閃閃發亮的大眼睛。

◆ I am drinking the sparkling wine.
我正喝著起泡沫的酒。

1038

sheer
ʃɪr
adj. 陡峭的；透
明的；全然的

◆ The hills rise sheer above the blue river
這些小山陡峭地矗立在藍色的河流上。

◆ The youth's behavior was just sheer bravado.
這小伙子的作為只是全然虛張聲勢。

1039

shower
ˈʃaʊə
n. 陣雨；淋浴

◆ A heavy shower drenched us yesterday.
昨天一場很大的陣雨把我們都淋溼了。

◆ I'd like a single room with a shower.
我要一間附設淋浴的單人房。

1040

famine
ˈfæmɪn
n. 飢荒；嚴重
短缺

◆ Drought has resulted in famine for a long time.
乾旱導致了長期的饑荒。

◆ The whole country faces famine and rampant disease.
整個國家面臨了饑荒及肆虐的疾病。

1041

stall
stɔl
n. 馬廄；攤位

◆ His mother set up a little stall to sell clothes.
他的媽媽擺了個小攤位來賣衣服。

◆ The groom led the horse out of the stall.
這位馬伕把這匹馬帶出馬廄。

1042

circus
ˈsɝkəs
n. 馬戲團

◆ The teacher took them to the popular circus.
這位老師帶他們去看這個受歡迎的馬戲團。

◆ The man is an animal trainer for the circus.
這人是這家馬戲團的馴獸師。

1043

bone
bon
n. 骨頭

◆ My sister has a broken bone in her hand.
我妹妹的手骨折了。

◆ Mary suffered from a broken bone in her foot.
瑪麗遭受腳骨斷裂之苦。

1044

skeleton
ˈskɛlətn̩
n. 骨骼;大綱

◆ Drinking milk can strengthen our skeletons.
喝牛奶可以強化我們的骨骼。

◆ There is a skeleton of a dinosaur displayed in the museum.
這博物館中陳列了一副恐龍的骨骼。

1045

usury
ˈjuʒərɪ
n. 高利貸

◆ He couldn't afford the usury so he escaped.
因為他負擔不起高利貸,他只得逃走。

◆ The rich man made money by practicing usury.
這位有錢人靠放高利貸賺錢。

1046

height
haɪt
n. 高度

◆ According to my height, what is my standard weight?
根據我的身高,我的標準體重是多少?

◆ Our family moved to Japan at the height of the emigration.
我的家人在移民高峰期移居到日本。

1047

plateau
plæˈto
n. 高原;平台

◆ The town is situated on a plateau among the mountains of the north.
這城市座落在北方群山環繞的高原上。

◆ The famous plateau extends for hundreds of miles.
這個著名的高原綿延了數百英里。

1048

assume
əˈsum
v. 假定……;採用

◆ I assumed you went on a trip to France.
我以為你去法國旅行了。

◆ All journalists assume that the famous singer will appear at the airport this morning.
所有的記者都以為這位知名歌手早上會出現在機場。

1049

bogus
ˈbogəs
adj. 假的;偽造的

◆ The clerk was fooled by his bogus identity card.
這店員被他的假身份證騙了。

◆ The government declared how to distinguish bogus from true bills.
政府宣布如何辨識偽鈔。

1050 ★

phony
'fonɪ
adj. 假的；偽造
的 *n.* 騙子

◆ It's very easy to create a phony identity and cheat others in cyberspace.
在網際空間中很容易製造一個假身份來欺騙其他人。

◆ You are using a phony credit card.
你使用的是一張偽造的信用卡。

1051

hypothesis
haɪ'pɑθəsɪs
n. 假設；假說

◆ The hypothesis for global warming had been proved.
全球性暖化的假設獲得證實。

◆ The hypothesis was invalidated by later findings.
後來的發現讓這個假設無效。

1052 ★

vacation
ve'keʃən
n. 假期

◆ The summer vacation usually begins in July.
暑假通常在七月開始。

◆ I'd like to take my vacation days starting tomorrow.
明天我要休假。

1053

recommend
,rɛkə'mɛnd
v. 做……建議；
推薦……

◆ He recommended this brand as a good substitute.
他推薦的這個品牌是不錯的替代品。

◆ Would you recommend any other nearby hotel?
你能為我推薦附近的飯店嗎？

1054 ★

mark
mɑrk
v. 做記號；打分
數 *n.* 記號

◆ The teacher marked the correct answers with checks.
老師在正確答案處打勾。

◆ There's a black mark on your shirt.
你的短袖上有黑色記號。

1055

outage
'autɪdʒ
n. 停電；中斷
供應

◆ The typhoon prostrated numerous trees and caused a power outage.
這場颱風弄倒許多樹，並且引起停電。

◆ There will be a power outage in my city tomorrow.
我的城市明天要停電。

1056

health
hɛlθ
n. 健康

◆ Keeping a good diet can bring you health.
保持良好飲食習慣能帶給你健康。

◆ Eating more vegetables is good for our health.
多吃蔬菜有益我們身體健康。

1057

fitness
ˈfɪtnɪs
n. 健康；言行
得體

◆ The fitness center has provided professional exercise instruction.
健身中心有提供專業的運動指導。

◆ He is a fitness fanatic who is in favor of vegetables.
他偏愛蔬菜，是個健身狂。

1058

detective
dɪˈtɛktɪv
n. 偵探

◆ I am crazy about detective novels and travelogues.
我對偵探小說和遊記十分入迷。

◆ A good detective needs to have incredible insight.
好的偵探需要極佳的洞察力。

1059

sneak
snik
v. 偷偷地走；溜
走

◆ The little girl sneaked into the masquerade party.
這個小女孩偷偷溜進這個化裝舞會。

◆ The soldier raised his gun and sneak forward .
這個士兵舉起槍偷偷前進。

1060

stowaway
ˈstoəˌwe
n. 偷渡者

◆ The stowaways used snide passports.
這些偷渡客使用假護照。

◆ There were five stowaways in the ship caught by the police.
警察抓到的這艘船上有五個偷渡者。

1061

steal
stil
v. 偷竊

◆ I heard that his new motorcycle was stolen.
聽說他的新機車被偷了。

◆ I'm pretty good at stealing bases, and sometimes disturb infielders' fielding.
我很擅長盜壘，有時候會擾亂內野手的守備。

1062

counterfeit
ˈkaʊntəfɪt
adj. 偽造的
v. 偽造……；仿造……

◆ She used a counterfeit passport to pass through customs.
她持假護照過海關。

◆ It is a crime to counterfeit document.
偽造文書是一種罪行。

1063 ★

---

hypocritical
ˌhɪpəˈkrɪtɪkl̩
adj. 偽善的；虛偽的

◆ Keep away hypocritical people if you can perceive them.
如果你能察覺到的話，遠離虛偽的人。

◆ Her hypocritical manners and greetings made me sick.
她偽善的態度和問候讓我作嘔。

1064

---

anonymous
əˈnɑnəməs
adj. 匿名的；不具名的

◆ An anonymous tipster has leaked confidential information to the press.
一位匿名密報者把機密的資訊洩露給新聞界。

◆ An anonymous donator contributed a great deal of money to the nursing home.
一位匿名的捐獻者捐了一大筆錢給療養院。

1065 ★

---

manual
ˈmænjʊəl
n. 參考手冊 *adj.* 用手操作的

◆ You can find a detailed explanation in the manual.
你在使用手冊中會找到詳細的說明。

◆ A blue-collar worker is one who performs manual labor and works in skilled trade.
藍領工作者是指那些從事體力勞動或以技能工作的人。

1066 ★

---

senate
ˈsɛnɪt
n. 參議院；立法機構

◆ The president called up a bill for the approval of both the Senate and the House .
總統提出一項議案，並要求參眾兩院的同意。

◆ The US senate vote against the agreement with China.
美國參議院投票反對與中國的協議。

1067

---

merchant
ˈmɝtʃənt
n. 商人 *adj.* 商業的

◆ That successful merchant gained considerable profits in a few months.
這位成功的商人在最近幾個月中獲得了可觀的利潤。

◆ The merchant supplies goods and food to them.
這位商人提供貨物與食物給他們。

1068

dealer
'dilə
n. 商人；發牌者

◆ The two women were the unwitting victims of a drug dealer who put a large quantity of heroin in their luggage.
毒販將大量的海洛因放入二個女人的行李中，讓她們成為不知情的受害者。

◆ I bought a used car from a car dealer.
我從車商那裡買了台二手車。

1069 ★

store
stor
n. 商店

◆ The store sells many cheap clothes.
這家店賣許多便宜的衣服。

◆ Liquor stores cannot sell alcohol to teenagers.
賣酒的店家不可以賣酒給青少年。

1070

promotion
prə'moʃən
n. 商品促銷；升級

全館大特賣

◆ He was very happy because he got a promotion.
他很高興因為他獲得了升遷。

◆ Tom is very depressed when he failed the promotion.
湯姆未能升職，感到非常沮喪。

1071 ★

chamber of commerce
'tʃembə əv 'kɑməs
n. 商會

臺灣商會聯誼

◆ The US Chamber of Commerce is the world's largest business federation.
美國商會是全世界最大的商業聯盟。

◆ The chamber of commerce helps local merchants a lot.
商會讓當地商人獲益良多。

1072

commercial
kə'mʃəl
adj. 商業的；商用的

全館八折！

◆ More and more people are learning commercial English for business purposes.
越來越多的人學習商用英語。

◆ The commercial property market is booming recently.
最近商業地產市場日益興盛。

1073 ★

brand
brænd
n. 商標；品牌

◆ Japanese girls love to buy famous brand purses.
日本女孩喜歡買名牌包。

◆ What brands of duty-free cigarettes and beer do you have?
你們有賣哪些牌子的免稅香煙和啤酒？

1074 ★

negotiate
nɪ'goʃɪet
v. 商議……條件；協商

一萬元好嗎？
不行！

◆ You can negotiate the unit price for large orders.
你如果大量訂購，單價可以再商議。

◆ The student union is currently negotiating with the school.
這個學生團體目前正和校方協議中。

1075 ★

sip
sɪp
v. 啜飲 **n.** 一小口

◆ She often sips a glass of red wine before dining.
她經常餐前啜飲一杯紅酒。

◆ Can I take a sip of brandy?
我能夠啜飲一口白蘭地嗎？

1076

dumb
dʌm
adj. 啞的；無言的

◆ She was struck dumb at the sight of a car accident.
看到車禍的場景，她嚇得說不出話來。

◆ The poor baby was dumb from birth .
這可憐的嬰兒出生就啞了。

1077

nation
ˈneʃən
n. 國家；民族

◆ The two nations' amity was as close as it ever had been.
這兩個國家的友好關係如同過去一般親密。

◆ People are the most important component of a nation.
人民是組成一個國家最重要的構成要素。

1078

congress
ˈkɑŋgrəs
n. 國會；立法機關

立法院

◆ The Congress has been debating the nationalization issue recently.
國會最近還在辯論國有化的議題。

◆ The Congress enacted a tax reform bill.
國會制定稅務改革法案。

1079 ★

state-run
stet ˌrʌn
adj. 國營的

國營造船公司

◆ The state-owned bank is open around the clock.
這家國有銀行二十四小時營業。

◆ The bad news tremendously reported by the state-run TV here.
這個壞消息被這間國營電視台大量報導。

1080

execute
ˈɛksɪˌkjut
v. 執行……；實施……；處死刑

Enter

◆ The company starts to execute the new policy.
這家公司開始執行新政策。

◆ The biggest problem now is how to execute the plan.
現在最大的問題是如何執行這個計劃。

1081 ★

charter
ˈtʃɑrtɚ
n. 執照；特許狀 **v.** 包租……

特許狀

◆ The drugstore is under charter to sell medicine.
這家藥房有販賣藥品的執照。

◆ Because of the charter, we can save from the investigation.
因為特許狀，我們可以從調查中節省開支。

1082

foundation
faʊnˈdeʃən
n. 基金會；基礎

和平基金會

◆ The foundation has been instituted for almost 10 years.
這個基金會已經設立將近十年了。

◆ The foundation of this great country is a great event in the history of mankind.
這個偉大國家的建立是人類歷史上的一件大事。

1083

basis
ˈbesɪs
n. 基礎；基本原理

◆ The basis of the professor's theory mostly came from foreign magazines.
教授的理論基礎絕大部分來自國外雜誌。

◆ Your salary is paid on a monthly basis.
你的薪水是按月來支付。

1084

fundamental
ˌfʌndəˈmɛnt.f
adj. 基礎的；根本的；根深蒂固的

◆ I have learned the fundamentals of the computer in senior high school.
我在高中時學習到電腦的基本常識。

◆ Making products marketable is a salesman's fundamental job.
讓產品賣得好是一個業務員的基本工作。

1085 ★

fortitude
ˈfɔrtə.tjud
n. 堅忍；剛毅

◆ He fights against his lung cancer with great fortitude.
他以極大的毅力來與肺癌對抗。

◆ The pianist was successful for her fortitude character.
這位鋼琴家因為她的堅毅而成功。

1086

firm
fɝm
adj. 堅定的；牢固的 **n.** 公司；行號

◆ She is a girl with firm principals.
她是一個有著堅定原則的女孩。

◆ It is one of his dreams to set up a firm with a great reputation.
開一家享有優良信譽的公司是他的夢想之一。

1087

insist
ɪnˈsɪst
v. 堅持；非要……不可

◆ He insisted that we should follow the plan.
他堅持我們應該按照計劃。

◆ She insists on taking a bus to Taipei.
她堅持要搭公車去台北。

1088 ★

adhere
ədˈhɪr
v. 堅持……；遵守……；黏著……

我會**堅持**到底!!

◆ She always adheres to what she wants. Thus, she made her dream come true.
她總是堅持她所要的，因此美夢成真。

◆ We decided to adhere to the proposal.
我們決定堅持這提案。

1089

rigid
ˈrɪdʒɪd
adj. 堅硬的；固定不動的；嚴格的

◆ If a thing is very rigid, it will not bend easily.
假如一個東西非常堅硬，就不會容易被折彎。

◆ A rigid diet and exercise plan will make your figure slim.
嚴格的飲食與運動計劃能讓你的身材苗條。

1090

pile
paɪl
n. 堆；大量

◆ Piles of garbage seriously affect the environment with odors.
許多成堆散發惡臭的垃圾嚴重影響環境。

◆ Your book got buried under a pile of letters.
你的書壓在一堆信件下面。

1091

stack
stæk
n. 堆；大量；書架 (雙面)

◆ She placed her clothes in a neat stack.
她把她的衣服整齊放一堆。

◆ Can you show me how to find books in the stacks here?
請告訴我如何在這些書架上找書，好嗎？

1092

extravagant
ɪkˈstrævəgənt
adj. 奢侈的；揮霍的

◆ It was the most extravagant purchase I have ever made.
它是我買過最奢侈的東西。

◆ The teenager was very extravagant with money.
這個青少年很揮霍金錢。

1093

marital
ˈmærətḷ
adj. 婚姻的

◆ Her marital life was exceptionally happy.
她的婚姻生活特別的快樂。

◆ This is a textbook on marital affairs.
這是有關婚姻事務的教科書。

1094

wedding
ˈwɛdɪŋ
n. 婚禮

◆ What date is your wedding?
你們的婚禮在什麼時候？

◆ The wedding will be held in the auditorium.
婚禮會在禮堂中舉行。

1095

dormitory
ˈdɔrməˌtɔrɪ
n. 宿舍 (同 dorm)

◆ He doesn't want to live in the dormitory next semester.
他下學期不想住宿舍了。

◆ The bedrooms are adjoined in the dormitory.
這棟學生宿舍間的臥室是相連的。

1096

hangover

ˈhæŋ͵ovɚ

n. 宿醉；遺物；
後遺症

◆ Peter was really drunk last night and got up this morning with a hangover.
彼得昨晚喝得很醉，而且今早起床時帶著宿醉。

◆ Sarah was totally drunk last night, but she paid for her misdemeanors this morning with a terrible hangover.
莎拉昨晚喝得爛醉，但今天早上的嚴重宿醉已讓她為行為失當付出代價。

1097

silent

ˈsaɪlənt

adj. 寂靜的；沉
默的

◆ All students were silent when the teacher came in.
當老師走進教室時，所有的學生都安靜無聲。

◆ The woman kept silent to avoid embroiling herself in the incident.
這位女人保持沈默以免在這件事裡受到牽連。

1098

density

ˈdɛnsətɪ

n. 密度；比重

◆ The city has a population density of ten people per square mile.
這城市擁有每平方公里十人的人口密度。

◆ Taiwan has a population density of over 600 people per square kilometer.
台灣擁有每平方公里六百人的人口密度。

1099 ★

intensive

ɪnˈtɛnsɪv

adj. 密集的；加
強的；徹底的

◆ The labor force is the main focus for intensive agriculture.
精耕式農業是以勞動力為主。

◆ In the new dynamic competitive environment, the traditional labor-intensive industry of Taiwan is no more competitive.
在新的動力競爭環境下，台灣傳統勞力密集的工業已不具任何競爭力。

1100

plot

plɑt

n. 密謀；故事
情節

◆ The plot was discovered before it was carried out.
這陰謀在實施之前就被發現了。

◆ His plot to assassinate the mayor was exposed.
他刺殺市長的陰謀曝光了。

1101

salvage

ˈsælvɪdʒ

v. 將……解救
n. 援救

◆ The firemen tried their best to salvage people from the fire.
消防員們盡力將人們救出火海。

◆ There is a little hope of her salvage during the violent storm.
在強烈的暴風雨中她的救援沒什麼希望。

1102

schedule

ˈskɛdʒʊl

v. 將列入……排
程 **n.** 時間表；
進度表

9:00 國文課
10:00 英文課
11:00 數學課

◆ That is scheduled for shipment the day after tomorrow.
後天將列入裝運的排程。

◆ What is the schedule for the full day tour?
一日遊的行程如何安排？

1103 ★

specialize
/ˈspɛʃəl.aɪz/
v. 專攻……；專門研究……

◆ Mike decided to specialize in engineering at college.
麥克決定在大學時專攻工程學。

◆ She specializes in maritime law.
她專攻海事法。

1104

speciality
/ˌspɛʃiˈæləti/
n. 專長；專業；名產

◆ My speciality at university is applied mathematics.
我大學時的專長是應用數學。

◆ Lobster is a speciality on the small island.
龍蝦是這個小島上的名產。

1105

expert
/ˈɛkspɝt/
n. 專家；能手

◆ The general manager is an expert at troubleshooting.
這位總經理是個排解糾紛的專家。

◆ The expert should be able to defuse the time bomb.
這位專家應該能拆除這枚定時炸彈。

1106

keynote speech
/ˈkinot ˌspitʃ/
n. 專題演講

專題演講

◆ He delivered a keynote speech in the school yesterday.
他昨天在學校做了一場專題演講。

◆ The senator had to give a keynote speech to the press club.
這位參議員必須對記者俱樂部作一場專題演講。

1107

slaughter
/ˈslɔtɚ/
v. 屠宰；屠殺

◆ Thousands of people were slaughtered in the war.
這場戰役中數以千計的人被屠殺了。

◆ They are really terrified to witness the slaughter.
他們親眼目睹這場屠殺，確實嚇壞了。

1108

bill
/bɪl/
n. 帳單；支票

◆ It's my turn to pay the bill.
輪到我付帳了。

◆ I will pay my bill by credit card.
我將用信用卡付帳。

1109 ★

sturdy
/ˈstɝdi/
adj. 強壯的；健壯的

營養午餐

◆ The enemy offered a sturdy resistance.
這個敵人展開了堅強的反抗。

◆ The sturdy young man removed the rock easily.
這個健壯的年輕人輕鬆地移開石頭。

1110

enforce
in'fors

v. 強制……；實施……

♦ Her parents enforced that she can't keep in touch with her ex-boyfriend.
她的父母強迫她不能跟前男友聯絡。

♦ The police enforced the constant vigilance to eradiate drug smuggling.
警方實施持續性的警戒以剷除毒品走私。

1111 ★

constrain
kən'stren

v. 強迫……；壓迫……

♦ I was constrained to do this work.
我被強迫去做這件工作。

♦ Is it really necessary to constrain yourself like that?
真的有必要像這樣壓制自己嗎？

1112 ★

backlash
'bæk.læʃ

n. 強烈反對；後座力

♦ Was there any backlash aimed at your policy?
針對你的政策有什麼反彈？

♦ There is not yet a backlash against the policy.
這個政策沒有產生反彈。

1113

bandit
'bændɪt

n. 強盜；土匪

♦ Their villages and crops were pillaged and destroyed by bandits.
他們的村莊和農作物被盜匪掠奪和破壞。

♦ The invading bandits plundered the town of food, money, and valuables.
這些入侵的強盜搶劫了這個城市的食物、金錢與珍寶。

1114

emphasize
'ɛmfə.saɪz

v. 強調……；加強……語氣

♦ The company greatly emphasizes the employees' work efficiency.
這家公司非常強調員工的工作效率。

♦ The importance of comity has to be emphasized in family relations.
在家庭關係中必須強調禮貌的重要。

1115 ★

score
skor

n. 得分；分數

♦ The final score in the soccer game was 3 to 2.
足球賽最後成績是三比二。

♦ Their team scored twenty-five points in the basketball game.
他們的隊伍在籃球賽中獲得二十五分。

1116 ★

roam
rom

v. 徘徊；漫步

♦ Don't let yourself roam the streets alone at night.
不要讓你自己夜晚單獨在街頭徘徊。

♦ He used to roam the streets at midnight.
他過去午夜常在街上閒逛。

1117

overflow
.ovəˈflo
v. 從……中溢出；泛濫 **n.** 過剩

◆ The river often overflows in the spring.
這條河經常在春天時氾濫。

◆ The overflow from the bath tub ran on to the floor.
浴缸的水溢出流到了地板上。

1118

emancipate
ɪˈmænsə.pet
v. 從……解放出來；使自由

◆ The Jews were emancipated until German evacuated.
猶太人直到德軍撤離才獲得自由。

◆ Emancipate the dog. It has been chained up for hours.
快解開這隻狗，牠被鎖了好幾個小時。

1119

situation
.sɪtʃuˈeʃən
n. 情況；處境；位置

◆ In light of the company's financial situation, there will be no annual bonus this year.
按照這家公司的財務狀況，今年將不會發年度紅利。

◆ His announcement to run for the election has made the situation more tenser.
他宣布參選後，局勢變得更緊張了。

1120 ★

emotion
ɪˈmoʃən
n. 情感；感情

◆ The fans' emotions were oscillating between desperation and hope.
球迷們的情緒在絕望與希望之間擺盪。

◆ She is void of emotion when she is exhausted.
當她疲憊時會變得毫無感情。

1121

roll
rol
n. 捲狀物 **v.** 使滾動；使捲起

◆ The chicken roll from KFC is very delicious.
肯德基的雞肉捲很好吃。

◆ Let's roll back the carpets and begin to work.
讓我們把地毯捲起來，而且開始工作。

1122

shortcut
ˈʃɔrt.kʌt
n. 捷徑；近路

◆ We take a shortcut through a field instead of following the road.
我們不走接下來的路，而改走經由田間的捷徑。

◆ The bad guy was always looking for a shortcut to fortune.
這壞蛋總是尋找致富的捷徑。

1123 ★

scanner
ˈskænə
n. 掃描器（電腦）

◆ How do I use the handy scanner?
我如何使用這台手提的掃描器？

◆ All scanners are busy. Would you like to wait?
所有的掃描器都在使用，你可以等嗎？

1124

sweep

swip

v. 掃落；掠過；吹襲

◆ My mother asked me to sweep and mop the floor.
我媽媽要求我掃地與拖地。

◆ I need someone to help me sweep the floor after the party.
舞會結束後，我需要有人幫我掃地。

1125

confer

kən'fɜ

v. 授予……；與人商量

◆ My best friend always confers useful advice upon me.
我最好的朋友總是給我有用的建議。

◆ He had some time to confer with his lawyer.
他挪出一些時間和律師商量。

1126

entitle

ɪn'taɪtl̩

v. 授予……名稱；使……有資格

◆ Long experience entitles you to have promotion.
長時間的經驗讓你有資格升遷。

◆ A person who is self-employed is not entitled to a statutory redundancy payment.
一個自由業的人士並不合乎法律上的遣散費補助。

1127

authorize

'ɔθə͵raɪz

v. 授權……；認可；批准

◆ One student of the class was authorized to act as the class leader during John's absence.
當約翰缺席時，班上的一位學生被授權當班長。

◆ The local government authorized a big housing project.
當地政府批准了一項大型蓋屋計劃。

1128

struggle

'strʌgl̩

v. 掙扎……；抗爭…… **n.** 奮鬥

◆ The climber's energy is flagging when he struggles up a hill.
當登山者傾力爬上山丘時便體力不濟了。

◆ Fish struggle for survival when they are caught by fishermen.
魚被漁夫捕獲時會奮力掙扎求生。

1129

沒有失敗的人，只有放棄嘗試的人

---

adopt
əˋdɑpt
vt. 採用；接受；
收養

看電影？
OK!

◆ The plan was adopted after many discussions.
這個計劃經過許多討論後被採納。

◆ This little boy was adopted into our family.
我們家領養了這個小男孩

1130

---

quest
kwɛst
vt. 探求……；尋
求……

◆ They went to the forest in quest of some valuable plants.
他們前往森林中尋求一些有價值的植物。

◆ The police was on a quest for further evidence.
警察正在尋找更多證據。

1131

---

trace
tres
vt. 探尋……的蹤
跡；痕跡；追蹤

◆ The cause of the fire in the forest was traced to the cigarette butts disposed by visitors.
這場森林火災的起因追溯到遊客亂丟菸蒂所致。

◆ The retired soldier spoke openly about the war without a trace of rancor.
這位退役士兵毫無怨恨地公開談論這場戰爭。

1132 ★

---

catch
kætʃ
vt. 接住；抓住

◆ The clever captain led our team to victory.
這位聰明的隊長帶領我們隊伍獲得勝利。

◆ The father threw the ball and his son caught it.
那位父親丟球給他的兒子接。

1133

---

proximity
prɑkˋsɪmətɪ
n. 接近；鄰近

◆ The cost of the car is in the proximity of 10,000 dollars.
這臺車的價格接近一萬美金。

◆ Their school is in close proximity to the city hall.
他們的學校鄰近市政廳。

1134

---

service
ˋsɝvɪs
n. 接待；維修

◆ You can get a free map at the service counter.
你可以在服務台拿到一份免費地圖。

◆ The good service of this restaurant has attracted many customers.
這家餐廳的優良服務品質，而吸引了許多客人。

1135

clerk
klɝk
n. 接待員；店員

◆ I asked the clerk to show me some skirts.
我要求店員拿幾件裙子給我看。

◆ The postal clerk has a lot of complaints about too many parcel posts.
郵局員工抱怨包裹郵件太多。

1136

touch
tʌtʃ
v. 接觸；聯繫；碰到

◆ He was so tall that he could touch the ceiling.
他夠高所以能碰到天花板。

◆ Please don't touch the television.
請不要碰到電視。

1137

sue
su
v. 控告……

◆ The woman sued her husband for domestic violence.
這女人因為家暴控告她的丈夫。

◆ You could be sued for breach of contract when it is not necessarily your fault.
即使不必然是你們的錯，也可能被控違約。

1138

control
kənˈtrol
v. 控制……；操縱……

◆ Forest fires are hard to be controlled.
森林火災很難受到控制。

◆ The patient's condition got under control temporarily.
病人的病情暫時獲得控制。

1139

introduce
ˌɪntrəˈdjus
v. 推薦；介紹

◆ Let me introduce the new purchasing agent to you.
讓我介紹新的採購人員給你認識。

◆ Let my introduce my professor to you.
讓我介紹我的教授給你認識。

1140 ★

swift
swɪft
adj. 敏捷的；快速的

◆ The artist drew my portrait with a few swift movements of his pencil.
這位藝術家以鉛筆快速畫出我的肖像。

◆ The couple are very swift to deny these rumors about divorce.
這對夫妻很快地否認這些有關離婚的謠言。

1141

ambulance
ˈæmbjələns
n. 救護車

◆ The injured motorcyclist was taken to the hospital by ambulance.
受傷的摩托車騎士被救護車送到醫院去了。

◆ Two ambulances dashed to the scene of the accident.
兩輛消防車火速前往意外現場。

1142

education
ˌɛdʒəˈkeʃən
n. 教育；學識
教養

◆ The government tries to promote 12-year compulsory education.
政府試著推動十二年國民義務教育。

◆ I want my children to have a secular education and be able to decide by themselves independently.
我希望我的孩子能接受普通教育，並能夠獨立做決定。

1143 ★

educate
ˈɛdʒʊˌket
v. 教育某人；實行訓練

◆ Where were you educated?
你上過哪些學校？

◆ As Joy was educated in the U.S.A., she has a good command of English.
因為喬伊在美國受教育，所以她精通英文。

1144

professor
prəˈfɛsə
n. 教授

◆ She was a professor of chemistry at Chicago University.
她是芝加哥大學的化學教授。

◆ My new neighbor is a professor.
我的新鄰居是一位教授。

1145

coach
kotʃ
n. 教練

◆ The coach of the local team decided to change its pitcher.
地主隊的教練決定要換投手了。

◆ Tom is an experienced coach of basketball.
湯姆是一個很有經驗的籃球教練。

1146

treaty
ˈtritɪ
n. 條約；協議

日韓合作條約

◆ A peace treaty was signed between the US and Vietnam.
美國和越南簽署了一份和平條約。

◆ Does the country have an extradition treaty?
這個國家有引渡條約嗎？

1147

pact
pækt
n. 條約；協議；
盟約

美日協防條約

◆ Two nations entered into a pact to improve foreign relations.
兩個國家締定條約來增進外交關係。

◆ The cession of the land is not mentioned in the pact.
割讓這塊土地沒有在這份合約中被提及。

1148

clause
klɔz
n. 條款；子句

合作條款

◆ The penalty clause of the contract specifies how much the fine is.
這些合約中的處罰條款訂出了罰金要罰多少。

◆ Since this non-compete clause is no longer legal, it needs to be updated.
既然這份競業禁止條款不再合法，它需要被更新。

1149

ladder
ˈlædə
n. 梯子

◆ He set a ladder against the wall.
他把梯子靠在牆上。

◆ My uncle fell off a ladder and broke his leg.
我叔叔從樓梯掉下來，並且跌斷腳。

1150

default
dɪˈfɔlt
v. 棄權；不履行
責任；違約

◆ The bankrupt boss was in default on a loan.
這位破產的老闆沒辦法對貸款負責任。

◆ The tennis player lost a game by default.
這位網球選手因沒有出席而輸掉比賽。

1151 ★

homicide
ˈhɑməˌsaɪd
n. 殺人；殺人
犯

◆ Great jealousy drove the man to commit homicide.
極大的嫉妒心導致他犯下殺人罪。

◆ The gangster has been charged with homicide
這個流氓被控殺人。

1152

liquid
ˈlɪkwɪd
n. 液體

◆ Be careful! Those are corrosive liquids.
小心！這些是腐蝕性液體。

◆ Gasoline is a volatile liquid.
汽油是一種易揮發的液體。

1153

thoughtful
ˈθɔtfəl
adj. 深思的；考
慮周詳的；體貼
的

◆ I think Bill should be more thoughtful with his words.
我認為比爾應該對他的談話更加深思。

◆ Although you're quite introverted by nature, I think
you're an easygoing and thoughtful girl.
雖然你生性內向，但是我覺得你是一位隨和且體貼的女孩。

1154

profound
prəˈfaʊnd
adj. 深奧的；淵
博的；深度的

◆ A student can gain profound knowledge at school.
學生在學校中可學到淵博的知識。

◆ Various kinds of strange fishes live in the profound
depth of the ocean.
各種不同的奇怪的魚類生活在海洋的深處。

1155

abstruse
æbˈstrus
adj. 深奧難解
的；難懂的

◆ Abstruse ideas are best understood with diagrams.
深奧難解的觀念輔以圖表，最容易被理解。

◆ Many people thought philosophy is too abstruse to
understand.
許多人認為哲學太過於深奧難解。

1156

blend
blɛnd

v. 混合……；調
和……

◆ You should blend milk and hot water together before feeding babies.
在餵嬰兒前，你應該將牛奶與熱水混合。

◆ The villa seems to blend into the surroundings.
這棟別墅和周圍的環境融合在一起。

1157

confuse
kənˈfjuz

v. 混淆……；使
困惑；誤認……

◆ John feels confused when facing a dilemma.
約翰對於左右為難的情況感到迷惘。

◆ We are all confused with his strange behavior.
我們都對他怪異的行為感到困惑。

1158

chaotic
keˈɑtɪk

adj. 混亂的；雜
亂無章的

◆ The traffic conditions are chaotic in Taipei .
台北的交通狀況很混亂。

◆ The atmosphere in the meeting is extremely chaotic.
這場會議的氣氛非常混亂。

1159

messy
ˈmɛsɪ

adj. 混亂的；難
以處理的

◆ There is too much stuff in his room, so it looks messy.
他的房間放了太多東西，所以看起來很雜亂。

◆ Your dinner table is always pretty messy.
你的餐桌總是很雜亂。

1160

shallow
ˈʃælo

adj. 淺的；膚淺
的

◆ His behavior seemed very shallow and immature.
他的行為似乎非常膚淺與不成熟。

◆ Several different species of fish inhabit these turbid shallow rivers.
數種不同的魚類生活在這些低淺而濁的河流中。

1161

add
æd

v. 添加；加上

99 ⊕ 1 = ?

◆ Please add some soda to the whisky.
請在威士忌中加蘇打水。

◆ Preservatives are added to some foods to prolong their expiration date.
有些食物會添加防腐劑以延長保存期限。

1162

sober
ˈsobə

adj. 清醒的；沒
喝酒的 **v.** 使清
醒

◆ You should talk to him when he is sober.
你應該在他清醒的時候跟他談談。

◆ A cup of tea may always sober me up.
一杯茶總能讓我清醒。

1163

recipe
ˈrɛsəpɪ
n. 烹飪法；祕訣

◆ I got a recipe for cookies from my mother-in-law.
我從我婆婆那得到做餅乾的食譜。

◆ This recipe asks for a liter of milk.
這份食譜需要一公升的牛奶。

1164

slam
slæm
v. 猛力關閉；用力丟下

◆ Slam the door, please.
請用力關上門。

◆ I love the powerful way he slammed dunk.
我愛上那種強力灌籃的方式。

1165

shove
ʃʌv
v. 猛推

◆ He shoved the heavy rock off the road.
他把這塊大石頭推離這條道路。

◆ Don't try to shove the heavy load onto others.
不要嘗試把重擔推給別人。

1166

speculate
ˈspɛkjəˌlet
v. 猜測……；推斷……

◆ I can speculate what will happen next.
我能夠猜出接下來要發生什麼。

◆ The policeman speculated about the criminal's motives.
警察猜測出這個罪犯的動機。

1167

suppose
səˈpoz
v. 猜想；設想；以為……

◆ Am I supposed to dress up?
我應該盛裝以赴嗎？

◆ Which gate are you supposed to board at?
你該去那個登機門登機呢？

1168

cash
kæʃ
n. 現金

◆ We give a special rebate of 10 percent for payment in cash.
我們給現金付款百分之十的特別折扣。

◆ The cash flow statement is concerned with the flow of cash in and cash out of the business.
現金流的報告是有關一個企業資金收入和支出的流通。

1169

phenomenon
fəˈnɑməˌnɑn
n. 現象；非凡的人事

◆ Gravity is a natural phenomenon.
地心引力是自然的現象。

◆ This phenomenon is not scientifically rational.
這個現象在科學上是不合理的。

1170 ★

realistic
/ˌriəˈlɪstɪk/
adj. 現實的；實際的

◆ We should be realistic about the prospects of our futures.
我們對於未來的願景應該要務實。

◆ My suggestion is that everything must be realistic.
我的建議是每件事必須要現實點。

1171

sphere
/sfɪr/
n. 球體；領域

◆ Most planets are spheres.
大多數行星是球體狀。

◆ Here a brand-new sphere was to open to him
這裡為他開啟了一個全新的領域。

1172

reason
/ˈrizn̩/
n. 理由

◆ The reason she quit is that she is going to get married.
她離職是因為要結婚了。

◆ For many years, he is dedicated in researching the reasons of dinosaurs' extinction.
多年來，他一直專注於研究恐龍絕種的原因。

1173

theory
/ˈθiərɪ/
n. 理論；學理

愛因斯坦相對論

$$E = mc^2$$

◆ Krashen's theory has had a great effect on English instruction.
卡森的理論對英文教學有很大的影響。

◆ It seems good in theory, but it doesn't work in practice.
理論上它似乎很不錯，但實際上卻行不通。

1174 ★

product
/ˈprɑdəkt/
n. 產品；成果；乘積（數學）

NEW

產品

◆ Our computer products will be available in the market next week.
我們的電腦產品在下星期要上市了。

◆ What are the selling points of your product?
你們產品的銷售重點是什麼？

1175 ★

skim
/skɪm/
v. 略讀；瀏覽；去除……

◆ I skimmed all my books before the exam.
我在考試前略讀了所有的書。

◆ You'd better skim the fat from the gravy for those patients.
你最好幫這些病人把肉湯中的油脂去掉。

1176

neglect
/nɪˈglɛkt/
v. 疏忽……；忽略……

◆ He was reprehended for neglecting his duty.
他因為怠忽責任而被譴責。

◆ That's a reason which you should not neglect.
那是一個你不能忽視的理由。

1177 ★

furious
ˈfjʊrɪəs
adj. 盛怒的；極憤怒的

◆ His wife is furious at being kept in the dark.
他的太太對被留在黑暗中大發雷霆。

◆ The man got furious when someone called his sobriquet.
有人叫他的綽號時，這個男子就會非常憤怒。

1178

fare
fɛr
n. 票價；車資

◆ How much is the fare to the subway station?
到地鐵車站要花多少錢？

◆ The air fare to Australia is quite expensive.
到澳洲的航空費用相當昂貴。

1179

immigrant
ˈɪməgrənt
n. 移民（自外國移入）

◆ The children of the immigrants easily assimilated into American culture.
新移民的小孩容易被美國文化同化。

◆ Immigrants from all over the world populate New York City.
來自全世界的移民在紐約市居住。

1180

transplant
træns'plænt
v. 移植（醫學）；移種；使遷移

◆ Doctors transplanted an artificial heart into a patient.
醫生為病人移植一顆人工心臟。

◆ Tomorrow they will transplant some trees to the other garden.
明天他們會把一部分的樹移植到另一個花園去。

1181

awkward
ˈɔkwəd
adj. 笨拙的；尷尬的；不便的

◆ You need to work hard because you are still awkward in performing your job.
你需要更努力，因為這份工作你做得還不夠熟練。

◆ The words he uses in his compositions are very awkward.
他在作文中使用的語法相當不熟練。

1182

stupid
ˈstjupɪd
adj. 笨的；愚蠢的

◆ The child is not smart, but he is not stupid either.
雖然這個小孩子不算聰明，但他也不笨。

◆ All the drunken man did was just stupid act.
那酒醉的男人所做的都只是愚蠢的行為。

1183

cable
ˈkebl̩
n. 粗索；纜索

◆ The truck used a cable to tow the car.
卡車使用粗纜拖這台汽車。

◆ Should I be responsible for the cable fee?
我需要負擔有線電視的費用嗎？

1184

rude
rud
adj. 粗魯無禮的

◆ He always answers others' questions in a very rude tone, and no wonder so many people dislike him.
他老用粗魯的語氣回答別人的問題，也難怪這麼多人討厭他了。

◆ You might at least apologize for your rude manner.
你至少該為你的魯莽行為道歉。

1185

rough
rʌf
adj. 粗糙的；表面不平的；艱難的

◆ The truck drove slowly across the rough ground.
這卡車緩慢地穿越這段崎嶇的道路。

◆ She has a really rough time after her parents die in a car accident.
當她的父母在車禍中喪生後，她的日子確實過得很艱難。

1186

coarse
kors
adj. 粗糙的；粗的；粗魯的

◆ The cowboy wore a coarse, rough coat and rode a mare.
這位牛仔穿著粗糙簡陋的大衣，並且騎一匹母馬。

◆ His coarse manners shocked everyone in the party.
他粗魯的行為嚇壞了宴會上的每個人。

1187

accumulate
əˋkjumjəˏlet
v. 累積……；堆積……

◆ You can stand on the top of the world if you accumulate enough knowledge.
你如果累積到足夠的知識，便能功成名就。

◆ He accumulated an impressive collection of stamps.
他累積了令人印象深刻的郵票收集。

1188 ★

observe
əbˋzɝv
v. 細心看；觀察到

◆ Birdwatchers will travel hundreds of miles to observe rare birds.
鳥類觀察家們即將旅行數百里去觀察稀有的鳥類。

◆ Anthropologists observe people's behavior.
人類學家觀察人類的行為。

1189 ★

bacteria
bækˋtɪrɪə
n. 細菌

◆ Lab scientists have to confront unknown bacteria all the time.
實驗室科學家們必須要一直面對未知的細菌。

◆ Biologists magnify bacteria with a microscope.
生物學家們使用顯微鏡來放大細菌。

1190

germ
dʒɝm
n. 細菌；微生物；幼芽

◆ Germs usually cause disease.
細菌通常會引起疾病。

◆ Wash your hands carefully so you don't get germs on the food.
你仔細洗手才不會把病菌沾在食物上。

1191

detail
ˊditel

n. 細節;詳情

◆ I'd like to discuss a few details over lunch.
有些細節我想在午飯時提出來討論。

◆ He generalizes what he speaks into the important details.
他歸納出他所講的重要細節。

1192 ★

terminal
ˊtɝmənl

adj. 終點的;終端的 **n.** 終點站

◆ Is this the right terminal for NW07?
這裡是西北航空 NW07 號班機的候機處嗎?

◆ After many defeats, the war ended for us in terminal victory.
經過許多失敗,我們以最終的勝利結束它。

1193 ★

statistics
stəˊtɪstɪks

n. 統計學;統計表

◆ Statistics on illness are used in planning health care.
疾病方面的統計學用在健保規劃上。

◆ These statistics show the trend of people's increasing consumption.
這些統計數字顯示民眾的消費增加趨勢。

1194 ★

habit
ˊhæbɪt

n. 習慣;習性

◆ Smoking is a bad habit; you had better try to quit now.
抽菸是一種壞習慣,你最好立刻戒掉。

◆ He cannot get rid of his bad inveterate habits.
他無法去除他根深蒂固的壞習慣。

1195

chat
tʃæt

v. 聊天;與……搭訕

◆ The lady chatted on and on about her rich fiance.
這位女士喋喋不休地談論她有錢的未婚夫。

◆ There are many chat rooms available on the Internet.
網際網路上有許多聊天室。

1196

ship
ʃɪp
n. 船；艦

◆ There is a big ship in the ocean.
海上有一艘大船。

◆ Our ship sails next month for Hong Kong.
我們的船下個月會啟程前往香港。

1197

stem
stɛm
n. 莖；幹(樹)；族系

◆ The thorny stem of a rose stabbed her.
玫瑰有刺的莖刺傷了她。

◆ My uncle dissevered branches from the stem.
我叔叔從樹幹上砍下許多樹枝。

1198

penalty
ˈpɛnḷtɪ
n. 處罰；罰款；刑罰

◆ The penalty for infringing on our patent rights is outlined in this contract.
有關侵犯到我方專利權的處罰，在這份合約中有概略提到。

◆ Some people hope for the abolition of the death penalty.
有些人希望廢除死刑。

1199 ★

protein
ˈprotiɪn
n. 蛋白質 **adj.** 含蛋白質的

◆ The patient needs more protein to build him up .
這個病人需要更多的蛋白質來增強體質。

◆ The fruit contains as much protein as the soya bean.
這種水果有和大豆一樣豐富的蛋白質。

1200

terminology
ˌtɝməˈnɑlədʒɪ
n. 術語；專有名詞

◆ You can find the meanings of terminologies in the glossary.
你能夠在專業詞典中找到這些術語的意義。

◆ Don't punish our brain with medical terminology.
別用醫學術語來讓我們傷腦筋。

1201

equipment
ɪˈkwɪpmənt
n. 設備；裝置

◆ He has great proficiency in fixing all household electrical equipment.
他對修理各種家電用品很在行。

◆ This store mainly sells the swimming equipment.
這家店主要出售游泳設備。

1202 ★

meager
/ˈmigə/
adj. 貧乏的；不足的；微薄的

◆ She could not support her children to study in England on her meager salary.
她無法靠她貧乏的薪水支持她的孩子們去英國念書。
◆ The single mother's present salary is rather meager.
這位單親媽媽目前的薪水相當微薄。

1203

sterile
/ˈstɛrəl/
adj. 貧瘠的；不能生育的

◆ Sterile land doesn't produce good crops.
貧瘠的土地不能生產好的農作物。
◆ His wife knew he was sterile before they got married.
在他們結婚前，他的太太就知道他不能生育。

1204

needy
/ˈnidɪ/
adj. 貧窮的

◆ The needy woman lived in a little wooden hut near the forest.
這位貧窮的女人住在靠近森林的一間小木屋。
◆ There are many needy families in our Chinese community.
我們華人社區有許多貧窮的家庭。

1205

indigent
/ˈɪndədʒənt/
adj. 貧窮的；貧困的

◆ The indigent student spends much time earning money.
這些貧窮學生花了許多時間在賺錢。
◆ People who live in the countryside are not always indigent.
住在鄉下的人們不會總是貧窮的。

1206

corrupt
/kəˈrʌpt/
adj. 貪汙的；不潔的

◆ The corrupt government will be overthrown one day.
這個貪汙的政府有一天會被推翻。
◆ The power makes people corrupt.
權力使人腐敗。

1207

avaricious
/ˌævəˈrɪʃəs/
adj. 貪財的；貪婪的

◆ The wolf is an avaricious animal.
狼是一種貪婪的動物。
◆ The lady is an avaricious person and seldom helps others.
這位女士是個貪婪的人，而且很少幫助別人。

1208

greedy
/ˈgridɪ/
adj. 貪婪的；貪吃的

◆ Everybody in the neighborhood knows that Mr. Wang is a greedy miser.
附近的每個人都知道王老頭是個貪婪的吝嗇鬼。
◆ The old couple were greedy and quarrelsome.
這對老夫婦貪心且喜歡爭吵。

1209

duty
ˈdjutɪ
n. 責任；稅；義務

◆ One of my duties is to file the letters.
我的職責之一是將信件歸檔。

◆ Would you please tell me what things have duties on them?
您可以告訴我哪些物品要納稅嗎？

1210

obligation
ˌɑbləˈgeʃən
n. 責任；義務

◆ You have an obligation to have your child receive a proper education.
讓孩子接受適當的教育是你的義務。

◆ If you had many obligations, you wouldn't be carefree.
假如你有許多責任，你將不會無憂無慮。

1211

responsible
rɪˈspɑnsəbḷ
adj. 責任重大的；負責的

◆ It is now generally acknowledged that Hitler was responsible for Germany's collapse.
現在普遍認為希特勒必須為德國的瓦解負起責任。

◆ The caretaker of the building is trustworthy and responsible.
這棟大樓的管理員是值得信任且負責任的。

1212 ★

upbraid
ʌpˈbred
v. 責罵；訓斥

◆ Mary's boss upbraided her for mistakes she made.
瑪麗的老闆責罵她所犯下的錯誤。

◆ Careless campers were upbraided for starting the forest fires.
粗心的露營者被責備是森林火災的禍首。

1213

forgive
fəˈgɪv
v. 赦免；原諒

◆ She forgives his ignorance and leaves silently.
她原諒了他的無知，並且沈默離去。

◆ She never forgave him for his lies.
她從未原諒他的謊言。

1214

absolve
əbˈsɑlv
v. 赦免……；寬恕……

◆ A political prisoner was absolved from his sins recently.
一位政治犯最近從他的罪狀中被赦免。

◆ Do not expect being absolved if you have already committed a crime.
假如你已經犯罪了，別期待被赦免。

1215

software
ˈsɔftˌwɛr
n. 軟體

◆ I need the setup wizard to help me install this software.
我需要裝置精靈幫我安裝這個軟體。

◆ His computer has a bootlegged copy of Windows software.
他的電腦使用盜版的視窗軟體。

1216 ★

overdraw

ˋovɚˋdrɔ

v. 透支；超支(如銀行帳戶)

◆ It was the first time he had ever overdrawn his account.
這是他第一次透支了他的帳戶。

◆ If you overdraw your bank account, you will be charged a fee.
假如透支銀行帳戶，你將會被收取費用。

1217

---

transparent

trænsˋpærənt

adj. 透明的；明顯的

◆ Frog's eggs are covered in a sort of transparent jelly.
青蛙的蛋是被一種透明的膠質物掩蓋。

◆ Her evil motives were transparent to us all.
對我們來說他的邪惡動機是明顯的。

1218

---

hike

haɪk

v. 途步旅行；急拉；價格提高

◆ I like to hike along the rivers.
我喜歡沿著河流健行。

◆ They enjoy going hiking on weekends.
他們喜歡在週末去健行。

1219

---

ventilation

ˌvɛntlˋeʃən

n. 通風；流通空氣

◆ This is a house with good ventilation.
這是一間通風良好的房子。

◆ They altered the hotel to improve its ventilation.
他們改裝旅館來改善通風設備。

1220

---

inflation

ɪnˋfleʃən

n. 通貨膨脹；脹大

◆ There is high inflation over price that rises for the commodities.
通貨膨脹嚴重，商品價格暴漲。

◆ Nowadays, inflation is under control.
現今通貨膨脹在控制中。

1221 ★

---

passage

ˋpæsɪdʒ

n. 通過；通行；段落

◆ The street is too narrow to allow the passage of a truck.
這街道太窄以至於無法讓卡車通行。

◆ You can get more details about computer memory in this passage.
你可以從這一段知道更多有關電腦記憶體的細節。

1222

---

speed

spid

n. 速度

◆ I was fined for speeding.
我因為超速被罰錢。

◆ The speed limit on this highway is 65 mph.
這條公路的速限是六十五英哩。

1223

velocity
vəˈlɑsətɪ
n. 速度；迅速

◆ The velocity of light can reach about 186,000 miles per second.
光速每秒鐘可達十萬八千六百英哩。

◆ Leopards can move with astonishing velocity.
美洲豹跑起來速度驚人。

1224

shorthand
ˈʃɔrt.hænd
n. 速記

油漆式速記法

◆ Being a stenographer, you must be good at taking notes in shorthand.
成為一個速記員，你必需精通用速記作筆記。

◆ The secretary took his speech down in shorthand.
這位祕書將他的演講速記下來。

1225

slander
ˈslændə
v. 造謠……；誹謗……

跟你說...

◆ The radio program slandered the politician by saying he committed corruption.
這廣播節目造謠說這位政治人物貪汙。

◆ She was fired because she liked to spread slanders in her company.
她被開除是因為她喜歡在公司散布造謠。

1226

uproot
ʌpˈrut
v. 連根拔起

連根拔起

◆ It will take an hour to uproot the tree.
將這棵樹連根拔起要花上一小時。

◆ Many people are uprooted from their home by the drought.
許多人因為這場乾旱而離開家園。

1227

link
lɪŋk
v. 連接……

◆ Workers linked the railroad carts together.
工人們把這些火車連結在一起。

◆ It is hard to realize how these events link to one another.
很難確認這些事件有彼此連結的關係。

1228

sequence
ˈsikwəns
n. 連續；排列；數列

◆ I can't remember the sequence of events.
我不能記住這些事件的順序。

◆ The popular ballet dancer made a sequence of dance movements.
這位受歡迎的芭蕾舞蹈家設計了連續的舞步。

1229

continuous
kənˈtɪnjʊəs
adj. 連續不間斷的

◆ We have stayed home for two days because of the continuous rain.
由於陰雨不斷，我們留在家裡二天。

◆ Continuous loud noise will gradually do harm to our hearing.
持續大聲的噪音會逐漸對我們的聽力造成損害。

1230 ★

consecutive
kənˈsɛkjətɪv
adj. 連續的;連貫的

◆ This is the second consecutive weekend that I've spent time on work.
這是第二個連續週末我把時間花在工作上。

◆ It has rained for three consecutive days.
這場雨連續下了三天了。

1231 ★

section
ˈsɛkʃən
n. 部分;區域;(街道)段

◆ I don't like the band's percussion section because it is too loud.
我不喜歡這樂團打擊樂的部分,因為太大聲了。

◆ Where can I find the produce section?
請問蔬果部在哪裡?

1232 ★

savage
ˈsævɪdʒ
adj. 野蠻的;兇暴的;猛烈的

◆ Tigers are barbarous and savage by nature.
老虎天生就是殘忍與兇暴的。

◆ The movie star was irritated by his savage attack recently.
這位電影明星被他最近猛烈的攻擊給激怒了。

1233

accompany
əˈkʌmpənɪ
v. 陪伴……;跟隨……

◆ You always accompany me during my hardest time.
在我最艱難的時刻,你總是陪著我。

◆ He accompanied me to the banquet.
他陪我參加晚宴。

1234

shade
ʃed
n. 陰暗;遮蔽…… *v.* 使陰暗

◆ We plan to sit in the shade of a large olive tree from sunburn.
我們打算坐在一棵大橄欖樹的樹蔭下以免曬傷。

◆ The beautiful woman's glamour throws other ladies into the shade.
這位美女的魅力讓其它女士黯然失色。

1235

shadow
ˈʃædo
n. 陰影;影子

◆ We have the shortest shadows at the noon.
我們在正午時分的影子最短。

◆ The shadow of death is on the patient's face.
死亡的陰影籠罩在病人的臉上。

1236

conspiracy
kənˈspɪrəsɪ
n. 陰謀;共謀

◆ He was part of a conspiracy to steal confidential documents from the company.
他密謀從公司竊取機密文件。

◆ Their conspiracy was brought to light finally.
最後他們的陰謀被揭露了。

1237

ware
wɛr
n. 陶器；物品；
器物

◆ The shop sells a great variety of wares.
這家商店販售各種的瓷器。

◆ This museum is famous for Chinese jade ware.
這個博物館以中國玉器聞名。

1238

trap
træp
n. 陷阱；圈套

◆ Hopefully, the kidnappers will fall right into our traps.
但願綁匪能正中我們的圈套。

◆ The kid gave a snicker when his trap worked out.
當這孩子的陷阱發揮作用時，他偷笑了一下。

1239

zenith
ˈzinɪθ
n. 頂點

◆ The mountain zenith was covered with snow.
這山頂覆蓋著積雪。

◆ Opera reached its zenith at the turn of the century.
歌劇在世紀之交達到高峰。

1240

trouble
ˈtrʌbl
n. 麻煩；煩惱

◆ My friends always help me when I get into trouble.
我的朋友在我有麻煩時，總是會幫助我。

◆ You should try to stay out of trouble.
你應該試著避免讓自己陷入麻煩。

1241

anaesthetic
ˌænəsˈθɛtɪk
n. 麻醉劑

◆ The effect of anaesthetic is to paralyze the patients' nerves during the operation.
麻醉劑的效果是在手術過程中麻痺病人的神經。

◆ Anesthetic must be used carefully for the patient.
對病人要小心使用麻醉劑。

1242

outstanding
aʊtˈstændɪŋ
adj. 傑出的；出
眾的

◆ His outstanding performance made his parents proud.
他傑出的表現讓他的雙親感到驕傲。

◆ The outstanding pianist always performed in diapason.
這位傑出的鋼琴家經常以全音域演奏。

1243 ★

create
krɪˈet
v. 創造……；產
生……

◆ God created heaven and earth.
上帝創造天堂與地球。

◆ This activity was created to teach students about respecting each other.
創造這個活動的目的是為了教導學生如何互相尊重。

1244

innovation
ˌɪnəˋveʃən

n. 創新；革新

◆ The innovation of transportation saves us a lot of time.
運輸工具的革新節省了我們許多時間。

◆ Anesthesia was a great innovation in medicine.
麻醉是醫學上重大的創新。

1245 ★

victory
ˋvɪktərɪ

n. 勝利；戰勝

◆ All of us are excited for his victory.
我們都為他的勝利感到興奮。

◆ The DDP won the overwhelming victories for the parliament election.
民進黨在國會選舉時贏得壓倒性的勝利。

1246

surpass
səˋpæs

v. 勝過……；超過……；凌駕

◆ You seem to surpass yourself in this race.
你似乎在這場賽跑中超越自己。

◆ The new actress's excellent performance has surpassed everyone's expectations.
這位新秀女演員的精湛表演出乎所有人意料之外。

1247

throat
θrot

n. 喉嚨

◆ It's said that salted water can cure a sore throat.
據說含鹽的水能治療喉嚨痛。

◆ I couldn't get that big chunk of meat down my throat.
我不能把這一大塊的肉吞下喉嚨。

1248

yell
jɛl

v. 喊叫……

◆ You could see he was full of malediction when he yelled at us.
當他對著我們大叫時，你可以看到他充滿了憎恨。

◆ I yelled to my friend and ran home yesterday。
昨天我對我朋友大叫一聲並跑回家。

1249

awake
əˋwek

v. 喚起；使覺醒

◆ Nothing can awake his interest in sports.
他對任何運動都提不起興趣。

◆ My grandfather lay awake all night and recalled the events of the past.
我爺爺整晚清醒地躺著，想起了許多往事。

1250

arouse
əˋrauz

v. 喚醒；喚起

◆ It took me some time to arouse my kid in the morning.
早上我花了一會才把孩子叫醒。

◆ Your bad behavior aroused our indignation.
你的惡行激起了我們的義憤。

1251

drink
drɪŋk
v. 喝…… *n.* 飲料

◆ You need to drink more water and take a rest.
你需要多喝水及休息。

◆ We sell only soft drinks to the underage.
我們只販售不含酒精的飲料給未成年者。

1252

solitary
ˈsɑləˌtɛrɪ
adj. 單獨的；唯一的

◆ Some animals are gregarious, but some tend to be solitary.
一些動物是群居的，但是有些則傾向離群獨居。

◆ The killer was placed in solitary confinement.
這個殺手被單獨監禁。

1253

single
ˈsɪŋɡl
adj. 單獨的；單一的

◆ Do you have a single room available for tonight?
你們今晚有單人房嗎？

◆ I am an advocate of single payer health care.
我是單一付款人醫療保健的提倡者。

1254

enclose
ɪnˈkloz
v. 圍住……；圈起……；隨函附寄

◆ She reminds me to enclose this check in it.
她提醒我要隨函附寄這張支票。

◆ The specification of the project has been enclosed herewith.
隨函附上這個計劃的詳細說明。

1255

besiege
bɪˈsidʒ
v. 圍攻；包圍

◆ The mayor was besieged by the press.
這位市長被媒體圍攻。

◆ The insurgent troops besieged the city.
這些暴動的軍隊包圍了這座城市。

1256

avenge
əˈvɛndʒ
v. 報仇；復仇

◆ She avenged the wrong that she suffered.
她為她所遭受的痛苦展開報復。

◆ In order to avenge himself, he killed all his enemies.
為了替自己報仇，他殺光了所有敵人。

1257

retaliate
rɪˈtælɪˌet
v. 報復……；復仇……

◆ The kidnappers retaliated by killing three hostages.
這些劫匪靠殺了人質來報復。

◆ The Afghanistan terrorists retaliated against the U.S. government with poisonous white powder.
阿富汗恐怖分子用有毒的白色粉末報復美國政府。

1258

reward
ri'wɔrd
n. 報酬；報答

◆ The company offered a reward to the indulgent employees who reached high efficiency.
公司給績效良好的員工獎勵。

◆ I think it is very rewarding to be a policeman.
我認為當警察是很值得的。

1259 ★

quote
kwot
v. 報價；引用……的話；舉例說明

◆ Were you able to quote all the items we need？
我們要的所有項目你都能報價嗎？

◆ The professor loves to quote Dickinson's verses in his class.
這位教授喜歡在課堂上引用狄金生的詩句。

1260

media
'midɪə
n. 媒介
（medium 的複數）

◆ Sometimes media is the bridge of communication between people and the government.
媒體有時是人民與政府之間的溝通橋樑。

◆ The wedding of century got massive media coverage.
這場世紀婚禮受到媒體廣泛報導。

1261 ★

affluent
'æflʊənt
adj. 富裕的；豐富的

◆ If a country is affluent in natural resources, it has a better condition to develop its industry.
如果一個國家資源豐富，會有較好條件可發展工業。

◆ Most affluent people live in this building.
大多數富裕的人士住在這棟大樓。

1262

respect
ri'spɛkt
v. 尊重……；敬重…… **n.** 尊敬

◆ Which teacher did you respect most during your college life?
在大學裡，你最尊敬哪一位老師？

◆ They bowed to their teacher in token of respect for him.
他們向老師鞠躬，表示對他的尊敬。

1263 ★

天下無難事，只怕有心人

---

seek
sik
v. 尋求；尋覓

◆ A judge seeks justice for everyone.
法官替每個人伸張正義。

◆ The homeless dogs are seeking a shelter from rain.
流浪狗正在找可以避雨的遮蓋物。

1264

---

nearly
'nɪrlɪ
adv. 幾乎；差不多

◆ The smoke nearly suffocated me.
這煙味差點讓我窒息。

◆ We have lived next door to each other for nearly ten years.
我們當鄰居幾乎快十年了。

1265

---

scarcely
'skɛrslɪ
adv. 幾乎不；幾乎沒有

太硬，幾乎咬不動

◆ This meat is so tough that the old man can scarcely chew it.
這塊肉太硬，所以這位老人幾乎咬不動。

◆ The young man could scarcely keep in his anger.
這位年輕人幾乎控制不住他的憤怒。

1266

---

hardly
'hɑrdlɪ
adv. 幾乎不；簡直不

我幾乎走
不動了！

◆ The car can hardly move in rush hour.
車子在巔峰時刻幾乎沒辦法移動。

◆ The aircraft can hardly land in the wide sea without a carrier.
若無航空母艦，飛機幾乎不可能在大海中著陸。

1267

---

circulation
ˌsɝkjə'leʃən
n. 循環（血液）；發行量；流通

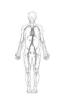

◆ Bad circulation of blood can cause a lot of sickness.
血液循環不良會引起許多疾病。

◆ The economic periodical has a national circulation.
這份經濟期刊有全國性的發行量。

1268 ★

---

sorrow
'sɑro
n. 悲痛；可悲之事

◆ Don't immerse too much in sorrow.
不要過度沉浸於悲傷之中。

◆ He expressed his sorrow at my mother's death.
他對我母親辭世表達悲痛之意。

1269

grief
grif

n. 悲傷；傷心的原因

◆ The widow is crying with grief for the loss of her husband.
這位寡婦因為失去了丈夫而正悲傷地哭泣。

◆ They were overwhelmed by grief when their daughter died.
當他們女兒過世時，他們悲痛不已。

1270

pessimistic
/ˌpɛsəˈmɪstɪk/

adj. 悲觀的

天快要塌下來了！

◆ He has been a pessimistic and negative person since he was a child.
他從小就是一個悲觀消極的人。

◆ Frustration predisposes him to be pessimistic.
挫折讓他傾向於悲觀。

1271 ★

notorious
/noˈtorɪəs/

adj. 惡名昭彰的

匿名告發

◆ The restaurant is notorious for its bad sanitation.
這家餐廳因為衛生不好而惡名昭彰。

◆ He wrote an anonymous letter to prosecute the notorious candidate.
他寫了一封匿名信來告發這位惡名昭彰的候選人。

1272

nasty
/ˈnæstɪ/

adj. 惡臭的；令人作嘔的

◆ There is a very nasty smell in the kitchen.
廚房有令人作嘔的味道。

◆ No one could stand the nasty river any more.
沒人能再忍受這條惡臭的河流。

1273

reign
ren

v. 掌握權力 *n.* 權勢；統治期間

統治50年

◆ Louis XIV reigned in France for over 70 years.
路易十四統治法國逾七十年。

◆ The king's reign lasted fifty years.
這國王的統治期間長達五十年。

1274

describe
/drˈskraɪb/

v. 描述……；敘述……

◆ Theoretical physicists like to use mathematics to describe certain aspects of Nature.
理論物理學家喜歡使用數學來描述自然界外觀。

◆ How would a friend describe you?
你的朋友都怎麼形容你？

1275 ★

submit
/səbˈmɪt/

v. 提交……；呈遞……；使服從

◆ The manager submitted his resignation to the board.
經理提交他的辭呈給董事會。

◆ I will not submit to your bullying and threatening.
我不會屈服在你的欺凌與威脅之下。

1276 ★

beforehand
bɪˈforˌhænd
adv. 提早地；預先地

提早起床做準備...

◆ In public speaking it is natural to feel nervous beforehand.
公開演講前會覺得緊張是很自然的。

◆ I am going to get everything ready beforehand.
我將會事先準備好每件事情。

1277

afford
əˈford
v. 提供；負擔起；買得起

◆ The girl was so penurious that she couldn't afford to pay the tuition.
這個女孩窮困到無法負擔學費。

◆ Helping others affords me happiness.
幫助別人帶給我快樂。

1278 ★

render
ˈrɛndɚ
v. 提供；給予；供給

投入50億美金
援助

◆ We are going to render these countries economic assistance.
我們將提供這些國家經濟援助。

◆ He is the man who renders good for evil.
他是一個以德報怨的人。

1279

safeguard
ˈsefˌgard
v. 提供……保護
n. 安全設施；護衛者

保管箱

◆ The program is developed for safeguarding the computer system against viruses.
這種程式的發展是用來保護電腦免於受病毒感染。

◆ The safeguard managed to purloin the money from the coffer.
警衛打算從箱櫃裡偷錢。

1280

offer
ˈɔfɚ
v. 提供給；表現出

最佳員工

◆ The company offered an annual premium to employers for their hard work.
這間公司提供每年的紅利給工作努力的員工。

◆ If the goods offer an excess of supply over demand, its price may be decreased.
如果貨物供過於求，價格可能會下跌。

1281

advocate
ˈædvəkɪt
v. 提倡……；主張…… **n.** 提倡者

世界和平

◆ We are advocates of women's rights.
我們是女權運動的提倡者。

◆ He strongly advocates world peace.
他強烈主張世界和平。

1282 ★

proposal
prəˈpozḷ
n. 提案；計劃；求婚

◆ He will not change his mind and accept our proposal.
他不會改變他的想法來接受我們的提議。

◆ Only a small minority of this group voted against the proposal.
只有這個團體的少數成員反對這項提案。

1283 ★

raise
rez
v. 提高；抬起；
養育……

拿起酒杯

◆ We have no plans to raise the salary at present.
我們目前沒有調薪方案。

◆ The chicks are raised in the yard.
小雞飼養在後院中。

1284

withdrawal
wɪðˈdrɔəl
n. 提款；撤回；
撤退

◆ Please fill out a withdrawal order.
請填寫提款單。

◆ U.S. troops have made a strategic withdrawal to regroup.
美軍戰略性撤退以重新整軍。

1285 ★

remind
rɪˈmaɪnd
v. 提醒；使想起

◆ Would you like my secretary to remind you？
你願意讓我的祕書來提醒你嗎？

◆ The song reminded me of my ex-boyfriend.
這首歌讓我想起前任男朋友。

1286

insert
ɪnˈsɝt
v. 插入……；嵌
入；添加……

◆ He inserted the crystal into the necklace.
他把水晶嵌入項鍊中。

◆ Could you insert my article into your periodical?
你能把我的文章加入你的期刊中嗎？

1287

plug
plʌg
n. 插頭；塞子
v. 把……塞住

◆ I put the plug into the socket for an electric light bulb.
我把插頭放入電燈泡的插座中。

◆ He hammered a wooden plug into the opening of the wine barrel.
他把一個木製的栓子釘進酒桶的桶口。

1288

save
sev
v. 援救；省下；
儲蓄

◆ The master tried to save the brindled cat away from the road.
主人試圖從路上救出斑紋貓。

◆ The lawyer presents a complete proof to save the innocent person.
律師提出完整的證據來營救這位無辜的人。

1289

rescue
ˈrɛskju
v. 援救……**n.** 營
救

◆ He rescued a cat in the middle of the road.
他在馬路中間救了一隻貓。

◆ The mayor praised the rescue team for their courage.
市長讚揚救難隊的勇氣。

1290

emit
ɪˈmɪt

v. 散發……；放射出……；發出聲音

◆ She emitted one shrill cry and then escaped.
她發出一聲尖叫，並且逃走了。

◆ The moon is emitting light through heavy clouds.
月亮在重重雲層中散發出光線。

1291

scatter
ˈskætɚ

v. 散播；散布

◆ She was told not to scatter this secret all over.
她被告知不要到處散播這個祕密。

◆ The old rich man hopes to be cremated and scattered from a plane into the sea.
這年老的有錢人希望被火化與從飛機上撒入海中。

1292

spot
spɑt

n. 斑點；場所；地點

◆ It'll be hard to remove the spot from the cloth.
很難把這衣服上的汙點去除。

◆ The policeman caught him on the spot.
警察當場逮到他。

1293

general
ˈdʒɛnərəl

adj. 普遍的；大概的 **n.** 將軍

◆ In general, everyone has the freedom of speech.
一般說來，每個人都有言論的自由。

◆ The general hospital has recently bought some medical apparatus.
這家綜合醫院最近買了一些醫學器材。

1294

sight
saɪt

n. 景色；視覺
v. 看見……

◆ This is my first time visiting New York. Could you recommend some sights?
這是我第一次參觀紐約。你能推薦一些風景名勝嗎？

◆ A large python was sighted near the river yesterday.
昨天有人在河邊看到一條巨蟒。

1295

view
vju

n. 景觀；視野

◆ Do you have a room with a nice view?
你們有好景觀的房間嗎？

◆ Could you tell me what your views on work are?
能談談你對工作的看法嗎？

1296

wisdom
ˈwɪzdəm

n. 智慧

別小看猴子的智慧

◆ We are waiting for the fortuneteller to utter words of wisdom.
我們正等著算命師發表充滿智慧的言論。

◆ I hope you can perceive god's wisdom.
我希望你能領悟上帝的智慧。

1297

maximum
ˈmæksəməm

n. 最大量；極大值；最高限度

◆ The maximum potential of human beings is beyond all imagination.
人類潛力的極限是無法想像的。

◆ If you drive over the maximum, you will get the fine.
開車超過最大速限，就會被處罰款。

1298 ★

minimum
ˈmɪnəməm

n. 最低限度；最小量

◆ Are you sure that a minimum order won't deter customers from purchasing?
你確定最低訂貨量不會阻礙消費者購買嗎？

◆ We need a minimum of 15 people to act this play.
我們需要至少十五人來演這齣戲。

1299 ★

initial
ɪˈnɪʃəl

adj. 最初的 **n.** 起首的字母

◆ The maple is deciduous near the initial winter.
楓樹接近初冬時會落葉。

◆ The incumbent was declared the winner from initial poll results.
從最初的投票結果，現任者得到獲勝。

1300 ★

favorite
ˈfevərɪt

adj. 最喜愛的；特別喜愛的人（物）

◆ There is a bust of my favorite singer on my desk.
我的桌上有一個我最喜愛歌手的半身像。

◆ April and August are my favorite months.
四月和八月是我最喜歡的兩個月份。

1301

term
tɝm

n. 期限；學期；術語

◆ Are there any exams at the end of this term?
這個學期有期末考嗎？

◆ He is about to begin his term as President.
他即將開始他的總統任期。

1302

expiration
ˌɛkspəˈreʃən

n. 期限截止；呼氣作用

◆ What was the expiration date of your passport?
你的護照什麼時候到期？

◆ Preservatives are added to some foods to extend their expiration date.
有些食物會添加防腐劑以延長保存期限。

1303 ★

prospect
ˈprɑspɛkt

n. 期望；展望；可能性

◆ There are good prospects for growth in the retail sector.
在零售部分會有很好的成長展望。

◆ He looks forward to the prospect of working at his favorite company.
他期待著有可能到他喜歡的公司上班。

1304 ★

futures
ˈfjutʃəz
n. 期貨

◆ Stock futures offer high leverage.
股票期貨提供了高槓桿操作。

◆ He continued his operations in stock futures.
他繼續進行他的股票期貨交易。

1305

forward market
ˈfɔrwəd ˌmɑrkɪt
n. 期貨市場

◆ How to invest in the forward market?
如何投資期貨市場？

◆ The forward market is facing a dramatic risk now.
這個期貨正面臨激烈的風險。

1306

plant
plænt
n. 植物 **v.** 種植

◆ He tried to plant cherry trees in Taiwan.
他試著在台灣栽種櫻桃樹。

◆ The plant has broad leaves with a reticulated vein structure.
這種植物有網狀葉脈結構的闊葉。

1307

bully
ˈbʊlɪ
v. 欺負(弱小)；恐嚇

◆ The little boy is always bullied by his neighbors.
這個小孩總是被他的鄰居欺負。

◆ Don't bully your sister! You have to take care of her well.
不要欺負你妹妹！你得要好好照顧她。

1308

cheat
tʃit
v. 欺騙；作弊

考試中...

◆ The student was punished for cheating on the exam.
那名學生因為考試作弊而受處罰。

◆ It is an improper act to cheat on tests.
考試作弊是不當的行為。

1309

fraud
frɔd
n. 欺騙；欺詐行為

◆ The man was found guilty of fraud.
這男人被發現犯了詐欺罪。

◆ The government fully investigated nefarious activities such as drug trafficking and fraud.
政府全力徹查邪惡的活動，如毒品走私及詐騙。

1310 ★

beguile
bɪˈgaɪl
v. 欺騙⋯⋯；迷惑⋯⋯

跟我走
壞人

◆ The salesman beguiled me into buying a fake.
這個業務人員騙我買了一個假貨。

◆ The candidate beguiled the voters with his good looks and grand talk.
這個候選人以英俊外表和流利口才迷惑選民。

1311

admire
əd'maɪr
v. 欽佩；讚美

◆ I admire him for his smooth talking.
我欽佩他的能言善道。

◆ The integrity of the judge is admired.
這位法官的正直是受到稱讚的。

1312 ★

hospitality
͵hɑspɪ'tælətɪ
n. 款待；好客

◆ The local people showed us great hospitality.
本地人民對我們非常好客。

◆ His hospitality left us a very good impression.
他的好客給我們非常好的印象。

1313

settlement
'sɛtḷmənt
n. 殖民地；和解；解決

台灣日治時期
1895~1945

◆ Great Japanese Empire had many settlements.
大日本帝國有許多殖民地。

◆ Two companies eventually reach an amicable settlement that was acceptable to both sides
兩家公司終於達成雙方都能接受的友好和解。

1314

debris
də'bri
n. 殘骸

◆ After the explosion, there was a lot of debris everywhere.
爆炸之後，到處都有許多殘骸。

◆ The soldier was buried beneath the debris.
這個士兵被埋在瓦礫下面。

1315

decrease
dɪ'kris
v. 減少

◆ The population of our city has gradually decreased.
我們城市的人口逐漸減少。

◆ Energy resources will continue to decrease if you don't start to conserve energy.
能源會持續的減少，如果我們不開始保留能源。

1316 ★

diminish
də'mɪnɪʃ
v. 減低；縮小(規模)

綠樹愈來愈少

◆ Relaxed life diminishes his morale.
悠閒的生活降低了他的士氣。

◆ The beauty of Antarctic glaciers is diminishing because of the changing global environment.
因為全球自然環境的改變，南極冰河的美景正在減少。

1317 ★

abate
ə'bet
v. 減退……；減少……；平息

請減低噪音

◆ No matter what his parents did for him, nothing could abate his rage.
不論他的父母為他做什麼，都無法平息他的憤怒。

◆ We must abate the noise in the neighborhood.
我們必須要降低鄰近地區的噪音。

1318

deduct
dɪ'dʌkt
v. 減除；扣除

◆ The firm deducts taxes from our wages.
公司從我們的薪水中扣稅。

◆ Could you deduct my rent from the deposit?
你能夠從押金中扣除我的房租嗎？

1319

slowdown
'slo.daun
n. 減速；怠工；攤牌

◆ The government tries to solve the question of economic slowdown this year.
政府嘗試去解決今年經濟下滑的問題。

◆ There has been a slowdown in the international trade this year.
這一年的國際貿易出現衰退。

1320

ferry
'fɛrɪ
n. 渡口；渡輪
v. 載運（船）

◆ The boat ferried the smuggled goods from the ships to the island.
這艘船從輪船載運走私品到島上。

◆ They need to pay the ferry charges.
他們需要付這渡輪的費用。

1321

wade
wed
v. 渡水；涉水

◆ The hunter waded across the shallow river.
這位獵人涉水穿越這條淺的河流。

◆ The adventurers climbed the mountains and waded across streams.
冒險家們爬過高山涉過溪流。

1322

workout
'wɝk.aut
n. 測驗；練習；訓練

◆ We often go to a gym for a workout.
我們經常到體育館練習。

◆ It is a good workout for your legs to walk up an incline.
在斜坡往上走對你的腳是個好的訓練。

1323

harbor
'hɑrbɚ
n. 港灣；避難所
v. 收容庇護

◆ During the typhoon the ships stayed in the harbor.
颱風期間船隻們停放在港中。

◆ The Statue of Liberty stands in New York Harbor.
自由女神像矗立在紐約港。

1324

desire
dɪ'zaɪr
v. n. 渴望……；想要……

◆ I've desired a new computer for a long time.
我渴望擁有一台新電腦很久了。

◆ The monk or nun are prohibited from giving in to carnal desires when they embrace Buddhism.
和尚或尼姑信奉佛教後，要禁絕世俗慾望。

1325 ★

futile

'fjutl̩

adj. 無用的；無效的；不重要的

◆ He tries to find the solution to the problem, but his efforts were futile.
他試圖找出問題的解決方式，但都徒勞無功。

◆ I am sure that resistance was futile.
我很確定反抗是徒勞無功的。

1326

inconceivable

ˌɪnkənˈsivəbl̩

adj. 無法想像的

◆ That car accident was inconceivable to us.
那場車禍是我們想像不到的。

◆ For a teenager to do that job is just inconceivable.
對一個青少年做那樣的工作是難以想像的。

1327

ignorant

'ɪgnərənt

adj. 無知識的；不知情的

◆ The moron is ignorant of even the most elementary facts.
這個傻瓜連最基本的事實都不知道。

◆ No one is ignorant of my name and address.
沒有一個人知道我的姓名與住址。

1328 ★

infinite

'ɪnfənɪt

adj. 無限的；極大的

◆ Each person has infinite potentials.
人人都有無窮潛力。

◆ The moor is filled with infinite desolation.
沼澤中滿是無限的荒蕪。

1329 ★

incompetent

ɪnˈkɑmpətənt

adj. 無能力的；無法勝任的

◆ He is incompetent as a manager of the computer company.
他無法勝任這家電腦公司的經理。

◆ It is obvious that the new programmer is incompetent.
這個新程式設計師很明顯無法勝任。

1330

不積小流，無以成江海

---

hopeless
ˋhoplɪs
adj. 無望的；絕望的

今年冠軍！
無望了！

◆ The hopeless man has no illusion about his future.
無助的男子對未來沒有幻想。

◆ The refugees feel hopeless about their future.
這些難民對未來感到無望。

1331

---

unquestionably
ʌnˋkwɛstʃənəblɪ
adv. 無疑地

我無疑地會愛你一輩子！

◆ She is unquestionably the best player in our team.
她無疑是我們隊伍中最好的選手。

◆ I believe that your goal can unquestionably be attained.
我相信你的目標無疑地能達成。

1332

---

vapid
ˋvæpɪd
adj. 無趣味的；平庸的；無生氣的

◆ The keynote of his speech was vapid yesterday.
昨天他演講的主題非常索然無味。

◆ She made a vapid comment about the politics.
她對政治做了一番乏味的評論。

1333

---

anguish
ˋæŋgwɪʃ
n. 痛苦；苦惱
v. 感到痛苦

?!?

◆ The difficult math question brings me great anguish.
這個困難的數學題目讓我很苦惱。

◆ She was in anguish over her failure.
她因為失敗而痛苦。

1334

---

ordeal
ɔrˋdil
n. 痛苦考驗；苦難

◆ The chemical treatment for cancer was a long, hard ordeal for her.
癌症的化學治療對她是一種長期與艱難的考驗。

◆ You must hang together through this ordeal.
你們必須團結才能通過這場考驗。

1335

---

enroll
ɪnˋrol
v. 登記……；使……成為會員；使入學

請登記姓名

◆ You will not be allowed to enter the building without enrolling your name.
你沒有登記姓名就不能進入這棟建築物。

◆ I am excited to enroll in the new exercise class.
我興奮地參加這個新的運動課程。

1336 ★

boarding pass
'bɔrdɪŋ pæs
ph. 登機證

◆ Here are your boarding pass and ticket with your baggage claim tag.
這是您的登機證、機票和行李提領單

◆ Please give your boarding pass and check in for Seattle at the transfer counter.
請到轉機櫃台拿往西雅圖的登機證並且報到。

1337

occur
ə'kɝ
v. 發生……；想到……

◆ It suddenly occurred to me that I have an important appointment tonight.
我突然想到晚上有一個很重要的約會。

◆ The expert said a second equinox occurs each year on September 22 or 23.
專家說每年的秋分在 9 月 22 或 23 日。

1338 ★

contrive
kən'traɪv
v. 發明……；設計……

◆ The man contrives a new kind of engine.
這位男人發明了一種新引擎。

◆ John had contrived a new tool for his factory.
約翰為他的工廠發明了一項新工具。

1339

invent
ɪn'vɛnt
v. 發明……；創造……

◆ Indians invented badminton during the period of colonization.
羽毛球是在殖民時期由印度人所發明。

◆ When were the computers invented?
電腦是什麼時候發明的？

1340

wreak
rik
v. 發洩出；施加……報復

◆ She always wreaks her bad temper on her husband.
她總把脾氣發洩在她的丈夫身上。

◆ She will wreak a terrible vengeance on her love rival.
她將對她的情敵施加可怕的報復。

1341

shoot
ʃut
v. 發射；開（槍）

◆ Shooting off crackers can be very precarious.
放鞭炮是非常危險的。

◆ The shooting was in pure self-defense.
開槍純粹是為了自衛。

1342

launch
lɔntʃ
v. 發射；新船下水；開始從事

◆ A new ship was launched from the shore.
這艘新船從岸邊下水。

◆ After a long period of preparation, they decided to launch the project.
經過一段長期的準備，他們決定要開始這個計劃。

1343

detect
dɪˈtɛkt
v. 發現……；查出……

◆ This police officer's job is to detect crime.
警察的工作是偵查犯罪。

◆ She detected her boyfriend's happiness in his voice.
她從男友的聲音中發現他的快樂。

1344 ★

discover
dɪˈskʌvə
v. 發現出；找到

◆ I've discovered a great restaurant nearby.
我在附近發現了一間很棒的餐廳。

◆ The man was surprised to discover how much the fine was.
這個人吃驚地發現罰金要花那麼多錢。

1345 ★

electric
ɪˈlɛktrɪk
adj. 發電的；帶電的

◆ Where did you buy these electric rice cookers?
你去哪裡買這些電鍋？

◆ My father will buy an electric heater because the winter is coming.
因為冬天近了，所以我爸爸要買台電暖爐。

1346

shortage
ˈʃɔrtɪdʒ
n. 短缺；不足

◆ Drought caused the water shortages in the summer.
旱災使夏天用水不足。

◆ A shortage of oil made gasoline more expensive.
石油短缺造成汽油更貴了。

1347 ★

scarce
skɛrs
adj. 稀有的；難得的

◆ Food and fuel were scarce throughout the war.
戰爭期間食物與燃料都缺乏。

◆ These flowers are very scarce in this country.
這些花卉在這些國家很稀有。

1348

revenue
ˈrɛvəˌnju
n. 稅收；總收入

政府稅收

◆ We must pay the taxes because they are one of the most important sources of the revenue.
我們必須繳稅，因為稅金是國家歲入最重要的來源之一。

◆ The lottery in Taiwan provides part of the government's revenue.
台灣的樂透彩券提供政府部分的稅收。

1349 ★

degree
dɪˈgri
n. 程度；等級；學位

◆ He has just got his M.A. degree.
他剛拿到文學碩士學位。

◆ This apparatus can offer a high degree of accuracy.
儀器裝備能提供高準確度。

1350

straightforward
.stret'fɔrwəd

adj. 筆直的；誠實的；正直的

◆ We took a straightforward route to the forest.
我們選了一條筆直通往森林的道路。

◆ He offered a straightforward apology to her for hurting her feelings.
他為了傷害了她的感情而坦白向她道歉。

1351

script
skrɪpt

n. 筆跡；腳本

◆ The invitation was written in her beautiful script.
這份邀請是用她優美的筆跡寫成。

◆ It is hard to interpret the meaning of those cursive scripts.
很難了解那些草寫手抄本的意思。

1352

equal
'ikwəl

v. 等於 **adj.** 相等的

◆ Five plus four equals nine.
五加四等於九。

◆ Twenty-nine minus sixteen equals thirteen.
二十九減去十六等於十三。

1353

equivalent
ɪ'kwɪvələnt

adj. 等值的；相等的

◆ A thousand grams are equivalent to one kilogram.
一千公克相當於一公斤。

◆ A dime is the equivalent to two nickels.
一角硬幣等於兩個五分硬幣。

1354 ★

grant
grænt

v. 答應……；授與…… **n.** 補助款

◆ My boss granted me extra time to finish the task before the deadline.
我的老闆答應在期限之前多給我些時間完成它。

◆ Many companies in Taiwan grant their old employees annuities after they retire.
台灣許多公司承諾資深員工退休後會發養老金。

1355

respond
rɪs'pɑnd

v. 答覆；回答

◆ She did not respond to my letter.
她沒有回我的信。

◆ Eager responses from the audience amplified the speaker's confidence.
聽眾熱烈回應讓演講者充滿信心。

1356

tactic
'tæktɪk

n. 策略；戰術

◆ Napoleon was an expert in military tactics because he always won his battles.
拿破倫是軍事戰術的專家，因為他總是贏得他的戰爭。

◆ The new tactic will be put into operation next year.
這個新策略下個年度要開始運作。

1357

ultraviolet
/ˌʌltrəˈvaɪəlɪt/
adj. 紫外線的

◆ Ultraviolet radiation from the sun can cause skin cancer.
太陽的紫外線幅射會引起皮膚癌。

◆ Don't expose yourself under the sun for too long because the ultraviolet rays may hurt you.
別曝曬在太陽底下太久，因為紫外線可能會對你造成傷害。

1358

---

aftermath
/ˈæftɚˌmæθ/
n. 結果；後果；餘波

◆ In the aftermath of the war, many children were unable to survive because they lost their parents during the war.
這場戰爭的結果讓很多孩童無法生存，因為他們在戰爭中失去了父母。

◆ The aftermath will be dealt with by my team.
這個後果將由我的團隊來善後。

1359

---

consequence
/ˈkɑnsəˌkwɛns/
n. 結果；重要性

攝取太多糖生病了......

◆ The unexpected consequence shock all of us.
這個意想不到的結果衝擊了我們所有人。

◆ The government's refusal to put enough money into the health care system will have destructive consequences.
政府拒絕投入足夠的金錢到健保體系，將會有破壞性的後果。

1360 ★

---

outcome
/ˈaʊtˌkʌm/
n. 結果；結論

戀愛了！

◆ The product has just come out, so we don't know the outcome yet.
這產品剛上市，所以還看不出銷售結果。

◆ It is impossible to predict the outcome of the negotiations with certitude.
要確實地預測談判後的結果，是不可能的。

1361 ★

---

absolute
/ˈæbsəˌlut/
adj. 絕對的；完全的

100%

◆ My father made an absolute mint of money in international trade.
我爸爸在國際貿易上賺了一大筆錢。

◆ The coffee pot is an absolute necessity in most homes nowadays.
咖啡壺在今天大多數的家庭中是個絕對必須品。

1362 ★

---

support
/səˈport/
v. 給……支持；支撐…… *n.* 支持

◆ The unemployed man has a family to support.
那個失業的男人有一個家庭要扶養。

◆ The government surcease any financial support to Peru.
政府終止對祕魯所有的經濟援助。

1363 ★

---

wax
/wæks/
v. 給……打蠟；蠟

◆ The luster of wax made the car shine.
蠟的光澤讓這台車發亮。

◆ You should use wax polish on wooden floor.
你應該在木製地板上打蠟。

1364

register
ˈrɛdʒɪstɚ
v. 給……登記；給……掛號 **n.** 收銀機

◆ I'd like to send this parcel by registered mail to Taiwan
我想用掛號寄這個包裹到台灣。

◆ The waiter stole money from a cash register in the shop.
這服務生偷走店裡收銀機的錢。

1365

irrigate
ˈɪrəˌget
v. 給……灌溉；沖洗傷口

◆ They irrigate their crops with water from this river.
他們用這條河裡的水灌溉農作物。

◆ The government has built canals to irrigate the fields.
政府建造河渠來灌溉田地。

1366

suggest
səˈdʒɛst
v. 給人……建議；給人……暗示

◆ He suggested that we take the plane to America.
他建議我們搭飛機去美國。

◆ I would suggest that you use this material instead of that.
我建議你使用這種原料來代替那種。

1367

cheer
tʃɪr
v. 給予喝采

◆ Can you cheer him on in Japanese?
你會用日文為他加油嗎？

◆ James's friends always cheer him up.
詹姆士的朋友總是給他鼓勵。

1368

comfortable
ˈkʌmfɚtəbl
adj. 舒服的；自在的

真好睡！

◆ I am not comfortable working with you.
和你一起工作我覺得不自在。

◆ The expensive chair is quite comfortable for me.
這張昂貴的椅子對我來說很舒適。

1369

menu
ˈmɛnju
n. 菜單

◆ Do you have a menu written in Chinese?
你有中文菜單嗎？

◆ May I have the menu for afternoon tea?
可以給我下午茶的菜單嗎？

1370

specious
ˈspiʃəs
adj. 華而不實的；外觀好看的；似是而非的

超喜歡喔！

◆ He likes to make specious claims to seem more knowledgeable.
他喜歡做些似是而非的主張，看起來較有學問。

◆ We wouldn't accept his specious explanation.
我們不能接受這似是而非的解釋。

1371

renowned
rɪˈnaʊnd
adj. 著名的；有
聲譽的

◆ Egypt is renowned for its magnificent pyramids.
埃及以其宏偉的金字塔而著名。

◆ Switzerland is renowned for its beautiful mountains.
瑞士以它的美麗山脈而著名。

1372

---

copyright
ˈkɑpɪˌraɪt
n. 著作權

◆ Copyright laws have become more and more important in the last fifty years.
在近五十年來，著作權法變得越來越重要。

◆ We discovered that you are using our copyrighted material without our permission.
我們發現你們沒有得到允許，就使用版權歸屬於我們的素材。

1373 ★

---

block
blɑk
n. 街區；一大塊
v. 封鎖

◆ The postbox is two blocks away from here.
郵筒距離這兒有兩條街。

◆ Don't block my way, I am in a hurry.
別擋路，我在趕時間。

1374 ★

---

judge
dʒʌdʒ
v. 裁判……；判
斷…… *n.* 法官

◆ It has been five years since the three young men were judged guilty.
自從這三名年輕人被判有罪以來已經五年了。

◆ Don't judge a man by his appearance.
不要根據外表來判斷一個人。

1375 ★

---

umpire
ˈʌmpaɪr
n. 裁判員 *v.* 仲
裁……

◆ The baseball player refused to accept the umpire's decision.
這位棒球隊員拒絕接受裁判的決定。

◆ The team refused to accept the umpire's decision.
這個球隊拒絕接受這個裁判的決定。

1376

---

cut
kʌt
v. 裁剪；切；割
n. 傷口

◆ My father cut the cake into five pieces.
爸爸把蛋糕切成五等份。

◆ The cut on my knee is getting better.
我膝蓋上的傷口已逐漸好轉。

1377

---

gap
ɡæp
n. 裂縫；缺口；
間隙

◆ She had gaps in her teeth.
她的牙齒中有裂縫。

◆ What can be done to solve the widening gap between the rich and poor in Taiwan?
對於解決台灣不斷加大的貧富差距，能夠做些什麼？

1378

breach
brit∫

n. 裂口；裂痕；
違反

◆ The employee sued his company for breach of contract.
這位員工控告他的公司違反合約。

◆ Your action is a breach of promise.
你的行為是違反承諾。

1379 ★

rift
rıft

n. 裂口；裂縫；
不和

◆ I found a rift on the door.
我發現門上有一道裂口。

◆ A deep rift had started in their friendship.
他們的友誼出現了一道很深的裂痕。

1380

vision
ˈvɪʒən

n. 視力；洞察力；
願景

◆ Tears make her vision vague.
淚水模糊了她的視線。

◆ The heavy fog blurred my vision while driving in the storm.
在大風雪中開車時，濃霧模糊了我的視線。

1381

visual
ˈvɪʒuəl

adj. 視覺的；光
學的

◆ Far-sightedness is a visual defect.
遠視是一種視覺上的疾病。

◆ They put emphasis on function rather than visual appeal.
他們在功能上加強，而不是視覺上的訴求。

1382

business
ˈbɪznɪs

n. 買賣；商業

◆ We do much business with foreign companies.
我們和許多外國公司有生意往來。

◆ They started a new business in China not long ago.
不久前他們在中國開始新的事業。

1383

charge
t∫ɔrdʒ

n. 費用；控制；
控訴

◆ Does this charge include dinner, service charge, and tax ?
這個費用包括晚餐、服務費和稅了嗎？

◆ You can download the software without charge.
你可以免費下載這軟體。

1384 ★

trade
tred

n. 貿易；行業
v. 交易……

◆ You will find a list of some of the industry trade press with corresponding contact information in the directory.
你將在這本電話簿中找到一些對應產業貿易通訊名錄的聯絡資訊。

◆ Our company does lots of trade with several foreign companies.
我們公司與幾間國外的公司有頻繁的貿易往來。

1385 ★

supermarket
ˈsupɚˌmɑrkɪt
n. 超級市場

◆ Can you bring me some drinks from supermarket?
你可以幫我到超級市場買一些飲料嗎？

◆ We bought some bread at the supermarket.
我們在超級市場買了一些麵包。

1386

exceed
ɪkˈsid
v. 超越……；超出……的範圍

◆ This question is too difficult for me, it exceeds my understanding.
這問題對我來說太難了，它超出我的理解力。

◆ If his liabilities exceed his assets, he may go bankrupt.
假如他的負債大於資產，他可能就破產了。

1387 ★

transcend
trænˈsɛnd
v. 超越……；優於……

◆ This question is too complicated for me, it has transcended my knowledge.
這問題對我來說太複雜了，已經超越我的學識。

◆ His ability to speak English transcends over all of us.
他說英文的能力已經超越了我們所有人。

1388

track
træk
n. 跑道；徑賽；蹤跡

◆ She represented our country to join the competition for track and field.
她代表我國參加田徑比賽。

◆ How can we judge a mutual fund by its track record?
我們如何能由一個共同基金的過去記錄來判斷呢？

1389

distribute
dɪˈstrɪbjut
v. 進行分配；使分布

◆ They had distributed food and water among the refugees.
他們把水和食物分配給難民。

◆ The mother distributes the candies to each kid.
母親把糖果分給每個孩子。

1390 ★

progress
ˈprɑgrɛs
n. 進步；發展

100分喔！

◆ If you want to make progress, you should practice more.
如果想進步，你應該多練習。

◆ He makes a great progress on English conversation.
他在英語會話方面有很大的進步。

1391 ★

mail
mel
n. 郵件；郵政
v. 郵寄

◆ Nowadays few people use aerogramme as air mail.
現在很少人用航空郵件寄航空信。

◆ A letter from my sister arrived in the mail today.
一封我姐姐寄的信，今天以郵件的方式送達了。

1392

rural
ˈrʊrəl
adj. 鄉村的；農村的

◆ Rural life is usually more peaceful and simple than city life.
鄉村生活通常比城市生活更為寧靜單純。

◆ My mother longs to lead a quiet rural life.
我媽媽渴望過一個安靜的鄉村生活。

1393

desert
dɪˈzɝt
v. 開小差；拋棄
n. 沙漠

◆ She deserted her husband and children for another man.
她為了其他男人放棄了丈夫和孩子。

◆ It is easy to get lost in the desert.
在沙漠中很容易迷路。

1394

initiate
ɪˈnɪʃɪˌet
v. 開始……；創始……

◆ It was silent until she initiated conversation by asking questions.
直到開始提問前她都相當安靜。

◆ It is silent until she initiated conversation by asking questions.
她打破沈默提出問題，並開始交談。

1395

exploit
ɪkˈsplɔɪt
v. 開發……；利用……

◆ You should exploit this opportunity to go abroad.
你應該利用這個機會到海外去。

◆ The government started to exploit a mine for searching a useful energy.
政府開始開礦以找尋可用的能源。

1396 ★

session
ˈsɛʃən
n. 開會；開庭

◆ I attended a session on the economy last week.
上週我參加一項經濟議題的會議。

◆ The bill will be enacted at the end of this session.
這項法案會在這屆會議結束時頒布。

1397

擁有希望的人擁有一切

---

gossip
/ˈɡɑsəp/
n. 閒話；八卦

◆ She loves to gossip with her friends.
她喜歡和朋友聊八卦話題。

◆ You can get any gossip in newspapers and magazines.
你能在報紙和雜誌上看到任何八卦。

1398

---

balcony
/ˈbælkənɪ/
n. 陽台

◆ I can see my school from our balcony.
我可以從我家陽台看到學校。

◆ The balcony juts out over the river.
這陽台伸出在河流上方。

1399

---

phase
/fez/
n. 階段；時期；
方面

◆ The time you spend in university is an important phase of your education.
你花在大學的時間對你的教育是個重要階段。

◆ The teenager is going through a difficult phase.
這個青少年正在經歷一個痛苦的階段。

1400 ★

---

rank
/ræŋk/
n. 階級；身分；
地位

◆ The man prostrated himself before rank and wealth.
這個人向階級及財富屈服。

◆ A chief executive officer (CEO) is the highest-ranking administrator in charge of an organization or a company.
一位執行長是管理一個組織或一家公司的最高階行政人員。

1401 ★

---

hierarchy
/ˈhaɪəˌrɑrkɪ/
n. 階級；等級

◆ There was a very rigid social hierarchy in ancient China.
古代中國有一種刻板的社會階級制度。

◆ Everyone has his own hierarchy of value in mind.
人人心中都有他自己的價值等級。

1402

---

eloquent
/ˈɛləkwənt/
adj. 雄辯的；有
說服力的

◆ The speaker made an eloquent appeal for children rights.
這位演講者為了兒童權利做了有說服力的訴求。

◆ The priest is a soul-stirring, eloquent preacher .
這位牧師是位振奮人心與有說服力的傳道者。

1403 ★

concentrate
ˈkɑnsn̩ˌtret

v. 集中；專心；
濃縮

◆ The teacher asks the students to concentrate on the class.
老師要求學生們專心上課。

◆ We must concentrate on our work.
我們必須專心工作。

1404 ★

---

collective
kəˈlɛktɪv

adj. 集合的；集
體的

◆ The successful invention was a collective effort.
這成功的發明是集體努力的成果。

◆ I do understand deeply the strength of the collective.
我深深了解到了集體的力量。

1405

---

employ
ɪmˈplɔɪ

v. 雇用……；使
從事於

◆ The factory employs over a thousand workers.
這家工廠雇用了超過一千名工人。

◆ You had better employ someone to oversee the play.
你最好雇人來監督這項計劃。

1406

---

cloud
klaʊd

n. 雲

◆ The sky was covered with dark clouds.
天空被烏雲覆蓋了。

◆ The shapes of clouds change all the time.
雲的形狀總是一直在變化。

1407

---

diet
ˈdaɪət

n. 飲食；規定
的飲食

◆ I am on a diet now.
我正在減肥。

◆ You won't get fat if you maintain a good diet.
保持良好的飲食就不會發胖。

1408

---

beverage
ˈbɛvrɪdʒ

n. 飲料

◆ Tea, coffee, wine and cola are beverages.
茶、咖啡、酒與可樂是飲料。

◆ Don't drink too many beverages; they will cause you harm.
別喝太多飲料，對身體有害。

1409

---

hustle
ˈhʌsl̩

v. 催促……；推
擠……

快一點！

◆ You can get there in time if you hustle.
假如你們快一點，就能夠及時到達那裡。

◆ My sister always hustles out of the house to catch the bus.
我妹妹總是從家裡趕著出門去搭巴士。

1410

epidemic

ˌɛpəˈdɛmɪk

n. 傳染病；流行病 *adj.* 地方病的

◆ There was a malaria epidemic in Florida last year.
去年佛羅里達有一場瘧疾傳染病。

◆ Many people died from the smallpox epidemic long time ago.
許多人在很久以前死於天花傳染病。

1411

arraign

əˈren

v. 傳訊；控告

◆ The suspect was arraigned on a charge of theft.
這名嫌疑犯被控偷竊。

◆ The young man is arraigned on a charge of murder.
這個年輕人被控謀殺。

1412

biography

baɪˈɑgrəfɪ

n. 傳記

◆ I like to read biographies more than novels.
我喜歡讀傳記勝過小說。

◆ The posthumous publication of the singer's biography aroused a lot of interest.
這位歌手過世後才出版的傳記引起很大的興趣。

1413 ★

tradition

trəˈdɪʃən

n. 傳統

◆ Four is considered an unlucky number in the Chinese tradition.
在中國的傳統上，「四」被認為是一個不吉利的數字。

◆ The custom is based mainly on Chinese tradition.
這個習俗主要建立在中國的傳統。

1414

legend

ˈlɛdʒənd

n. 傳說；傳奇故事

◆ The little girl likes the legend of the unicorn very much.
那個小女孩很喜歡獨角獸的傳說。

◆ In the West, there are many legends about centaurs.
在西方有許多半人馬的傳說。

1415

transmit

trænsˈmɪt

v. 傳遞……；傳播……

◆ Do all kinds of mosquitoes transmit malaria?
是否所有的蚊子都會傳播瘧疾？

◆ The secretary transmitted the messages to the boss.
祕書把消息傳達給老闆。

1416

propagate

ˈprɑpəˌget

v. 傳播……；使普及；使繁殖

◆ Scientist's duty is to propagate scientific knowledge to people.
科學家的責任是傳播科學知識給一般民眾。

◆ Most plants propagate themselves by seeds.
大多數植物靠種子來繁殖。

1417

creditor

ˋkrɛdɪtə

n. 債權人

◆ Our creditors are knocking on our doors.
我們的債權人開始催債了。

◆ The creditor postdated the check to a month from today.
債權人從今天開始將支票延長一個月。

1418

---

incision

ɪnˋsɪʒən

n. 傷口；切口

◆ The incision on my finger is very painful.
我手指上的傷口非常痛。

◆ The deep incision has just been stitched up.
這道很深的傷口已經被縫合。

1419

---

wound

wund

n. 傷口；創傷
v. 使受傷

◆ The nurse carefully bandaged the patient's flesh wound.
這位護士小心地用繃帶包紮這位病患肌肉的傷口。

◆ He had two wounds on his body.
他的身上有兩處傷口。

1420

---

damage

ˋdæmɪdʒ

n. 傷害；損害

◆ My suitcase is badly damaged.
我的皮箱被嚴重破壞。

◆ The typhoon caused great damage to the crops.
颱風對農作物造成很大的損失。

1421 ★

---

harm

hɑrm

v. 傷害；損傷

◆ Smoking may harm your lungs.
抽煙會對你的肺部帶來傷害。

◆ The accident did great harm to him.
那場意外對他造成很大的傷害。

1422

---

bias

ˋbaɪəs

n. 傾向；偏見

偏愛蕭邦的音樂家

◆ The first impression often causes the bias.
第一印象往往會造成偏見。

◆ Some people have a bias against Chinese products.
有些人對中國的產品有偏見。

1423 ★

---

dump

dʌmp

v. 傾倒……；倒
垃圾 *n.* 垃圾堆

◆ We should put our trash in the dump, not on the street.
我們應該把垃圾放在垃圾場，而不是街上。

◆ The municipal waste dump pollutes our environment.
這個城市的垃圾處理場汙染了我們的環境。

1424

diligent
/ˈdɪlədʒənt/
adj. 勤勉的

◆ Tommy is very diligent in learning English.
湯米非常努力學英語。

◆ Not every student is as diligent as Tom; he studies twelve hours a day.
不是每個學生都像湯姆一樣勤勉用功的；人家每天唸十二小時的書。

1425

smell
/smɛl/
v. 嗅；聞 *n.* 氣味

◆ She doesn't like things that smell bad.
她不喜歡聞起來臭的東西。

◆ The dog was attracted by the smell of the delicious food.
狗受到這份美食的香味引誘。

1426

sob
/sɑb/
v. 嗚咽……；啜泣……；啜泣聲

◆ The girl sobbed over her sad fate.
這女孩在啜泣她悲慘的命運。

◆ The old lady started to sob uncontrollably.
這老女人開始嗚咽了起來。

1427

circumference
/səˈkʌmfərəns/
n. 圓周

◆ The circumference of the circle is 25 centimeters.
這圓的圓周是二十五公分。

◆ This round table has a circumference of 10 feet.
這個圓桌的圓周有十英呎。

1428 ★

mass
/mæs/
n. 塊；大量

◆ There are masses of dark clouds in the sky.
天空中有大量的烏雲。

◆ A mass of people get together for the demonstration in the town.
大批民眾聚集鎮上示威。

1429

jealous
/ˈdʒɛləs/
adj. 嫉妒的

我比你美多了!

◆ The queen was jealous of the princess' beauty.
皇后嫉妒公主的美貌。

◆ The woman speaks with an acidulous tone when she is jealous of someone.
這女人嫉妒別人時，講話就很酸。

1430

microwave
/ˈmaɪkrəˌwev/
n. 微波爐

◆ It is quite convenient to use a microwave to heat up food.
使用微波爐加熱食物相當方便。

◆ These microwave foods are the most convenient of all.
這些微波食品是其中最為方便的。

1431

breeze
briz
n. 微風

◆ The yellow ribbon fluttered in the breeze.
這黃色的緞帶在微風中擺動。

◆ I like the beach because I can enjoy the sea breeze.
我喜歡海邊，因為可以享受海風。

1432

microprocessor
ˌmaɪkroˈprɑsɛsɚ
n. 微處理機

◆ A personal computer uses a microprocessor chip as its CPU.
一台個人電腦使用一塊微處理器晶片當它的 CPU。

◆ I've got a laptop with an advanced microprocessor.
我有一台有先進微處理機的膝上型電腦。

1433

dim
dɪm
adj. 微暗的；無
光澤的；朦朧的

◆ It's easy to become nearsighted by reading under a dim light constantly.
經常在昏暗的燈光下讀書很容易近視。

◆ The light was too dim for my mother to read.
這光線對我媽媽閱讀來說太暗了。

1434

wonder
ˈwʌndɚ
v. 想……；想知
道……

◆ I wonder why he can't come to my wedding.
我很想知道他為什麼不能來參加我的婚禮。

◆ I wonder if you would have time to meet me on Monday.
不知道你星期一有沒有時間跟我見面。

1435

notion
ˈnoʃən
n. 想法；意圖；
意見

◆ Because of his silly notion, we got lost in the jungle.
因為他的愚蠢意見，我們在叢林裡迷路了。

◆ I have no notion of what you mean.
我不知道你的意思是什麼。

1436

casualty
ˈkæʒʊəltɪ
n. 意外；傷者

◆ The airplane crash caused heavy casualty according to the first reports.
根據最初的報導，空難意外傷亡慘重。

◆ My uncle read through the casualty list anxiously
我叔叔焦急地把傷亡名單看一遍。

1437 ★

accident
ˈæksədənt
n. 意外事故；
不測

◆ The accident delayed the train for over three hours.
這場意外使得火車延遲了三個小時。

◆ She didn't tell anyone about the accident.
她沒有告訴任何人這個意外事件。

1438 ★

opinion
əˈpɪnjən
n. 意見；信念

◆ In my opinion, you shouldn't refuse his help.
我的看法是你不應該拒絕他的幫忙。

◆ The mayor remains impervious to public opinion.
市長對輿論還是不為所動。

1439 ★

meaningful
ˈminɪŋfəl
adj. 意味深長的；有意義的

◆ It is a meaningful explanation about Olympics Game.
它是一則關於奧運意味深長的解釋。

◆ Motherhood is very meaningful to most women.
母職對大多數女人來講十分有意義。

1440 ★

mock
mɑk
v. 愚弄；不尊重

◆ The bad boys mocked the lame woman.
這群壞男孩嘲笑這位跛腳的女人。

◆ Peter loves to use the word "morons" to mock his classmates.
彼得喜愛使用「傻瓜」這個字來嘲笑同學。

1441

affection
əˈfɛkʃən
n. 愛情；情感

◆ He thanked his mother with genuine affection.
他真情流露地感謝他的母親。

◆ If you like him, just show your affection.
你如果喜歡他，就向他表明愛意。

1442

shame
ʃem
n. 感到羞恥 **v.** 使丟臉

◆ His fatuous behavior made all his friends feel shame.
他愚蠢的行為讓朋友感到羞愧。

◆ He felt no shame and no remorse.
他沒感到羞恥與後悔。

1443

sentiment
ˈsɛntəmənt
n. 感情；情操

◆ Should reason be guided by sentiment?
理性會被感情所引導嗎？

◆ There is no place for sentiment in business.
生意上不能感情用事。

1444

sensational
sɛnˈseʃənl
adj. 感覺上的；轟動的；極棒的

◆ You look sensational in that red evening dress!
妳穿紅色禮服看起來棒極了。

◆ This play was a truly sensational performance.
這場表演確實是轟動的演出。

1445

deliberate
dɪˈlɪbəˌret
v. 慎重考慮……
adj. 故意的；慎重的

◆ She is still deliberating his proposal.
她仍然在慎重考慮他的求婚。

◆ The man solved the problem in his deliberate and decorous way.
這人利用他謹慎得體的方式解決了問題。

1446 ★

discredit
dɪsˈkrɛdɪt
v. 損害名譽；使丟臉；使懷疑

◆ The employee discredited her boss's good name with ugly gossip.
這員工用醜陋的八卦來損壞她老闆的好名聲。

◆ Her new theories were discredited by the scholars.
她的新理論受到學者的質疑。

1447

stagger
ˈstæɡɚ
v. 搖晃走路；使吃驚

◆ The old man staggers across the road.
這個老人蹣跚地穿越馬路。

◆ His strong resolution had begun to stagger.
他強烈的決心開始動搖。

1448

swing
swɪŋ
v. 搖擺；搖動
n. 鞦韆

◆ The palm trees along the road swung in the wind.
沿路上這些棕櫚樹在風中搖盪。

◆ The kids used the tree as a swing.
這些孩子把樹木當鞦韆玩。

1449

search
sɝtʃ
v. 搜尋；調查

◆ The police officer searched every room for evidence.
這位警官搜尋了每間房間來找證物。

◆ The judge issued the police a warrant to search the suspect's house.
法官發給警方搜索票來搜查嫌犯的房子。

1450

porter
ˈportɚ
n. 搬運工人；腳伕

◆ I'm looking for a porter, would you get me a porter, please?
我正在找個搬行李的人，請幫我找一下好嗎？

◆ Porters carry passengers' luggage from the airport to a taxi outside.
腳伕幫忙乘客把行李從機場搬到外面的計程車。

1451

rob
rɑb
v. 搶劫；盜取

不要臉！

錢包拿出來

◆ Pirates boarded the ship and robbed the passengers.
海盜登上船，並且搶劫乘客。

◆ The terrorists were plotting to rob the famous bank.
這些恐怖份子計劃搶這間知名銀行。

1452

adore
əˈdor
v. 敬重……；崇拜……；疼愛

◆ He adored the movie Titanic so much that he bought the DVD.
他熱愛鐵達尼電影，所以買了它的 DVD。

◆ I adore kids and like being around them.
我疼愛小孩而且喜歡在他們身邊。

1453

allude
əˈlud
v. 暗示……；影射……

◆ What are you alluding to just now?
你剛才在影射誰？

◆ Although the teacher didn't mention the name, but everyone knows whom she was alluding to.
雖然老師沒有說出名字，但大家都知道她暗指誰。

1454

obscure
əbˈskjʊr
adj. 暗的；不清楚的

◆ The direction of that country's policy is still obscure.
那個國家的政策方向仍然晦暗不明。

◆ The meaning of his words is obscure and hard to understand.
他話中的意思模糊，而且難以了解。

1455

interview
ˈɪntəˌvju
v. 會見……；採訪…… **n.** 面談

◆ If you can successfully have an exclusive interview with that star, it will be big news.
如果你能成功地獨家採訪到那位明星，那會是個大新聞。

◆ Could you tell me your name and interview number?
可以告訴我你的名字和面試號碼嗎？

1456 ★

accounting
əˈkaʊntɪŋ
n. 會計 (學)

會計學

◆ The mechanism for budget accounting needs revising.
預算會計結構需要修訂。

◆ Wait a moment, please. I will transfer you to our Accounting Department.
請稍等，我將為你轉接到會計部門。

1457

council
ˈkaʊnsḷ
n. 會議；委員會

◆ The city council had monthly meetings.
這都市委員會每月開會。

◆ He represents the richest ward on the council.
他在這個委員會中代表最富裕的行政區。

1458 ★

fabulous
ˈfæbjələs
adj. 極好的；難以置信的；傳說的

◆ The museum has a fabulous collection of antique objects.
這間博物館有許多難以置信的古物收藏。

◆ The marathon runner has fabulous endurance.
這位跑步者有難以置信的忍耐力。

1459

utmost
ˈʌt͵most
adj. 極度的；最遠的

◆ They offered the utmost help during my hardship.
在我困難的時候，他們提供了最大的幫忙。

◆ The thrift of water is of the utmost importance during the drought.
在乾旱時期節省用水是最為重要的。

1460

desperate
ˈdɛspərɪt
adj. 極度想要的；奮不顧身的；絕望的

◆ A mother is always desperate to protect her children.
母親總是奮不顧身保護她的孩子們。

◆ He was desperate when he went bankrupt.
當他破產時，他陷入絕望中。

1461

limit
ˈlɪmɪt
n. 極限；邊界

◆ The speed limit on this highway is 65 mph.
這條高速公路的速限是六十五英哩。

◆ Working hours are limited by ordinance.
工作時間被法令所限制。

1462 ★

excruciating
ɪkˈskruʃɪˏetɪŋ
adj. 極痛苦的；難以忍受的

◆ I felt excruciating pain while I had a car accident.
出車禍時我感到極大的痛苦

◆ The pain in my leg was excruciating.
我的腳痛難以忍受。

1463

extremely
ɪkˈstrimlɪ
adv. 極端地；非常地

◆ Their lawyer was extremely sedulous in preparing their case.
律師為他們的案子非常聚精會神地準備。

◆ I am extremely sorry to hear that your father passed away.
聽到你父親過世，我感到非常難過。

1464 ★

精誠所至，金石為開

---

ravenous
ˈrævənəs

adj. 極餓的；貪婪的

◆ The child has a ravenous appetite after school.
放學後這孩子餓極了。

◆ The ravenous wolves hunted for prey.
這些饑餓的狼群獵取獵物。

1465

---

totalitarian
to.tælə'tɛrɪən

adj. 極權主義的
n. 極權主義者

◆ North Korea is a absolutely totalitarian state.
北韓是一個絕對極權主義的國家。

◆ Russia was once a totalitarian state.
俄國曾經是一個極權國家。

1466

---

concept
ˈkɑnsɛpt

n. 概念；觀念

◆ Can you explain this abstract concept again?
你可以再解釋一次這個抽象概念嗎？

◆ The teacher uses one example to make the students understand the concept.
老師使用一個實例讓學生了解概念。

1467 ★

---

mar
mɑr

v. 毀損；破壞

◆ A scar on his right cheek marred his appearance.
他左臉頰的疤痕損傷了他的外表。

◆ Such a cheating event would mar your marriage.
如此的外遇事件將會損害你的婚姻。

1468

---

communicate
kə'mjunə.ket

v. 溝通……；交際

◆ We all found it hard to communicate with the grumpy man.
我們發現要和暴躁的人溝通很困難。

◆ We all found it hard to communicate with the irascible man.
我們所有人都發現和易怒的人溝通很困難。

1469 ★

---

stream
strim

n. 溪流；潮流

◆ This fertile territory is watered by numerous limpid streams.
這片肥沃的土地是由許多清澈溪流所澆灌。

◆ I've never seen the stream of lava from a volcano in my life.
我一生中從未見過火山噴出的熔岩流。

1470

temperature
ˈtɛmprətʃɚ
n. 溫度；體溫

◆ The temperature rises year by year because of the green house effect.
氣溫因為溫室效應而年年上升。

◆ The weather is fair, and the temperature is 82 degrees Fahrenheit.
天氣晴朗，而氣溫是華氏八十二度

1471 ★

camera
ˈkæmərə
n. 照相機

◆ Digital cameras are more and more popular now.
數位相機現在越來越流行了。

◆ Another hobby of mine is taking pictures with my precise single-lens camera.
我另一個嗜好就是用我那部精密的單眼相機拍照。

1472

tend
tɛnd
v. 照料……；照管……；有……傾向

◆ You'd better tend to your own affairs.
你最好管好你自己的事務。

◆ I tend to stick to fresh vegetables for cooking.
我傾向堅持用新鮮蔬菜來烹飪。

1473

harassment
həˈræsmənt
n. 煩惱的事物；煩擾

寶寶睡
得好嗎？

◆ My company prohibits any form of sexual harassment.
我們公司禁止任何形式的性騷擾。

◆ Do you want to accuse him of sexual harassment?
你要控告他性騷擾嗎？

1474

local
ˈlokḷ
adj. 當地的

當地的水果

◆ He works at a local bank.
他在本地的一間銀行工作。

◆ I'd like to set my watch to the local time.
我想將我的錶調整到當地時間。

1475

confederate
kənˈfɛdərɪt
n. 盟友；共犯
v. 使結盟

日韓聯盟會議

◆ Bill and Jack are confederates to steal the car.
比爾和傑克是偷這輛車的共犯。

◆ The country agreed to confederate with the neighboring countries finally.
這個國家最後同意與鄰近國家結盟。

1476

ally
ˈælaɪ
n. 盟邦；同盟者
v. 使結盟

◆ America and Great Britain were allies in World War II.
美國和大英帝國在第二次世界大戰時是盟邦

◆ The United States is a close ally of Taiwan.
美國是台灣的親密盟友。

1477

short
ʃɔrt
adj. 矮的；短的

◆ The barber cut my hair very short.
理髮師把我的頭髮剪得很短。

◆ The city was forced to yield after only a short siege.
這個城市只被短期的圍困，就被迫投降了。

1478

fragment
ˈfrægmənt
n. 碎片；片斷

◆ The vase fell to the floor and broke into fragments.
這花瓶掉到地板上，而且破裂成碎片。

◆ Middle East had always been politically fragmented .
中東在政治上總是四分五裂。

1479

scrap
skræp
n. 碎片；廢料
v. 報廢

◆ A crumpled scrap of paper was found in her palm.
在她的手掌中發現一張皺掉的碎片。

◆ All I could do was sell it for scrap.
我能做的就是把它當廢物賣掉。

1480

crash
kræʃ
n. 碰撞 *v.* 使失
敗；使破產

◆ A lot of people were killed in the plane crash.
許多人在墜機意外中喪生了。

◆ The stock market crash caused panic among businessmen.
股市崩盤引起商人們的恐慌。

1481 ★

inhibit
ɪnˈhɪbɪt
v. 禁止；抑制

◆ We inhibit the children from playing by the railroad.
我們禁止孩童在鐵路旁遊玩。

◆ Smoking is inhibited in some public places.
吸煙在某些公眾區域是禁止的。

1482 ★

forbid
fəˈbɪd
v. 禁止……；不
許……

◆ I'm sorry but it's forbidden to park here.
很抱歉此處禁止停車。

◆ Swimming is forbidden in the lake.
這個湖中禁止游泳。

1483

embargo
ɪmˈbɑrgo
n. 禁止……出
入港口；禁運

◆ The government has put an embargo on the imports of opium.
這個政府對進口的鴉片展開禁運。

◆ The prime minister has lifted the embargo on all imports.
總理對所有進口產品解除禁運。

1484

chopstick
ˈtʃɑpˌstɪks
n. 筷子

◆ I taught Mr. Brown how to use chopsticks.
我教布朗先生使用筷子。

◆ My friend from Germany doesn't use chopsticks very well.
我從德國來的朋友不太會用筷子。

1485

economical
ikəˈnɑmɪkl̩
adj. 節省的；節約的

◆ International trade plays a very important role in the economical field of Taiwan.
國際貿易在台灣的經濟領域中扮演極重要的角色。

◆ Entrepreneurs can promote economical growth in Taiwan.
在台灣企業家們提高了經濟成長。

1486 ★

frugality
fruˈgælətɪ
n. 節儉

◆ His frugality helped him become the richest man in the world.
他的節儉幫助他成為世界首富。

◆ We should learn the frugality of our parents.
我們應該學習我們父母的節儉。

1487

thrifty
ˈθrɪftɪ
adj. 節儉的；節約的

◆ The old man has an excessively thrifty and industrious character.
這老人有一種格外節儉和勤勞的性格。

◆ My father is an architect in a building company and my mother is a thrifty housewife.
我的父親是建設公司的建築師，而我的母親是位勤儉的家庭主婦。

1488

bind
baɪnd
v. 綁；捆；裝訂……

◆ He bound the box with a strong rope.
他用粗繩綁這箱子。

◆ Binding is very hard to learn for a child.
孩童要學裝訂非常困難。

1489

abduct
æbˈdʌkt
v. 綁架；誘拐

◆ The robber tried to abduct the rich man for ransom.
這強盜企圖綁架這位有錢人來索取贖金。

◆ The gangster had attempted to abduct the two children.
這流氓嘗試綁架這兩個小孩。

1490

longitude
ˈlɑndʒəˌtjud
n. 經度

◆ The city destroyed by the earthquake lies at a longitude of 25 degrees west.
這座被地震摧毀的城市位於西經二十五度。

◆ Our position is at longitude 36 degrees east.
我們的位置是在東經三十六度。

1491

agent
ˈedʒənt
n. 經紀人；代理商；間諜

◆ Thank you for your proposal of acting as our company's agent.
謝謝你做為我們公司代理人的企劃案。

◆ The double agent takes James as his alias.
這位雙面間諜以詹姆士當他的化名。

1492 ★

manager
ˈmænɪdʒɚ
n. 經理人；管理人

◆ He was promoted to a manager.
他升職當上經理了。

◆ The manager will hold a review meeting tomorrow.
經理明天要召開檢討會議。

1493

downturn
ˈdaʊntɝn
n. 經濟衰退；不景氣

◆ You had better save enough cash to survive an economic downturn.
你最好維持足夠的現金來度過經濟衰退。

◆ The current economic downturn has only just started.
這次的經濟衰退才剛開始。

1494 ★

recession
rɪˈsɛʃən
n. 經濟衰退；引退

◆ The continuing recession made the price of stocks slump.
持續的經濟蕭條使得股市價格大跌。

◆ The man was unfortunately laid off by the company during the recession.
這位男士很遺憾地在不景氣時被公司解雇了。

1495 ★

economist
ɪˈkɑnəmɪst
n. 經濟學家

◆ An economist is a professional in the social science discipline of economics.
經濟學家是社會科學學門中的經濟學專業人士。

◆ The economy is slumping, but economists don't notice the magnitude of the problem.
經濟正在衰退，但是經濟學家沒有注意到問題的嚴重性。

1496

experience
ɪkˈspɪrɪəns
n. 經驗；經歷

◆ Her abundant working experiences made her stand on a vantage point in our company.
她的豐富工作經驗讓她站在一個有利地位。

◆ The salary is commensurate with your experience and position.
薪水與你的經驗和職等相稱。

1497

flock
flɑk
n. 群（禽類或牲畜）；群眾

◆ A flock of geese swam in the river.
一群母鵝在河中游泳。

◆ Flocks of sheep graze in the meadow.
好幾群羊在草地上吃草。

1498

crowd
kraud
n. 群眾；一夥
v. 使擁擠

◆ The crowd flows into the department store during the holidays.
假日期間，人群湧入百貨公司。

◆ The influx of customers crowded the shop.
顧客們的湧入擠爆了這家商店。

1499

brain
bren
n. 腦；頭腦

◆ His brain was severely injured during the accident.
他在這場意外中造成腦部嚴重的傷害。

◆ He gets the first prize because he has a good brain.
他頭腦聰明，所以拿第一名。

1500

lump
lʌmp
n. 腫塊 *v.* 使成團；笨重地走

◆ The surgeon excised the lump from her liver.
這個位外科醫生切除她的肝臟腫塊。

◆ She found a lump in her right breast last year.
她去年發現右邊乳房有一個腫塊。

1501

tiptoe
ˈtɪp.to
n. 腳尖 *v.* 用腳尖走路；踮著腳走

◆ My sister walked into the room on tiptoe.
我妹妹踮著腳尖走進房內。

◆ The nurse tiptoes upstairs so as not to wake the patient.
這位護士踮著腳上樓，以免吵醒病人。

1502

abdomen
æbˈdomən
n. 腹部

哇!我有150公斤了!

◆ Baby kangaroos live in a pouch on their mother's abdomen.
小袋鼠住在媽媽的育兒袋裡。

◆ My mother often feels pain in her abdomen.
我媽媽時常感覺到腹部疼痛。

1503

diarrhea
ˌdaɪəˈriə
n. 腹瀉

◆ He has trouble with diarrhea now because he ate something bad yesterday.
因為他昨天吃了不好的東西，現在腹瀉。

◆ In fact, the cause of diarrhea are numerous.
事實上，引起腹瀉的原因很多。

1504

board
bord
n. 董事會；委員會 *v.* 登機（船）

◆ He has recently joined the board of the company.
他最近加入了該公司的董事會。

◆ Your flight will be boarding in 30 minutes.
你的班機在三十分鐘後登機。

1505

funeral
'fjunərəl
n. 葬禮；追悼會

◆ The priest prayed for peace upon the soul of the dead during the funeral.
牧師在葬禮上祈禱，願已逝的靈魂能夠安息。

◆ John went to his grandfather's funeral ceremony in the morning.
約翰早上前往他的祖父的葬禮。

1506

compensate
'kɑmpən.set
v. 補償；賠償

◆ Since half of the shipment will be delayed, I expected to be compensated.
既然有一半的出貨將會延遲，我期望得到賠償。

◆ The company compensated the woman for her inconvenience.
公司因為造成這位女士的不便而賠償她。

1507 ★

decorate
'dɛkə.ret
v. 裝飾；裝修房屋

◆ The room was decorated with fake flowers.
這個房間以假花來裝飾。

◆ The pub was decorated with a rustic appearance by putting horseshoes and old guns on the walls.
這間酒吧用馬蹄鐵、老槍裝飾牆面，有鄉村風貌。

1508

ornament
'ɔrnəmənt
n. 裝飾品

◆ She has many artificial flowers as ornaments in her living room.
在她的客廳中了用很多人造花當裝飾品。

◆ The shop stocks a wide range of garden ornaments, such as statues and fountains.
這家商店存放了多種的花園裝飾品，例如雕像和和噴泉。

1509

spreadsheet
'sprɛd.ʃit
n. 試算表

◆ I spent much time learning how to use Excel spreadsheets.
我花了很多時間學習如何使用 Excel 試算表。

◆ Can you convert the spreadsheet to html ?
你能把試算表轉成 html 文件嗎？

1510

trick
trɪk
n. 詭計；惡作劇

◆ The magician's amazing trick surprised Helen.
這位魔術師的驚人技巧讓海倫嚇了一跳。

◆ Don't be fooled by his delusive tricks.
不要被他騙人的技巧給愚弄。

1511

specification
.spɛsəfə'keʃən
n. 詳述；規格書；說明書

◆ Will you let us have the specifications ?
規格書可以給我們嗎？

◆ Have you received a new product of this detailed specification?
你們有這份詳細規格說明書上的新產品嗎？

1512 ★

scrutinize
ˈskrutn̩ˌaɪz
v. 詳細審查；細看

◆ The lawyer scrutinized all the documents about the case.
這律師仔細檢查了與這案子有關的文件。

◆ You must more closely scrutinize each case.
你必須更仔細檢查每個案子。

1513

overstate
ˌovɚˈstet
v. 誇大陳述；言過其實

有空來坐坐

◆ Don't overstate your importance or no one will believe you.
別誇大自己的重要性，否則沒有人會相信你。

◆ It's hard to overstate my dissatisfaction
很難誇大形容我的不滿。

1514

boast
bost
v. 誇耀；吹噓

◆ She always boasts to us how rich she is.
她總在我們面前誇耀自己多麼有錢。

◆ A modest man will never boast of his learning.
一個謙虛的人不會吹噓自己的學識。

1515

sincere
sɪnˈsɪr
adj. 誠心的；真誠的

◆ He gave a sincere apology for the mistakes he made.
他為所做的錯誤表示真誠的道歉。

◆ Please accept my sincere congratulations.
請接受我最衷心的祝賀。

1516

capitalist
ˈkæpətəlɪst
n. 資本家；資本主義者

◆ The stingy capitalist is in possession of a large fortune.
這個小氣的資本家擁有大量財富。

◆ In the capitalist country cash is the king.
在這資本主義國家，現金就是一切。

1517

fund
fʌnd
n. 資金；基金
v. 為……提供資金

 專案基金

◆ The company has set up a special fund to hold special party.
公司設立一項特別基金來舉辦特別的派對

◆ This project of Ministry of Science and Technology needs a great sum of funds.
這個科技部的專案需要一大筆資金。

1518

resource
rɪˈsors
n. 資源；錢財

 開發綠能資源

◆ Arabia is a country with abundant oil resources.
阿拉伯是石油資源豐富的國家。

◆ The college library is an important resource for learning.
大學圖書館是學習的重要資源。

1519 ★

kneel
nil
v. 跪著；跪下

◆ The old woman knelt down to pray in the church.
這老女人在教堂中跪下來禱告。

◆ People kneel when they pray at church.
人們跪下在教堂中祈禱。

1520

---

dive
daɪv
v. 跳水；潛水；潛心研究

◆ He dived into the lake to save a little boy.
他跳進湖中救起這個小男孩。

◆ My brother dived into his new job with great zest.
我弟弟滿懷熱情地投入新工作。

1521

---

skip
skɪp
v. 跳來跳去；輕躍；跳讀

◆ The bad student was culpable because he always skipped classes.
因為這壞學生總是翹課，應該受到譴責。

◆ You can skip the sentences that you don't understand.
你可以跳過不懂的句子。

1522

---

bailout
ˈbel.aʊt
n. 跳傘；緊急財務援助

◆ A bailout is an act of giving money to a company to rescue it from financial difficulties.
緊急財務援助是種把錢給一家公司，並將它從財務困境中解救出來的行為。

◆ Bailout is an activity for the brave people.
跳傘是屬於勇者的活動。

1523

---

avoid
əˈvɔɪd
v. 躲開……；避開……；撤銷……

◆ She left the house earlier today because she wanted to avoid a traffic jam.
她今天比較早出門，因為她想要避開塞車。

◆ You should avoid blaming your students.
你應該避免責備你的學生。

1524

---

elude
ɪˈlud
v. 躲避……；逃避……

◆ The tiger succeeded in eluding the hunters.
這隻老虎成功地躲過這些獵人。

◆ If you chase the monkey, it will elude you.
假如你追逐這猴子，牠會躲避你。

1525

---

dodge
dɑdʒ
v. 躲避……；閃開……

◆ Would you like to go playing dodge ball with us?
你想和我們一起打躲避球嗎？

◆ It is impossible for a man who committed a crime to dodge the responsibility.
一個人不可能犯了罪還逃得掉該負的責任。

1526

minor
ˈmaɪnə

adj. 較小的；少數的 *n.* 未成年人

◆ Don't waste a lot of time to focus on the minor points.
不要在小處浪費許多時間。

◆ You will not be considered as a minor once you are older than 18 years old.
如果你超過十八歲就不是未成年人了。

1527

encounter
ɪnˈkaʊntə

v. 遇到⋯⋯；遭遇⋯⋯；和⋯⋯交戰

◆ Mary has encountered many troubles recently.
瑪麗最近遇到很多麻煩。

◆ Stay calm if you encounter adventitious situations.
如果遇到突發狀況時要保持鎮定。

1528 ★

playground
ˈpleˌɡraʊnd

n. 遊樂場；操場；運動場

◆ Let's go play on the playground.
我們去操場玩。

◆ Several children were skipping in the playground.
好幾個孩子在操場上跳躍。

1529

motion
ˈmoʃən

n. 運動；動機；運轉

◆ She is mad because nobody understands what her motion is.
她因為沒人了解她的動機而感到不悅。

◆ The new security system has a very sensitive motion sensor that will detect any irregular movements in the building.
新的保全系統有非常敏感的動作感應器，會偵測檢查建築物裡任何不正常的動作。

1530

exercise
ˈɛksəˌsaɪz

n. 運動；習題；演習

◆ Exercises can make your body healthy.
運動能保身體健康。

◆ Our homework today is to do the exercise at the end of chapter nine.
我們的家庭作業，是做第九章後面的習題。

1531

sport
sport
n. 運動；體育活動

◆ What is your favorite sport?
你最喜歡的運動是什麼？
◆ Nothing can awake his interest in any sport.
他對任何運動都提不起興趣。

1532

athlete
ˋæθlɪt
n. 運動員

◆ My brother is an outstanding athlete.
我兄弟是位出色的運動員。
◆ The athlete won two gold medals in the Olympics.
這位運動員在奧林匹克運動會上獲得兩塊金牌。

1533

freight
fret
n. 運貨（船）；運輸

◆ The aircraft carries both freight and passengers.
這架飛機上乘載貨物與乘客。
◆ Who is the shipper of the freight?
這批貨的託運人是誰？

1534

allergic
əˋlɝdʒɪk
adj. 過敏的

◆ Some people are allergic to seafood.
有些人對海鮮過敏。
◆ Are you allergic to any medicine?
你有對任何藥物過敏嗎？

1535

process
ˋprɑsɛs
n. 過程；常規；製作方法

◆ What are the processes of applying for a scholarship?
申請獎學金的流程是什麼？
◆ The process of generating the power from the motor often needs time.
從馬達產生電力的過程常常需要時間。

1536 ★

fault
fɔlt
n. 過錯

◆ The man endeavors to make up every fault he made.
這個人努力彌補他犯的每一個錯。
◆ It needs some courage for one to acknowledge his own fault.
要一個人承認自己的錯誤需要一點勇氣。

1537 ★

apologize
əˈpɑlədʒaɪz
v. 道歉；認錯

◆ I apologized for an outburst of anger yesterday.
我為昨天的勃然大怒來道歉。

◆ We apologize for the inconvenience.
我們很抱歉帶來不便。

1538 ★

achieve
əˈtʃiv
v. 達成；到達

◆ He has achieved his goal in less than five years.
他不到五年就達成了他的目標。

◆ Please achieve all these tasks in one day.
請在一天之內完成所有的工作。

1539

defy
dɪˈfaɪ
v. 違抗……；挑戰；蔑視危險

不要講話！

◆ Mother will be angry if you defy her again.
假如你再次違抗媽媽，她將會生氣。

◆ The solider defied the order of the military law.
這名軍人違抗軍法命令。

1540

violate
ˈvaɪəˌlet
v. 違背……；對……的違反

闖紅燈

◆ Don't violate laws or you would be punished.
不要違反法律，否則你將會被處罰。

◆ The doctor has been accused of violating medical ethics.
這名醫生被控違反醫療道德。

1541 ★

retail
ˈritel
n. 零售 *adv.* 以零售方式地

◆ She made the bread herself and sold it by retail.
她自己做麵包，並以零售方式賣出。

◆ There are good prospects for growth in the retail sector.
零售部門成長的展望很樂觀。

1542 ★

electricity
ˌɪlɛkˈtrɪsətɪ
n. 電；電流；電學

◆ We should decrease the use of electricity to conserve energy.
我們應該節省用電以保護能源。

◆ Water can act as a medium to conduct electricity.
水可以當成導電的媒介。

1543

scenario
sɪˈnɛrɪˌo
n. 電影腳本；情節

◆ She told me about the scenario of her new movie.
她告訴了我她新電影的腳本。

◆ The plot of the play is just a hackneyed boy-meets-girl scenario.
這齣戲的劇情就是一個平庸的男孩遇見女孩的情節。

1544

voltage
/ˈvoltɪdʒ/
n. 電壓

◆ What is the voltage of electricity supply in Taiwan?
台灣電力供應的是什麼電壓？

◆ Has its voltage been exceeded?
電壓有超過嗎？

1545

reserve
/rɪˈzɝv/
v. 預定……；保留……權利

◆ I'd like to reserve a seat from New York to Kaohsiung.
我想預約一個從紐約到高雄的機位。

◆ I want to reserve a double room.
我想訂一間雙人房。

1546 ★

anticipate
/ænˈtɪsəˌpet/
v. 預料……；預期……；預先考慮

預料拿冠軍

◆ We can hardly anticipate what will happen to us in the future.
我們很難預料未來會發生什麼事。

◆ I really anticipate your coming. I can't wait to see you.
我真的期待你來，我等不及要見到你了。

1547

rehearsal
/rɪˈhɝsl/
n. 預演；演練

彩排

◆ The play is in rehearsal tonight.
這戲劇今晚要排練。

◆ Claques were hired by the theater to make a loud applause during the rehearsal.
鼓掌觀眾是戲院雇用來在彩排時鼓掌喝采的。

1548

budget
/ˈbʌdʒɪt/
n. 預算；安排

我的預算不夠！

◆ How much of the budget do you spend in this program?
這個計劃中你花費了多少預算？

◆ There is an exiguous budget on education in the country.
這個國家的教育預算很缺乏。

1549 ★

stubborn
/ˈstʌbən/
adj. 頑固的；倔強的；頑強的

還不起床！

◆ I don't want to talk with such a stubborn man.
我不想和這樣一個頑固的人說話。

◆ Recession is a stubborn phenomenon, which won't just disappear overnight.
不景氣是頑強的現象，不會一夜之間消失。

1550

rear
/rɪr/
v. 飼養……；養育…… **n.** 後面

◆ The ticket office is at the rear of the station concourse.
售票處在車站大廳的後面。

◆ Please disembark through the rear exit.
請由後方機尾處下機。

1551

tame
tem
adj. 馴服的；溫順的

◆ My pet is as tame as a sheep.
我的寵物就像綿羊一樣溫馴。

◆ The lion proved to be tame when the trainer stuck his head inside its mouth.
當這訓練師把他的頭伸入獅子口中時，證明獅子是溫馴的。

1552

applaud
ə´plɔd
v. 鼓掌；拍手喝采；贊許

◆ The audience applauded the winner ardently.
觀眾熱情地為這勝利者鼓掌。

◆ He showed his modesty when people applauded his achievement.
當人們對他的成就喝采時，他表現了謙遜。

1553 ★

inspire
ɪn´spaɪr
v. 鼓舞……；給某人信心

◆ A truly good friend inspires me with many precious experiences.
真正的好朋友會以許多珍貴的經驗鼓舞我。

◆ He gave a noteworthy speech that many teenagers are inspired.
他發表了一場讓很多年輕人都受到鼓勵的出色演說。

1554 ★

encourage
ɪn´kɝɪdʒ
v. 鼓勵……；使……有勇氣

加油!

◆ My mother encouraged me to join the basketball team.
媽媽鼓勵我加入籃球隊。

◆ Abstinent belief is commonly accepted and encouraged by some religions.
節制的信念普遍受到某些宗教的接受與鼓勵。

1555 ★

servant
´sɝvənt
n. 僕人；佣人

◆ The rich family keeps thirty servants.
這富有的家庭養了三十個僕人。

◆ The prince made friends with his servants despite their social status.
不管他們的社會地位，這位王子與他的僕人們成為朋友。

1556

division
də´vɪʒən
n. 劃分；除法；部門

$$\frac{x}{y}$$

◆ There are four police divisions around this area.
這附近有四個警察分局。

◆ The editor agreed upon a division of the book into fourteen units.
編輯同意將這本書切割分成十四個單元。

1557

divide
də´vaɪd
v. 劃分……；分割……

◆ The president divided the company into two major departments.
董事長將公司分成兩個主要部門。

◆ Europe is usually divided into five parts.
歐洲通常被分為五個部分。

1558

partition
parˈtɪʃən
v. 劃分……；分割…… **n.** 分隔物

◆ The workers partition my office into three cubicles.
這些工人們將我的辦公室分隔成三個小隔間。

◆ My father partitioned off part of the house as a garage.
我爸爸將房子一部分隔開做車庫。

1559

abhor
əbˈhɔr
v. 厭惡……；憎惡……

厭惡比我美的

◆ Most people abhor those parents who abuse their children.
大多數人痛恨那些虐待小孩的父母。

◆ Penny abhors people who have bad manners.
潘妮痛恨談吐態度不佳的人。

1560

noisy
ˈnɔɪzɪ
adj. 嘈雜的；喧嘩的

◆ The teacher ejected the noisy student from the classroom.
老師把這位吵鬧的學生趕出教室。

◆ It's too noisy outside for me to sleep.
外面吵到我睡不著。

1561

carnival
ˈkɑrnəvl
n. 嘉年華會；園遊會

◆ The most famous carnival in Europe was in Venice.
歐洲最著名的嘉年華會是在威尼斯。

◆ The carnival parade was a magnificent spectacle.
這場嘉年華會的遊行相當壯觀。

1562

graph
græf
n. 圖表

◆ The graph shows a bulge in the price of gold.
這圖表顯示黃金價格的上漲。

◆ Could you recommend some books on computer graphs?
你能推薦一些電腦圖表的書嗎？

1563 ★

diagram
ˈdaɪəˌgræm
n. 圖表；圖樣

◆ The teacher uses diagrams to explain the mathematical principles.
老師用圖表來解釋數學原理。

◆ A flowchart is a diagram, which shows the stages of a process.
流程圖是一種能展示程式步驟的圖形。

1564 ★

pattern
ˈpætən
n. 圖案；模範；模型

◆ The pattern on this dress is very interesting.
這件洋裝上的圖案非常有趣。

◆ She prefers clothing with arabesque patterns.
她較喜歡阿拉伯式圖案的衣服。

1565

solidarity
.sɑlə'dærətɪ
n. 團結一致

◆ Your party is based on solidarity forever.
你們政黨是建立在永久的團結上。

◆ Their sense of solidarity is very high.
他們的團結意識非常高昂。

1566

snatch
snætʃ
v. 奪取；奪走

◆ The girl's brother snatched the ice cream from her hand.
這女孩的哥哥從她的手上奪走冰淇淋。

◆ Sometimes bears snatch food from aquatic birds.
有時候熊會搶走水鳥的食物。

1567

hatch
hætʃ
v. 孵化；策劃

◆ Hen's eggs take nearly 20 days to hatch out.
母雞下的蛋幾乎要二十天才孵化。

◆ They hatched up a plot to overthrow these oppressors.
他們策劃推翻這些壓迫者。

1568

truth
truθ
n. 實話；真理

我說的都是真話…

◆ Because he is grumpy, no one likes to tell him the truth.
因為他的脾氣暴躁，沒有人喜歡對他說真話。

◆ The witness took an oath of truth to the court.
證人向法庭發誓所言屬實。

1569

betray
bɪ'tre
v. 對……不忠；
出賣……

對妻子不忠的男人

◆ The traitor betrayed his country.
賣國賊背叛自己的祖國。

◆ The man asseverated that he would take a revenge on the one who betrayed him.
這個男人鄭重地說他會報復背叛他的人。

1570 ★

tempt
tɛmpt
v. 對……加以誘
惑；引誘……

◆ The offer of a free TV tempted her to buy the car.
一台免費電視的誘惑讓她買了這輛車。

◆ The man is always tempted by stripper.
這男子總是被脫衣舞孃誘惑。

1571

swap
swɑp
v. 對……作交換

◆ He offered to swap his laptop for hers.
他提議和她交換筆電。

◆ Can I swap your diamond for my ruby?
我能夠用我的紅寶石和你交換鑽石嗎？

1572

agree
əˈgri

ⅴ 對……表示同意；答應……

◆ We agreed with the President's new proposal.
我們贊同總統的新提案。

◆ I don't agree with your opinion.
我不同意你的看法。

1573

threaten
ˈθrɛtn

ⅴ 對……恐嚇；對……威脅

錢拿出來!

◆ The labor union is threatening to call a strike for one day.
勞工團體提出罷工一天的威脅。

◆ Humanity was threatened by nuclear war.
人類受到核子戰爭的威脅。

1574 ★

prosecute
ˈprɑsɪˌkjut

ⅴ 對……起訴；提出控告

你被起訴了!

◆ Peter's father was prosecuted for drunk driving.
彼得的父親酒駕被起訴。

◆ All the politico's proponents are prosecuted for the bribery.
這名政客所有的擁護者皆因賄賂而被起訴。

1575

worship
ˈwɝʃəp

ⅴ 對……崇拜；禮拜……

◆ People in Taiwan regularly prepare some food to worship their ancestors on certain dates.
台灣民眾習慣在特定的日子裡準備一些食物祭祀祖先。

◆ Chicken and pork are often used as oblation to worship ancestors.
雞肉和豬肉經常用來作為祭拜祖先的祭品。

1576

detest
dɪˈtɛst

ⅴ 對……深惡痛絕；厭惡

討厭!

◆ The teacher detests those students who deceive and tell lies.
這位老師厭惡那些欺騙和說謊的學生。

◆ The workers detest his critical manner.
這些工人討厭他吹毛求疵的態度。

1577

impeach
ɪmˈpitʃ

ⅴ 對……提出懷疑；彈劾……

政見發表會

說到做到嗎?

◆ The governor was impeached because of the scandal.
州長因為醜聞遭到彈劾。

◆ We must impeach the police officer for taking bribes.
我們要彈劾這位警官收取賄賂。

1578

warn
wɔrn

ⅴ 對……提出警告

◆ My father always warns me not to go out alone at night.
我父親常警告我不要在晚上單獨出門。

◆ Noah was assigned to warn people about the diluvial event.
諾亞被指定去警告人們大洪水的事件。

1579

supervise
ˋsupɚˏvaɪz
v. 對……進行監督；管理

管理部

◆ Her job is supervising the company's operations in Japan.
他的工作是監督這家公司在日本的運作。

◆ The UK had supervised Hong Kong for 150 years.
英國曾經管理香港一百五十年。

1580 ★

suspect
səˋspɛkt
v. 對……懷疑；對……起疑心
n. 嫌疑犯

我懷疑…

◆ I suspect he has some ulterior motive in his plan.
我懷疑他的計劃中暗藏玄機。

◆ The agent was suspected of treason.
這個代表被懷疑叛國。

1581

opponent
əˋponənt
n. 對手；反對者

◆ In the second round, his opponent wins in an overwhelming victory.
第二回合，他的對手獲得壓倒性的勝利。

◆ I hope to beat my opponent in the run-off.
我希望在決賽時擊敗對手。

1582 ★

contrast
ˋkɑntræst
n. 對比；對照；差別

◆ There is a remarkable contrast between the two pictures.
這兩張圖畫有極顯著的對比。

◆ The clothing designer likes the contrast of the white skirt with the black blouse.
這位服裝設計師喜歡白色裙子與黑短衫間的對比。

1583 ★

opposite
ˋɑpəzɪt
adj. 對立的；相反的

北韓
南韓

◆ My aunt lives opposite to me.
我姑姑住在我家對面。

◆ We have opposite opinions on this matter.
對於這事情我們有相反的意見。

1584

treat
trit
v. 對待；對……進行招待

◆ Many people like to treat their pets as kids.
很多人喜歡將寵物當成小孩對待。

◆ The pet might be amenable if you treat it with your heart.
如果真心以待，寵物也會順從的。

1585

screen
skrin
n. 幕；螢幕

◆ I don't like sitting near the computer screen.
我不喜歡坐離電腦螢幕太近。

◆ A multi-screen cinema is the best amenity in a sports center.
運動中心裡的多螢幕電影院是最好的設施。

1586

thorough
/ˈθɝo/
adj. 徹底的；完全的；十足的

徹底檢查

◆ I went to the hospital for a thorough health check-up.
我去這所醫院做一個徹底的健康檢查。

◆ The mechanic gave the car a thorough going-over.
這位技工給這台車一次徹底的檢查。

1587

manner
/ˈmænɚ/
n. 態度；樣子

很乖喔！

◆ A good manner can make your personal image better.
良好的態度可以使你有更好的形象。

◆ The customers were piqued by the waiters' bad services and manners.
侍者糟糕的服務和態度激怒了客人。

1588 ★

jog
/dʒɑg/
v. 慢跑

◆ I go jogging every morning.
我每天早上都去慢跑。

◆ My father goes jogging every morning.
我父親每天去慢跑。

1589

routine
/ruˈtin/
n. 慣例；常規

5點下課了

◆ The doctor wants to do some routine urine tests.
醫生想要做一些例行尿檢。

◆ All that you've mentioned are some routine work.
您剛才所提的都是一些例行工作。

1590 ★

deadline
/ˈdɛdˌlaɪn/
n. 截止日期

時間到了！

◆ What is the deadline for submitting the quotation?
什麼時候是報價的截止日期？

◆ He is sanguine about getting the work finished before the deadline.
他對在期限內完成工作很樂觀。

1591 ★

summary
/ˈsʌmərɪ/
n. 摘要

摘要

◆ The assignment is to write a summary of this article.
這次的作業是寫出這篇文章的摘要。

◆ The speaker gave sententious summary instead of copious speech.
演講者提出簡潔的摘要而不是冗長的演說。

1592 ★

raze
/rez/
v. 摧毀；夷平

◆ After the fierce earthquake, many buildings were razed to the ground.
經過這場激烈的地震後，許多房子都被夷為平地。

◆ Numerous buildings are razed to the ground suddenly.
突然間大量房屋被摧毀為平地。

1593

demolish
dɪˈmɑlɪʃ

v. 摧毀……；改變……的立場

◆ A fire demolished many buildings on the street.
一場大火摧毀了這條街上的許多大樓。

◆ They're going to demolish that old building under the special situation.
在某種特殊情況下，他們準備拆除這棟老舊大樓。

1594 ★

blackmail
ˈblæk.mel

v. n. 敲詐；勒索

◆ The men tried to blackmail the senator by speaking about his scandal.
這人以說出醜聞來敲詐這位參議員。

◆ The man was sent to prison for blackmail.
這男人因為勒索而進監獄。

1595 ★

banner
ˈbænɚ

n. 旗；旗幟；橫幅

◆ On National Days, many people carried our national banner on the streets.
每逢國定假日，許多人在街上拿著我們的國旗。

◆ You need to spread out the banner so I can write on it.
你必須把旗幟展開，我才能在上面寫字。

1596

flag
flæg

n. 旗子 v. 使枯萎；懸旗於……

◆ The Canadian flag has a red maple leaf in the center.
加拿大的國旗有一片紅楓葉在中央。

◆ Her interest in swimming has begun to flag.
他對游泳的興趣逐漸消退了。

1597

marketable
ˈmɑrkɪtəbl

adj. 暢銷的；有銷路的

◆ Our new products will be well marketable in your country.
我們的新產品在你們國家會賣得很好。

◆ The silk dress is a widely marketable product.
這種絲質洋裝是種大量暢銷的產品。

1598 ★

積土而為山，積水而為海

---

float
ˈflot
v. 漂浮；浮動

◆ There are floating objects on the sea.
　海上有漂流物體。

◆ The dead fish floating on the lake are fetid.
　漂浮在湖面上的死魚發出惡臭。

1599

---

maneuver
məˈnuvə
n. 演習；策略

◆ The army performed a military maneuver last week.
　陸軍在上週舉行軍事演習。

◆ Each summer, the army goes on maneuvers to test its equipment and its readiness to fight.
　每年夏天軍方演習以測試裝備及戰鬥的意志力。

1600

---

extinguish
ɪkˈstɪŋgwɪʃ
v. 熄滅……
(火)；使消失

◆ Please extinguish your cigarettes.
　請將你的香煙熄滅。

◆ It took a few days to extinguish the large forest fire.
　花了幾天才撲滅這場森林大火。

1601 ★

---

bear
bɛr
n. 熊；承擔；
忍受

◆ We ran away from the bear.
　我們從熊的身邊跑走。

◆ Many couples had to bear long periods of separation during the war.
　戰爭時許多夫妻必須忍受長期分離。

1602

---

petty
ˈpɛtɪ
adj. 瑣碎的；小
器的；小規模的

分到10%的財產

◆ The daughter only received a petty share of her father's wealth.
　這女兒只有接受到他父親財產的一小部分。

◆ He wastes his time on petty details that no one else cares about.
　他浪費時間在那些沒有人關心的瑣碎小事。

1603

---

mad
mæd
adj. 瘋狂的；惱
怒的

◆ I feel I shall go mad when you quarrel with me .
　當你跟我爭吵時，我感覺自己要瘋了。

◆ You must be joking or else you are mad .
　你一定是開玩笑，不然就是瘋了。

1604

aim

em

v. 瞄準⋯⋯；針對⋯⋯ **n.** 目標

◆ This book aims at giving a general outline of the subject.
這本書針對這個主題來提出整體性大綱。

◆ He aimed the gun at the a bear.
他把槍瞄準一隻熊。

1605

racial

ˈreʃəl

adj. 種族的；人種的

◆ His ridiculous speech on racial discrimination agitates the public.
他對種族歧視荒謬的演說煽動了群眾。

◆ The racial discrimination causes a serious problem in society.
種族歧視造成嚴重的社會問題。

1606

species

ˈspiʃiz

n. 種類；物種

◆ Dolphins are a protected species.
海豚是受保護的物類。

◆ Both kangaroo and koalas belong to the species of the marsupial.
袋鼠和無尾熊都屬於有袋動物。

1607

accolade

ˌækəˈled

n. 稱讚；盛讚；獎品

◆ His behavior won everyone's accolade.
他的行為獲得每個人的讚賞。

◆ The best accolade that parents give their children is their support.
父母給孩子最好的獎勵就是他們的支持。

1608

elaborate

ɪˈlæbərɪt

adj. 精心製作的 **v.** 精心設計；詳細說明

◆ They make an elaborate celebration in order to give her a surprise.
為了要讓她驚喜，他們精心設計了慶祝活動。

◆ Peter concocted an elaborate excuse for being absent.
彼得為自己的缺席捏造精心設計的藉口。

1609

shrewd

ʃrud

adj. 精明的；敏銳的

精明的狐狸

◆ He is shrewd enough to take care of himself.
他足夠精明來照顧自己了。

◆ She is a shrewd saleswoman who knows how to persuade people to buy her products.
她是一位精明的銷售員，知道如何說服人們去買她的產品。

1610

elite

eˈlit

n. 精英；出類拔萃者

◆ The Southeast Asian country was governed by a small elite group of political and military officers.
這個東南亞國家是被少數政治和軍事精英集團所統治。

◆ They all are the elite of the society.
他們全都是社會的精英。

1611

psychiatrist
saɪˈkaɪətrɪst
n. 精神科醫生

◆ He is always under the pressure, so he goes to see a psychiatrist.
他總是壓力重重，所以去看了精神科醫生。

◆ It was declared by the psychiatrists that the killer is insane.
心理醫生們宣稱這位殺人犯有精神病。

1612

computer-literate
kəmˈpjutəˈlɪtərɪt
adj. 精通電腦的

◆ When employers interview prospective employees, they always want to make sure candidates are computer-literate.
當雇主應徵未來的員工時，他們總希望確認面試者能精通電腦。

◆ If someone is computer-literate, they have enough skill to use a computer.
假如有人是懂電腦的，他們就有足夠技巧來使用電腦。

1613 ★

accurate
ˈækjərɪt
adj. 精確的；準確的

◆ Her idea is absolutely accurate about this financial prophesy.
她對於這項財務預測的意見是非常精確的。

◆ The young photographer is a laity at taking accurate focal length and point.
這位年輕的攝影師對於取得精確的焦距和焦點是外行人。

1614 ★

exquisite
ˈɛkskwɪzɪt
adj. 精緻的；絕妙的

◆ These stamps are very exquisite and pleasing.
這些郵票都十分地精緻且討人喜歡。

◆ She bought an exquisite diamond necklace.
她買了一條精緻的鑽石項鍊。

1615

selection
səˈlɛkʃən
n. 精選；入選者

老歌精選集

◆ The library has a good selection of western classic literature.
這間圖書館有很好的西方古典文學精選。

◆ That bakery has a fine selection of cakes.
這家麵包店有很好的蛋糕供我們選擇。

1616

net
nɛt
n. 網；網狀物
adj. 淨值的

◆ The fisherman uses fishing nets to catch fish in the river.
這漁夫使用魚網在這條河流中補魚。

◆ The net weight of this bag of coffee bean is 200 grams.
這袋咖啡豆淨重二百公克。

1617

cyberspace
ˈsaɪbəˌspes
n. 網際空間

◆ It's very easy to create a phony identity and cheat others in cyberspace.
在網際空間中很容易製作一個假身份來欺騙其他人。

◆ Someone would like to live in the cyberspace.
有些人喜歡生活在網際空間。

1618

Internet
/ˈɪntɚˌnɛt/
n. 網際網路

◆ The Internet helps us learn.
網際網路幫助我們學習。

◆ Do you like surfing the Internet?
你喜歡上網瀏覽嗎？

1619

tight
/taɪt/
adj. 緊的；牢固的

◆ The skirts are a bit tight around my waist.
這些裙子在我腰部附近有點緊。

◆ They have planned a tight agenda of travel.
他們計劃了一份緊湊的旅遊行程。

1620

emergency
/ɪˈmɝdʒənsɪ/
n. 緊急；緊急事件

◆ What sort of emergency equipment did you prepare at that time?
當時你們準備了什麼緊急逃生裝備？

◆ His potential ability was exposed during the emergency.
他的潛力在緊急的時候顯露出來。

1621 ★

urgent
/ˈɝdʒənt/
adj. 緊急的；急迫的

◆ The family is in urgent need of help.
這個家庭急需幫忙。

◆ People in the past used the telegram to send urgent messages.
以前人們用電報來傳遞緊急消息。

1622 ★

tension
/ˈtɛnʃən/
n. 緊張；焦急；張力

◆ Gary quit the school because of heavy tension.
蓋瑞因為精神高度緊張而休學。

◆ The tension between the two countries has eased off a little.
這兩個國家間的緊張關係已經緩和一些。

1623

nervous
/ˈnɝvəs/
adj. 緊張的；神經的

◆ I am nervous because it's my turn to make presentation today.
我好緊張，因為今天輪到我做報告了。

◆ She is too nervous to express her opinions.
她太緊張而說不出意見。

1624

focus
/ˈfokəs/
v. 聚焦於 *n.* 焦點；集中點

◆ This chapter focuses on the history of Taiwan.
本章的重點在於台灣歷史。

◆ I think Emily likes to be the focus of attention.
我認為愛蜜莉喜歡成為注意的焦點。

1625 ★

amass
ə'mæs
v. 聚積；聚集

◆ Helen has amassed working experience and been a professional leader for many years.
海倫累積了工作經驗，而且多年以後成為一位專業的領導者。

◆ If you want to amass a fortune, you need to work hard.
假如你想累積一筆財富，你需要努力工作。

1626

rotten
'rɑtn̩
adj. 腐敗的；發臭的

◆ It is important to refrigerate your food to prevent it from becoming rotten.
冷凍你的食物對於防止食物腐壞是重要的。

◆ A crowd wanted to overthrow the rotten government.
群眾們希望推翻這個腐敗的政府。

1627

compete
kəm'pit
v. 與……競爭；對抗

◆ We will compete with the State champion team.
我們將要和州冠軍隊競爭。

◆ Five teams from different counties competed with each other for a large reward.
五個來自不同縣的隊伍為了巨額的獎金互相競爭。

1628

dispute
dɪ'spjut
v. 與……辯論
n. 爭論

◆ The legislators have disputed this policy for a long time.
立法委員為此政策已爭論多時。

◆ The dispute estranged him from his friend.
這場爭論讓他和朋友疏遠了。

1629 ★

wrestle
'rɛsl̩
v. 與……摔角；搬動……；努力解決

◆ Men like to watch cruel wrestling shows most.
男人最愛看殘酷的摔角秀。

◆ It took two men to wrestle the heavy table into suitable place.
動用了兩個人才把這張很重的桌子搬到適合的地方。

1630

incur
ɪn'kɝ
v. 蒙受……；遭致……

◆ He incurred the wrath of his wife.
他惹來他太太的報復。

◆ His disobedience incurred his father's umbrage.
他的不服從招致他父親的憤怒。

1631

suffer
'sʌfɚ
v. 蒙受……痛苦

◆ He often suffers from a stomachache.
他經常會胃痛。

◆ My aunt is suffering from severe mental disorder.
我姑媽正患有嚴重的精神錯亂。

1632

vapor
ˈvepɚ
n. 蒸氣

◆ Boiling water turns into vapor.
煮沸的水轉變為蒸氣。

◆ Vapor is water in the form of a gas.
蒸氣是一種氣態的水。

1633

---

evaporate
ɪˈvæpəˌret
v. 蒸發

◆ The pool of water on the ground will evaporate soon.
地上的這池水將會很快蒸發。

◆ If you heat the water, it will evaporate.
假如你把水加熱，水會蒸發掉。

1634

---

pale
pel
adj. 蒼白的

◆ Suffering from cancer makes him look pale.
罹患癌症使他看來蒼白。

◆ At the news of the car accident she turned pale.
她聽到這場車禍的消息，臉色變得蒼白。

1635

---

lid
lɪd
n. 蓋子；眼瞼

◆ He broke open the lid of the box with a hammer.
他用鎚子把這箱子的蓋子敲開。

◆ I put a lid on the box yesterday.
我昨天在這箱子上加蓋。

1636

---

fabricate
ˈfæbrɪˌket
v. 製造……；
裝配……；杜
撰……

那邊有隻恐龍

◆ The excuse was fabricated and completely untrue.
這個藉口是杜撰的，而且完全不是事實。

◆ He fabricated an excuse to rationalize his fault.
他杜撰一個藉口來合理化他的錯誤。

1637

---

produce
prəˈdjus
v. 製造出；使產
生

◆ As long as it's in the process of being patented, we can start producing.
只要專利已經在申請中，我們就可以開始生產。

◆ Without muscles, it is impossible for the body to produce the movements.
沒有肌肉，身體不可能產生動作。

1638 ★

---

matter
ˈmætɚ
v. 認為……有關
n. 事情；課題

◆ I have nothing to do with this matter.
我和這事毫無瓜葛。

◆ It doesn't matter whether he agrees to help us or not.
他是否答應幫我們已經不重要了。

1639

recognize
/ˈrɛkəg.naɪz/

v. 認得出；辨別出；意識到

◆ The student recognized that he had made a mistake.
這位學生承認他犯了錯。

◆ I could hardly recognize your voice.
我幾乎認不出你的聲音

1640

distinguish
/dɪˈstɪŋgwɪʃ/

v. 認清楚；區別出……；使顯著

◆ It is hard to distinguish her from her sister.
很難區別出她和她妹妹的長相。

◆ My costume designer is distinguished for his originality.
我的服裝設計師以獨創性聞名。

1641 ★

oath
/oθ/

n. 誓約；發誓

◆ The witness took an oath of truth to the court.
這位證人向法庭發誓所言屬實。

◆ The old man took an oath to quit drinking alcohol.
這老人發誓說他戒酒了。

1642

lure
/lur/

v. 誘惑…… **n.** 引誘品；魅力

◆ Fishermen use lures to attract and hook fish.
漁夫們使用誘餌來吸引並釣魚。

◆ The officer couldn't resist the lure of money.
這位官員無法抵抗金錢的誘惑。

1643

language
/ˈlæŋgwɪdʒ/

n. 語言

◆ How many languages do you speak?
你會說幾種語言？

◆ It is very difficult for foreign students to overcome language barriers.
外國學生很難克服語言的障礙。

1644

misunderstand
/ˌmɪsʌndəˈstænd/

v. 誤解……；誤會……

◆ You misunderstood my words completely.
你完全誤解我的話了。

◆ The man tried to make everything explicit to avoid a misunderstanding.
這位男人嘗試把每件事表達清楚，以避免誤會。

1645

deluxe
/dɪˈlʌks/

adj. 豪華的；高檔的

◆ The rich man lives in a deluxe villa.
這有錢人住在一間豪華的別墅。

◆ The prince lived in a large and deluxe castle.
這位王子住在一座豪華的大城堡。

1646

luxurious
lʌɡˈʒʊrɪəs
adj. 豪華的；奢侈的

外太空旅行

◆ The rich man lives under a prodigal and luxurious lifestyle.
富人過著浪費豪奢的生活。

◆ This luxurious suite is clean and tidy.
這個豪華套房又乾淨又整齊。

1647

splendid
ˈsplɛndɪd
adj. 豪華的；華麗的

華麗的宮殿

◆ The dome of the castle is very splendid.
這個城堡的圓頂是非常壯觀的。

◆ The royal wedding was a splendid affair.
這個皇室婚禮盛大豪華。

1648

banish
ˈbænɪʃ
v. 趕走……；放逐

把這叛徒驅逐出境！

◆ The king banished the betrayer from the country.
國王將這叛徒驅逐出境。

◆ She tries to banish sorrow from her thoughts.
她嘗試從她的想法中趕走悲傷。

1649

auxiliary
ɔɡˈzɪljərɪ
adj. 輔助的；後備的 **n.** 輔助者

◆ The advanced system includes a backup auxiliary system
這個先進系統包括一個後備輔助系統。

◆ The operational base offered a nursing auxiliary to the combat troops.
作戰基地為戰鬥部隊提供了附屬的護理機構。

1650 ★

tap
tæp
v. 輕拍；接通水源 **n.** 閥門

◆ He'll perform in the tap dance show tonight.
他將在今晚的踢踏舞秀表演。

◆ He cleaned his hands in the water from the tap.
他用水龍頭的水洗手。

1651

contempt
kənˈtɛmpt
n. 輕視；恥辱

髒死了！

◆ I feel contempt for his impoliteness to the elderly.
他對老人家的無禮讓我感到不屑。

◆ Such behavior is beneath contempt.
如此的行為令人不齒。

1652 ★

despise
dɪˈspaɪz
v. 輕視……；看不起

You Loser！

◆ All of his friends despise his treatment of his parents.
他所有朋友都唾棄他對待父母的方式。

◆ I have nothing but despise for such a person.
對這樣的人我只有唾棄。

1653

disparage
dɪˈspærɪdʒ
v. 輕視……；誹謗……的名譽

◆ Tom's theory was widely disparaged by scientists.
湯姆的理論廣泛地被科學家們輕視。

◆ You should not disparage his achievements.
你不應該輕視他的成就。

1654

slight
slaɪt
adj. 輕微的；微小的

輕微的疼痛

◆ The Chinese Petroleum Corp. made a slight reduction in the price of oil.
中國石油公司微降了石油的價格。

◆ The patient has a slight wheeze in his chest.
這個病人的胸部發出輕微的氣音。

1655

deliver
dɪˈlɪvə
v. 遞送；運送；傳達

◆ When can you deliver my order?
什麼時候我訂的貨能送來？

◆ The products you ordered were delivered three days ago.
您訂購的產品在三天前就送出去了。

1656 ★

excursion
ɪkˈskɝʒən
n. 遠足；短程旅行

◆ We are planning for our excursion next week.
我們正在為下週的遠足作準備。

◆ They are very happy because they are going on an excursion.
他們很高興因為他們要去遠足了。

1657

distant
ˈdɪstənt
adj. 遠的；遠離的

好遠哦！

◆ He is very distant with his family after he got out of prison.
自從他出獄後，他與他的家人漸行漸遠。

◆ In a way, he is a distant relation of mine.
就某種意義而言，他是我的遠房親戚。

1658

acid
ˈæsɪd
adj. 酸味的 *n.* 酸

◆ The metal cover is fretted with the acid.
這金屬蓋子被酸腐蝕了。

◆ Acid rain is recognized as a serious environmental problem.
酸雨被認為是一種嚴重的環境問題。

1659

sour
saur
adj. 酸的

◆ Milk turns sour when it coagulates.
牛奶凝固時會變酸。

◆ I don't like lemonade because it is too sour for me.
我不喜歡喝檸檬汁，因為太酸了。

1660

bank
bæŋk
n. 銀行

◆ Most banks open at 9:00 and close at 3:30.
大部分的銀行都在九點開門，三點半關門。

◆ A bank draft is a check where the payment is guaranteed to be paid by the issuing bank.
銀行匯票是一種由發行銀行保證付款的支票。

1661

banker
ˈbæŋkə
n. 銀行家；銀行業者

◆ Foreign bankers are very optimistic about the country's economic future.
國外銀行業者對這個國家的經濟前景感到非常樂觀。

◆ My boss has applied to the banker for a loan
我老闆已向銀行業者申請貸款。

1662

galaxy
ˈgæləksɪ
n. 銀河；一群傑出人物

◆ Each galaxy contains myriads of stars.
每一個銀河系都有無數的恆星。

◆ We will see a galaxy of musicians in tonight's concert.
我們在今晚的音樂會上看到一群傑出的音樂家。

1663

silverware
ˈsɪlvəˌwɛr
n. 銀器

◆ Could you place the classical silverware on the table for dinner ?
你能將這古典銀器擺放在晚宴桌上嗎？

◆ The waitress rubbed up the silverware with a clean wiper.
這位女侍者以一塊乾淨的抹布擦拭銀器。

1664

impediment
ɪmˈpɛdəmənt
n. 障礙物；殘障；口吃

◆ A critical impediment to development is the country's huge foreign debt.
巨額外債是我國發展的主要障礙。

◆ No impediment could shake my determination.
沒有阻礙能動搖我決心。

1665

重複是學習之母

want
wɑnt
v. 需要……

◆ Do you want some more coffee?
你要再來點咖啡嗎？

◆ Do you want a regular or king-sized bed?
你要一個普通或特大號的床？

1666

realm
rɛlm
n. 領土；國土；領域

◆ He is very outstanding in the realm of literature.
他在文學的領域非常著名。

◆ The king rules his realm with benevolent policies.
這個國王用仁慈的政策統治他的國土。

1667

collar
'kɑlə
n. 領子；衣領

◆ The police seized the thief by the collar.
警察一把抓住小偷的衣領。

◆ What size of collar is this shirt?
這件襯衫的衣領尺寸是什麼？

1668

pilot
'paɪlət
n. 領航員；駕駛員

◆ The airline pilot spoke to the passengers during the flight.
飛行時這位飛機駕駛員對乘客說話。

◆ The pilot climbed into the cockpit and waved to the crowd.
這位駕駛員爬入駕駛座艙，並和群眾揮手。

1669

scope
skop
n. 領域；範圍

◆ Calculus is outside the scope of my math knowledge.
微積分在我的數學知識領域之外。

◆ Your question is beyond the scope of my research.
你的問題超過了我研究的領域了。

1670 ★

typhoon
taɪ'fun
n. 颱風

颱風最新動態

◆ This typhoon didn't cause serious damage.
這個颱風沒有造成很嚴重的傷害。

◆ The typhoon brought a lot of trouble to the town.
那個颱風給城鎮帶來很多的麻煩。

1671

stand-off
ˈstænd.ɔf
n. 僵持局面 *adj.*
冷漠的

◆ This could lead to another diplomatic stand-off.
這可能導致另外一種外交僵局。

◆ The selfish miser had a stand-off nature.
這位自私的守財奴有一種冷漠的天性。

1672

tariff
ˈtærɪf
n. 價目表；關稅；
運費

◆ May I have the tariff for your products?
能給我看你們產品的價目表嗎？

◆ The government is going to increase the tariff on imported cars.
政府準備對進口車增加關稅。

1673 ★

apparatus
ˌæpəˈretəs
n. 儀器；器官；
機械裝置

◆ The hospital has recently bought some medical apparatus.
這家醫院最近買了一些醫學器材。

◆ Each apparatus in this room is very expensive. You got to take care of them very carefully.
在此房裡的每部儀器都很昂貴，你得小心照管。

1674

acute
əˈkjut
adj. 劇烈的；急
性的；激烈的

◆ The patient fell ill with acute respiratory disease.
這位病人患有急性呼吸系統疾病。

◆ Suddenly, he had acute pain in his chest.
他胸口突然一陣劇痛。

1675

nausea
ˈnɔzɪə
n. 噁心；作嘔

◆ The patient suffers from a headache, nausea, and vomiting.
這位病人正受頭痛、噁心和想吐之苦。

◆ My uncle experienced nausea after eating sea food.
我叔叔吃了海鮮感覺噁心。

1676

accrue
əˈkru
v. 增加；利息孳
生

◆ Many benefits accrue to society with perfect social welfare.
完美的社會福利為社會帶來許多好處。

◆ Knowledge will accrue to you from reading a lot.
多閱讀將會增加知識。

1677

increase
ɪnˈkris
v. 增加……；加
大……

◆ The trade surplus of our country increased rapidly over the past few years.
我國的貿易順差在過去幾年裡迅速增長。

◆ The prices keep increasing these years.
這幾年間物價一直持續上揚。

1678 ★

tomb
tum
n. 墳墓

◆ Egyptian pyramids are tombs and monuments to dead rulers.
埃及金字塔是死去統治者的墳墓與紀念碑。

◆ They found this authentic diamond in an ancient tomb.
他們在古代墳墓中發現了這顆真鑽。

1679

---

prudent
ˈprudn̩t
adj. 審慎的；小心的

新生兒照顧

◆ The investor made some prudent financial decisions and earned a lot of money.
這個投資者做了一些審慎的財務決定，而且賺了不少錢。

◆ Isn't it prudent of you to marry the bad guy?
你嫁給這個壞蛋是明智的嗎？

1680

---

generous
ˈdʒɛnərəs
adj. 寬大的；慷慨的

◆ The rich man is generous in giving help to the poor.
這位有錢人對於助窮人很大方。

◆ It was most generous of you to lend me the car.
你借車給我真是太慷慨了。

1681

---

width
ˈwɪdθ
n. 寬度

2.0 m
6′- 6″

◆ What is the desk's width?
這桌子有多寬？

◆ How many centimeters is the width of the rectangle?
這個長方形的寬度是多少公分？

1682

---

lenient
ˈlinjənt
adj. 寬容的；不嚴厲的

◆ Mothers are always lenient towards their children.
母親對自己的孩子總是寬容不嚴厲。

◆ The judge was lenient with the criminal.
這位法官對這罪犯很寬容。

1683

---

spacious
ˈspeʃəs
adj. 寬敞的；廣闊的

車內舒適又寬敞

◆ The old lady lived in a spacious house alone.
這位老女人獨自住在一間寬敞的房子裡。

◆ The dormitory is neither spacious nor comfortable.
這家學生宿舍既不寬敞也不舒適。

1684

---

broad
brɔd
adj. 寬闊的；廣泛的

理論太廣泛要縮小範圍

◆ He had broad shoulders and stalwart arms.
他有寬闊的肩膀與健壯的手臂。

◆ Your theory is too broad; you need to narrow it down.
你的理論太廣泛了，需要把涵蓋的範圍縮小。

1685

resume
rɪˈzjum
n. 履歷 *v.* 重新開始；取回

◆ The applicant is required to submit a resume.
這位申請者被要求交一份履歷表。

◆ The TV show will resume after this commercial.
廣告後這個電視節目將會重新開始。

1686 ★

widespread
ˈwaɪdˌsprɛd
adj. 廣布的

◆ The forest fires were widespread through the mountains.
這場森林大火蔓延了這幾座山。

◆ Higher rates of unemployment caused widespread poverty.
較高的失業率會引起廣泛的貧窮現象。

1687 ★

advertisement
ˌædvɚˈtaɪzmənt
n. 廣告；宣傳

◆ Advertisement can stimulate customers to buy goods.
廣告能夠刺激消費者買東西。

◆ The advertisement signboard should be conspicuous.
廣告看板應該要能醒目。

1688

billboard
ˈbɪlˌbord
n. 廣告牌；看板

明天放假！

◆ Can you type up an official notice and post it on the billboard by noon?
你能在中午之前，起草一份正式公文貼在公布欄嗎？

◆ The billboard in a rubric is brilliant.
這個紅色標題的廣告牌很鮮明。

1689

broadcast
ˈbrɔdˌkæst
v. 廣播 *n.* 廣播節目

◆ The famous program is broadcasted every Sunday night.
這個知名的節目都在週日晚間播出。

◆ She is listening to an overseas broadcast program.
她正在聽海外的廣播節目。

1690 ★

influence
ˈɪnfluəns
v. 影響…… *n.* 影響力；權力

◆ Psychologists think that one's mental condition influences his external behavior.
心理學家認為一個人的心理狀況影響著他的外在行為。

◆ His past failure causes a great influence on his thoughts.
過去的失敗對他的想法造成很大的影響。

1691 ★

celebrate
ˈsɛləˌbret
v. 慶祝……；過節

◆ Chinese people celebrate the Lunar New Year.
中國人慶祝農曆新年。

◆ All my friends came to celebrate my birthday.
所有的朋友都來慶祝我的生日。

1692 ★

gloomy
/ˈglumɪ/
adj. 憂鬱的；陰暗的

◆ This weather makes people feel gloomy.
這樣的天氣讓人感到憂鬱。

◆ The neighbors regarded the gloomy man as something of an enigma.
鄰居們認為這名憂鬱男子是個謎。

1693

---

skyscraper
/ˈskaɪˌskrepə/
n. 摩天大樓

◆ A new skyscraper has been built near our company.
我們公司附近建造了一棟新的摩天大樓。

◆ The architect has good spatial skills in building a skyscraper from plans on paper.
從紙上作業看來，這位建築師對於蓋這座摩天大樓有很好的空間運用技巧。

1694

---

friction
/ˈfrɪkʃən/
n. 摩擦；衝突；摩擦力

鞋底的**摩擦力**

◆ I was not intending to cause any friction between you and him.
我沒有打算在你和他之間引起任何衝突。

◆ You need to put oil in machinery to reduce the friction .
你需要把油放在機器中以減少磨擦。

1695

---

pacify
/ˈpæsəˌfaɪ/
v. 撫慰……；使平靜

◆ The mother pacified the baby by feeding her some milk.
媽媽藉著餵牛奶來安撫女嬰。

◆ We need troops to pacify that country.
我們需要更多軍隊去平定那個國家。

1696

---

seed
/sid/
v. 播種 *n.* 種子

◆ They seeded the field with wheat.
他們在田地中播種小麥。

◆ My father scattered the seeds in the land.
我爸爸在土地上撒上種子。

1697

---

quantity
/ˈkwɑntətɪ/
n. 數量；數目

◆ What is the minimum quantity I need to order to use my credit card ?
如果要使用信用卡訂購，最低訂貨量是多少？

◆ The police seized a quantity of pornographic publications.
警察查扣了大量的黃色書刊

1698 ★

---

provisional
/prəˈvɪʒənl/
adj. 暫時的；臨時的

◆ They set a provisional government to appease people.
他們設立一個暫時的政府來安撫民眾。

◆ All these agreements are provisional today.
今天所有協議都是暫時的。

1699

time-out
ˈtaɪmˈaʊt
n. 暫停；休息

◆ I took time-out from studying to go to watch TV.
我暫停讀書去看電視。

◆ Now you can take time-out for yourself.
現在你可以為了自己休息了。

1700

outrage
ˈaʊtˌredʒ
n. 暴行；違法
行為；憤慨

◆ These terrorist attacks are an outrage against society.
這些恐怖分子的攻擊對社會是一種暴行。

◆ The police's remarks caused public outrage.
警方的言論引起公眾的憤慨。

1701 ★

storm
stɔrm
n. 暴風雨

◆ The weather forecast says that there will be storms.
氣象報告指出，暴風雨即將來臨。

◆ The captain remained unperturbed throughout the raging storm.
這位船長在暴風雨肆虐期間都保持沉著。

1702

mob
mɑb
n. 暴徒；幫派；
民眾

◆ Mobs gathered in front of the city hall to protest new tax policies.
群情激憤的群眾聚集在市政府前抗議新的稅務政策。

◆ One of the police officers was hacked to death by the mob.
其中一位警官被暴民給砍死。

1703

outburst
ˈaʊtˌbɜst
n. 暴起暴落 (情
緒)

◆ I apologized for an outburst of anger yesterday.
我為昨天的勃然大怒來道歉。

◆ I was really horrified by her outburst .
她的暴怒讓我驚訝。

1704

plummet
ˈplʌmɪt
v. 暴跌；快速落
下

◆ Home prices have plummeted in this shopping district.
這個商店區的房價往下暴跌。

◆ The bank stocks continue to plummet recently.
最近銀行股票持續暴跌。

1705 ★

instrument
ˈɪnstrəmənt
n. 樂器；工具

◆ The doctor used an instrument to check the girl's teeth.
醫生用器具檢查女孩的牙齒。

◆ Can you play any traditional Chinese instruments?
你會彈奏中國的傳統樂器嗎？

1706

bullish
ˈbʊlɪʃ
adj. 樂觀的;看漲的

◆ A bullish trend in the stock market refers to rising stock prices.
股票市場的樂觀趨勢是指股票價格呈現上漲。
◆ The bullish stock market is on the turn.
看漲的股票市場轉變了。

1707

optimistic
ˌɑptəˈmɪstɪk
adj. 樂觀的;樂天派的

◆ She is optimistic to overcome any difficulty.
她樂觀地克服任何困難。
◆ I think I'm reasonably optimistic by nature.
我想我的天性是相當樂觀的。

1708 ★

downstairs
ˈdaʊnˈstɛrz
adv. 樓下地

◆ He went downstairs about ten minutes ago.
他大概在十分鐘前下樓的。
◆ The host fell downstairs and broke his leg.
這位男主人掉下樓,並且摔斷腿。

1709

stair
stɛr
n. 樓梯

◆ It's dangerous to run down the stairs.
用跑的下樓梯很危險。
◆ Go down the stairs and turn left over there.
順著樓梯下去左轉就是。

1710

standard
ˈstændəd
n. 標準;規格

◆ The airline has strict safety standards.
航空公司有嚴格的安全標準。
◆ According to my height, what is the standard weight?
根據我的身高,標準體重是多少?

1711 ★

sign
saɪn
n. 標誌;號誌
v. 在……簽名

◆ What does this sign mean?
這個標誌是什麼意思?
◆ The two companies have signed a trade agreement for two years only.
兩家公司簽了一紙只有二年的貿易契約。

1712

headline
ˈhɛdˌlaɪn
n. 標題;新聞提要

◆ What are the headlines in today's newspaper?
今天報紙的頭條新聞是什麼?
◆ Please give this article a impressive headline.
請給這篇文章一個印象深刻的標題。

1713

label
ˈlebl
n. 標籤；稱號
v. 貼標籤

◆ The label on the bottle says not to take more than five tablets a day.
瓶子上的標籤說明一天不能服用超過五片。

◆ The man was unable to slough off the stigmatizing label of criminal.
這人無法擺脫「罪犯」這個侮辱的標籤。

1714 ★

model
ˈmɑdl
n. 模型；模特兒

◆ He spent twenty five thousand dollars buying a model car.
他花了兩萬五千元買了一台模型車。

◆ No matter when you buy a printer, the manufacturer will release new models soon.
無論你何時購買印表機，廠商會很快的又出新的式樣。

1715 ★

ambiguous
æmˈbɪgjʊəs
adj. 模糊的；模稜兩可的

◆ Whenever I ask him a question, he always gives me an ambiguous answer.
無論什麼時候我問他問題，他總是給我模擬兩可的答案。

◆ The wording of the contract is ambiguous, so both interpretations are valid.
這份合約用字模稜兩可，所以兩種解讀都有效。

1716 ★

specimen
ˈspɛsəmən
n. 樣品；標本

◆ The doctor needs a specimen of your blood.
這位醫生需要你的血液樣本。

◆ The little girl used pins to impale the butterfly as the specimen.
小女孩用針刺穿蝴蝶當做標本。

1717

sample
ˈsæmpl
n. 樣品；標本

◆ Would it be possible for me to take a sample back with me？
我能否帶個樣品回去？

◆ Mary did the research by adopting the method of using random samples.
瑪麗用隨機採樣的方式做研究。

1718 ★

sloppy
ˈslɑpɪ
adj. 潦草的；草率的

◆ I can't understand his sloppy handwriting.
我無法了解他潦草的字跡。

◆ I don't like his sloppy demeanor about the event.
我不喜歡他對這事件草率的態度。

1719

humid
ˈhjumɪd
adj. 潮溼的

◆ The weather is humid in Taiwan.
台灣的天氣是潮溼的。

◆ The air is so humid, it seems that it is going to rain.
空氣如此潮溼，看來快下雨了。

1720

damp
dæmp
adj. 潮溼的 *n.* 溼氣

◆ The weather in Taipei is too damp to get used to.
台北天氣太潮溼以至於不能習慣。

◆ Before the raining day, the air was always muggy and damp.
下雨之前，空氣總是悶熱潮溼。

1721

skillful
ˈskɪlfəl
adj. 熟練的；有技術的

◆ She bought the handicraft from a skillful old man.
她向這位有技藝的老人買這件手工藝品。

◆ The employee is skillful enough to control the new machine.
這位員工足夠熟練來操控這台新機器。

1722 ★

zealous
ˈzɛləs
adj. 熱心的

◆ Mary is zealous about helping the poor.
瑪麗熱衷於幫助窮人。

◆ The salesman seems very zealous to answer customers' questions.
這個業務員非常熱心地回答顧客的問題。

1723

zest
zɛst
n. 熱情；熱心；風趣

◆ He entered into our schedules with zest.
他熱情地參與我們的計劃。

◆ She joined in the games with unrestrained zest.
她滿懷熱情地參加這項比賽。

1724

trophy
ˈtrofɪ
n. 獎杯；獎牌；戰利品

◆ The racecar driver held the trophy up high after he won the race.
這位賽車選手在贏得比賽後，高舉起他的獎杯。

◆ The final winner was presented with a gold trophy.
這位最後的勝利者得到一份金盃。

1725

scholarship
ˈskɑləˌʃɪp
n. 獎學金

◆ My scholarship didn't cover all my expense so I found a part-time job.
我的獎學金不夠我所有的開銷，因此我兼差打工。

◆ Can I apply for the scholarship?
我可以申請獎學金嗎？

1726

insure
ɪnˈʃʊr
v. 確保……安全；給……買保險

◆ The company should insure their employees.
公司應替他們的員工投保。

◆ I'd like to insure this package, please.
這個包裹我打算投保。

1727

confirm

kənˈfɝm

v. 確認……；使堅定

密碼正確

◆ I am calling to confirm our luncheon appointment.
我打電話來是想確認午餐的約會。

◆ I need to confirm my flight departure time.
我需要確認我的班機起飛時間。

1728 ★

range

rendʒ

n. 範圍；種類
v. 將……分等級

◆ I am sorry, because that is out of our price range.
抱歉，因為那已經超出我們的價格範圍。

◆ The vintage wine produces a whole range of gustatory sensations.
葡萄酒產生出所有範圍的味覺感受。

1729 ★

line

laɪn

n. 線；隊伍 *v.* 排隊……

◆ Many people stand in line for free tickets.
很多人排隊等著拿免費的票。

◆ Where should I line up?
我該在哪排隊？

1730

cue

kju

n. 線索；暗示

◆ I gave Mary a cue, but she missed it.
我給了瑪麗一個暗示，不過她沒注意。

◆ I'll give you the cue when you're to stop.
當你要停止時，我會給你暗示。

1731

clue

klu

n. 線索；端倪

◆ The detective breaks the criminal case by clues.
這位偵探經由線索偵破此犯罪案件。

◆ There is no clue to the identity of the robber.
沒有確認這強盜身份的線索。

1732

業精於勤，荒於嬉

---

editor
ˈɛdɪtɚ
n. 編輯

◆ He is the chief editor of this newspaper.
他是這家報社的主編。

◆ The editor has conglomerated different articles into a famous magazine.
這位編輯聚集了不同的文章到一本有名的雜誌。

1733

---

scriptwriter
ˈskrɪpt.raɪtɚ
n. 編劇；作家

趕寫劇本中...

◆ The scriptwriter adapted the famous novel for the screen.
這編劇家將這本著名小說改編成電影。

◆ He has worked as a film scriptwriter before。
他過去曾經當過電影編劇。

1734

---

weave
wiv
v. 編織

◆ My mother is an expert in weaving small rugs.
我媽媽是編織小地毯的專家。

◆ My grandmother weaved the sweater by woolen yarn as the gift on Christmas Day.
我奶奶用羊毛紗線織毛衣當作耶誕禮物。

1735

---

glue
glu
n. 膠水

◆ This glue can bond with impervious substances like glass and metal.
這膠水可將不滲透物質如玻璃和金屬黏在一起。

◆ This glue doesn't stick very well.
這種膠水黏得不太牢。

1736

---

stalemate
ˈstel.met
n. 膠著狀態

帥

將

◆ Now they are reaching a stalemate on the negotiations.
目前他們的協商呈現一個膠著狀態。

◆ All the meetings ended in stalemate.
所有的會議都以僵局結束。

1737

---

sanitary
ˈsænə.tɛrɪ
adj. 衛生的；清潔的

◆ We wash our hands before eating for sanitary consideration.
基於衛生考量，吃東西前要先洗手。

◆ He worked hard to improve the sanitary conditions of the school.
他非常努力去改善這間學校的衛生情況。

1738

satellite
ˈsætl̩.aɪt
n. 衛星

◆ The moon is a satellite of the Earth.
月球是地球的衛星。

◆ The satellite had a camera that took pictures of Venus and Mars.
衛星上的相機拍了金星和火星的相片。

1739

conflict
ˈkɑnflɪkt
n. 衝突；爭執
v. 與……衝突

◆ The conflict became serious without any reasons.
這個衝突毫無理由地越趨嚴重。

◆ The two countries involved in the conflict seem to be drawing closer to a rapprochement.
這二個捲入衝突的國家似乎拉近距離恢復友好關係。

1740 ★

impact
ˈɪmpækt
n. 衝擊；影響

◆ The mayor's speech made a great impact on me.
市長的演說對我造成很大的衝擊。

◆ The greatest impact of his mother's death is likely to be psychological.
他母親死亡的最大影響可能是心理層面。

1741 ★

review
rɪˈvju
v. 複習；回顧；審閱

◆ Please review this contract and sign your name at the bottom.
請審核這張合約並且在底下簽名。

◆ I would like to review the statistics in about a month.
我想在一個月左右時再來審視一下統計數字。

1742 ★

facsimile
fækˈsɪməlɪ
n. 複製；傳真

◆ I will send you a facsimile of the letter.
我將寄給你這封信件的副本。

◆ Can you help me operate a facsimile machine?
你能幫我操作這台傳真機嗎？

1743

duplicate
ˈdjupləkɪt
adj. 複製的 **v.** 複製……；使再發生

◆ The matter of duplicate human beings involves the ethic issue.
複製人的問題牽涉到倫理上的議題。

◆ The researcher had trouble duplicating the original results.
這位研究員對於複製原來的結果有困難。

1744 ★

complex
ˈkɑmplɛks
adj. 複雜的；複合的 **n.** 情結

◆ It is not easy to solve this complex problem.
要解決這個複雜的問題並不容易。

◆ Life is getting more complex and difficult nowadays.
現今生活是變得越來越複雜與艱難。

1745 ★

intricate
/ˈɪntrəkɪt/
adj. 複雜的；難懂的

◆ He gave me an intricate problem, and I don't know how to solve it.
他給我出了一個複雜的難題，而且我不知道如何解答。

◆ The intricate machine requires a skilled operator.
這台複雜的機器需要一個熟練的操作員。

1746

class
/klæs/
n. 課；班；等級；階級

◆ The Chinese class begins at 8:00 a.m..
國文課八點開始。

◆ Would you please tell me how many absentees we have in this class today?
你能告訴我今天這堂課有幾人缺席嗎？

1747

detention
/dɪˈtɛnʃən/
n. 課後留校；拘留

留校

◆ The young man was in detention because of stealing.
這年輕人因為偷竊被收押。

◆ We are placing the thief in criminal detention.
我們將這小偷進行刑事拘留。

1748 ★

course
/kors/
n. 課程；過程；路線

◆ She took a course in psychology.
她選讀了一門心理學課程。

◆ Which courses are you taking for next semester?
你下學期修了哪些課？

1749 ★

investigate
/ɪnˈvɛstəˌget/
v. 調查……；研究……

◆ The police start to investigate the bribery between the politicians.
警方開始調查政客之間的受賄。

◆ Several cases of malfeasance in the financial world are currently being investigated.
許多在金融界發生的惡行案例，現在被拿出來調查。

1750 ★

adjust
/əˈdʒʌst/
v. 調整；修整

◆ I adjust my alarm clock before I go to bed every night.
我每晚睡覺前都會調整鬧鐘。

◆ Could you adjust the brakes for me?
你能幫我調整剎車嗎？

1751

reference
/ˈrɛfərəns/
n. 談及；參考；查詢

◆ That student used many foreign periodicals as the reference for his senior project.
那個學生用很多外國期刊作為他大四研究計劃的參考書目。

◆ You may leave your key at the reference desk
你可以把你的鑰匙留在詢問台。

1752 ★

request
rɪˈkwɛst

v. 請求給予；要求某事

◆ Do you have any special request for your room?
對您的房間有什麼特別要求呢？

◆ We were requested to arrive at the airport before ten o'clock.
我們被要求在十點前到達機場。

1753 ★

petition
pəˈtɪʃən

n. 請願

◆ Local residents signed a petition to remove the governor.
當地的居民簽署一項請願來撤換州長。

◆ The residents presented their petition to the authorities.
這些居民向當局提出訴願。

1754 ★

thesis
ˈθisɪs

n. 論文；論題

◆ Without handing in the thesis by the end of May, she couldn't graduate from the graduate school this summer.
要是沒有在五月底前繳交論文，她就無法在今年夏天自研究所畢業。

◆ The professor checked the student's thesis and vouched for the accuracy of the information.
教授檢查學生的論文並且保證資料的正確性。

1755

forum
ˈforəm

n. 論壇；廣場

公共論壇

◆ This is a forum for computer and technology.
這是一個有關電腦與科技的討論會。

◆ There is a fair in the town forum.
城市廣場那裡有個市集。

1756

appreciate
əˈpriʃɪˌet

v. 賞識；感激；重視

Thank You!

◆ Tommy feels upset because no one can appreciate his talents.
湯米覺得沮喪因為無人欣賞他的才華。

◆ I appreciated his imperturbability at the dangerous moment.
我欣賞他在危險時刻時的冷靜。

1757 ★

pedantic
pɪˈdæntɪk

adj. 賣弄學問的；學究派的

我上知天文，下知地理...

◆ The more he has learned , the more pedantic he is.
他學得越多，越會賣弄學問。

◆ The professor talks quickly, with pedantic precision.
這位教授講話快速，有著學究般的精準。

1758

step
stɛp

v. 踏步；踩 **n.** 腳步

◆ The driver stepped on the gas and the car accelerated.
這駕駛踩油門讓車子加速前進。

◆ You must watch your step so as not to fall down.
你必須小心你的腳步以免摔倒。

1759

alternate
'ɔltə.net
v. 輪流；交互

◆ Most experienced farmers alternate crops.
大部分有經驗的農夫會輪種農作物。

◆ We saw each other on alternate Sundays.
我們每隔一星期見一次面。

1760

shift
ʃɪft
n. 輪班
v. 變換……；更動……

◆ If the machine can work three shifts per day, it can easily pay for itself in a year.
如果這機器能每天以三班制來運作，那麼一年就可輕易回本了。

◆ The office is staffed around the clock with three shifts.
這間辦公室配置日夜不斷的三班制。

1761

profile
'profaɪl
n. 輪廓；外形；簡介

◆ I turned my head and saw the profile of this clown.
我轉過頭，看見這個小丑的側影。

◆ She spent much money remedying her prognathous profile.
她花了許多錢治療下巴突出的外形。

1762

proper
'prɑpɚ
adj. 適合的；恰當的

看書保持距離

◆ According to proper etiquette, you should not have the seat next to her.
依照正統的禮儀，你不應該坐在她旁邊。

◆ To discipline a child for his bad behavior by removing his dinner is not a proper way of education.
用不能吃晚餐來懲處孩子不好的行為是不適當的教育方法。

1763

fit
fɪt
adj. 適合的；適當的

◆ Is the dress fit for you?
洋裝合身嗎？

◆ He's very drunk and is not fit to drive.
他喝得很醉不適合開車。

1764

timely
'taɪmlɪ
adj. 適時的；及時的

及時完成任務

◆ But for your timely help we couldn't have finished the work on time.
有你及時的幫忙，我們才能準時完成這項工作。

◆ We are very grateful to you for your timely help .
我們非常感謝你的及時幫忙。

1765

keen
kin
adj. 銳利的；敏銳的

◆ He has a keen mind, so nothing can escape from him.
他有一個敏銳的頭腦，所以沒有什麼事能瞞得過他。

◆ Foxes have a keen sense of smell.
狐狸有很敏銳的嗅覺。

1766

sale
sel
n. 銷售；促銷拍賣

◆ The department store is having a sale.
這家百貨公司正在舉行促銷拍賣。

◆ According to the latest news, the military sales to Taiwan might be postponed for political reasons.
根據最新消息，對台軍售案可能會因政治因素暫緩。

1767

sharp
ʃɑrp
adj. 鋒利的；尖銳的

◆ Be careful with the sharp knife.
小心使用尖銳的刀子。

◆ There has been a sharp decrease in the country's trade surplus.
這個國家的貿易順差銳減。

1768

pave
pev
v. 鋪……路面；鋪設……

客廳鋪地毯

◆ Workers are paving the destroyed road.
工人們正在鋪設被破壞的馬路。

◆ The ground of the hall is paved with red rug.
這個大廳的地面鋪滿紅色地毯。

1769

shock
ʃɑk
n. 震驚；衝擊

◆ The movie star's suicide was a shock to me.
那位影星的自殺令我非常震驚。

◆ It was a real shock to hear that the company would have to close.
聽到這家公司要關門真是讓人震驚。

1770

foster
ˈfɔstɚ
v. 養育；領養
adj. 收養的

◆ The girl's uncle fostered her after her parents died in an accident.
在父母車禍去世後，這女孩的叔叔領養她。

◆ There is one foster child in his family.
他的家庭有一個收養的小孩。

1771

aftershock
ˈæftɚˌʃɑk
n. 餘震

◆ The aftershock is still horrible after a main earthquake.
主震之後的餘震仍然可怕。

◆ Aftershock is not discontinuous still now。
現在餘震還尚未間斷。

1772

balance
ˈbæləns
n. 餘額；結帳
v. 使平衡

◆ It is essential to balance one's budget.
平衡我們的預算是必要的。

◆ The minimum balance on your checking account is $100.
你的支票存款最低餘額是美金一百元。

1773 ★

steer
stɪr
v. 駕駛……；操
縱……

- ◆ It's quite difficult to steer the car through the narrow street.
  駕駛汽車穿過狹窄的街道很困難。
- ◆ The mariners learned how to tie ropes and steer the ship.
  這位船員學習如何捆綁繩索和駕駛船。

1774

reckless
ˈrɛklɪs
adj. 魯莽的；不
計後果的

- ◆ We are all scared by his reckless driving.
  他莽撞的駕駛把我們都給嚇壞了。
- ◆ Some of the taxi drivers are very reckless.
  有些計程車駕駛是非常魯莽的。

1775

rash
ræʃ
adj. 魯莽的；輕
率的 *n.* 疹子

- ◆ Don't go making any rash decisions about your future!
  別做任何有關你未來的魯莽決定。
- ◆ It was rather rash of you to make a decision without the second consideration.
  你沒有多考慮就下決定，實在太輕率了。

1776

dawn
dɔn
n. 黎明 *v.* 開始
明白；醒悟

- ◆ We leave for the airport at dawn.
  黎明時我們動身去機場。
- ◆ Plan your year in spring and your day at dawn.
  一年之計在於春，一日之計在於晨。

1777

utensil
juˈtɛnsl̩
n. 器皿；用具

- ◆ This store sells stainless steel cooking utensils.
  這家店販售不鏽鋼炊具。
- ◆ I prefer metal utensils to plastic ones.
  我喜歡金屬的器具勝於塑膠器具。

1778

appliance
əˈplaɪəns
n. 器具；電器

- ◆ Do you need any electrical appliances?
  您需要一些電器用品嗎？
- ◆ This store supplies home appliances.
  這家店有提供家用器具。

1779

organ
ˈɔrgən
n. 器官；管風
琴

- ◆ Cancer cells erode his internal organs day by day.
  癌細胞一天一天地侵蝕他的內臟器官。
- ◆ Many hospitals are waiting for the donation of organs to save the patients.
  許多醫院等待器官捐贈來救病人。

1780

jam
dʒæm
n. 壅塞；困境；
果醬

◆ I was stuck in a traffic jam on my way to work.
在我去工作的路上遇到了塞車。

◆ The traffic jams always block the roads for more than one hour during rush hour.
在尖峰時刻，交通壅塞經常堵住道路超過一個小時。

1781

strive
straɪv
v. 奮鬥；努力

◆ He strived to overcome his bad habits.
他努力來克服他的壞習慣。

◆ We all have to strive for our good future.
我們全部都必須為美好的未來奮鬥。

1782

scholar
'skɑlɚ
n. 學者

國學大師

◆ My teacher is a scholar of Chinese literature.
我的老師是位中國文學學者。

◆ The scholar's theory is no longer tenable now that new facts have appeared.
由於新事實的出現，這位學者的理論不再站得住腳。

1783 ★

apprentice
ə'prɛntɪs
n. 學徒 *v.* 當學徒

拜名師學藝

◆ He works in the factory as an apprentice during his summer vacation.
暑假時他在一家工廠當學徒。

◆ My grandfather learned carving as an apprentice to a master craftsman.
我祖父在一位工藝大師那當學徒學習雕刻。

1784

semester
sə'mɛstɚ
n. 學期

本學期上課開始

◆ How many courses are you taking this semester?
你這學期修了幾門課？

◆ My advisor asked me to take three courses this semester.
我的指導顧問要求我這學期修三門課。

1785 ★

credential
krɪ'dɛnʃəl
n. 憑證；證書

中華民國
技術證
G1103744836
吳小華73.02.01
級別：丙 級
有效日 109.03.02

◆ The young man has the perfect credentials for the job.
這位年輕人對這份工作完全夠資格。

◆ Can you show me your credentials?
你可以出示證件嗎？

1786

war
wɔr
n. 戰爭

◆ The two countries have been at war for three months.
這兩個國家已經交戰三個月了。

◆ The soldier showed great courage during the war.
這位士兵在戰爭時展現很大的勇氣。

1787

battle
ˈbætl̩
n. 戰鬥;戰役

◆ He finally succeeded in the battle of life.
他終於在這場生命戰役中成功了。

◆ The hero showed great valor in the battle.
這位英雄在戰場上展現出極大的英勇。

1788

---

strategy
ˈstrætədʒɪ
n. 戰略;策略

◆ The company decided to adopt a monolithic brand strategy.
這家公司決定採用單一品牌戰略。

◆ The president held a discussion about making a strategy to boost the stock market.
總統為了振興股市召開討論會來訂定政策。

1789

---

own
on
v. 擁有;承認
adj. 自己的

◆ Everyone is responsible for his own work.
每個人都要為自己的工作負責。

◆ Mind your own business!
少管閒事!

1790

---

hug
hʌg
v. 擁抱

◆ She hugged her son passionately.
她熱情地擁抱她的兒子。

◆ My sister hugged the doll and threw it into the air.
我妹妹抱著這個娃娃,並且把它擲向空中。

1791

---

manipulate
məˈnɪpjə.let
v. 操作……;運用……

◆ Do you know how to manipulate the washing machine?
你知道怎麼操作這台洗衣機嗎?

◆ The osteopath carefully manipulated my damaged shoulder.
這位整脊專家小心地處理我的肩膀。

1792 ★

---

handle
ˈhændl̩
v. 操縱……;處理…… *n.* 把手

◆ We can't handle these price increases of yours.
我們無法接受你們提高價錢。

◆ Sometimes being stubborn only makes things hard to handle.
有時候頑固只會令事情難以處理。

1793

---

ensure
ɪnˈʃʊr
v. 擔保……成功;確保……

◆ The police ensure that he will be safe before taking the witness stand.
警方擔保他出庭作證之前都會是安全的。

◆ No one can ensure the true genesis of the universe.
沒有人能確認宇宙的真正起源。

1794

batch
bætʃ
n. 整批；整組

◆ The last batch of students' assignments was due yesterday.
最後一批學生的作業昨天要交。

◆ The accountant has signed a batch of cheque.
這個會計簽發了一批支票。

1795 ★

overall
ˌovəˈɔl
adj. 整體而言的；全面的

◆ The lantern illuminated the overall house.
這燈籠照亮整間房子。

◆ The overall situation is worsening day by day.
總體的情況一天比一天惡化。

1796 ★

plain
plen
adj. 樸素的；明白的 **n.** 平原

◆ The mountain became an alluvial plain after a decade later.
一百年後，這座山變成了沖積平原。

◆ My father's devotion to art is plain to see.
我爸爸對藝術的熱愛是顯而易見的。

1797

root
rut
n. 樹根 **v.** 根除……

◆ The plant has not struck root yet.
這棵植物還沒有生根。

◆ The mayor declared to root out crime in the city.
市長聲稱要根除這個城市中的犯罪。

1798

bridge
brɪdʒ
n. 橋；橋樑

◆ Trust is the most important bridge to maintain a good marriage.
信任是維持美滿婚姻最重要的橋樑。

◆ I visited the Golden Gate Bridge in San Francisco last year.
我去年去看了舊金山的金門大橋。

1799

繩鋸木斷，水滴石穿

---

airport
ˋɛr͵port
n. 機場

◆ She sent her driver to pick the important customer up at the airport.
她派私人司機去機場接這位重要客戶。

◆ When will you arrive at the airport?
你幾點會到機場？

1800

---

opportunity
͵ɑpəˋtjunətɪ
n. 機會

◆ Thank you for the opportunity to speak with you today.
今天感謝你們讓我有機會跟你們談。

◆ The only opportunity to recover your health is to go back for the chemotherapy.
你恢復健康的唯一機會，就是回去接受化療。

1801 ★

---

machine
məˋʃin
n. 機器

◆ Please put your dirty clothes into the washing machine.
請把髒衣服放進洗衣機裡。

◆ The candy vendor machine is broken again.
這台糖果販賣機又壞掉了。

1802

---

historic
hɪsˋtɔrɪk
adj. 歷史著名的

自由女神
落成 1886年10月28日

◆ The book is talking about something historic.
這本書是談論歷史上的某些事件。

◆ This famous historic event happened In the Victorian era.
這件著名的歷史事件發生在維多利亞女王時代。

1803 ★

---

vehement
ˋviəmənt
adj. 激烈的；強烈的；熱烈的

◆ There is usually a vehement argument between the politicians.
政治人物之間通常有激烈的爭論。

◆ After a vehement battle, the enemy was forced to surrender.
經過一次激烈的戰鬥後，敵人被迫投降了。

1804

---

violent
ˋvaɪələnt
adj. 激烈的；劇烈的；暴力的

◆ The woman is always bruised by her violent husband.
這女人經常被她暴力的丈夫打得鼻青臉腫。

◆ Don't be so violent to your children.
別對你的孩子暴力相向。

1805 ★

militant
ˈmɪlətənt

adj. 激進的；好鬥的；交戰的

◆ Militant labor unions are going on strike to support their demands.
激進的勞工工會將用罷工來爭取他們的訴求。

◆ The cripple is always militant in struggle.
這位殘障人士總是鬥志高昂。

1806

radical
ˈrædɪkl̩

adj. 激進的；根本上的 **n.** 激進份子

◆ His ideas are too radical to catch on.
他的想法太激進，以至於無法理解。

◆ The politician took up a radical position on this issue.
這位政治家對這個議題採取激烈的立場。

1807

spur
spɜ

v. 激勵……；促進…… **n.** 鼓舞

加油喔！

◆ Many shops cut prices just before New Year in an attempt to spur sales.
許多商店在新年前降價是為了刺激銷售。

◆ She started for Thailand on the spur of the moment.
她一時興起去了泰國。

1808

combustion
kəmˈbʌstʃən

n. 燃燒

◆ They burn the flammable garbage in a combustion chamber.
他們在燃燒室中燒毀可燃性的垃圾。

◆ The government plans to build a combustion furnace to burn garbage.
政府計劃建造一個焚化爐來焚燒垃圾。

1809

pry
praɪ

v. 窺視；刺探

◆ He often pried into other people's private affairs.
他經常窺探別人的私事。

◆ I do not desire to pry into those gossips.
我不想要去探聽這些八卦。

1810

diabetes
ˌdaɪəˈbitɪs

n. 糖尿病

Diabetic Foot

◆ My grandma was hospitalized because of the diabetes.
我祖母因為糖尿病而住院治療。

◆ The doctor diagnosed her illness as diabetes.
醫生診斷她患了糖尿病。

1811

relative
ˈrɛlətɪv

n. 親戚；親族 **adj.** 相對的

◆ We used to visit our relatives during Chinese New Year.
以前我們在農曆過年時會去拜訪親戚。

◆ The ruling oligarchy in that country is composed of one family and their relatives.
那個國家的執政寡頭是由一個家族及其親戚所組成。

1812 ★

autograph
ˈɔtə.græf
n. 親筆（簽名）

◆ May I have your autograph in this document?
你可以在這公文上簽名嗎？
◆ May I have your autograph on the cover of your CD?
你可以在你 CD 的封面上簽名嗎？

1813

sarcastic
sɔrˈkæstɪk
adj. 諷刺的；譏諷的；挖苦的

真好笑！

◆ Her sarcastic tongue caused everyone to dislike her.
她譏諷的言論導致每個人討厭她。
◆ His sarcastic comment hurt her feelings.
他的諷刺言論傷害了她的感情。

1814

promise
ˈprɑmɪs
n. 諾言；答應
v. 向……保證

一生一世
愛你

◆ You can provide me with the information you promised.
你可以把你承諾的資訊提供給我。
◆ He promised that he wouldn't be late anymore.
他保證不會再遲到了。

1815

murder
ˈmɝdə
n. v. 謀殺；兇殺

◆ The defendant pleaded not guilty to the charge of murder.
這位被告對於謀殺的指控辯護自己無罪。
◆ The police have no clues to the murder.
警方對那樁謀殺案絲毫沒有半點線索。

1816 ★

import
ˈɪmport
v. n. 輸入；進口

◆ We import a lot of agricultural products from Japan.
我們從日本進口了大量的農產品。
◆ Those exotic tulips are imported from Holland.
這些外來的鬱金香是從荷蘭進口。

1817 ★

export
ɪksˈport
v. n. 輸出；出口

◆ According to the statistics, this major product accounts for more than 50% of the exports.
根據統計資料，這項主要產品佔出口值的百分之五十以上。
◆ In order to export animal by-products, we will need a permit.
我們必須有許可才能出口動物副產品。

1818 ★

transfusion
trænsˈfjuʒən
n. 輸血；資金注入

◆ The injured man had to be given a blood transfusion immediately.
這個受傷的男子必須立刻進行輸血。
◆ The patient contracted AIDS from a blood transfusion.
這位病人因為輸血而感染愛滋病。

1819

pipe
paɪp
n. 輸送管子

◆ A crack on the pipe was found out.
這條管子上的裂口被發現了。

◆ The plumber went down to the cellar to fix the leaky pipe yesterday.
昨天水管工人到地窖去修理漏水的管子。

1820

radiation
redɪˊeʃən
n. 輻射；輻射能

◆ The workers may receive a heavy dose of radiation.
這些工人受到大劑量的輻射。

◆ Radiation from the sun is attenuated by the Earth's atmosphere.
從太陽來的輻射線會被地球大氣層減弱。

1821

office
ˊɔfɪs
n. 辦公室

◆ He went to the office at nine o'clock.
他九點去辦公室。

◆ How far is it from your house to the post office?
從你家到郵局有多遠？

1822

comply
kəmˊplaɪ
v. 遵守……；順從……；服從

◆ You should comply with what your boss asks you to do.
你必須順從老闆要你去做的事。

◆ Everyone should comply with the law.
每個人都應該遵守法律。

1823

follow
ˊfɑlo
v. 遵循；跟隨

◆ Please follow the instructions in the manual.
請遵照使用手冊上的指示。

◆ They follow the religious creed loyally.
他們忠誠地遵從宗教的信條。

1824

select
səˊlɛkt
v. 選擇；挑選

◆ The teacher selected a student to participate in the speech contest.
老師選了一位學生參加演講比賽。

◆ As a banquet manager, you should select the best server to be at the head table.
做為一個宴會經理，你應該在首桌選一個最好的侍者。

1825 ★

genetics
dʒəˊnɛtɪks
n. 遺傳學；遺傳性

DNA

◆ On the basis of genetics and biology, scientists produced thirty GM babies.
以遺傳學和生物學為基礎，科學家們創造了三十個基因改造寶寶。

◆ Inbreeding is not good for human genetics.
近親交配無益於人類遺傳。

1826

omit
o'mit
v. 遺漏；疏忽

◆ He omitted several steps in the experiment and the experiment failed.
他在實驗中漏了幾個步驟所以失敗了。

◆ I omitted to buy fish from my shopping list.
我的購物清單中疏忽了買魚。

1827

---

bequest
bɪ'kwɛst
n. 遺贈；遺產

◆ The house was a bequest from his only uncle.
這棟房子是來自他唯一叔叔的饋贈。

◆ She left bequest of money to all her staff.
她對所有的員工都留下了饋贈。

1828 ★

---

tin
tɪn
n. 錫；罐頭

◆ Is that can made of tin or steel?
這個罐頭是錫或鐵製成的？

◆ You can only open a tin of food with a opener.
你只能使用開罐器打開罐頭食物。

1829

---

error
'ɛrə
n. 錯誤；過失

◆ There is an error in spelling.
有一個拼字錯了。

◆ His small error in this job was a mere inadvertence.
他在這個工作上的小錯誤僅僅是一個疏忽。

1830

---

false
fɔls
adj. 錯誤的；不正確的

◆ Your conclusion is based on a false premise.
你的結論是建立在一個錯誤的前提下。

◆ The manager's false decision made the business have great pecuniary loss.
這位經理決策錯誤，使這筆生意在金錢方面損失慘重。

1831

---

optional
'ɑpʃənl
adj. 隨意的；可選擇的

◆ The charge for going into the casino is optional.
進去賭場的花費是選擇性的。

◆ Literature and art at university should be optional.
文學和藝術在大學應該是選修。

1832 ★

---

random
'rændəm
adj. 隨機的；偶然的

◆ The inspection list is arranged in a random order .
這份檢查名單是隨機安排。

◆ Is this a random road check for drunk driving ?
這是酒駕的隨機道路臨檢嗎？

1833

284

sculpture

'skʌlptʃɚ

n. 雕刻；雕刻術
v. 從事雕刻

◆ Tom teaches sculpture in the elementary school.
湯姆在國小裡教雕刻。

◆ The statue was sculptured from a stalactite.
這雕像是用鐘乳石雕刻的。

1834

statue

'stætʃʊ

n. 雕像

◆ The citizens planned to erect a statue of the President.
市民打算要立一座總統的雕像。

◆ The noted magician, David, made the Statue of Liberty disappear amazingly.
著名的魔術師大衛，神奇地讓自由女神像消失。

1835

stationary

'steʃən.ɛrɪ

adj. 靜止的；固定的

◆ She stands stationary saying nothing.
她靜靜地站著不說話。

◆ The taxi crashed into a stationary bus in the street.
這輛計程車撞上街上一台靜止不動的巴士。

1836

silence

'saɪləns

n. 靜默；沉靜

◆ The man's silence is construed as the expression of anger.
這男人的沈默被詮釋為是發怒的表示。

◆ The girl shows her opposition by silence for the unfair treatment.
女孩對於不公平待遇，以沈默表示反抗。

1837

headache

'hɛd.ek

n. 頭痛

◆ She took some medicine to relieve her headache.
她服用一些藥來減輕她的頭痛。

◆ The poor old man was afflicted with a headache.
這貧窮的老人為頭痛所苦。

1838

napkin

'næpkɪn

n. 餐巾

◆ Will you please give me more paper napkins, too?
也請給我多一點紙巾好嗎？

◆ A napkin folded into the shape of a water lily was on each table in the restaurant.
餐巾折成荷花的形狀，放在這餐廳中的每張桌子上。

1839

dessert

dɪ'zɝt

n. 餐後甜點

◆ What kind of dessert do you serve?
你們有供應哪些點心呢？

◆ Sir, what would you like for dessert, cake or ice cream?
先生，您想要什麼點心？蛋糕或冰淇淋？

1840

curator

kjuˈretə

n. 館長；管理者

◆ The curator of London museum is my father's friend.
倫敦博物館的館長是我爸爸的朋友。

◆ The curator of a library takes charge of importing the foreign books.
圖書館館長負責進口外國書籍。

1841

---

duck

dʌk

n. 鴨；鴨肉

◆ Have you ever tried Peking duck?
你曾經嚐過北京烤鴨嗎？

◆ Fowls include chickens, ducks, and geese, but usually we refer fowls to chickens only.
家禽包括了雞，鴨及鵝，但「禽」多只用來指稱「雞」。

1842

---

quality

ˈkwolətɪ

n. 優良；品質；特色

◆ How is the quality of the water here?
這裡水的品質如何？

◆ Some professors work hard on their dissertation, and completely ignore their teaching quality.
有些教授專心致力於他們的論文，而完全忽略了其教學品質。

1843 ★

---

coupon

ˈkupon

n. 優待券；多次通聯票

◆ I have ten coupons for the restaurant.
我有十張這間餐廳的優惠券。

◆ Well, with these coupons, your total is $57.00.
嗯，有了這些折價券，你的總價是五十七元美金。

1844 ★

---

voucher

ˈvautʃə

n. 優待券；收據；保證人

◆ People will be able to buy anything with consumer vouchers in Taiwan.
人們可以在台灣使用消費券來買任何東西。

◆ Could I use this voucher to pay for my meal？
我能用這張餐券來付餐費嗎？

1845 ★

---

elegant

ˈɛləgənt

adj. 優美的；文雅的

◆ The woman looked elegant in her new dress.
這穿著新衣的女人看起來優雅美麗。

◆ The sad lady wears an elegant white suit.
這位悲傷的女士穿著一件優雅的白色套裝。

1846

---

delicacy

ˈdɛləkəsɪ

n. 優雅；柔弱；佳餚

◆ Her delicacy attracts people's attention.
她的優雅引起人們的注意。

◆ The local people regard the fish as a great delicacy .
當地人認為這種魚是種極佳的美味。

1847

graceful
'gresfəl
adj. 優雅的；得體的

◆ We admired the graceful poise of the ballerina.
我們欣賞這個女芭蕾舞者的優雅姿勢。

◆ Though graceful and fluid while swimming, ducks are somehow ungainly on land.
雖然鴨子划水時優雅又流暢，但是牠們上岸後卻有點笨拙。

1848 ★

savings account
'seviŋz ə.kaunt
n. 儲蓄存款帳戶

◆ I'd like to withdraw $50 from my savings account.
我要從儲蓄帳戶戶頭提領五十元美金。

◆ Savings accounts pay the depositor interest but checking accounts don't.
儲蓄存款帳戶付給存款人利息，但支票存款帳戶沒有。

1849

depot
'dipo
n. 儲藏所；倉庫；軍械庫

◆ The soldiers' weapons were put in the depot.
士兵們的武器放在這個軍需庫中。

◆ The general asked the soldiers to guard the ammunition depot.
這位將軍要求士兵們保護彈藥庫。

1850

repository
rɪ'pazə.tɔrɪ
n. 儲藏處；倉庫

◆ The repository is filled with famous paintings.
這間儲藏室充滿知名的油畫。

◆ The library became a repository for police files.
這間圖書館成為警方檔案的儲藏庫。

1851

squash
skwaʃ
v. 壓扁……；粉碎…… **n.** 迴力球

◆ I squashed an insect with my foot.
我用我的腳壓扁一隻昆蟲。

◆ I could make nothing of the rules of squash.
我搞不懂迴力球規則。

1852

crush
krʌʃ
v. 壓碎；壓壞

◆ My grandmother uses a pestle and mortar to crush spices.
我的祖母用杵和臼來碾碎香料。

◆ Don't crush this box; there are vases inside.
別壓壞這盒子，裡面有花瓶。

1853

aid
ed
v. 幫助；支持 **n.** 助手

◆ Please give him first aid.
請幫他急救。

◆ Foreign aid is needed to ameliorate the effects of the 921 earthquake.
需要國外援助來改善九二一地震帶來的影響。

1854

plea
pli
n. 懇求；呼籲

◆ The rich man ignores the hungry man's pleas for food.
這個有錢人不理會這個饑餓男人施捨食物的懇求。

◆ His lawyer advised him to plea bargain.
他的律師勸他認罪協商。

1855 ★

appeal
ə'pil
v. 懇求……；
向……求助；引
起興趣

他向我們尋求支援

◆ He appeals to us for support.
他向我們尋求支援。

◆ The film greatly appealed to young audiences.
這部電影深深吸引了年輕觀眾。

1856

payable
'peəbļ
adj. 應支付的；
到期的

該付房租了！

◆ The payment of the household appliance is payable in installments.
這款電器用品的付款可以分期付款。

◆ The first month's rent is necessary to be payable in advance.
第一個月的租金必須提前支付。

1857

candidate
'kændə.det
n. 應考者；候選
人

◆ Mike is a candidate for the principal of the university.
麥克是這所大學的校長候選人。

◆ The candidate avers that he will do something to boost the economy.
這位候選人堅稱他會著手振興經濟。

1858 ★

drama
'drɑmə
n. 戲劇

演太空人

◆ He disguised himself as a beast in the drama.
在這齣戲劇中，他假扮成一隻野獸。

◆ All of the audience felt moved after seeing the lachrymose drama.
所有聽眾在欣賞過這齣感人熱淚的戲劇後都深受感動。

1859

wipe
waip
v. 擦；擦淨

◆ The housecleaner wiped the mirror with a soft cloth.
這位打掃者用一塊柔軟的布擦鏡子。

◆ The worker stood up to wipe the sweat off his face.
這位工人站起來擦去臉上的汗水。

1860

erase
ɪ'res
v. 擦掉；消除

◆ Time cannot erase my memories of childhood.
時間無法抹掉我童年的回憶。

◆ I tried to erase the idea from my mind.
我嘗試把這個念頭從我腦海中抹去。

1861

scrape
skrep

v. 擦掉……；刮掉……

◆ I scraped off the apple peel before eating it.
我吃蘋果之前先把皮刮掉。

◆ I had my arm scraped yesterday.
我的手臂昨天擦傷了。

1862

inspect
ɪnˋspɛkt

v. 檢查……；查閱……

◆ You are very welcome to inspect the winning bid.
我們歡迎你來查閱得標者。

◆ Father inspected the roof for leaks.
爸爸檢查屋頂的漏水。

1863 ★

censor
ˋsɛnsɚ

n. 檢查員

◆ The film was rejected by the censors again.
這部電影再度被電檢人員否絕。

◆ The controversial sections of the report were excised by the official censors.
這份報告有爭議的部分被官方檢查人員刪去。

1864

moisture
ˋmɔɪstʃɚ

n. 溼氣；水份

◆ Plants absorb moisture from the soil.
植物從土壤中吸收水份。

◆ This special material will repel heat and moisture.
這種特殊材料能防熱與防潮。

1865

abuse
əˋbjuz

v. n. 濫用；辜負；虐待

◆ Don't abuse parents' trust, just tell them the truth.
不要辜負父母的信任，就跟他們說事實。

◆ I never abuse my power in my office.
在辦公室中我從未濫用權利。

1866

耐心是一切聰明才智的基礎

---

turnover
'tɝn.ovɚ
n. 營業額；交易額；翻轉

營業額不錯喝!
coffee

◆ Turnover of E-commerce via Internet grew fast in Taiwan.
在台灣透過網際網路的電子商務營業額成長快速。
◆ The coffee shop has a turnover of 5,000 dollar a week.
這間咖啡店每週有五千美金的營業額。

1867 ★

---

gain
gen
v. 獲得；到達

恭喜!

◆ He gained a lot of weight after breaking his leg since he was unable to exercise.
他腿骨折之後胖了許多，因為他不能去運動。
◆ He gained a lot of money from the lottery.
他玩樂透贏了很多錢。

1868

---

obtain
əb'ten
v. 獲得；取得；通行

◆ He obtains the opportunity to study abroad.
他獲得出國留學的機會。
◆ At last, their company obtained the mining prerogative.
最後他們公司獲得了採礦的特權。

1869 ★

---

acquire
ə'kwaɪr
v. 獲得；取得；養成

◆ Tina acquires everything she wants after spending lots of money.
汀娜付出了相當多金錢後，得到了她想要的每件東西。
◆ Helen acquired some renown because of her eloquent debate.
海倫辯才無礙贏得一些名氣。

1870 ★

---

outfit
'aut.fɪt
v. 獲得配備；裝備 *n.* 全套服裝

◆ She wore a beautiful outfit to the wedding.
她穿著一套美麗的服裝出席婚禮。
◆ He wore an outlandish outfit including pink pants and green sneakers.
他穿了一套有粉紅褲子與綠色運動鞋的怪異服裝。

1871

---

win
wɪn
v. 獲勝；贏

◆ Did your team win the game?
你們隊伍比賽獲勝了嗎？
◆ My favorite baseball team won the game yesterday.
我最喜歡的棒球隊昨天贏得比賽了。

1872

surroundings

sə'raundiŋz

n. 環境

◆ Ben spent a few weeks getting used to the new surroundings.
班花了數星期去習慣新環境。

◆ Lots of Scorpio people have the insight into the surroundings.
許多天蠍座的人有洞悉周遭環境的能力。

1873

environment

in'vairənmənt

n. 環境；情境

◆ Today's topic in class was how to improve our environment.
今天課堂上的專題是如何改善我們的環境。

◆ My living environment is very quiet.
我的居家環境十分地安靜。

1874 ★

cancer

'kænsə

n. 癌症

◆ She got breast cancer last year.
她去年得了乳癌。

◆ The old man died of liver cancer.
這位老先生因為肝癌而過世。

1875

momentary

'momən.tɛrɪ

adj. 瞬間的；短暫的

◆ The old woman had a momentary cessation of breathing three minutes ago.
三分鐘前這個老太太有短暫的呼吸停止。

◆ The singer caught a momentary glimpse of the audience.
這位歌手短暫地瞥了一下觀眾。

1876

sew

so

v. 縫紉

◆ Could you sew this button onto my shirt?
你能把這鈕扣縫在我的襯衫上嗎？

◆ My mother was taught sewing when she was very young.
我媽媽非常年輕時就被教導縫紉。

1877

gross

gros

n. 總收入 *adj.* 總的；全部的

◆ I invest my gross income to the stock.
我將所有的收入投資在股票上。

◆ The gross national product has increased 10 percent this year.
國民生產總值今年增加了百分之十。

1878 ★

mileage

'maɪlɪdʒ

n. 總英哩數

◆ The mileage is free, but you have to fill up the gas when you return the car.
哩數是不計費的，但是還車時您必須將汽油加滿。

◆ What mileage does your car do per gallon?
你的車每加侖可行駛多少哩程數？

1879

01 02 03 04 05 06 07 08 09 10 11 12 13 14 15 16 17 18 19 20 21 22 23 24 25 26 27 28 29 30

aggregate
'ægrɪgɪt
adj. 總計的 *n.* 集體 *v.* 使聚集

總計2000元

◆ The citizens in the city came to the aggregate number of a million.
這城市中的市民總數目達到一百萬。

◆ Society is not just an aggregate of individuals, but races.
社會並不只是個人的集合體,更是種族的集合體。

1880

total
'totl
adj. 總計的 *n.* 總額;總數

總計有3隻!

◆ The total population of Taiwan is over twenty million now.
現在台灣的總人口已超過二千萬人了。

◆ I have three cats and two dogs in total.
我總共養了三隻貓、兩隻狗。

1881

prosperous
'prɑspərəs
adj. 繁榮的;成功的;茂盛的

◆ She chose to live in one of the outlying suburbs instead of prosperous city.
她選擇住在偏遠的郊區,而不是繁榮的市區。

◆ Taipei and Kaohsiung are prosperous cities in Taiwan.
台北與高雄在台灣是繁榮的都市。

1882

coalition
ˌkoə'lɪʃən
n. 聯合;聯盟

◆ Many small parties have united to form a coalition in Japan.
在日本許多小黨已經結成聯盟。

◆ They formed a coalition government after the election.
選舉後他們組成了一個聯合政府。

1883

boycott
'bɔɪkɑt
v. n. 聯合抵制

我們都不參加!

◆ People in the city boycotted irrational laws.
這城市中的居民聯合抵制不合理的法律。

◆ They declared a boycott against all North Korean goods.
他們聯合抵制北韓的產品。

1884 ★

contact
'kɑntækt
n. 聯繫;隱性眼鏡 *v.* 與……聯繫

◆ We usually don't have much contact with our classmates after university graduation.
大學畢業後,我們就不常聯絡。

◆ I am very near-sighted and wearing a pair of contact lens now.
我近視很深而且現在戴著隱形眼鏡。

1885 ★

clever
'klɛvə
adj. 聰明伶俐的

◆ My dog is very clever, and it can catch a ball.
我的狗很聰明,能夠接球。

◆ Even the clever men ignored that simple rule.
即使聰明人都會忽略簡單的規則。

1886

smart
smɑrt
adj. 聰明的

◆ Those smart students get good grades and go to college.
那些聰明的孩子得到好成績，而且進了大學。

◆ He is no less smart than his elder brother.
他和他的哥哥一樣精明。

1887

sound
saund
n. 聲音 **v.** 聽起來

有聽到我的聲音嗎？

◆ Did you hear that sound?
你有聽到那個聲音嗎？

◆ I was awakened by a gruesome sound of explosion.
我被一陣可怕的爆炸聲嚇醒。

1888

shrug
ʃrʌg
v. 聳聳肩

◆ I feel sorry for orphans, but what can I do to help them? said Ray, shrugging.
雷聳聳肩說：「我對這些孤兒感到難過，但是我能做什麼來幫助他們？」

◆ He shrugs his shoulders, saying that he doesn't know anything.
他聳聳肩膀，說自己什麼也不知道。

1889

cholesterol
kəˈlɛstəˌrol
n. 膽固醇

◆ If you know more about cholesterol, you can reduce your risk for a heart attack or stroke.
假如你了解膽固醇越多，你就能減少心臟病和中風的危險。

◆ Bean foods are without any fat and cholesterol.
豆類食物不含任何脂肪和膽固醇。

1890

timid
ˈtɪmɪd
adj. 膽怯的；怕羞的

◆ The little girl is as timid as a lamb.
這小女孩像小羊一樣膽怯。

◆ He is too timid to get up to the top of the building.
他太膽小而上不了這棟建築物的頂端。

1891

interim
ˈɪntərɪm
adj. 臨時的；暫時的 **n.** 過渡期

臨時住所

◆ There was an interim of two years between the two civil wars.
兩次內戰中有兩年的過渡期。

◆ Could you give me an interim receipt?
你能給我一張臨時收據嗎？

1892

lift
lɪft
v. 舉起；提高

◆ The bridegroom lifted the bride's veil and kissed her.
這位新郎掀起新娘的面紗而且親吻她。

◆ We lifted the lid and sniffed the aroma of fresh vegetable soup.
我們掀開蓋子聞了聞新鮮蔬菜湯的香味。

1893

spiral
spaɪrəl
adj. 螺旋形的
n. 螺旋 *v.* 螺旋
形上升

◆ A snail's shell is spiral in form.
蝸牛殼的形狀是螺旋形的。

◆ Their profits in this factory began to spiral up .
這家工廠的獲利開始螺旋狀上升。

1894

screw
skru
n. 螺絲釘 *v.* 使
栓緊

◆ You should use some tools to tighten the screw.
你應該使用一些工具來栓緊這個螺絲釘。

◆ Please turn the screw to the left to tighten it.
請將螺絲釘向左旋緊。

1895

humble
ˈhʌmbl̩
adj. 謙恭的

◆ The student is so humble that most teachers like him.
這學生相當謙恭，所以每個老師都喜歡他。

◆ You are welcome to my humble home at any time.
任何時間都歡迎你光臨寒舍。

1896

rumor
ˈrumɚ
n. 謠言 *v.* 謠
傳……

◆ Rumor has it that Jean divorced again and will fall in love again soon.
謠言傳出珍再度離婚，並且很快墜入情網。

◆ It's rumored that she went mad after her divorce.
傳說她在與她先生離婚後就瘋了。

1897 ★

earn
ɝn
v. 賺取……；謀
生

◆ How much do you earn every month?
你每個月賺多少錢？

◆ A man earns a lot of money from a lottery overnight.
人可以靠中樂透一夜致富。

1898

avert
əˈvɝt
v. 避免……；防
止……

◆ He averted failure with hard work and study.
他努力工作和讀書來避免失敗。

◆ In order to avert chaos in her room, she tidies her room every day.
為了避免房間零亂，她每天將房間整理得井然有序。

1899

haven
ˈhevən
n. 避風港；避
難所；停泊處

◆ The jungle is a haven for wildlife.
這個叢林是野生動物的棲息地。

◆ In the storm we took a haven under a big tree.
暴風雨時我們找了棵大樹當避風港。

1900

resort
rɪˈzɔrt
n. 避暑勝地 **v.** 訴
諸於；依賴

◆ The occupancy rate is up to 90% during the summer vacation at the resort hotel.
這家度假飯店在暑假期間的住房率上升到百分之九十。

◆ When his polite requests failed, he resorted to threats.
當他禮貌的請求失敗後，他便訴諸恐嚇。

1901

shelter
ˈʃɛltɚ
n. 避難所；庇護
物 **v.** 使掩蔽

◆ The wanderer always took shelter for the night in an abandoned house.
流浪漢總是找廢棄的房子當作庇護所過夜。

◆ The house sheltered us from the storm last night.
昨晚這房子在暴風雨中庇護我們。

1902 ★

invitation
ˌɪnvəˈteʃən
n. 邀請書；請帖

聖誕舞會邀請函

◆ Thank you very much for your invitation.
非常謝謝您的邀請。

◆ He passes up the invitation of a costume party.
他拒絕了一場化妝舞會的邀請。

1903

yet
jɛt
adv. 還（沒）

還沒吃飯
出去玩吧！

◆ Dad is not at work yet.
爸爸還沒開始工作。

◆ Have you prepared for tomorrow's English quiz yet?
你準備好明天的英文小考了嗎？

1904

ugly
ˈʌglɪ
adj. 醜的；難看
的

◆ To be candid, I think his car is very ugly.
坦白說，我覺得他的車很醜。

◆ The employee discredited her boss's good name with ugly gossip.
這員工用醜陋的八卦來損壞她老闆的好名聲。

1905

scandal
ˈskændl̩
n. 醜聞；恥辱

貪污洗錢

◆ Some magazines thrive on spreading gossip and scandal.
一些雜誌熱衷於散布八卦和醜聞。

◆ The crowd hissed at the politician involved in a scandal.
群眾對這位身陷醜聞的政治人物發出噓聲。

1906 ★

anchor
ˈæŋkɚ
n. 錨

◆ The anchor secured the boat's location during the storm.
錨能讓船在暴風雨中停放在安全的位置。

◆ The ship lay at anchor in the harbor during the gale.
這艘船刮大風時停泊在港灣中。

1907

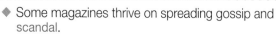

seclusion
sɪˋkluʒən
n. 隱居；隔離

隱居生活

◆ The ancient poets always liked to live in the peace and seclusion of the area.
古代的詩人們都喜歡過著安詳樂居的生活。

◆ She lives in seclusion apart from her friend for many years.
她多年來離開朋友過著隱居生活。

1908

---

hide
haɪd
v. 隱藏；躲避

◆ His sister likes to hide behind the bedroom door.
他妹妹喜歡躲在房門後面。

◆ Are you trying to hide something from your boss?
你想對你老闆隱瞞一些事嗎？

1909

---

conceal
kənˋsil
v. 隱藏……；隱瞞……；保守祕密

◆ He tries to conceal everything from the police.
他試圖對警察隱瞞一切。

◆ Some authors wrote novels under pseudonym to conceal their names.
有些作者用筆名寫小說來隱藏他們的名字。

1910

---

cling
klɪŋ
v. 黏住；纏住；堅持

◆ The kid clings to his grandmother.
這小孩纏著他的祖母。

◆ Mary clings to finish the challenging task until the last moment.
瑪麗堅持到最後，完成這有挑戰性的任務。

1911

---

sticky
ˋstɪkɪ
adj. 黏的；易卡住的

◆ I feel uncomfortable because my hands are sticky.
因為我的雙手黏黏的，覺得不太舒服。

◆ There's some sort of sticky and dirty fluid on the bathroom floor.
浴室的地板有種黏稠與骯髒的液體。

1912

---

nod
nɑd
v. 點頭；打盹

◆ Don't nod in the class.
不要在課堂上打瞌睡。

◆ He greets his friend by nodding his head.
他向朋友點個頭打招呼。

1913

---

order
ˋɔrdɚ
v. 點餐……；訂購…… *n.* 順序；匯票

24H
點餐服務中心

◆ I ordered breakfast at 7:30 but it hasn't come yet.
我七點三十分點了早餐，但是到現在還沒送來。

◆ I want to buy a money order for $200.
我要一張二百元美金的匯票。

1914

series

ˈsɪrɪz

n. 叢書；系列節目；接連

◆ A series of cascades flow into the stream from large boulders.
一連串的小瀑布從大圓石中流入溪流。

◆ The archaeologist discovered a series of underground caves and passages.
考古學家發現了一連串的地下洞穴與通道。

1915

reimburse

ˌriːmˈbɜs

v. 歸還……；補償……

◆ The department store reimbursed me for the amount they had overcharged me.
百貨公司把對我超收的錢退還給我。

◆ I will reimburse what you lent me tomorrow.
我明天將歸還你借我的錢。

1916

amenity

əˈmɛnətɪ

n. 禮儀；親切；舒適

◆ We should show our amenities to visitors in Taiwan.
在台灣我們對觀光客要展現禮貌。

◆ A multi-screen cinema is the best amenity in a sports center.
運動娛樂中心裡的多螢幕電影院是讓人覺得最愉快的環境。

1917

simple

ˈsɪmpl

adj. 簡單的

◆ I like simple games like jumping rope.
我喜歡像跳繩這類簡單的遊戲。

◆ A space simulator can be as simple as a spacecraft simulation program running on your PC.
一個太空模擬器能夠簡單的像太空船模擬程式般在你的桌上電腦上運行。

1918

concise

kənˈsaɪs

adj. 簡潔的；概括的

◆ Can you make a concise summary of this chapter?
你能就此章做出簡潔的摘要嗎？

◆ She made a concise conclusion without verbiage.
她毫無廢話地做了一個簡潔的結論。

1919

curriculum vitae

kəˈrɪkjələm ˈvaɪtə

n. 簡歷表

◆ I've read your curriculum vitae on the website.
我已經在網站上看過你的簡歷表。

◆ Please attach a copy of your curriculum vitae and a recent photograph.
請附上一份履歷表與近照。

1920 ★

career

kəˈrɪr

n. 職業；事業；經歷

◆ She is not interested in a stage career.
她對舞台的工作沒興趣。

◆ He has serious aspirations to a career in education.
他對教育事業有認真的抱負。

1921 ★

blueprint
ˈbluˌprɪnt
n. 藍圖；設計圖

◆ The company has drawn up a blueprint for future development.
這家公司已經規劃出未來的發展藍圖。

◆ There is a slight inaccuracy in your new blueprint.
在你的新藍圖中有一點小誤差。

1922

---

belittle
bɪˈlɪtl
v. 藐視；輕視

◆ A man becomes a loser as long as he belittles himself.
一個人只要看輕自己就成了輸家。

◆ Those who cheat on exams belittle their potential.
那些考試作弊的人藐視了他們的潛力。

1923

---

bug
bʌg
n. 蟲子；竊聽器（美）

◆ There are many bugs in the evening during summer.
夏天的傍晚有許多蟲子。

◆ There might be a bug in your program.
你的程式中可能有一個錯誤。

1924

---

caution
ˈkɔʃən
n. 謹慎；警告

◆ He always arranges everything with caution.
他總是謹慎安排每一件事。

◆ Her father asks her to drive with caution.
他爸爸要求他小心開車。

1925 ★

---

transfer
trænsˈfɝ
v. 轉車（飛機）；轉移；搬移

◆ Where can I transfer to a bus for the Golden Gate Bridge?
我在哪裡可以換車到金門大橋？

◆ The patient was transferred to a bigger hospital.
那位病人被轉送到另一家較大的醫院。

1926 ★

---

turn
tɝn
v. n. 轉彎；轉動；輪流

◆ Amid the students' protests, the teacher turned the TV off.
在學生的抗議聲中，這位老師關上了電視。

◆ The fans took turns to shake hands and take pictures with the singer.
歌迷們輪流與那位歌手握手及合照。

1927

---

hospital
ˈhɑspɪtl
n. 醫院

◆ All the doctors in the hospital are on stand-by.
這家醫院的所有醫生正待命中。

◆ The hospital imported the latest surgical techniques.
這家醫院引進了最新外科技術。

1928

medical
ˈmɛdɪkl̩
adj. 醫學的

◆ The hospital has recently bought some medical apparatus.
這家醫院最近買了一批醫學器材

◆ It's impossible for doctors to be omniscient about all medical knowledge.
醫生不可能對所有的醫學知識無所不知。

1929

grocery store
ˈɡrosərɪ ˈstor
n. 雜貨店

◆ I want to buy some frozen food from the grocery store.
我想在這間雜貨店買些冷凍食品。

◆ Do you know where the nearest grocery store is?
你知道最近的雜貨店在哪裡嗎？

1930

theme
θim
n. 題目；主題

就業與未來

◆ The main theme of our discussion was juvenile delinquency.
我們討論的主要題目是少年犯罪。

◆ Would you please expatiate the theme of the novel for me?
你可以為我詳述這部小說的主題嗎？

1931 ★

spoil
spɔɪl
v. 寵壞……；破壞……

通通買給你

◆ The little boy is spoiled because he is the only child at his home.
因為那個小男孩是獨生子，所以被寵壞了。

◆ I haven't seen the movie, so don't spoil it for me by telling me what happens.
這電影我還沒看，所以別告訴我劇情以免毀了我的樂趣。

1932

sluggish
ˈslʌɡɪʃ
adj. 懶散的；怠倦的

◆ An abundant lunch makes my brain sluggish in the afternoon.
豐盛的午餐讓我下午時頭腦變得遲緩。

◆ The medicine makes me feel rather sluggish.
這種藥讓我感覺懶洋洋。

1933

流淚撒種的，必歡呼收割

---

doubt
daʊt
v. 懷疑……；不
相信…… *n.* 疑
惑

◆ I have never doubted his words.
我從沒懷疑過他的話。

◆ The authenticity of the antique is beyond doubt.
這件古董的真實性毋需懷疑。

1934

---

skeptical
ˈskɛptɪkl̩
adj. 懷疑的；多
疑的

◆ I'm rather skeptical about the impetuous decision.
我相當懷疑這個衝動的決定。

◆ The majority of people were skeptical about this
solution.
大多數人懷疑這個解決方案。

1935

---

scramble
ˈskræmbl̩
v. 攀爬……；使
倉促行動；炒蛋

◆ These climbers began to scramble up the mountain.
這些登山者開始向上攀登這座山。

◆ Do you want your eggs scrambled, boiled, or fried?
你要炒蛋、煮蛋或是煎蛋？

1936

---

brutal
ˈbrutl̩
adj. 獸性的；殘
忍的

◆ His brutal treatment of his children will always be a blot
on his reputation.
他對小孩的殘忍虐待將永遠成為他名譽上的汙點。

◆ It was brutal of you to do that.
你做那件事很殘忍。

1937

---

stable
ˈstebl̩
adj. 穩定的

◆ The economic growth of this country is stable.
這個國家的經濟成長很穩定。

◆ My older brother is a man of stable character.
我哥哥是一個穩定可靠的人。

1938 ★

---

signature
ˈsɪgnətʃɚ
n. 簽名；署名

◆ He faked my signature to get money from my bank
account.
他偽造我的簽名從我銀行帳戶拿錢。

◆ The demonstrators delivered a petition with four
thousand signatures to the authority.
示威運動者們向當局展示有四千人簽名的請願書。

1939 ★

fasten
'fæsn̩
v. 繫住；閂住；抓牢

◆ Remember to fasten your seat belt after you get in the car.
記得上車入座之後要繫上安全帶。

◆ The kid cannot fasten the shoe buckle by himself.
這個小男孩不會扣緊他的鞋帶扣。

1940

tablet
'tæblɪt
n. 藥片

◆ The doctor asked me to take one tablet after meals.
醫生要求我飯後服下一片藥片。

◆ These tablets make me feel drowsy.
這些藥片讓我昏昏欲睡。

1941

witness
'wɪtnɪs
n. 證人；目擊者；證明

◆ The judge appealed for witnesses to come forward and offer crucial information.
法官請求傳喚證人上前，提供關鍵性的消息。

◆ Unimpeachable evidence and witness made the case break.
挑不出瑕疵的證據和目擊者破了此案。

1942 ★

attest
ə'tɛst
v. 證實……；作證……

◆ You have to attest to the truth of his words.
你必須確定他話中的真實性。

◆ The evidence attests his innocence.
這個證據證實了他的清白。

1943 ★

evidence
'ɛvədəns
n. 證據；證物

◆ There is no evidence to prove his theory.
沒有證據來證明他的理論。

◆ The judge exonerated the defendant from being sentenced because of insufficient evidence.
法官因證據不足，免除了被告的罪名。

1944 ★

approve
ə'pruv
v. 贊成；批准

◆ Have we approved the new prices with the marketing department ?
我們已經得到行銷部門批准新價格了嗎？

◆ We assume that my manager will approve of the plan.
我們以為經理會贊成這個計劃。

1945 ★

patronage
'petrənɪdʒ
n. 贊助；支持；光顧

◆ We thank you for your patronage sincerely.
我們衷心感謝你的光顧。

◆ The famous hotel has a large patronage.
這家著名的旅館有很大的顧客群。

1946

sponsor
'spɒnsə
n. 贊助……*v.* 贊
助者；主辦人

◆ Do you know what you will do for money since we are not sponsoring you？
既然我們無法贊助你，你在金錢方面要怎麼辦？

◆ You need a sponsor to get a working visa.
你需要一位保證人才能得到工作簽證。

1947 ★

resign
rɪ'zaɪn
v. 辭去……工
作；聽從於

◆ Rumor has it that she will resign.
謠言傳出她將會辭去工作。

◆ The statesman succumbed to the public pressure and resigned.
這位政治人物屈服於大眾的壓力並且辭職。

1948

frontier
frʌn'tɪr
n. 邊境；邊疆；
新領域

◆ Both countries often fight each other because of the indefinite frontiers.
因為不確定的邊境關係，這兩個國家經常交戰。

◆ Thailand has frontiers with Burma and Combodia.
泰國和緬甸與柬埔寨交接。

1949

brink
brɪŋk
n. 邊緣

◆ The haggard woman is standing on the brink of the cliff.
這位發狂似的女人站在懸崖的邊緣。

◆ There are many lilies on the brink of the pond.
池塘邊有很多的百合花。

1950

rim
rɪm
n. 邊緣

◆ The rim of the bowl is made of gold.
這個碗的邊緣是黃金做的。

◆ Andy's glasses have gold rims.
安迪的眼鏡鑲著金邊。

1951

edge
ɛdʒ
n. 邊緣

◆ He put the glass on the edge of the table.
他將玻璃杯放在桌子邊緣。

◆ The airport is situated on the edge of the town.
這個機場座落在城市的邊緣。

1952

margin
'mɑrdʒɪn
n. 邊緣；界限

◆ The election was won by a margin of 5,000 votes.
這場選舉以五千票差額勝利。

◆ I can't sacrifice our profit margin that much.
我不能犧牲那麼大的淨利率。

1953

joint
dʒɔɪnt
n. 關節;接合點;
聯合的

◆ My doctor put my bone into the joint again
我的醫生將我的骨頭接回關節處。

◆ The joint venture meeting was very successful.
那個合資的會議十分成功。

1954

shut down
ʃʌt daʊn
v. 關機;停業

◆ The owner made a unilateral decision to shut down the factory despite the workers' protests.
老闆不顧員工抗議,一意孤行將工廠關閉。

◆ The worker shut down upon his anger and sat down.
這位工人壓住怒火,並坐了下來。

1955

inexplicable
ɪnˈɛksplɪkəbl
adj. 難以理解
的;原因不明的

◆ The inexplicable disappearance of Tom worried me.
湯姆令人不解的消失讓我憂慮。

◆ The mayor's mistake was not so inexplicable now.
現在這位市長的錯誤不是那麼令人難以理解。

1956

illegible
ɪˈlɛdʒəbl
adj. 難以辨認
的;無法閱讀的

◆ I could not say that his handwriting is really illegible.
我不得不說他的字跡真的很難辨認。

◆ The book is too old to be illegible.
這本書太舊了以致無法閱讀。

1957

reverse
rɪˈvɝs
v. 顛倒;使反轉
adj. 反向的

◆ However, I'm not expecting to reverse my decision.
然而,我不預期我會改變決定。

◆ The court of appeals reversed the original verdict and set the prisoner free.
這個訴願法庭退回原先的判決,並且釋放這位囚犯。

1958

scam
ˈskæm
n. 騙局;詐欺
v. 欺騙……

◆ The old man got involved in a scam unluckily.
這位老人不幸地捲入一場騙局。

◆ You should not scam other players in this game.
你不應該在這場遊戲中欺騙其他玩家。

1959

dissuade
dɪˈswed
v. 勸阻;阻止

◆ I dissuaded her from going to London alone.
我勸阻她單獨前往倫敦。

◆ His failure did not dissuade him from trying again.
他的失敗並沒有阻止他再度嘗試。

1960

reprimand

ˋrɛprəˏmænd

v. 嚴斥；訓斥；斥責

◆ Her boss reprimanded her for carelessness.
她的老闆因為粗心而斥責她。

◆ The military court reprimanded the solider for going out without permission.
軍事法庭申斥未獲許可而外出的士兵。

1961

---

stern

stɜn

adj. 嚴苛的；嚴厲的

◆ Stern discipline did not achieve the expected result.
嚴格紀律並沒有達到預期的結果。

◆ Stern as my father is, he is full of sympathy.
我爸爸雖然嚴格，卻富有同情心。

1962

---

serious

ˋsɪrɪəs

adj. 嚴重的；認真的

◆ My friend has a serious cut on his knee.
我朋友的膝蓋上有道嚴重的傷口。

◆ What do you think the most serious social problem is?
你認為最嚴重的社會問題是什麼？

1963 ★

---

strict

strɪkt

adj. 嚴格的；嚴厲的

◆ He is the strictest father I've ever seen.
他是我見過最嚴厲的父親。

◆ I will not sign this contract with such a strict non-compete clause in it.
我不會簽有如此嚴格競業禁止條款在其中的合約。

1964

---

austere

ɔˋstɪr

adj. 嚴格的；嚴厲的

◆ He had no austere words or criticism.
他沒有嚴厲的言詞或批評。

◆ The man had an austere childhood because it was during the Vietnam War.
這男人有個嚴峻的童年，因為當時正值越戰。

1965

---

severe

səˋvɪr

adj. 嚴厲的；苛刻的；嚴重的

◆ He is very severe with his students.
他對他的學生很嚴格。

◆ He's suffering from severe mental disorder.
他患有嚴重的精神錯亂。

1966

---

dour

dʊr

adj. 嚴厲的；悶悶不樂的；固執的

◆ He is very dour with his children.
他對他的孩子很嚴厲。

◆ His dour personality makes it difficult for us to get close to him.
他固執的個性讓我們很難接近他。

1967

hang
hæŋ

v. 懸掛；吊起；逗留

◆ Please hang your coat on the hook.
請把你的外套掛在鉤子上。

◆ She likes to be idle and hang around all day.
她喜歡整日發呆閒晃。

1968

devote
dɪˈvot

v. 獻身於……；將奉獻給……

◆ The artist devoted himself to painting.
這位藝術家獻身於油畫。

◆ We need to devote money to save our community.
我們需要捐款來拯救我們的社區。

1969 ★

mineral
ˈmɪnərəl

n. 礦物

◆ Can you give me a bottle of mineral water?
給我一瓶礦泉水好嗎？

◆ Spa water is very good for the skin because of the minerals it contains.
溫泉水因為含有礦物質，所以對皮膚很好。

1970

rivalry
ˈraɪvlrɪ

n. 競爭；競賽

◆ The two countries were in a fierce rivalry.
兩個國家處於激烈的競爭。

◆ There is great rivalry between the two companies.
這兩家公司之間有一場很大的競賽。

1971

competition
ˌkɑmpəˈtɪʃən

n. 競賽；貿易競爭

◆ Sally came in first in the beauty competition.
莎莉在選美比賽中獲得第一名。

◆ She was delegated to take part in a chess competition.
她代表參加一場西洋棋競賽。

1972

inherit
ɪnˈhɛrɪt

v. 繼承……；遺傳某特徵

◆ Tom inherited his father's fortune.
湯姆繼承他父親的財產。

◆ It is the result of natural selection acting on inherited variation.
作用在遺傳變種上的結果就是物競天擇。

1973

heir
ɛr

n. 繼承人

◆ He is the lawful heir of the kingdom.
他是這王國的合法繼承人。

◆ He was the sole heir to the property.
他是這筆財產的唯一繼承人。

1974

ongoing
/ˈɑn.gɔɪŋ/
adj. 繼續的；前進的

◆ An ongoing feud between two neighbors led to violence.
在這兩個鄰居間持續的紛爭導致了暴力。

◆ My mother has had an ongoing headache recently.
我媽媽最近有持續性的頭痛。

1975

alert
/əˈlɜt/
adj. 警覺的；有注意力的

◆ Most animals are naturally alert, especially when they are in danger.
大多數的動物特別當它們身處險境時，會自然地警覺。

◆ The airline station was closed for three hours because of a security alert.
因為安全警報，航空站關閉三小時。

1976

agenda
/əˈdʒɛndə/
n. 議程；會議事項

◆ Since we have difficulty staying on topic, I made an agenda.
既然我們專注在主題上有困難，我訂了一份議程。

◆ The committee has drawn up a new agenda.
這個委員會起草了一個新議程。

1977 ★

acrophobia
/ˌækrəˈfobɪə/
n. 懼高症

◆ Do you know how to overcome acrophobia?
你知道如何克服懼高症嗎？

◆ Why is he free from acrophobia when standing in a high-rise elevator?
為什麼他站在高樓的電梯上卻沒有懼高症？

1978

debate
/dɪˈbet/
v. n. 辯論；爭論；討論

◆ The politicians have debated this issue for a long time.
政治人物長期辯論著這個問題。

◆ Helen acquired some renown because of her eloquent debate.
海倫的辯才無礙讓她贏得一些名氣。

1979 ★

grin
/grɪn/
v. 露齒而笑

◆ The chubby and naughty boy usually grins at me.
這位圓胖頑皮的男孩時常對我露齒而笑。

◆ All you can do is to grin and bear it.
你所能做的就是笑笑而且承擔它。

1980

consultant
/kənˈsʌltənt/
n. 顧問

工程顧問

◆ The consultant gave us some proposals in point.
這位顧問給了我們一些中肯的建議。

◆ They employed the professor as a consultant.
他們聘請這位教授為顧問。

1981 ★

expel
ɪkˈspɛl

v. 驅逐；趕走；
開除

◆ The king expels the slave from the country.
國王將這名奴隸驅逐出境。

◆ The miscreant was expelled from his town.
這個異教徒被驅逐出城。

1982

urge
ɝdʒ

v. 驅策……；力
勸……

◆ My parents urges me to study in the Untied States.
我父母力勸我去美國念書。

◆ We will urge them to adhere to the peace agreement .
我們將會力勸他們遵守這份和平協議。

1983

authority
əˈθɔrətɪ

n. 權鑑；專家

◆ Who gave you the authority to enter my room?
誰允許你進我的房間？

◆ I have it on good authority that any dissenting opinions are brusquely pushed aside.
我有權威消息證明任何反對意見都被粗率地推到一邊去。

1984 ★

sprinkle
ˈsprɪŋkl̩

v. 灑在……上；
用……點綴

◆ Sprinkle a little salt on the French fries .
在薯條上灑一點鹽。

◆ He sprinkled water on the flowers in the morning.
他早上幫這些花灑水。

1985

palpitate
ˈpælpə͵tet

v. 顫動（心臟）；
急速跳動

◆ My heart palpitates whenever I see him.
無論何時我看到他，心臟都會急速跳動。

◆ My heart palpitates when I am surprised .
當我受驚嚇時，心臟會急速跳動。

1986

slim
slɪm

adj. 纖細的；苗
條的

◆ I wish I was as slim as the movie star.
我希望和那個電影明星一樣苗條。

◆ The man looks slimmer than his wife.
這個男人看起來比他的妻子還瘦。

1987

logical
ˈlɑdʒɪkl̩

adj. 邏輯的；合
理的

◆ The professor still flunked him last semester because his paper was not logical.
教授上學期仍然當了他，因為他的報告不合邏輯。

◆ He always can make a logical conclusion after discussion.
經由討論後，他總是能夠做出有邏輯的結論。

1988

autopsy

ˈɔtɑpsɪ

n. 驗屍

◆ He is going to carry out an autopsy in the hospital.
他正前往醫院進行驗屍。

◆ The forensic expert always finds out the evidence by the autopsy.
法醫總是透過驗屍來找到證據。

1989

---

astonishment

əˈstɑnɪʃmənt

n. 驚訝的事物

◆ The kid was struck dumb with astonishment.
這小孩驚訝地說不出話來。

◆ To our astonishment, my parents arrived on time.
讓我驚訝的是我父母準時到來。

1990

---

gym

dʒɪm

n. 體育館

天天到健身房

◆ He went to the gym on Sundays.
他每逢週日都到健身房。

◆ He went to the gym to train himself everyday.
他每天都到體育館訓練自己。

1991

---

weight

wet

n. 體重

我有50公斤！

◆ Would you weigh this letter for me, please?
請幫我秤這封信的重量好嗎？

◆ At the airport, if the baggage is over the weight limit, the passenger has to pay for the overweight.
在機場裡如果行李超重，旅客就必須為超重部分付費。

1992

---

soul

sol

n. 靈魂；心力

◆ Christians believe that the soul lives forever.
基督徒們相信靈魂永生。

◆ May my grandfather's soul rest in the heaven.
但願我爺爺的靈魂在天國能得到安息。

1993

---

fence

fɛns

n. 籬笆；柵欄
v. 擊劍

◆ Father built an extensive fence around our house.
爸爸在房子的四周裝上大量的籬笆。

◆ A fence is used to separate the areas of different races.
圍籬用來區隔不同種族的地區。

1994

---

sightseeing

ˈsaɪtˌsiɪŋ

n. 觀光；遊覽

倫敦

◆ What's the best way to do my sightseeing?
什麼是觀光的最好方式？

◆ Where can I get information on sightseeing in the city?
哪裡可以拿到本市的觀光資訊？

1995

spectator

'spɛktetə

n. 觀眾；旁觀者

◆ When the popular actress was awarded an Oscar, many spectators stood and clapped.
當這受歡迎的女演員得到奧斯卡獎時，觀眾起立並喝采。

◆ Thirty thousand spectators watched the play-off game.
三萬名觀眾觀看這場延長賽。

1996

---

audience

'ɔdɪəns

n. 觀眾；讀者

◆ Hope Radio as the broadcasting station has a large audience.
希望廣播電台有廣大的聽眾。

◆ The singer's outstanding performance won the plaudits of the audience.
這位歌手傑出的表現贏得觀眾的喝采。

1997 ★

---

binding

'baɪndɪŋ

n. 鑲邊；裝訂；捆綁

◆ Binding is very hard to learn for a child.
孩童要學裝訂非常困難。

◆ Something is used for securing or binding.
用來固定或捆綁的某些東西。

1998

---

fringe

'frɪndʒ

n. 鑲邊；邊緣
adj. 額外的；附加的

◆ The family live on the western fringe of Taipei.
這個家庭住在台北的西邊。

◆ What sort of fringe benefits are involved?
還有哪些額外的福利呢？

1999

---

acclaim

ə'klem

v. 讚揚……*n.* 喝采

◆ Her successful artwork has won her international acclaim.
她成功的藝術品幫她贏得了國際上的讚揚。

◆ The famous novel received great acclaim.
這本著名的小說獲得很大的讚揚。

2000

單字	詞性／字義	頁碼
abroad	*adv.* 在國外；到國外	53
absolute	*adj.* 絕對的；完全的	214
academic	*adj.* 大學的；學術的；學院的	15
accident	*n.* 意外事故；不測	225
accomplish	*v.* 完成……；實現……	71
accumulate	*v.* 累積……；堆積……	188
accurate	*adj.* 精確的；準確的	252
acknowledge	*v.* 承認……；回覆；打招呼	113
acquire	*v.* 獲得；取得；養成	290
admire	*v.* 欽佩；讚美	207
admit	*v.* 承認；容許入場	113
adolescent	*adj.* 青少年期的	125
advantageous	*adj.* 有益的；有利的；有助的	60
adverse	*adj.* 不利的；逆向的；有害的	18
advice	*n.* 忠告；消息	112
advocate	*v.* 提倡……；主張……　*n.* 提倡者	202
affair	*n.* 外遇；事情	39
affect	*v.* 使影響；使感動	101
afford	*v.* 提供；負擔起；買得起	202
agenda	*n.* 議程；會議事項	306
agent	*n.* 經紀人；代理商；間諜	234
agreement	*n.* 協議；協定；同意	108
allow	*v.* 允許	21
alternative	*adj.* 二者擇一的；替代的	12
altitude	*n.* 海拔；高度	152
ambiguous	*adj.* 模糊的；模稜兩可的	267
amend	*v.* 修正……　*n.* 賠罪；補償	145
analyze	*v.* 分析……；解析……	23
anonymous	*adj.* 匿名的；不具名的	170
apologize	*v.* 道歉；認錯	241
appease	*v.* 使平靜；使撫慰	82
appendix	*n.* 附錄	125
applaud	*v.* 鼓掌；拍手喝采；贊許	243
application	*n.* 申請書；申請	46

單字	詞性／字義	頁碼
appreciate	*v.* 賞識；感激；重視	273
approve	*v.* 贊成；批准	301
arrange	*v.* 安排；預備	56
assassinate	*v.* 行刺；糟蹋	65
assistant	*n.* 助手；助教	68
association	*n.* 協會；聯想；社團	108
astonish	*v.* 使……驚訝；使吃驚	80
astronaut	*n.* 太空人	25
attest	*v.* 證實……；作證……	301
attorney	*n.* 律師；法定代理人	131
auction	*n.* 拍賣　*v.* 把……賣掉	114
audience	*n.* 觀眾；讀者	309
authority	*n.* 權威；專家	307
automatic	*adj.* 自動；必然的	63
auxiliary	*adj.* 輔助的；後備的　*n.* 輔助者	257
available	*adj.* 可用的；有空的	37
aware	*adj.* 知道的；察覺的	121
awful	*adj.* 可怕的；嚇人的	37
background	*n.* 背景；經歷	140
balance	*n.* 餘額；結帳　*v.* 使平衡	275
ballot	*n.* 投票；選票	74
ballyhoo	*n.* 宣傳；廣告　*v.* 大肆宣傳	130
bankrupt	*adj.* 破產的	156
bargain	*v.* 討價還價　*n.* 交易	162
batch	*n.* 整批；整組	279
behalf	*n.* 利益；代表	67
behave	*v.* 表現出……；舉止	123
beneficial	*adj.* 有益的；有利的	60
benefit	*n.* 利益；好處；恩惠	67
bequest	*n.* 遺贈；遺產	284
betray	*v.* 對……不忠；出賣……	245
bias	*n.* 傾向；偏見	223
bill	*n.* 帳單；支票	176
biography	*n.* 傳記	222

單字	詞性／字義	頁碼
convenient	*adj.* 方便的；便利的	28
copyright	*n.* 著作權	216
corporation	*n.* 股份（有限）公司	122
council	*n.* 會議；委員會	228
counterfeit	*adj.* 偽造的 *v.* 偽造……；仿造……	170
coup	*n.* 政變	134
coupon	*n.* 優待券；多次通聯票	286
course	*n.* 課程；過程；路線	272
crash	*n.* 碰撞 *v.* 使失敗；使破產	232
crime	*n.* （法律上）罪；不道德行為	10
crisis	*n.* 危機；難關	49
crucial	*adj.* 決定性的；重要的	76
culture	*n.* 修養；文化	146
curriculum vitae	*n.* 簡歷表	297
damage	*n.* 傷害；損害	223
dangerous	*adj.* 危險的；不安全的	50
deadline	*n.* 截止日期	248
dealer	*n.* 商人；發牌者	171
debate	*v. n.* 辯論；爭論；討論	306
decrease	*v.* 減少	207
default	*v.* 棄權；不履行責任；違約	183
defect	*n.* 缺點；過失	160
defend	*v.* 保衛……；防禦……；替某人辯護	126
delay	*v.* 使……延誤；耽擱	79
delegate	*n.* 代表團；委派代表 *v.* 授權……	33
deliberate	*v.* 慎重考慮…… *adj.* 故意的；慎重的	227
deliver	*v.* 遞送；運送；傳達	258
demolish	*v.* 摧毀……；改變……的立場	249
density	*n.* 密度；比重	175
depression	*n.* 沮喪；意志消沉；不景氣	118
describe	*v.* 描述……；敘述……	201
desire	*v. n.* 渴望……；想要……	208
destroy	*v.* 破壞……；毀掉……；使失效	156
detail	*n.* 細節；詳情	189
detect	*v.* 發現……；查出……	212

單字	詞性／字義	頁碼
detention	*n.* 課後留校；拘留	272
develop	*v.* 使發展；使進化；沖洗底片	97
devote	*v.* 獻身於……；將奉獻給……	305
diagram	*n.* 圖表；圖樣	244
diminish	*v.* 減低；縮小（規模）	207
direction	*n.* 指示說明；方向	132
directory	*n.* 電話簿；目錄	111
discard	*v.* 拋棄……；丟棄……	114
discover	*v.* 發現出；找到	212
discuss	*v.* 討論……；商議……	162
display	*v.* 展覽……；陳列	148
dispute	*v.* 與……辯論 *n.* 爭論	254
distinguish	*v.* 認清楚；區別出……；使顯著	256
distribute	*v.* 進行分配；使分布	218
disturb	*v.* 打擾……；使不安	43
diverge	*v.* 使分歧（道路）；使離題	81
diversify	*v.* 使有變化；使多元化	85
donate	*v.* 捐贈給	149
downturn	*n.* 經濟衰退；不景氣	234
draft	*n.* 草稿；通風裝置 *v.* 打草稿	161
drawback	*n.* 缺點；短處；障礙	159
duplicate	*adj.* 複製的 *v.* 複製……；使再發生	271
economical	*adj.* 節省的；節約的	233
edition	*n.* 版；版本	119
education	*n.* 教育；學識教養	182
effective	*adj.* 起作用的；生效的	164
effort	*n.* 努力；成就	68
element	*n.* 元素；成分；要素	21
eligible	*adj.* 合格的；合意的	50
eliminate	*v.* 消滅……；消除……；排除……	154
eloquent	*adj.* 雄辯的；有說服力的	220
embassy	*n.* 大使館；大使館（全體人員）	14
emergency	*n.* 緊急；緊急事件	253
emphasize	*v.* 強調……；加強……語氣	177
employee	*n.* 受雇者；員工	109
encounter	*v.* 遇到……；遭遇……；和……交戰	239

單字	詞性／字義	頁碼
encourage	v. 鼓勵……；使……有勇氣	243
encryption	n. 加密	36
enforce	v. 強制……；實施……	177
enroll	v. 登記……；使……成為會員；使入學	210
enterprise	n. 企業；進取心	48
environment	n. 環境；情境	291
equipment	n. 設備；裝置	190
equivalent	adj. 等值的；相等的	213
escape	v. 逃脫；逃走	165
estimate	v. 估計……；評價……；估算	65
evidence	n. 證據；證物	301
exaggerate	v. 把……誇張化；使擴大	73
examination	n. 考試（同 exam）	63
exceed	v. 超越……；超出……的範圍	218
excellent	adj. 特優的；傑出的	154
excuse	v. 原諒……；寬恕…… n. 藉口	147
execute	v. 執行……；實施……；處死刑	172
expand	v. 使展開；使擴大	91
expenditure	n. 消費；消費量；消耗時間	153
exploit	v. 開發……；利用……	219
explosive	n. 炸藥 adj. 爆炸性的；暴躁的	136
export	v. n. 輸出；出口	282
extinguish	v. 熄滅……（火）；使消失	250
extremely	adv. 極端地；非常地	229
fatal	adj. 致命的；命運的	140
fault	n. 過錯	240
feasible	adj. 可實行的；可能的；合理的	38
feature	n. 容貌；特徵	148
flexible	adj. 易彎曲的；有彈性的；可變通的	117
fluctuate	v. 使波動；使起伏	89
focus	v. 聚焦於 n. 焦點；集中點	253
formal	adj. 正式的；形式上的	44
found	v. 建立；創立；創辦	130
fraud	n. 欺騙；欺詐行為	206
fundamental	adj. 基礎的；根本的；根深蒂固的	173

單字	詞性／字義	頁碼
future	n. 未來	43
global	adj. 全球的；球形的；世界性的	49
government	n. 政府	133
graceful	adj. 優雅的；得體的	287
grade	n. 分數；階級；年級	23
graph	n. 圖表	244
gross	n. 總收入 adj. 總的；全部的	291
guilty	adj. 有罪的	61
haggle	v. 討價還價	162
hardship	n. 辛苦；困苦	78
hardware	n. 五金	21
highlight	v. 使突出；強調…… n. 最精彩部份	91
hijack	v. 劫持（飛機）；強取（貨運）	68
historic	adj. 歷史著名的	280
horrible	adj. 可怕的；可憎的	37
hypothesis	n. 假設；假說	168
ignorant	adj. 無知識的；不知情的	209
illegal	adj. 非法的	125
impact	n. 衝擊；影響	271
import	v. n. 輸入；進口	282
improve	v. 使改良；使改善	87
include	v. 包括；包含	36
incorporate	v. 使合併；使包含；組成公司	83
increase	v. 增加……；加大……	261
infinite	adj. 無限的；極大的	209
inflation	n. 通貨膨脹；脹大	193
influence	v. 影響…… n. 影響力；權力	263
information	n. 消息；知識	153
ingredient	n. 配料；成份	165
inhibit	v. 禁止；抑制	232
initial	adj. 最初的 n. 起首的字母	205
innovation	n. 創新；革新	197
insider trading	n. 內線交易	22
insist	v. 堅持；非要……不可	173
inspect	v. 檢查……；查閱……	289
inspire	v. 鼓舞……；給某人信心	243
instruct	v. 指示……；通知……；指導	132

單字	詞性／字義	頁碼
population	*n.* 人口；全體居民	12
portable	*adj.* 可攜帶的	38
portfolio	*n.* 文件夾；作品集；投資組合	28
probable	*adj.* 可能的；可能發生的；有希望的	38
process	*n.* 過程；常規；製作方法	240
produce	*v.* 製造出；使產生	255
product	*n.* 產品；成果；乘積（數學）	186
progress	*n.* 進步；發展	218
promotion	*n.* 商品促銷；升級	171
proposal	*n.* 提案；計劃；求婚	202
prospect	*n.* 期望；展望；可能性	205
protect	*v.* 防護；保護	79
qualify	*v.* 使合格；使適任	84
quality	*n.* 優良；品質；特色	286
quantity	*n.* 數量；數目	264
quarter	*n.* 四分之一；一刻鐘；（美金）25 分	38
quota	*n.* 配額；限額	165
range	*n.* 範圍；種類 *v.* 將⋯⋯分等級	269
rank	*n.* 階級；身分；地位	220
ratify	*v.* 批准⋯⋯；認可⋯⋯	72
ratio	*n.* 比例	30
realize	*v.* 使了解；使領悟；將⋯⋯實現	81
recession	*n.* 經濟衰退；引退	234
recommend	*v.* 做⋯⋯建議；推薦⋯⋯	168
reference	*n.* 談及；參考；查詢	272
refund	*v.* 退還；償還	165
refuse	*v.* 拒絕⋯⋯ *n.* 廢物	115
relative	*n.* 親戚；親族 *adj.* 相對的	281
relax	*v.* 使放鬆；使輕鬆	88
release	*v.* 使放開 *n.* 釋放；發布（新聞稿）	88
religious	*adj.* 宗教的；謹慎的	111
renew	*v.* 重新開始；使更新	143
representative	*n.* 代表；代理人；典型人物	33
reputation	*n.* 名聲；名譽	51
request	*v.* 請求給予；要求某事	273
research	*n.* 研究；調查	137

單字	詞性／字義	頁碼
reserve	*v.* 預定⋯⋯；保留⋯⋯權利	242
resource	*n.* 資源；錢財	237
respect	*v.* 尊重⋯⋯；敬重⋯⋯ *n.* 尊敬	199
responsible	*adj.* 責任重大的；負責的	192
result	*v.* 作為⋯⋯結果；導致於 *n.* 結果	67
resume	*n.* 履歷 *v.* 重新開始；取回	263
retail	*n.* 零售 *adv.* 以零售方式地	241
retain	*v.* 保留⋯⋯；持續維持；雇用⋯⋯	126
retire	*v.* 使退休；使退役	93
retrieve	*v.* 重新得到；取回⋯⋯	143
revenue	*n.* 稅收；總收入	212
review	*v.* 複習；回顧；審閱	271
revise	*v.* 修改；修訂	145
reward	*n.* 報酬；報答	199
rotate	*v.* 使旋轉；使輪流；由⋯⋯輪值	94
routine	*n.* 慣例；常規	248
royalty	*n.* 王權；王室；版稅	31
ruin	*v.* 使成廢墟；使毀壞	84
rumor	*n.* 謠言 *v.* 謠傳⋯⋯	294
sample	*n.* 樣品；標本	267
scandal	*n.* 醜聞；恥辱	295
schedule	*v.* 將列入⋯⋯排程 *n.* 時間表；進度表	175
scheme	*n.* 計劃；方案；陰謀	141
scholar	*n.* 學者	277
scientific	*adj.* 科學（上）的	137
scope	*n.* 領域；範圍	260
score	*n.* 得分；分數	177
secondary	*adj.* 中等的；次要的；第二的	20
section	*n.* 部分；區域；（街道）段	195
security	*n.* 安全；保安	55
select	*v.* 選擇；挑選	283
semester	*n.* 學期	277
seminar	*n.* 研討會；討論會	137
separate	*v.* 使分離 *adj.* 分開的	81
serious	*adj.* 嚴重的；認真的	304
shareholder	*n.* 股東	122

單字	詞性／字義	頁碼
shelter	*n.* 避難所；庇護物 *v.* 使掩蔽	295
shortage	*n.* 短缺；不足	212
shortcut	*n.* 捷徑；近路	178
signature	*n.* 簽名；署名	300
significant	*adj.* 重要的；重大的；顯著的	142
situation	*n.* 情況；處境；位置	178
skillful	*adj.* 熟練的；有技術的	268
slogan	*n.* 口號；廣告用語	13
social	*adj.* 社交的；社會的；關於社會的	121
software	*n.* 軟體	192
solve	*v.* 使解決；給……解答	99
source	*n.* 來源；泉源	106
souvenir	*n.* 紀念品	138
specification	*n.* 詳述；規格書；說明書	236
sponsor	*v.* 贊助…… *n.* 贊助者；主辦人	302
stable	*adj.* 穩定的	300
staff	*n.* 全體人員；全體職員	49
standard	*n.* 標準；規格	266
stationery	*n.* 文具	28
statistics	*n.* 統計學；統計表	189
status	*n.* 地位；身份；狀態	53
strike	*v.* 使擊出；使撞擊	103
style	*n.* 風格；款式	144
subjective	*adj.* 主觀的；個人的	32
submit	*v.* 提交……；呈遞……；使服從	201
substitute	*v.* 以……代替 *n.* 代理人；代用品	33
succeed	*v.* 使成功；使繼續	84
summary	*n.* 摘要	248
supervise	*v.* 對……進行監督；管理	247
supply	*v.* 供給……；補充…… *n.* 補給品	106
support	*v.* 給……支持；支撐…… *n.* 支持	214
surf	*v.* 作衝浪運動；在網路上迅速瀏覽資料	66
survive	*v.* 使存活；使……劫後餘生	84
synonym	*n.* 同義字	51

單字	詞性／字義	頁碼
tariff	*n.* 價目表；關稅；運費	261
temperature	*n.* 溫度；體溫	231
tenure	*n.* 任期；保有	48
terminal	*adj.* 終點的；終端的 *n.* 終點站	189
theme	*n.* 題目；主題	299
theory	*n.* 理論；學理	186
threaten	*v.* 對……恐嚇；對……威脅	246
timetable	*n.* 時刻表	150
tolerant	*adj.* 容忍的；寬恕的	147
trace	*v.* 探尋……的蹤跡；痕跡；追蹤	180
trade	*n.* 貿易；行業 *v.* 交易……	217
transaction	*n.* 交易；處理；買賣	47
transcript	*n.* 抄本；副本；成績單	73
transfer	*v.* 轉車（飛機）；轉移；搬移	298
transform	*v.* 使變化；使變形	105
turnover	*n.* 營業額；交易額；翻轉	290
undergraduate	*adj.* 大學生的	15
uniform	*n.* 制服 *adj.* 相同的；一致的	107
update	*v.* 使更新	87
upgrade	*v.* 使升級；提高……品質	82
urgent	*adj.* 緊急的；急迫的	253
vegetarian	*n.* 素食者	158
violate	*v.* 違背……；對……的違反	241
violent	*adj.* 激烈的；劇烈的；暴力的	280
volunteer	*n.* 志願者；義工	71
voucher	*n.* 優待券；收據；保證人	286
wage	*n.* 工資；薪水	17
warranty	*n.* 保證書；保證；擔保	126
waste	*v.* 浪費；使消耗	152
wealth	*n.* 財富；豐富	163
weapon	*n.* 武器；兵器	118
welfare	*n.* 平安；福利；福祉	41
widespread	*adj.* 廣布的	263
withdrawal	*n.* 提款；撤回；撤退	203
witness	*n.* 證人；目擊者；證明	301
yield	*v.* 出產（水果）；使屈服；讓與	35

國家圖書館出版品預行編目資料

NEW TOEIC新多益單字圖像記憶法／吳燦銘作 －－ 初版.
－－ 臺中市：晨星，2016.10
面； 公分. －－（Guide book；358）

ISBN：978-986-443-165-6（平裝）

1.多益測驗 2.詞彙 3.學習方法

805.1895   105013265

Guide Book 358

NEW TOEIC 新多益單字圖像記憶法

作者	吳燦銘 ◎ 策劃 油漆式速記法 外語研發團隊
編輯	余順琪
封面設計	李莉君
美術編輯	張蘊方
創辦人 發行所	陳銘民 晨星出版有限公司 台中市407工業區30路1號 TEL：（04）23595820　FAX：（04）23550581 E-mail：service@morningstar.com.tw http：//www.morningstar.com.tw 行政院新聞局局版台業字第2500號
法律顧問 承製 初版	陳思成 律師 知己圖書股份有限公司　TEL：（04）23581803 西元2016年10月15日
郵政劃撥 讀者服務專線	22326758（晨星出版有限公司） （04）23595819＃230
印刷	上好印刷股份有限公司

定價 380元

（如書籍有缺頁或破損，請寄回更換）

ISBN：978-986-443-165-6

Published by Morning Star Publshing Inc.

Printed in Taiwan

All rights reserved.

版權所有‧翻印必究

2016/12/31前填妥本回函卡投入郵筒
就有機會抽到黑板月曆貼
把學習計劃貼在書桌前，陪你用功30天！

以下資料或許太過繁瑣，但卻是我們瞭解您的唯一途徑
誠摯期待能與您在下一本書中相逢，讓我們一起從閱讀中尋找樂趣吧！

姓名：＿＿＿＿＿＿＿＿＿　性別：□ 男　□ 女　　生日：　　／　　／

教育程度：＿＿＿＿＿＿＿＿

職業：□ 學生　　　□ 教師　　　□ 內勤職員　　□ 家庭主婦
　　　□ SOHO族　　□ 企業主管　□ 服務業　　　□ 製造業
　　　□ 醫藥護理　□ 軍警　　　□ 資訊業　　　□ 銷售業務
　　　□ 其他 ＿＿＿＿＿＿＿＿＿＿

E-mail：＿＿＿＿＿＿＿＿＿＿＿＿＿　聯絡電話：＿＿＿＿＿＿＿＿＿＿

聯絡地址：□□□＿＿＿＿＿＿＿＿＿＿＿＿＿＿＿＿＿＿＿＿＿

購買書名：NEW TOEIC新多益單字圖像記憶法

‧本書中最吸引您的是哪一篇文章或哪一段話呢？＿＿＿＿＿＿＿＿＿＿＿＿＿

‧誘使您 買此書的原因？

□ 於 ＿＿＿＿ 書店尋找新知時　□ 看 ＿＿＿＿ 報時瞄到　□ 受海報或文案吸引
□ 翻閱 ＿＿＿＿ 雜誌時　□ 親朋好友拍胸脯保證　□ ＿＿＿＿ 電台DJ熱情推薦
□ 其他編輯萬萬想不到的過程：＿＿＿＿＿＿＿＿＿＿＿＿＿＿＿＿＿

‧對於本書的評分？（請填代號：1. 很滿意 2. OK啦！ 3. 尚可 4. 需改進）

封面設計 ＿＿＿＿　版面編排 ＿＿＿＿　內容 ＿＿＿＿　文／譯筆 ＿＿＿＿

‧美好的事物、聲音或影像都很吸引人，但究竟是怎樣的書最能吸引您呢？

□ 價格殺紅眼的書　□ 內容符合需求　□ 贈品大碗又滿意　□ 我誓死效忠此作者
□ 晨星出版，必屬佳作！□ 千里相逢，即是有緣 □ 其他原因，請務必告訴我們！
＿＿＿＿＿＿＿＿＿＿＿＿＿＿＿＿＿＿＿＿＿＿＿＿＿＿＿＿＿

‧您與眾不同的閱讀品味，也請務必與我們分享：

□ 哲學　　　□ 心理學　　□ 宗教　　　□ 自然生態　□ 流行趨勢　□ 醫療保健
□ 財經企管　□ 史地　　　□ 傳記　　　□ 文學　　　□ 散文　　　□ 原住民
□ 小說　　　□ 親子叢書　□ 休閒旅遊　□ 其他 ＿＿＿＿＿＿＿＿＿＿＿

以上問題想必耗去您不少心力，為免這份心血白費

請務必將此回函郵寄回本社，或傳真至（04）2359-7123，感謝！

若行有餘力，也請不吝賜教，好讓我們可以出版更多更好的書！

‧其他意見：

407

台中市工業區30路1號

晨星出版有限公司

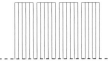

更方便的購書方式：

（1）網站：http://www.morningstar.com.tw
（2）郵政劃撥　帳號：22326758
　　　　　　　戶名：晨星出版有限公司
　　　　　　　請於通信欄中註明欲購買之書名及數量
（3）電話訂購：如為大量團購可直接撥客服專線洽詢

◎ 如需詳細書目可上網查詢或來電索取。
◎ 客服專線：04-23595819#230　傳真：04-23597123
◎ 客戶信箱：service@morningstar.com.tw